Raven, Tell A Story

Anne Donaghy

For my future great, great grandchildren, with the hope that their world is far more tolerant and peaceful than ours.

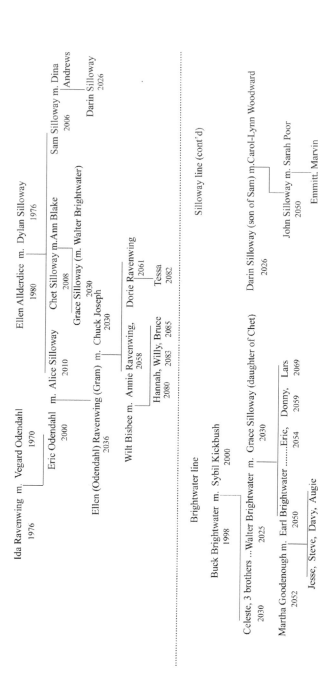

Ida Ravenwing m. Vegard Odendahl
1976   1970

Ellen Allderdice m. Dylan Silloway
        1980   1976

Eric Odendahl m. Alice Silloway
          2000   2010

Chet Silloway m.Ann Blake
            2008

Sam Silloway m. Dina Andrews
          2006

Darin Silloway
2026

Grace Silloway (m. Walter Brightwater)
2030

Ellen (Odendahl) Ravenwing (Gram) m. Chuck Joseph
2036   2030

Wilt Bisbee m. Amie Ravenwing,
                          2058

Dorie Ravenwing
2061

Tessa
2082

Hannah, Willy, Bruce
2080   2083   2085

Silloway line (cont'd)

Darin Silloway (son of Sam) m.Carol-Lynn Woodward
2026

John Silloway m. Sarah Poor
2050

Emmitt, Marvin
2076

Brightwater line

Buck Brightwater m. Sybil Kickbush
1998   2000

Celeste, 3 brothers ...Walter Brightwater m. Grace Silloway (daughter of Chet)
2030   2025   2030

Martha Goodenough m. Earl Brightwater ......Eric, Donny, Lars
2052   2050   2054   2059   2069

Jesse, Steve, Davy, Augie
2081   2083   2086   2091

Note: Dates are birthdates.
Tessa and Hannah Ravenwing, Jesse Brightwater, Emmitt and Marvin Silloway are third cousins whose great, great grandparents are Ellen Allderdice and Dylan Silloway.

ACKNOWLEDGEMENTS

Working on this story, using storytelling and myth throughout, I discovered Sean Kane's book *Wisdom of the Mythtellers*. Kane brings us the stories of Étaîn, Raven, and The Woman Who Married The Bear (among others), all told by elders from cultures shaped by these myths. His book opens new and wonderful vistas which I am still exploring.

I am indebted to him, and to the authors listed below, for their inspiration and piercing insights. Their works are cited in the Notes section at the back of this book.

And to the RWW (Rainier Writing Workshop) mentors, particularly Ann Pancake—the most inspirational and encouraging writing mentors on the planet—Thank you.

Works Cited:

Bringhurst, Robert and Reid, Bill. *The Raven Steals the Light.*

Coast Salish artist Joe Jack, www.joejack.com. Cowichan Salish Legend. *Bluejay.*

Dauenhauer, Nora Marks and Richard, editors. *Haa Tuwunaagu Yis, for Healing Our Spirit: Tlingit Oratory.*

Estés, Clarissa Pinkola. *Women Who Run With the Wolves.*

Kane, Sean. *Wisdom of the Mythtellers.*

Neruda, Pablo. *The Essential Neruda: Selected Poems* (bilingual edition).

I. Raven

We are not human beings on a spiritual journey. We are spiritual beings on a human journey.
—Teilhard de Chardin

1. January 2091–September 2092

When I was eight years old, I drowned for fifteen minutes. One moment I was flying over smooth, black lake ice—my mukluk bottoms slick as the ice, it really was like flying, the low lakeshore birches whizzing past and snowmantled Ptarmigan mountain on the south side of our lake coming closer—and then the world upended and I dropped into nothingness and the cold of outer space. A second later my brain shut down.

I was under the icy water long enough for some of the village kids to race across the ice, fortunately close to the shore, and sprint to their homes to find parents to help. Jesse Brightwater found his dad first. Jesse's a year older than me and I'd considered him a bug up until that moment that he saved my life.

Earl Brightwater smashed the ice in a wide circle with a heavy tree limb he'd carried out with him. He was shouting at the kids to stand way back when the ice broke under him, too, but later he said that he was going to jump in anyway. And it was sunlight as well as Earl Brightwater that saved me, for the sun came out right then, around the dark clouds we'd had for so long that winter, light goldened straight through eight feet of glacier lake water and Earl saw me curled up like I was asleep on the stony lake-bottom. He dove down and grabbed my parka and lifted me up through the watery gold light, heaved me up onto the shelf of ice that would hold my weight, yelled at Jesse to lie flat on the ice so it wouldn't break, so he could pull me back away from the water.

It took Earl another minute or two to get himself out, his weight breaking off the ice each time he tried to lunge out on it. Jesse had pulled the bundle of wet that was me over the ice away from the water, and was edging toward Earl with that heavy branch that Earl had carried out when a few other dads finally got there carrying two by four boards they lay on the ice for him.

Water steaming and streaming off him, Earl Brightwater climbed back to his feet and hefted me over his right shoulder and jogged over the ice with me bouncing away until I started gasping and breathing again.

He took me straightaway to the little house Gram and I lived in next to the lakeshore. Gram was the village healer; she was raising me since I didn't have parents. Every other kid had their parents; well, a few kids had dads who'd left for the city, but at least they knew who their dads were. Not me. My mom had left for the city to become a resistance fighter, and she had come home to have me, to give me to Gram, but then she returned to the city and never came back. No one in our village ever met or even heard of my dad.

I'd pestered Gram a lot over this—pester was her word—*why had my mother left me, just barely born, with Gram so she could go back to the resistance? what's a resistance? what were they resisting? who is my father?* Oh, and another—it seemed that my weird colored eyes must have come from my father, and that made me wonder all the more if my father had been, well at least not quite normal. All through the year leading up to me going through the ice I'd ask and ask, until Gram would tug her going-white hair and sit me down on the doorstep with a basket of herbs to sort through (or, half the year she'd sit me in a chair by the fireplace) *to quiet your brain,* she'd say. *Tessa, you have to quiet your brain or you will never hear a thing.* And regarding the color of my eyes, my irises were only slightly different from everyone else's, lacking color, pale gray with slightly darker rims that emphasized how pale they were. Paying attention to kids who teased me about them (*Pale Eyes!*) would just be an invitation for them tease me all the more.

Calm yourself, Tessa, was Gram's mantra, *be still, and pay attention.*

The funny thing about going through the ice when I was eight was that it actually did seem to quiet my brain. Gram and I laughed about that later. But not then, of course. When it happened she was afraid that I hadn't come completely back.

I woke up to the sound of someone praying and the air filled with the scent of burning sage and sweetgrass, which in our village meant heavy-duty healing. I opened my eyes to see Gram standing in front of the sweet-burning fire on the hearth of our main room, her arms lifted up, her eyes closed in concentration. Her uplifted arms, in the robe she was wearing, cast a shadow on the wall across the room from me.

"Raven!" I exclaimed. That's exactly what the shadow looked like. And suddenly I remembered that when I had gone through the dark hole in the ice, I'd had a dream. Raven and I had gone somewhere together.

Gram's eyes opened wide, she dropped to her knees and hugged me tight against her scratchy robe. She was crying, which surprised me. She seldom cried; her steady state was calm, looking like she was thinking, a little distance away from the rest of us behind her dark eyes. I figured that was part of being the village healer. Somebody had to be listening, always paying attention to things that other people were missing.

"God sent you back to us, Tessa," she said, holding me a little way away from her chest so she could look into my eyes. "There is a reason he sent you back to us."

"Noooo," I said. "It was Raven, Gram. He was as big as me, he was there helping me."

She rocked back on her heels, looking thoughtful. Her dark eyes crinkled at the corners. "You and your ravens."

I shook my head. "No, it was *Raven* in my dream. He was as big as me. He was talking to me and I was talking to him."

She kept looking at me and I could feel her thinking. "I pray to God," she said. "Earl Brightwater now, he prays to Saint Pope Francis. And I do believe Tucky Lotts"—he was the old guy who lived in the rundown cabin beyond ours—"I believe old Tucky prays to someone named Jim Beam." She was smiling now. "I know Raven a bit myself, and I'm sure he does fit in somewhere."

"I'll pray to Raven," I said.

She smiled and pulled me in against her again. "That's fine. All that really matters is that we pray."

~

Gram loved to tell stories. She had a wide range of them, from her granny Ida's Tlingit and Coast Salish stories of Raven and the creation of the world, to Celtic folktales she learned as a child from her other grandmother, granny Silloway, and even a thrilling, true story from five hundred years ago of one of granny Silloway's ancestors named Penelope Van Princes, who was shipwrecked and then set upon by natives on the shores of what later became New Jersey. Granny Silloway, who was named Ellen, who Gram was named after, passed on to Gram a book with a faded red cloth cover that had pages and pages of lists of family names going back more than five hundred years, and other stories in it too, though the Penelope Van Princes story was by far the most exciting of them.

Our village had a small library of battered books which had arrived a few at a time over the decades, carried through the mountains from the city to the main house, but Gram served as the repository of myths and folktales. Usually it was just me and Gram snuggled in the cushions of the small couch beside the fireplace, but also there were storytelling nights at the village main house for whoever wanted to come and listen. Mostly it was older people, but Jesse Brightwater was almost always there, and a few of my Silloway cousins too. Sometimes we had native drums as accompaniment, and singing. By the time I came along, Gram had retired as master storyteller for the village, though she loved doing guest appearances. Usually it was auntie Annie, my mother's older sister, who did the honors, but other people took turns, sometimes with a little fun competition, and us kids were doing storytelling in school and thinking that some day we'd be the ones to sit in the big chair by the fireplace in the big room of the main house.

Just after my going through the ice, Gram and I began our own story of "Girl and Raven." This fit partly because our family name was Ravenwing, which Gram chose when she was young and spent a few years with granny Ida's family by that name, still living in a Tlingit village way south down the coast. But also before I went through the ice I was known as the girl who talked with ravens, since I always called back whenever they flew by and sometimes one even wheeled on the wing and came back for a second look down at me, which I took as the biggest compliment in the world. So Gram and I began building stories about me and ravens.

Gram called it "the girl and the raven" but in my mind it was "girl and Raven." It started with them meeting in a dream the girl had, and their adventures went on from there, sometimes in dreams, and sometimes in the physical world, kind of an interweaving between the two since that's how Gram saw the world, and how I grew up understanding it.

Gram told me about the ancient Celts' "thin places," those sites where the spirit world drew close. Where there was some back and forth across the boundary between the physical and the metaphysical. We lived in such a place, but I don't think it was because it was an old sacred spot, since we lived deep in the young mountains of the north-northwest and it wasn't likely (in my mind anyway) that people could have lived here earlier than Gram's grandparents, the settlers. More likely it was because of Gram, who was someone who was comfortable with the thought of living with the spirit world, and the spirits seemed comfortable living with her.

Gram's granny Ida had left a Tlingit village from the coast farther south and ended up in the city, married a Norwegian named Vegard Odendahl, the grandson of sailors drawn to our coast of snowy mountains so much like Norway's. I had a pin, supposedly his, of a Viking ship that Gram gave me as a gift, *To keep safe for always* (whether I was to keep it safe, or it would keep me safe, I didn't know). Besides the Raven stories that she loved to tell, granny Ida also had a story about what it was like to meet and marry a Viking. So Gram said. They lived in the city for a while until they moved to the mountains with granny and grampa Silloway and some friends, all of them seeing it as an escape to freedom while those they left behind in the city saw it as a crazy leaving behind of safety, comfort and the civilized world. Gram's parents, Erik Odendahl and Alice Silloway, were teenagers in the new village. They grew up and got married and had Gram, who was an only child like me.

~

We usually had village story and game nights on the first and third Saturdays of the month. This first story night after my falling through the ice, a slightly larger than usual crowd gathered in the main house—my auntie Annie, my cousin Hannah who was two years older than me and as bossy and ever-present as a big sister, and Hannah's two younger brothers Willy and Bruce; there were a bunch of Brightwaters, including Jesse, who sat down next to me, with Hannah on my other side; a single line of creaky white haired elders sat in rough wooden chairs at the back; and another bunch of Silloway cousins crowded between Jesse and the tall wooden pillar supposedly carved by great great grampa Vegard at the east end of the house. The radiant heat floor warmed us right through as we sat cross-legged on it. Gram had told me the story of the building of it when she was a girl, the main house heat pump powered by the solar film on the roof, which had been replaced only once, fifty years later. *We all began to get soft after that,* she liked to say, and I thought she was joking a little, but I couldn't quite tell. *Living in the village took a lot more toughness when we only had a couple of woodstoves, and all the cabins had for heat was fireplaces.*

I'd always been grateful that I wasn't around back then. Some of Gram's stories about those early days made me think that my grampa Silloway (his first name was Dylan, but for some reason we always called him grampa Silloway) might have wished that he hadn't been

11

around back then either. He wasn't handy with tools like grampa Vegard; he was a quiet man who loved nothing more than reading his books, and he wrote books too (we had those, as well as the one with the red cover that was filled with our family tree). That first winter, when the settlers lived in yurts that kept getting snowed on, grampa Silloway didn't come out for weeks, so it was said.

The smooth wooden walls on the inside of the main house— two walls covered with bright-colored murals, brilliant reds and turquoises mingled with white and black, colors of the coastal Tlingit and Haida, and another wall with a painting our school classes just started, with lots of yellow in it for the sun and the textures and greens of all of the different trees and shrubs and mosses on the mountainslopes around our lake—these were separated from the rough outer log walls by thick foam panels. The building was planned and crafted by my great great grandfather Vegard the Viking, who fortunately was hugely strong as well as skilled with tools. The cabins the settlers built that first year, while they hunkered in yurts with snow so heavy on some nights that people (definitely not my grampa Silloway) were designated roof shovelers, also were built with inches of foam insulation and insulated windows.

How'd they get all that stuff up here into the mountains? I pestered Gram when I was younger. *How'd they get the water pipes up here, and the solar panels? Nobody could carry composting toilets this far, even grampa Vegard!*

She told me that Jesse Brightwater's family always have been the ones who raised and kept the work horse teams who did all the hauling, from logs for building from the valley to the south that has the bigger trees, to three-day long trips to haul supplies from the city thirty miles away. It was actually forty-five miles, since with the horses they had to go around, not over, three lines of mountains. And some building materials long ago, Gram told me, were flown in right onto the lake by a floatplane.

I knew what jets and airplanes were since we saw them nearly every day high in the sky, headed to or from the city. I'd never seen one up close, though, and only twice I'd seen small airplanes, ones that flew low and had loud engines. *But a plane that could land on water?!*

She made no further comment about floating planes, but added that there always had been an artist or two in the village skilled at carving the yellow cedar hauled up by the horses, creating art to be bartered in the city for pipes and steel and foam panels, and even composting toilets. I'd seen Jesse get his first lessons at carving cedar and alder, wielding sharp knives and blades as Earl carefully watched him and guided his hands at times.

Hannah and Jesse both sat quietly on the warm floor, watching the stragglers come through the main door. As usual I was the squirmer. Hannah pinched me, as was her custom when she finally got fed up with me, and I pinched her back, but harder, which made her glare, black brows drawn in straight lines over her squinched dark eyes. "Tessa, you're such a brat!"

I stopped paying attention to Hannah and looked at Gram, who had taken the storyteller's seat that night. She was wearing her wrap-around long wool sweater of rich, deep green, her equivalent to the ceremonial robe which she wore only in private, when she was working a healing. I was expecting her to tell a Raven story, but instead she announced she was going to tell a story from long, long ago, from a green place far, far away called Ireland.

Hannah and I smiled at each other, in truce again. Gram was going to tell our favorite one about the fly! The fly was only in a part of the story, but it was the best part because that's when we could call out the lines that we'd learned. And we always laughed over how funny it was that a human could become a fly, such a pretty little fly at that, and then later become a human again. But the whole tale was about transformations and back-and-forthing between the world of humans and the world of the gods, the Danaans as they were called in Ireland. We loved it even if we didn't, at ages eight and ten, understand much of it. Mostly it was a lot of kings, some of them gods in disguise, falling in love with a beautiful woman named Étain, over hundreds of years. And of course there was an evil witch queen, jealous of Étain's beauty, who cast a spell *with a wand of scarlet rowan-tree* and Étain became a puddle of water.

But the heat of fire and the heat of air and the heat of the sodden earth turned the pool of water into a chrysalis, Gram half-sang, half-spoke from her chair in the front of the room, *And the chrysalis became a fly. And sweeter than flutes and harps and horns was the voice of that fly and the humming of its wings.*

Here us kids loudly hummed a few notes. I always tried to hit the highest pitch I could. Jesse, at nine, could hit a higher note than me which was so unfair. But I always tried to beat him at it. Hannah poked me again for being too loud.

Its eyes were like jewels in the dark, and its radiance and fragrance could take hunger and thirst away from any man.

Hannah and I always sniggered here, the thought of a fly having eyes like jewels, and being radiant and sweet! But we had to make sure we sniggered quietly, or Gram would send us a stern look.

And she shed from her wingtips a spray of droplets that could cure sickness in anyone she went with. It was Midir she went with, following him in his travels throughout his land. He knew it was his Étain, and during the time she was with him in the shape of a fly, he was nourished and never took a woman. He used to fall asleep to the humming of her wings, and if someone who did not love him came near, she would awaken him.

Midir was a god, but also a man. All right, I could sort of get that, but what I loved was the idea of a fly hanging around, humming you to sleep with its tiny wings, and waking you up if danger approached. Hannah and I usually giggled at this part, too, because last summer (it seemed that flies were pretty scarce in winter, sleeping somewhere in the cabin walls) I had tried to train a fly. It did seem to like to hang out on my arm and run up to my shoulder, but it kept flying away, no matter how gentle I was with it. I was proud that I never once had injured it, but was sad that it didn't seem to like me all that much.

But in the story, the evil witch came back. And Fuamnach the witch caused big winds to blow for seven years so that the little fly couldn't find any place to rest in all of Ireland. But finally she found Aengus, the son of the king of Ireland.

Gram continued: *The Mac Óc* (this was the other name for Aengus) *folded her in his cloak, and he carried her to his house, to a sun-bower with bright windows for going in and out. Aengus slept every night by her side, comforting the little fly until the lustre of happiness returned to her again. That sun-bower was full of the fragrance of herbs, and Étain grew stronger in the aroma of them.*

I loved the thought of that little fly regaining *the lustre of happiness* in a garden full of sun and herbs. That was what I wanted to be able to do for injured or sick creatures.

~

Gram often took in injured or sick birds and animals, sometimes at the same time she was helping heal injured or sick people. The summer of my ninth birthday, an immature hawk with a broken wing came to live with us. *Buteo jamaicensis calurus*, Gram taught me, commonly called the red-tailed hawk, familiar bird of the northwest with a wild screaming cry that fortunately we never heard in our little cabin. Our young male came to stay for a few months while his right wing healed. Gram rigged up a splint for it out of balsawood and super glue and after the first couple of days, the hawk left the splint alone, as if he understood what it was for. He hung out in our ceiling rafters and dropped down rather clumsily twice a day for his meal of dead red squirrel or shrews, which Gram paid well for, since trapping and killing even shrews was something I could never get myself to do. Jesse was her best supplier. The hawk let Gram hand him back up into the rafters after his meals, then he spent what seemed like hours preening his feathers. After that he just sat there and stared down at us.

He made me feel like a mouse. I knew he was just about to pounce on me. After about a week of this, one early evening after dinner I turned and glared back up at him and he turned his head away, looking off into the shadows between the roof and the rafters, as if he was a little embarrassed to be caught staring. When I looked away, I felt his eyes on me again. I got up and walked over and stood right under him, looking up again. This time he didn't look away. His golden eyes reflected the bright summer evening sunlight that reached through our west window and lit up the whole main room of our cabin. His white belly was speckled and streaked with brown, and he had the funniest white puffy-feathered legs that reminded me of old-fashioned pantaloons I'd seen in pictures in books. He didn't have a red tail yet. Gram said that would come in a year or two. But it was his eyes that drew me in and wouldn't let me go.

"Gram," I heard myself say. "This hawk is sad."

She was reading a book in her favorite chair by the window. She set the book down in her lap. "See if he wants to come down to you."

It felt like he wanted *me* to come up to *him*, so I climbed up the heavy bookcase on the wall near where he sat, so I could be close to him. Gram always had stern words for me when I climbed the bookcase, but I just couldn't help it, I loved climbing up it and sitting on it and looking down. She started to say something now, and then stopped and just watched me.

"Hey," I whispered to the hawk. "I'm here for a visit." I scootched to the edge of the bookcase just below the rafter he was sitting on. We looked at each other for a minute, then he shuffled a little to look away, so I looked away, then glanced back to see him with his head bent under his wing—as funny as a person glancing over his shoulder—peeking back at me. We just sat up there like that for a few minutes. Then I slowly put my right arm out toward him. He shuffled another step away. I stayed like that for a few minutes until my arm started tingling and I needed to move a little so it wouldn't go to sleep. After another minute he shuffled a couple of steps closer.

He had quite a beak. Big and strong and wicked sharp. I'd seen him tear into squirrels with it, tossing bits of fluffy fur into the air impatiently as he worked to get to the meat. But it didn't scare me somehow. I could feel his curiosity. He liked having me up there for a visit.

Gram said that when red-tailed hawks were mature they did courtship flights, tumbling through the air with aerobatic maneuvers, females as well as males. And they mated for life. I suddenly, desperately hoped that this bird's wing would heal quickly so he could fly south out of the mountains and down the valleys in the fall and find some other red-tailed hawks and then do his courtship flying in the spring.

My right arm was still cocked out toward him, tingling again, but he was shuffling over toward me, slowly, not quite looking at me. I was careful not to look directly at him either. Then I felt the sharp grab of his talons. He hummucked up my arm, talons stabbing through the thin fabric of my shirt—next time I'd wear two shirts!—and there he was on my right shoulder, shifting around a little because he was so big compared to my little shoulder perch.

"Ah," said Gram, not moving in her chair. "I see you've made friends."

"I think he wants to come down and look out the window."

"You'd better be careful, Tessa. I don't think you can climb down the bookcase with that bird on you."

Of course I didn't listen. I climbed down very slowly so as not to scare him. It took me at least fifteen minutes, but I did it, and he stayed gripped to my shoulder. Once down I slowly walked across the room to our picture window that looked out on the lake, and sure enough, he was happy looking out.

We did this often until Gram deemed him finally healed enough to be set free. I was the one he launched from, holding my arm out, wrapped with a dish towel tied with leather straps that Jesse made, patterned after what falconers used in a book he'd just read. The hawk rose into the air with swift beats of unfurled wings, nearly knocking me over, and for one moment he hung there, paused, that one moment needed for the pieces of his wild bird brain to settle back in place. He glanced down at me. Then he turned his head and sighted down the green valley and I watched him grow smaller, smaller, until he was just a speck against the blue. He turned down the next valley, to the south, and was gone.

~

After that Gram started asking me to help her when people brought in hurt birds or little animals. There were some sad failures, like the mouse babies who died because I couldn't find anything close enough to mouse milk to drop into those tiny pink mouths that quivered shut as they got weaker and weaker and then died. I cried for hours until Gram told me to buck up and figure out what went wrong so I'd know how to do better next time. *Sometimes we do all we can but we just can't quite get it right and then we have to let it go so we can try again next time. And hopefully next time it will go better.*

Jesse brought us a red squirrel with a broken leg the summer after the red-tailed hawk. The squirrel was a side casualty on a hunting trip Jesse and a few of the other kids had taken down the valley with their dads. He arrived at our house in a pouch cinched shut to prevent his escape. When Jesse held it out to me I couldn't say anything at first, I was so amazed by the incessant kicking and punching that was going on from inside.

"What's in there?" I asked, though clearly it was a demon of some sort.

"Crazy dude squirrel," Jesse said. "Took me a half hour to catch him even with his broken leg, everyone wanted to leave him, and me by then, but I felt so bad and I knew you'd want to help him."

"Don't open that sack yet!" Gram warned. "Let's get something to put him in first or he'll be all over this house and we'll never catch him."

Jesse and I made a little cage of chicken wire we found at the supply shed in back of the main house. Well, it was my idea but Jesse made it. I was—I still am—kind of like my great great grampa Silloway when it comes to tools. We brought the cage back to our cabin and Gram reached into the pouch, wearing a glove, and gently pulled out the squirming squirrel. She made Jesse and me sit down and hold still, *and for God's sake be quiet, Tessa!* under penalty of tongue lashing. She'd rigged up a tiny plastic pull-on splint for his leg while Jesse was building the cage.

"If we don't get this on him now, we never will," she muttered under her breath. She began singing softly. I recognized one of her healing ditties that she used on creatures and small children. *Warmth of sun and cool of night, blue of lake and green of light, here we greet you in this place! Spirit helpers send us grace...*

Sitting quietly on my chair, I felt soothing calm all around me. The squirrel stopped squirming. Gram gently touched its bent leg with her bare hand, humming, then repeating her song. With one quick movement she straightened the leg, the squirrel twitched once, then was quiet in her hands.

"Tessa, hand me the splint that's in my lap, would you?" she spoke quietly.

I moved slow as I could, relieved that I wasn't scaring the squirrel, and picked up the tiny white plastic coil in her lap, and held it up for her to take. Back in my chair I marveled at Gram's dexterity as she slipped it on the squirrel's tiny leg.

When we put him in the cage, the squirrel shot out like a drop of the sun, pure red gold energy seeking its source. Even with a splinted front leg. Wow, wouldn't that have been something, I thought, him loose in the cabin, pinging off every piece of furniture and us?

He finally calmed down after a few hours in a quiet dark corner of our main room.

Gram made me sit right next to his cage every day for an hour. "Sing the healing song softly," she said. "Learn how to be calm and how to send out that calmness."

I made up my own songs too. The squirrel calmed as the days passed, though it felt like this was mostly depression at being stuck inside a house with humans. But he began to come up to me, curious, hoping I'd brought him food, which I always did. Nuts and sunflower seeds from Gram's cache that Jeremy the trader to the city supplied her with regularly, and the tiny pinecones that I gathered from the mountain hemlocks that hemmed our cabin on its north side and rose up the steep slope of the mountain to our north, getting smaller and shrubbier as they climbed higher, providing good cover for the birds and small creatures, and for Hannah and me when we had the chance to slip up there and play amongst their knotted and twisted trunks, under the canopy of their dark and interlaced branches.

Then Gram announced we could let the squirrel loose in the house—*and Tessa, I'm trusting you to be extra careful whenever you go in or out the door*—the intermediate stage of his rehabilitation, as Gram called it.

He loved the rafters. He loved leaping from the rafters even more, and I swear he sat up there waiting until I was about to pass below, and then he launched into the air and parachuted down on my head or my arms. He never did it to Gram. He scratched almost as much as the hawk but he couldn't help it; that was just part of being a squirrel. I loved him and wanted to keep him for a pet but Gram put a dark view on that.

"We're helping him heal so he can go back to his own life, Tessa." Then she looked thoughtful and added, "I think it's time I talked with you about the role of the healer."

Her dark eyes held onto mine when she said this and it felt like they held on so tight I couldn't look away even if fifty squirrels came running in through our door.

"What do you know about healing, Tessa?" Gram asked.

"Um, some people do it. You do it, sometimes you use herbs and uh, usually you use songs..." I stammered, realizing that I knew nothing about it at all.

"Can I be a healer, Gram?" It kind of burst out of me.

Her dark brows began to move into her frown that made me hold my breath and try to become invisible. "It's probably the hardest thing you could ever become," she said finally, "and even then it's not up to you. You are called to it. Either you're a healer or you aren't. But if you want to find out, we'll find out."

Okay. I sat there waiting for our first lesson. But she only said, "Sit where you're sitting for an hour and see if the squirrel comes up to you. And think of everything you know about healing."

She picked up her collecting basket and slipped out the door.

A golden-crowned sparrow sang its three descending notes from a bushy mountain hemlock close to our cabin. *Oh dear me...*

I sat. I didn't squirm. I thought about Gram, my only example of a healer. She was a little different from everyone else in the village. She was raising me because someone needed to, but if it weren't for that, she would be living alone. She once had a husband but he left, *off to the city* she told me once when I asked her, and she never talked about him. I did know that he was half Tlingit, so both my mother and auntie Annie were somewhere between quarter and half Tlingit.

Gram sometimes smiled, and every once in a while she laughed, but usually she was serious, and almost always she seemed to be... listening. Gram heard, and even saw, things that no one else did. And they seemed to be sobering things. Things you had to be careful about.

Sometimes she stayed up all night praying over someone who'd come to her for help. Sometimes she fasted for a day. Or two. She cried when people walked out our door shaking their heads, not believing that they could be healed. She cried when they died. Her crying was silent, and oddly there was something of that red-tailed hawk in it, something a little fierce. I'd seen Gram cry over a brand new baby in someone's arms—usually people cried with happiness over babies, at least that's what it seemed to me the few times I'd seen it, but somehow Gram didn't seem like she was crying like the other women. I wondered. It seemed like she was crying for another reason, and it wasn't happiness.

Either you're a healer or you aren't, she said. And if it's a calling, how does a person know when she's getting the call?

I reached the point of thinking that maybe I didn't really want to be a healer. But from what Gram said, maybe it wasn't up to me after all?

Suddenly the squirrel leaped onto my shoulder from the bookcase and scared me so much I fell off the chair. He thought it was a game.

~

For some time I had begged to be allowed to climb the mountain that rose out of our backyard to close our small valley off to the north. Gram always shook her head and said that I was too young. Then one day she said I could. She called it "walking the mountain." *Go walk the mountain,* she said, *alone, with just your thoughts, and with your eyes and ears open. Be still and pay attention.*

She didn't cut me completely free—I needed to stay within sight of the village—but since it was a four thousand foot mountain and our village was at about a thousand feet in the valley, it was a good climb she was letting me do at the age of ten. Hardly anyone ever went up there as there was always plenty to do around the village or in the neighboring valleys and it would be kind of rare for someone to just take an afternoon and climb one of the mountains for the view. There were plenty of mid-sized to large-sized animals I could potentially meet up there—no moose as they stayed down in the valleys or followed the treeline that climbed a quarter of the way up the mountains around us—but mountain goats, lynx, foxes, every once in a while a fierce wolverine, and even more infrequently a wolf (these we never saw, but every once in a while we heard them calling from the mountain heights). And there definitely were black bears around. I'd seen a few of them already in my young life, but they didn't really scare me as I knew they would leave me alone unless I did something really stupid like come between a mother and a cub, or between a bear and its kill. So the wildlife didn't worry me, and I hoped to see some of it once I started climbing.

The mountain's name was Mount Snow, not terribly imaginative, but accurate. Like everything else around home, it wasn't a name on a map. It was our white guardian to the north in winter and even in the warmest summers a couple of snow patches still held on, resisting melting, at the very top. Though not many people in the village climbed it, a hundred years of occasional traffic had left a clear path once you'd left the scrubby hemlocks behind and got up into the shrubby juniper bushes and, even higher up, the tough mountain grass and moss. My eyes followed the thread of a path zigzagging upward, around a rocky knob about halfway up, over to the western ridge where it dipped up and down with the rocky bumps of the mountain's big shoulder. I was ready for it.

When I stepped out of the last of the hemlocks, the sun poked through fast-running high clouds and shone warm on my dark hair. I was glad for the cool, freshly-filled water bottle in my small backpack, along with my pouch of nuts and dried fruit, and a spare jacket. *When you walk the mountain, you always carry a spare layer,* Gram had said, *because you never know what the weather might bring, and it's always easy to take off layers, but not as easy to find them if you didn't bring them.* I was comfortable in my pants and long-sleeved shirt but I was pretty sure that up top near those snow patches—and I *would* be there soon; even though this was my very first time walking the mountain, my determination was unbounded—I was pretty sure that it would be colder up top.

Ravens gronked overhead, their play-on-the-wind call. I gronked back, spreading my arms out like wings, wishing I was up there with them. They ignored me.

The higher I climbed, the more I could see in every direction but north, which still was blocked by the shoulder of the mountain above me. So far it was just more mountains. All had rocky and snow-patched summits, rock and ice both shining under the warming sun, and every mountain rose from the dark green of the hemlocks and spruce of the valleys. But on each mountain there was a wonderful in-between zone of bright emerald green in the summer, lush green of mosses and berry bushes and dwarf birch leaves. Every autumn this bright green turned to deep crimson, as if the mountains all pulled furry red robes over their middles to stay warm. And you suddenly noticed how many aspens and cottonwoods were down in the valleys, for they all turned brilliant gold, just below that red.

Your Silloway great-great grandparents both grew up a long away from here, Gram told me once, *in a place called Vermont, and when they moved up here at first they complained about how they missed the autumn colors from the East. But then your grampa Silloway realized that the colors here are every bit as beautiful, it's just that he hadn't been looking in the right places.*

On another rest break, stopping just below the mountain's ridge, I found my sun cap in the bottom of my pack and pulled it over my hair which now felt hot from the sun. I wasn't as grateful as usual to have Gram's and auntie Annie's glossy black Tlingit hair. It did help make up for not getting their dark brown eyes like my cousin Hannah got. My skin wasn't quite as dark as Hannah's either, and sometimes in the summer I got sunburned. Before I left this morning Gram rubbed some white lotion on my nose and cheeks and chin, for a little protection, she said. It had a slightly bitter chemical smell to it that I didn't like.

Now I could see over Ptarmigan, the mountain that hemmed our valley to the south. It was a lower mountain, which was good, for in winter when the sun was low, it still reached over the mountain's ridges to our village. It was for this sun that my great great grandparents and the other settlers built the village up against the northern mountain with the broad valley open to the west. Ptarmigan was a lower mountain than the others, but broad as a bulwark, with tiny lakes in the hollows of its heights. Valleys fingered off to the south on the other side of it to—yes! water glinted in the distance. The bay that reached into the mountains for more than twenty miles. Water glinted under the sun, a mile across, and steep mountains rose up on its other side, marching off to the south in interminable lines. I'd seen the bay once before, the summer I turned eight, when Gram and I got to ride in a wagon with Jesse's family as Earl drove the horses down for harvesting yellow cedar.

Eighty years earlier my ancestors planted several groves of yellow cedar in the sheltered valley at the edge of the bay. Ever since then Brightwater family members have driven draft horses down to haul harvested logs back up to our village for the carvers to turn them into boat paddles and masks to sell or barter in the city for supplies. As I sat on the dusty rock of my mountain, my eyes picked out the ferny texture of the cedars against the darker spruce and hemlock.

I sat still and paid attention—Gram would be proud—and right then something shifted in my brain. One familiar piece slid to the side and a bright new piece suddenly slipped over it. Up until then I'd lived my life in a valley. Now I was looking from above. I could see how the world was beginning to fit together.

Time to move on. My steps were slower now that the going was steeper, but I was as determined as ever. An irritation on my left heel told me that maybe that second layer of socks wasn't quite doing the job, even with such well-worn boots. Auntie Annie liked to say that that was the best part about hand-me-downs—*already broken in!*—but sometimes the fit wasn't quite right, and in this case Jesse's younger brother Steve's feet were wider than mine. My breathing came faster. But I loved being out and moving under the sun, in the cool breeze that flowed over the ridge just above me. I'd left behind the shrubby green zone of stunted grasses and oddly furry wildflowers (I wondered if that was what kept them warm in the long blasted mountain winters) and came out into the upper zone of dusty rock. The blue sky turned to dark blue above me.

I was on the ridge. The whole north face of the mountain dropped off almost straight down into a narrow valley on the other side. A lake, smaller than ours and rounder, shone down there under the midday sun but you could see that it had that same bit of milky glacial blueness in it that ours had. On cloudy days our lake looked almost opaque, pale blue, and on the darkest days the water reminded me of jade stone, cool, smooth and greenish. This lake was toward the east end of its valley, like ours, with a spur of Mount Snow dropping down to wall off its east end. I didn't see any signs of habitation, no clearing next to the lake for cabins, no thin tendrils of woodsmoke rising, no fields painstakingly cleared over the generations for crops and for hay for the horses. It was a wild, empty valley and a small lake with no one living near it.

I turned to follow the ridge trail as it climbed east to the summit. As I climbed, I hoped that when I got to the top, I could get a glimpse of the city far to the west. I knew it was only about thirty miles as the ravens flew, though when the traders made the trip with the draft horses it was much farther since they had to go around the mountains and keep to the valleys. Recently I pestered Jesse's dad for information on the city, since he always did the trip with the horses, being the horse handler.

"Lotta people," was all Earl Brightwater said at first. Jesse smiled at this; he and I were with Earl in the barn, helping to brush the draft horses, which meant climbing up on rough wooden boxes so we could reach their shoulders. They always held still for us, though, closing their eyes as we brushed, loving it.

"Please, please, *please* tell more?" I tried to be as winning as Étaîn when she was a fly, but I don't think I came very close.

Jesse's dad huffed. He reminded me of his horses, a little scary he was so large, and kind of quiet, but gentle. "Well, lotta noise too," he said. When he saw the disappointment on my face, he set down the harness he was untangling and leaned on the haunch of my horse and looked at me. "Not a place for you, honey." He called women "honey"—well, not my Gram, but everyone else. "It's a hard place. Easy place to get hurt in."

That was all I was going to get. Jesse told me later he'd heard his dad talk about people getting shot by Orion police in the streets, and the supply party never carried guns with them, even though they might have the opportunity to kill game along the way to bring home for food, because guns would make Orion suspicious, *and anyone with a gun is someone who's got something to protect, something that might be valuable to someone else.*

You mean they'd take things from us if they could?

Well, sure. Dad says don't give Orion the chance and we'll be okay. Layin' low is the way to go.

I nodded then as if I understood—not wanting to seem ignorant to Jesse, who was like a big brother to me, someone to look up to and measure up to. I wanted to be strong like him, and clever at making things. But I knew even then that I couldn't be a hunter. And there was the name Orion again, *the Hunter.*

When I was very little, maybe four or five, when I heard that name I thought of the constellation in the sky, the Hunter, up there so clear and near over our heads in fall, winter, and spring, the three bright stars of his belt, the arms raised in attack, hunting dog at his heels, and knowing that my mother had died somehow fighting him, I was afraid. But my cousin Hannah explained to me that the Orion in the stars was a good hunter, just like the people in our village who went out in hunting parties to bring home meat to share. The Orion my mother had been fighting was bad people in the city who told everyone what to do, and if you weren't in agreement with them you'd get banished, or, even worse, put in camps.

I nodded then, too, as if I understood, but I didn't understand what banished meant, and camps were good things, weren't they? When Gram and I had gone down to see the yellow cedars with Jesse's family, we'd camped overnight and had a campfire and good food and singing.

At ten years old I didn't know much more. Orion was police, who were bad people, who wanted the people who lived in the city to do what they told them to do. If you didn't want to obey Orion, you didn't want to be noticed by them because they might put you in camps somewhere. But this meant that there were people besides us who weren't Orion and who didn't agree with Orion. How many of them were out there? Were there other villages in the mountains like us, people living on their own, some of them going off to fight Orion?

Gram told me that my mother died fighting Orion in the city. I wanted to see the city. As I steadily walked east, up the summit ridge, I was sure that I would be able to turn at the top and see the city in the distance. I could imagine lots and lots of big buildings, and noise of people and machines as Earl Brightwater mentioned, with big open space for landing the jets that so often flew overhead, getting lower as they cleared the mountains and headed for the city. But I couldn't picture how a city could send enough light up into the night sky to light up the clouds to the west. How could people make that much light?

I made myself wait until the tower of rocks higher than me that marked the very top of Mount Snow. Then I turned around and looked to the west. More mountains. The mountains between me and the city were higher than the mountain I was standing on. Tears sprang up in my eyes, and I understood that this was really why I wanted to climb up this mountain. I was hoping for a glimpse of the city.

A raven flew by right then. *Graaaawk!* He tumbled on the air, playing. He could see the city easily if he flew just a little higher. He could fly to the city with hardly any trouble at all.

I pulled on my jacket, feeling a chill for the first time, then meandered over to see if I could look down on our village—I'd broken my promise to Gram to keep home in sight the whole time, oh well—and I found a mossy spot on the ridge that gave a good view down on our valley. Our village was tiny from my raven's eye view. There was the main house up on the grassy slope near the west end of the lake. Cabins scattered above it and below it, nestled between the alders that liked growing along the lakeshore and the mountain hemlocks that liked growing at the feet of Mount Snow. Maybe three dozen cabins in all, one hundred or so people. Our cabin was the next to last one farthest east in the valley with a nice view of the lake... there, my eyes found it... a thread of woodsmoke rose from its chimney, Gram sending me a signal no doubt. More cabins had been built at the west end of the lake where the rushing river began its tumble down the valley over rough rock, screened in places by the alders. Jesse's family's cabin was among those, and there was the horse barn above it, with three acres of grassy field beyond it, field that seemed so huge when I was standing down there outside the barn but now was a tiny green square.

Suddenly I was hungry, and I opened my pack and pulled out my snack of nuts and dried fruit. I found a small piece of paper stuck in the little canvas pouch that we used for carrying snacks. Gram's handwriting: *I packed a little extra for you to share. Remember, be still and pay attention!*

I looked around. I'd seen ravens flying overhead, but that was it for wildlife. I munched for a moment, not intending to save any of my snack for anyone, but then just before getting up to leave, I scattered a handful of dried cranberries and blueberries over the stony ground. A nice treat for a raven.

I discovered that going down was at least twice as fast as going up. Pretty soon I'd descended so far that I was about to lose my view.

I stopped to sit on the moss for one more look to the south, to the bay, before I was down in the valley again. I really didn't want to go back down.

One more long drink from my water bottle, the last of my water but I figured I'd be home soon. I opened up my snack pouch for one last nibble, and I heard a whistle on the breeze, sharp and short, more like a warning call. I turned my head to look all around. Nothing. The whistle again. Then I saw the noisemaker—a hoary marmot sitting up on his haunches, probably guarding his burrow, only twenty yards away.

An answering whistle, then a second marmot bundled over the moss on short legs, over to the first one. Much bigger than the arctic ground squirrels we called parkie squirrels, these were almost knee high to me, burley with thick, rippling coats of silver fur, accented by bushy brown tails and brown faces and paws. Big sniffy noses with long whiskers. They stood up on their hind legs and touched noses. Oh, this was as good as a fly with lustrous eyes!

They dropped down on all fours, each looking around for a moment, then started my way, stepping, pausing, sniffing. I made myself into a statue. They came closer. And closer. I began trembling as I worked so hard to hold absolutely still. I heard the scratch of their claws on the moss as they came right up to me. Scratch, scratch, sniff, sniff. I could have reached out and touched them, but of course that would have made them run off. So I held absolutely still, my eyes wide and taking them in.

One was braver than the other. The female, I was sure of it. She took two steps closer and sniffed my boots. Oh, I could barely stand it! The male, farther away, jumped back, which startled her and made her jump back. But after a second she came forward again to sniff my boots and then my pant legs above my boots. I wondered what I smelled like. And if they had ever sniffed humans before. My hand twitched from wanting to reach out and touch her.

She didn't seem to think much of me, though, and turned back to the more timid one. Suddenly they both stood up on their hind legs and put their front paws on each other's shoulders. They took little steps back and forth, holding on with their paws, and it looked just like they were dancing.

I nearly died from holding my breath, to keep from bursting out laughing. Marmots dancing!

27

My laugh of delight made them drop to their feet and scramble away. I wished I could stay the rest of the day up there with them. I wondered if there was a burrow big enough for me, too, and if I could share it with them for the night. But no, I had to get back to the village and Gram.

I scattered a handful of nuts and dried cranberries on the moss before leaving.

"Bye guys," I whispered. They'd gone to their burrows, but I was pretty sure they'd come back as soon as I was gone.

Down the mountain. The trail forked as it neared the village—I hadn't noticed this on the way up, I only noticed the path I was on from our house—and now I chose the right hand path, the longer way home that took me past the Brightwater barn and horses and then up through the village.

"Ho, little Ravenwing!" Earl Brightwater called out to me as I walked along the pasture fence. Sometimes he called me that and it made me happy. "Where've you been to?"

"I just climbed the mountain!"

He leaned against a fencepost and pushed back his broad-brimmed felt hat. "Well now." He glanced up the mountain. "I was up there once a long, long time ago."

"Did you see the marmots?"

"The whats?"

"The marmots that live up there. They put their paws on each others shoulders and dance!"

Earl Brightwater smiled and shook his head. "Well, I never."

I waved at him and kept walking, turning left after his barn and up the main path through the village. It was quiet, late afternoon, everybody off doing something. The only other person I saw was Tucky Lotts, sagging on the wooden bench outside the main house, eyes shut in the late afternoon sun. Grizzled whiskers covered his cheeks and chin, shrubby gray hair poked out in all directions from under his cowboy hat with a bald eagle tailfeather sewn in.

I hoped I'd get past him without him opening his eyes—he said some strange things sometimes and I never knew what to say back—but no luck. His eyes opened and he raised his right hand in a little wave.

I waved back and kept walking, calling out, "I was up the mountain!"

Tucky suddenly exclaimed, "Marmots!" At least I thought that was what he said.

I paused and looked at him. "Yes, I saw them. They were dancing!"

He nodded vigorously and said something else, I had no idea what. Then he looked sad. "Empty," he said. I think.

I pulled off my backpack, opened it up and pulled out the snack pouch that still had a few handfuls in it. I tossed the pouch to him and he caught it out of the air with both hands. "From Gram," I said. He could return it, or not. If Gram wanted it back, we knew where to find him.

He gave me a gappy grin. He waved again, I waved back and kept on heading home.

~

"Have you wondered why we so often tell stories and folk tales?" Gram asked after I'd told her all about the dancing marmots and the wonderful views from high up on the mountain. I couldn't answer the *why* part; all I knew was that the legends and fairy tales were as much a part of me as air and water.

But as I thought over my day of walking the mountain, something else clicked in my mind. "Somebody has an adventure," I said. "That's usually how the stories start, isn't it?"

Gram looked surprised, then she smiled a little. "You're right, Tessa. They almost always start with somebody getting called to an adventure."

We were sitting on the rock step below our cabin door where we often sat on late afternoons in summer when the sun shone down and warmed the stone. We faced down the valley, the lake perfectly still on our left, mirroring the mountain to the south. The rest of the village lay slightly below us.

"At the heart of every one of those adventures is the mystery of callings and boundaries and thresholds," Gram said, looking down the valley over the village instead of looking at me. "Raven is one of the threshold guardians. Since time immemorial he's been seen that way, not just by the Tlingits and other natives here, but also by the Celts, on the other side of the world. That tells you something, doesn't it? But you have to also remember that he's a trickster. He's your friend, but it might be best not to trust him entirely."

I thought of the beginning of the Haida creation story called

"Raven Travelling." It was another of the main house story-night favorites, and we kids had small parts in it which made it fun, and I'd learned whole lines of it without trying to. The story began with Raven flying over the sea in darkness looking for a place to land and rest. In those days there was even more sea than there was today. And Raven did something strange: he pushed right through the sky into another world.

> *Now when the Raven had flown a while longer,*
> *the sky in one direction brightened.*
> *It enabled him to see, they say.*
> *And then he flew right up against it.*
> *He pushed his mind through and pulled his body after.*

And in that story, and in the Tlingit story of Raven bringing the sun, moon and the stars to humans, Raven used his trickery to become human for a time, to live with a chief's family so he could complete his mission of creating a world for the gods to live in, or of putting the sun, the moon and the stars in the sky so the humans could have light.

"This is very important, Tessa," Gram said, turning her head to look at me. "Like Raven, the healer also crosses back and forth over the thresholds, across the boundaries. There is great power in that, and great peril as well."

Great peril echoed in my mind. I wasn't quite sure what peril was. But it felt familiar.

I took a deep breath and looked left, over the lake to the birches on the far shore. They were just beginning to turn autumn gold, something I hadn't noticed until that moment. Even from up on the mountain looking down, I hadn't noticed.

Then I remembered where I'd heard the word *peril*. It was in the dream I had when I fell through the lake ice. Raven was there standing next to me and I heard the words *peril and joy*. I didn't know if Raven spoke them or not, but they echoed inside me even as I didn't quite understand what they were about.

"Peril means danger, right, Gram?"

She nodded. Then she looked away, back down the valley over the village. I felt released enough from her attention to be able to think again. That dream. Raven was there with me and we had gone somewhere. We *flew* somewhere. And I felt joy. The words *peril and joy*

30

had reverberated through the dream, but I felt only joy.

I told Gram what I remembered about the dream, and she looked thoughtful. "We have spirit helpers," she said. "Probably they are there for all of us, but not many people seem to be aware of them. They are essential for the healer, though." She turned her eyes on me again. "Think hard, Tessa. Which feels more like a spirit helper to you, the dancing marmots or Raven?"

I didn't have to think hard at all; I knew right away. "The marmots are my friends. Raven is my spirit helper."

"Probably the most powerful of all," Gram said softly, still looking at me. "But he's not the power. He comes and goes with it, he crosses the thresholds, he serves the power, or sometimes he doesn't, since he's Raven. He can be your helper and the one that you talk to, Tessa, but he's not the one you pray to. I want you to take some time over the next few days and think on this: who do you pray to?"

~

I thought Gram might be talking about God. Some Haida and Tlingit stories that took place so long ago it was called "time immemorial," talked about a Transformer, which fascinated me. Might that also be God? The Celts had gods and goddesses, but it seemed like there was a being beyond them, greater than they, something very big and mysterious. But, to me, awfully vague.

There was a Christian priest in our village who led Sunday services in a small house next to the main house, who talked about God and forgiveness of our sins and hearing God's voice in our lives. I'd gone a few times with Jesse, whose family went every Sunday, along with maybe a third of our village. God was definitely a "he." There were crosses and statues of Jesus and the Virgin Mary, and people prayed holding beads in their hands. People who were what they called *baptized* walked up front to drink out of a cup and eat wafers handed out by the priest. I wasn't baptized—I was pretty positive I wasn't, knowing Gram—so I couldn't do that, but I was always curious and watched Jesse's every move. There wasn't much that was vague, except maybe the part about a holy ghost. That I didn't get at all.

"You pray to God, right, Gram?" I asked her a couple of mornings later, partly to let her know I was working on my homework, partly to get whatever hints I could.

"I do." Gram kept washing dishes in the sink and handing them to me to dry. The plates were cold since the water early in the morning hadn't had time to get warmed in our rooftop solar system. "Where do you think God is, Tessa?"

I looked out the window over the sink. It gave a wonderful view up the lake since our cabin sat only about thirty yards up on the bank above the water, with no alders between us and the shore. "He's out there, he's bigger than us and our world, bigger than Raven or the spirit helpers." That seemed safe to say.

Gram tapped my forehead lightly with her soapy right index finger. "God is a mystery. God is within each of us, not 'out there' anywhere. The Celts saw God as the ultimate circle, and the ultimate mystery. And best not to let anyone talk to you about God as a 'He' and tell you that you need to atone for your sins in order to be able to talk with God. Too many people try to control the idea of God, wanting something concrete like statues and crosses. They want the tangible, they're afraid of mystery. Don't be afraid of mystery, Tessa."

She'd never hesitated in letting me go to church with Jesse and his family, and I realized she had been letting me make decisions on my own as to what I believed. *Mystery*, I thought. *Peril and joy.*

"Is it God who you ask to heal people, Gram?"

She pursed her lips and looked away, out at the lake. "You're going to need to keep thinking on all of this for a long time, Tessa. This is an awful lot at once. But remember this: asking isn't going to get you very far. Most of our asking is more like demanding. Even when we add 'please' to it."

After a moment's pause, while wind sighed through the hemlocks on the other side of our cabin, Gram added, "Think of seeking healing as more like seeking a blessing. And it's not you seeking a blessing, it's you putting yourself *into* a blessing for someone or something else. You become part of that blessing. Maybe you can be the vehicle for the blessing."

~

The day after that conversation at the sink, I was walking home from school, downhill from the main house and not in a very good mood because my teacher that year, Mrs. Mack, moved me to a corner because she said I'd exceeded my talking-during-class quota for the year. And she didn't answer all of my questions about why the seas rose around the world sixty years ago, and I was beginning to suspect that was because she didn't really know why, and I hated it when people didn't come out and say they didn't know something. So I was kicking stones down the path, then noticed Jesse's younger brother Steve and his buddy Jacob Lotts, old Tucky's great-nephew, tossing something black back and forth between them. A wing fluttered. I was on them in an instant.

"Give that to me *right now*." I was prepared to do absolutely anything to get it away from them.

They were both about my size, maybe not quite as tall but a bit heavier and just starting to come into some muscles. Steve opened his mouth and I didn't even give him the chance to speak.

"Now!"

He held out a limp raven. "He was already like this, honest, Tessa."

"Well you sure weren't helping him feel any better, were you?" The raven was still warm, but limp, with a film just beginning to come down over his wonderful blue baby-raven eyes. He was a baby raven but he still completely filled both my hands. I felt my heart give a painful squeeze and stay shut. The whole world seemed to get darker. I could barely breathe.

I took careful steps through the sedges and mud that separated the path from the pebbly lakeshore, and as I carried the raven, I began singing under my breath—I barely had the breath for it, but I did—the first healing song of Gram's I'd learned: *Warmth of sun and cool of night, blue of lake and green of light, here we greet you in this place! Spirit helpers send us grace...* I added, *Raven, be here with your own, send a blessing to see him flown.*

At the edge of the lake I lifted the raven up toward the cobalt blue sky and heard myself singing, *Fly with the west wind, fly with the east. Soar on the south wind until you find north. Fly with blessing, little raven.*

Something happened that I didn't understand at all, but it seemed like a perfectly natural thing to happen. My hands tingled. A surge of pulsing current swept down from my hands through my body. I felt like a lightning rod, a human conductor. My hands felt hot with fire.

Then it was over and I slowly lowered my hands. The raven twitched as if waking from a dream, and the next thing I knew we were staring into each other's eyes. It looked very surprised. I'm sure I looked surprised too. He opened his black wings, flapped once, twice, then took off with a hoarse cry. He flew low over the water headed east, slowly climbing higher as he went. I blinked my eyes several times because the world had become very bright.

"Holy shit!" Steve Brightwater shouted, and he and Jacob took off running down the path for their homes.

I suddenly needed to sit down, so I just dropped to the cool pebble beach and stayed sitting with my arms around my knees, turned back to watch the tiny black dot of the raven get smaller and smaller as he flew down the lake.

2. September–October 2092

"And the girl blessed the little raven, and Raven blessed it, too, and the girl lifted the little raven up and it suddenly spread its wings and flew away," Gram said as she smoothed the blanket over me and kissed my forehead.

"And it flew back the next day with its best friend," I added. "Gram, wouldn't it be nice if it *did* come back to visit me? I wish it would."

Gram was smiling a little as she turned away from my bed. "That sort of thing doesn't happen very often, Tessa. And if he did, how would you know him?"

"Oh, I'd know him." She was moving for the door and I wasn't ready to go to sleep. "Gram, *what* was that tingling that moved through my hands? I can't sleep until I know."

I heard her sigh. She turned and looked at me, then slowly walked back and sat down on the edge of my bed. She smoothed back from her forehead her black-with-white-threads-through-it hair, a typical gesture when she was settling in to deep thought.

"The tingling feeling and the burning heat," she said slowly, "where did it feel it came from? From inside you, working out, or from outside you, working in?"

"From outside me." No doubt about it.

Ah, I was catching on to why she was thinking so hard. Earlier she said that God was within us, not a force outside of us. But what I felt was definitely *other*.

"You know how we talked about God being a mystery?" Gram said. "Well, you're getting some lessons on mysteries early on. You aren't going to be able to understand this yet, Tessa, and in fact you may never feel you really understand it. I can't say that I understand it, myself."

This was sobering. I looked to Gram as the person who understood everything.

"What were you thinking when you first took that raven into your hands?" Gram asked. "What were you feeling?"

I thought hard for a moment and put myself back there. "I was mad at the boys for playing with it, but as soon as I held it, I felt... well, it was kind of weird. It felt like my heart was squeezing and I could hardly breathe, and the whole world began getting dark."

She was silent for a moment, looking at me in the evening dimness gathering in my room. It was early September, no longer a bedtime with the sun still shining high in the sky like an invitation like it did all through the summer months.

"Were you afraid?"

I shook my head. "All I could think of was wanting the raven to get better. So I tried singing your healing song, even though I could barely sing, and I added a little bit of my own, wanting it to be a blessing, like you said..."

"And that's when you lifted him up, and felt that power run through you," Gram added when I faltered.

I nodded. I could feel her thinking hard again. I felt the words *great power and great peril.*

"Tessa," Gram said, and paused, and went on, "you pick up what other people, or birds, or animals are feeling?"

I nodded again. I hadn't thought about this before. It just seemed normal to me. I did it all the time with the creatures that we took in to help heal; there seemed no barrier between them and me. With people it was different, which was a good thing since there were so many people around, and who would want to be picking up what's going on inside one hundred people around you all day long? I'd learned the steady-state feeling of each of the people closest to me, and liked leaving it at that.

"Well, I'll give you another mystery to mull over," Gram said with a little more energy, as if she was hoping to wrap up this bedtime session. "Gifts run through our family, gifts that are—well, a bit out of the ordinary. Like being able to help people or animals heal, or like knowing events in the future that are drawing near."

"Our family," I repeated. "You mean, like from granny Ida and grampa Vegard, and granny and grampa Silloway?"

Gram nodded. "Your great great granny Ida was a legendary healer. On the other side of the family, my mother's side, your great great grampa Dylan Silloway was... well, he was different, we'll just leave it at that. A good and kind man, but someone so sensitive to the energies of the people around him that he needed to protect himself most of the time."

Huh. This explained a lot of questions I'd had about my great great grampa Silloway. Of course it also raised many more.

"The important thing to think about," Gram said, "is how to use those gifts, how to become a blessing by using those gifts." She paused, then she added, "And how to be protected in being the conductor that those gifts work through."

She kissed my forehead. Time for me to go to sleep.

"God?" I asked.

Gram nodded. "God protects us, though we have to do our share as well. Sleep tight little Ravenwing."

~

More homework. This was hard. Gram was making me sit for an hour, doing absolutely nothing, in my favorite place on a rocky shelf that stuck out above the gnarled hemlocks of the lower reaches of Mount Snow. It was my favorite place because when you sat there, you felt like the lake was at your feet, within the sheltering arms of the mountains north and south. But instead of doing what I usually did, like singing and building little houses out of hemlock twigs and moss, and watching for ravens, I now had to sit absolutely still on the rocks, my hands open and resting on my knees, my eyes half open, my mind calm and open.

Be still and pay attention.

Gram said that while God was our guide, and Raven was my spirit-helper, the lake was important for me too. "It can be your spirit place," she said when I skeptically squinched my face up at her before I left the cabin. She had handed me a wool rug I could use for sitting on, to make the rocks a little more comfortable. "You're going to learn how to be completely there, in that place," she said. "You are letting that place go all the way deep inside you, so that it is always there for you to call on when you need it."

"For the power?" I was frowning, trying to understand.

"For itself. Perhaps it is behind the power for the blessing."

I wanted to tell her that this was the lake that tried to kill me, didn't it? I wasn't so sure I wanted to spend special time with this lake!

She bent down—Gram was pretty short, actually, and at ten I was suddenly all legs and arms, so she wasn't much taller than me anymore and didn't have to bend down far—and her dark eyes were smiling into my eyes.

"It's a powerful lake, Tessa. Our ancestors chose to live here. They chose this lake. Or maybe it chose them? It's neither good nor bad, that's not how powerful things work. We have to respect the power and understand where we are in relation to it. What's important now is for you to be still and pay attention and understand this lake as best you can, and let it understand you."

I tried, though everything in me was struggling against doing it. I guess that was why I related so well to that drop-of-red-gold-sun squirrel. I myself was always the noisiest and most energetic creature in the room.

I kept thinking, *how can a lake understand a person?!* But there was something about this lake... perhaps because it was one of those thin places between real and... everything else. Perhaps many spirits were drawn to it.

There was a wind up higher, along the mountain ridges, and its hushing sound grew louder as I grew quieter inside. Every few minutes I heard a distant cry from a raven up there, playing the ridges. Down below the lakewater was still, though. The lake was doing its mirror game on this cloudy day with no bright sun to interfere: the smooth, green lakewater perfectly reflected the golding birches and cottonwoods along the shoreline, and above them the fur of midmountain showed an auburn tinge now as the berry bush leaves turned crimson. I was just high enough up on Mount Snow that I couldn't see the top of the mountain to the south reflected in the lake. Just the colors and textures of golds and reds with gray rock above them, all in the mirror water.

I was not exactly obeying Gram's instructions, as my eyes were wide open and staring at the lake. I imagined away all of its water. This was fairly easy to do if you spent enough time looking up and down the steep mountain slopes above the water—you could picture how steep the roots of the mountains were, down below the water, smooth gray rock, how they narrowed down, finally settling into a rocky bottom floor way, way down. It would take me hours to climb down, just as it had taken a couple of hours to climb to the top of Mount Snow. And from the very bottom, way deep in the dark hollow that would only get a little sun in the very middle part of the day in the very middle part of the summer, you would be looking seven thousand feet up—more than a mile!— to the summit of Mount Snow, against a sky almost blue-black it was so far away.

Our two mountains, Mount Snow to the north and Ptarmigan to the south, didn't quite meet at the east end of the lake. Both mountain ridges sharpened to a narrow canyon, and a river ran through, and into the lake, always rushing and full with water from the snowfield draped over the taller mountains to the northeast. Jesse told me once that the snowfield ran for miles and miles and miles, it would take a person days to cross it on skis, and there were deep crevasses in the ice that were so deep they were pretty much bottomless, so if you fell in one of those your body might never be found. One of his uncles skied up there once, and came back to tell the story.

The east end of our lake was the end I didn't know very well, the mysterious end. I decided to spend some time down there as soon as Gram would let me. I'd follow the path down the lake, just above the shore, the path kept open by trail parties from our village smacking back the brushy alders and willows every couple of years. This trail eventually ran alongside the river in the canyon and came out on the east side in another valley, where people hunted in the fall, and fished, too.

The local fishes, the ones always around, even in winter (and always there was someone out there on the ice in midwinter jigging a line up and down in the frosty cold, putting out clouds of steam and pulling fish up through the ice), our fish were rainbow trout, sleek arctic greyling, and the char which were gray with pink polka dots, with the wonderful name of Dolly Varden. They were important food for our village. But best of all were the salmon, much more exotic because of how they came and went—a small mystery in themselves, I realized as I looked down at the lake.

When I was very little, it just seemed to me that sometimes the salmon were there and sometimes they weren't, and who knew how that happened? But once I was ten and paying more attention, I remembered Gram's stories about how the salmon fry (those that weren't eaten as eggs by the greedy Dolly Varden and greyling and trout) grew up in our lake and then, somehow, the lake seemed too small for them and something called them to swim away, down the river, through the valleys, to the bay and then to the sea. They were gone in the sea for a while—maybe three years?—but then something called them back, and the real mystery was that somehow they knew how to come back out of the wide, wide sea to that very river that they had come out of. They found the mouth of the river, and then swam up the river against the current, all the way back to our lake where they had been baby salmon. They arrived back home in wonderful shades of red, the males with yellow-green heads and the funniest beaks and big humps on their backs. We called them "humpies" of course.

But as I was growing older, fewer salmon came back to us, so we had to be very careful to only eat a few, gratefully. Jesse had some Brightwater uncles who, when the first salmon were sighted swimming up under the log bridge over the mouth of our lake, trudged down to the lakeshore and made a cedarsmoke fire and said prayers, thanking God and thanking the salmon for coming back to feed us. Gram and Auntie Annie always joined them, bringing Hannah and her brothers and me. Auntie Annie always made a little speech about salmon running up the streams, but also running through the veins of the people, and Hannah and I always giggled at the thought of humpies inside people.

Hannah. We actually hadn't giggled together for a while. I hadn't seen as much of her as usual, and when I did see her, she didn't talk as much to me. She was acting more like the grownups now. What was with that? Another mystery.

I looked away from the lake, lifting my face to the mountain ridges. I closed my eyes and listened. Ravens again.

~

"It has been said..." Gram trailed off and looked across the main house right at me. "It has been said..." and we all could hear the words that followed right after, hanging in the air: *though of course we can't know for sure.* This was Gram's favorite way of beginning a story. Of course we all liked *Long, long time ago*, but *It has been said* kicked the whole endeavor up another notch in the realm of possibilities.

Her second *It has been said* was the cue for someone to call out, and this time it was white-haired Lester Goodenough, "Heck, we never know anything for sure anyway!" Everyone in the room laughed, and Gram began telling the Haida story of Raven Travelling.

When she said the lines about Raven pushing his mind through the sky and pulling his body after, for the first time it occurred to me that it wasn't him pushing his *head* through the sky, and pulling his body after, like I'd always thought—he pushed his *mind* through first. This added new mystery to the story and made me wonder what else I was missing.

And after pushing through the boundary of the sky, Raven was in a new place where there were people:

> *There were five villages strung out in a line.*
> *In the northernmost, the headman's favoured daughter*
> *had just given birth to a child.*
> *When evening came, and they were sleeping,*
> *the Raven peeled the skin off the newborn child, starting at the feet,*
> *and put it on.*
> *Then he laid down in the child's place.*

For a while Raven lived in the village as a baby boy, doted on by the grandfather. But he was hungry since he was Raven as well as a baby, and he needed real food, so at night when everyone in the house slept, he sneaked out and found himself things to eat. But the story kept it a secret what he was bringing back to roast on the fire and eat. And more mysterious than that, Raven was being watched by something very strange.

> *Something that was half rock, living in the back corner, watched him.*
> *While he was gone, it continued to sit there.*
> *He brought something in in the fold of his robe.*
> *In front of his mother, where the fire smoldered,*
> *he poked at the coals.*
> *He scooped out a cooking spot with a stick,*
> *and there he put the things that he carried.*
> *As soon as the embers had charred them, he ate them.*
> *They slithered.*
> *He laughed to himself.*
> *Therefore he was seen from the corner.*

After a couple of nights of this, there was wailing in the villages in the morning, and it turned out that all of the people (except the grandfather's family) were each missing an eyeball. That was what Raven had been eating in the night.

"Ewwwwwwwwww!" All of us kids shouted in unison.

I'd heard this story many times before and always had been grossed out over the eyeball part, but this time it struck me that Raven was cruel (skinning the baby? the laughing to himself as the eyeballs slithered—how could they slither?—and the horror of having someone dig out one of your eyeballs while you slept!). And what was that thing, *Something that was half rock, living in the back corner,* watching. The story didn't say anything more about it, just that it watched, and after Raven went out *it continued to sit there.*

This was just about the creepiest thing I had ever heard.

But an elder figured out the nighttime raids, and the people were onto Raven. All the people walked outside and called for the baby of the favored one.

And as soon as the people had gathered,
they stood in a circle, bouncing him up as they sang him a song.
After a while they let him fall,
and they watched him go down.
Turning round to the right he went down through the clouds
and struck water.
Then as he drifted about, he kept crying.
After his voice grew tired, he slept.

Raven fell downwards, through the clouds.

His adventures continued. He continued to transform.

~

Back up in my spot above the lake a few days later, trying to be still and pay attention to the lake and not to how cold I was getting now that it was late September and chilly breezes flowed over Mount Snow, I heard a sudden *whuh-whuh-whuh* of wing beats and opened my eyes to see a pair of ravens settle in the hemlocks just twenty yards away. They'd flown in without calling, which seemed unusual for ravens. I sat absolutely still so as not to scare them, and smiled to myself over how I actually *could* be extremely still and attentive. Selectively.

But the ravens didn't seem to care a bit about me—and ravens always noticed you, even if you held still as a statue, so of course they knew I was sitting there when they came in to land. This pair of ravens began making the most amazing sounds, and I thought I knew pretty much every sound a raven made, all of the wild calls on the wing whether in play or in pointing out food down below, the warnings and invitations and queries from the treetops. Now they were making quiet sounds, whispers. They were almost melodic. It was like two people saying sweet and loving things to each other, half-singing. Their heads were close together and from time to time one sidled closer and they bobbed their heads a little, all the while making this wonderful murmuring song.

It was as magical as the marmots, but in a quiet way.

"I heard ravens singing," I announced to Hannah when I met her on the path on my way home.

She stopped walking and frowned. It seemed to me that Hannah had been doing a lot of frowning lately. Her hair was pulled tight into long braids and she was neatly dressed in a warm-looking green wool tunic over gray wool leggings, all in very tidy contrast to my shorter, wild-as-usual hair and well-mended jeans and dirty sweatshirt. Tidy and all put together, but really she looked kind of pale and tired.

"Ravens don't sing, Tessa," she said.

"They do, too." I put my hands on my hips, ready for a fight, even if it was only verbal.

But she just shook her head and kept walking.

"Hannah!" I called after her. "Where are you going?"

"I have to go home." Her voice drifted back to me.

I arrived back at my home feeling unjustly treated. Even a fight would have been better than her turning her back on me and walking away.

"What's bothering you?" But Gram sounded like she didn't want to hear much from me either. She was sorting and tying herb bundles—sage, oregano, meadowsweet—readying them for hanging to dry from the rafters. The whole cabin filled with sweet and piercing herb fragrance.

"What's with Hannah?"

Gram looked at me for a moment sort of speculatively. Then she went back to her herbs.

"It might be better if you ask her yourself."

I made a scoffing sound. "She hardly talks to me anymore. Want me to help tie things up?"

"That would be nice, dear. Thank you." Gram moved over and made room for me at the end of our wooden table piled with springy masses of green. I'd tied herbs before with her and it wasn't a bad job, but really I was hoping she'd talk more about Hannah. She didn't.

But two days later Gram and I had a berry picking outing with Auntie Annie and Hannah, and I could tell that Gram was hoping that us girls would talk to each other.

We walked down the lake path, past the path up to my sitting spot, and then began climbing over grass and tundra around the hemlocks to the wide swath of berry bushes that looked now like a soft, crimson belt around Mount Snow's middle. Every fall we came here with woven cedar-strip baskets on our backs to pick berries. Every year we chose clear late September days when the wind was cold on our backs but the sun was warm on our faces. Faint barking came from the sky and I lifted my face—surprised every time—to see wild geese skeining up, making that long journey south to somewhere for the winter. Sometimes you could count a hundred V's of geese in an hour, there were so many of them.

The mountain blueberries were small and firm, tasty but not great for eating like a snack. They were much better in muffins and pancakes in the winter, and Gram made good jam with them too. But because they were small, the picking went slowly and I got bored quickly. Gram and Auntie Annie talked from time to time, working bushes not too far apart from each other, but Hannah seemed to want to be off on her own, farther away. So I had to do things like count the geese overhead and watch for any other autumn migrants that we sometimes caught glimpses of, like cranes with their long legs trailing behind them. And our own summer birds liked to gang up before migrating, so sometimes we were treated to several ruby-crowned kinglets competing with their funny little warbly songs from the hemlocks just below us.

But there wasn't much bird action this day.

I heard a distant shout down below, turned and saw a canoe on the lake, two people in it, paddling east in our direction. The person in the stern stopped paddling and waved—I think at us. I waved back, spreading my aqua blue sweatshirt open so it was easy to see.

"Brightwaters?" I heard Gram say to Auntie Annie.

Auntie straightened up and shaded her eyes to see better into the bright sun. She was about Gram's size, short and plump, but her black hair was glossy and free of any white, and she wore it shoulder length and tucked behind her ears, kind of stylish. Her snug and faded jeans looked hip, too.

"No, I think it's a couple of Silloways. Marvin and Emmitt, I'd bet." Auntie glanced over at me, and Hannah a little ways down the slope from me. "How're you girls doing?"

Hannah just grunted. I said, "Oh, fine."

Then Hannah fell to her knees. She dropped her basket and it rolled over, spilling berries everywhere. She looked like she was just about to crash face-first into the sea of bushes all around us. Auntie moved in a flash. She dropped her own basket and dashed through the berry shrubs to catch Hannah in her arms and hold her up against her chest. Gram moved surprisingly quickly too, to kneel at Hannah's side, looking into her face.

I was left standing there staring, my mouth open. Then I stumbled a few tentative steps forward until I stood a few feet away from Gram. Hannah was breathing in gasps, her eyelids fluttering, her hands grasping at the air. Gram reached out for Hannah's hands and talked to her softly. I couldn't hear what she was saying.

In another moment Hannah was quiet, breathing normally, looking like she was asleep. Auntie and Gram looked at each other. Gram talked softly to Auntie, and Auntie nodded. Gram gave a big sigh, a sad sigh, and then she looked over at me.

"She'll be okay, Tessa."

Auntie lifted Hannah, Gram reaching out and helping with Hannah's legs, because as strong as Auntie was, Hannah was nearly her size. They carried Hannah a few steps over to a grassy patch in the midst of the berry bushes, and laid her down with care. I crept over to join them. Auntie put an arm around my shoulders.

"She's okay, Tessa, don't you worry."

She looks okay now, I was thinking, but she definitely did not look okay a minute ago.

Hannah opened her eyes and looked right at me. Her eyes opened wider and she started to sit up, but both Auntie and Gram put their hands out to stop her.

"Just lie still a few minutes, Sweetie," Auntie said.

"The canoe!" Hannah breathed. Her eyes still had a wild look. "The canoe! We'll drown!"

I turned and looked down on the lake, checking on the canoe, half expecting to see it roll over right then. But no, the guys—my distant cousins Marvin and Emmitt Silloway, twins, big boys about sixteen years old which made them gods to me—they were fishing and nothing was happening.

"They're okay," I said to Hannah. "Nobody's drowning."

She shook her head, her eyes still wide open so that I could see white all around her brown-black irises. "No, it's us, Tessa! We'll drown!"

45

~

"You know how I said that gifts, not exactly ordinary gifts, run through our family?" Gram said to me when we were in our cabin, emptying our smaller than usual haul of berries into a bowl. We were back from all walking slowly to Auntie's cabin, Auntie and Gram each with an arm around Hannah and me carrying Hannah's basket as well as mine, until we got to the path where Hannah said she could walk okay, she just needed to go slowly.

I nodded when Gram looked at me to make sure I was listening to her. Oh, I was. I so needed to know about Hannah.

"Well, there's a gift of Seeing in our family," Gram said, and I heard the capital S when she said it. "Those who have it generally don't see it as a gift, but as a... as something hard, something one has to learn how to live with." I could feel her thinking as she spoke. "It seems that you have been gifted with power for healing, and that Hannah has inherited the gift of Seeing."

"Seeing what, Gram?"

"Seeing events in the future," she said slowly. "Things that *may* happen, but they don't necessarily have to happen."

At first all I could think about was how Hannah looked when she was Seeing. Hannah on her back, her eyes rolled up in her head, choking, her hands clutching the air. I shuddered.

"I thought Hannah was dying." My voice came out in a tiny whisper.

Gram reached out her arm for me and I stepped in and snuggled against her shoulder. "Oh, Sweetie, it must have been hard for you to see," she said. "Sometimes it hits her like a seizure, and that's hard for her, and for anyone with her."

"She Sees the future, Gram?" And then a couple of thoughts fell together in my mind and my heart gave a startled thump. "You mean Hannah and I are going to drown!?"

Gram put her hand on my arm. She gave me her *Listen very carefully to me, young lady* look. "You and Hannah will *not* drown, as long as you pay attention to what Hannah just Saw."

"How do we do that?"

"You don't get in any damn canoes, Tessa!" Gram carried the bowl of berries over to the sink, but didn't do anything with it, just looked out the window at the lake. "At least for a while."

I walked over to stand near her right elbow. She might not want to talk any more, but I needed to. "So it's kind of like Hannah gets warnings?"

Gram nodded. "Yes, think of it that way."

I looked out at the lake too. The canoe with my cousins in it was way down at the east end, tiny now, just a dark shape with two bumps at either end of it.

"Okay," I said. "I won't get in any canoes."

"Promise me that, Tessa?"

"Promise." I really wasn't tempted to, since I didn't trust the lake. This was such an easy promise to make that I almost forgot it.

~

Two weeks passed. The nights were cold enough now that a skim of ice formed on the lake, but it melted off when the sun beamed on it during the day. Brilliant gold leaf medallions spun down from the aspens and birches along the lake shore, carpeting the shore path, and those that got caught up in the thin ice at night slowly settled through the clear water during the day. All of the geese had flown south.

School was out for the day and I was happy as I walked down the hill from the main house, toward the lake. Jesse was just behind me, talking with Bobby Kickbush, one of his best buddies, who was also his cousin. Some older kids were ahead of us, already down at the lakeshore, skipping stones. And then I noticed a distant snarling, growling sound from down the valley behind us. I was still high enough up on the trail to be able to look down the valley to the west, but I couldn't see anything that could be making the sound. Then... an airplane! Much, much closer than any airplanes I'd ever seen before high in the sky. It was invisible at first because it was low, amongst the greens and browns and grays of the valley.

Suddenly it was on us, huge and so low it was positively scary, heading for the lake.

The engine roared as the plane flew right above our heads. It was white with green stripes and numbers on its sides, with big white wings and a tall, square tail, with canoelike silver things hanging down on either side of its body. Floats! When I was very little and pestering Gram about how an airplane could land on the water, she had described big silver floats.

Jesse and Bobby shouted at the same second I let out a shout. *It's going to land in the water!*

We took off running down the rest of the hill to the shore, our eyes never leaving the plane. It was a ways out now, flying down the lake away from us. The engine got quieter and the plane got lower and lower, closer to the water, then suddenly the floats splashed water into the air. The plane settled on the water and the sound of the engine died away.

Jesse, Bobby and I joined the bigger boys on the shore. My cousins Marvin and Emmitt pounded down the hill we had just come down, whooping past us, headed for the dock where their canoe was tied up alongside three other canoes belonging to other families but lent out all the time, the casual borrowing system that usually worked until there was a moment when everyone wanted to go out at the same time and no canoes on the dock and then there was some shouting about god damn kids always taking the canoes. But then it was all forgotten 'til next time.

The floatplane was just sitting out there, halfway down the lake. There was no engine sound at all. We heard a sputter, like the engine was trying to start again, then silence. The plane was just drifting out there ever so slowly away from us, pushed by the breeze that almost always came up the valley from the west.

"Let's go get 'em!" Marvin shouted—he was the twin who always wore the backwards ball cap—and everybody on the beach started running behind them for the dock and the canoes.

"Come on, Tessa!" Jesse called back to me.

I sprinted after him and Bobby.

There was a general melee at the dock with everyone trying to cram into the four canoes. Jesse called to me from the one he was clambering into, but my cousin Emmitt grinned up at me through the lanky brown hair falling across his face, as he untied the Silloway canoe.

"Want to come with us, little Ravenwing?"

Another Silloway third cousin, Jenna, who was only a year younger than the twins, was climbing in and the canoe was wobbling on the water, and my breath was wobbling at the thought of being invited in by the godlike big kids—and then I heard my name being called in the distance. It was Hannah, steaming down the hill to the shore as fast as her chubby legs could take her, braids flying out behind her.

"Tessa! Tessa! Don't you dare!" she shouted.

Oh crap. I looked back at Emmitt, who gave a grin and a shrug and pushed the canoe away from the dock and started paddling away.

"Tessa!" It was Jesse calling from another canoe. There was room between him and Bobby, it was waiting for me...

I looked back at Hannah, still barreling my way. I never thought I'd want to go out in a canoe on this lake, and when I really, really, really wanted to go, well there would be a hell of a price to pay, and the wrath of Hannah seemed more fearsome than the thought of drowning.

"Go ahead, Jesse," I told him. "I'll stay here with Hannah."

Slow steps took me back down the dock to the shore. Behind me the excited shouts and laughter faded as the canoes pulled away down the lake toward the floatplane. Hannah met me where the dock met the rocky shore. Was she grateful that I decided to stay behind? Not at all. She glared at me.

"Tessa, you almost went with them!"

"But I didn't, did I?"

We slowly walked over the rocky beach to the path and up it a little ways to a grassy bank that gave a view down the lake.

"You almost went with them!" Hannah said again as she plopped down on the grass.

"Well, I didn't." I stayed standing, watching the canoes, a bit spread out now with Emmitt and Marvin's well into the lead. There was one straggler canoe, Jesse and Bobby. They were paddling hard but even I could see they were only about half as efficient as the bigger boys. I wished with all my heart I was sitting next to Jenna. I wanted to see that airplane!

The adults started showing up. Earl Brightwater jogged down the path to us and paused, staring hard down the lake.

"Damn kids," he muttered. "Not one lifejacket out there."

Lester Goodenough walked by us wearing a kayak on his head. He was Jesse's great uncle on his mother's side, old, with white hair, but he was wiry and tough and known to carry his kayak this way, up and down the hill to the lake from his cabin. He knew what would happen if he left it at the dock, even without a paddle.

"Ho there, Earl," Lester said as he passed us. "Think it's Chuck?"

"Who else?" Earl said back. "Say, keep an eye on those younger boys out there for me, wouldya?"

"Sure will!"

"Who's Chuck?" I asked Earl Brightwater.

He glanced down with a little surprise, like he'd forgotten Hannah and I were next to him. "Well, maybe best you ask your Gram that. Looks like she's just about here."

There was a scrambling and a puffing on the trail behind us and sure enough, it was Gram, loose black and white hairs flying in the breeze, her face flushed up, but she was trying not to look like she'd hurried down as fast as she could from our cabin.

"Oh, girls!" she exclaimed when she saw us, and she plopped down on the grass next to us. It wasn't an *oh-girls-are-you-in-for-it-now* tone, but instead it was like a sigh of relief. "You didn't go."

"Of course not," I said.

Hannah glared at me but kept silent.

Gram was still catching her breath, looking down the lake at the canoes trying to catch up to the plane. Lester's kayak was already in the water and he was dipping his paddle side to side, skimming away from us like a waterbug.

"Who's Chuck?" I asked her.

She quickly looked at me, then up at Earl Brightwater, who gave a little shrug.

"That," she said, nodding down the lake, "is your grandfather."

"I have a grandfather?" I thought of Jesse's grandfather, Walt Brightwater, who seemed ancient, bent over a walking stick whenever I saw him on the village paths, long white hair in braids on his shoulders; so gnarled and old he was scary, except he laughed a lot and liked to keep wrapped candies in his pockets to give to us kids when he saw us.

Gram wouldn't say much about ours right then, except that he hadn't been to the village in "a while," not since Hannah and I were toddlers, so that's why we didn't remember him. She walked on down to the dock to talk with a few more of the grownups who'd showed up, waiting and looking down the lake. I sat there hoping that our grandfather had candy like Jesse's. But even if he didn't—he had an airplane!

"I remember him," Hannah said softly after Gram had left.

I looked over at her, suddenly jealous.

"I remember him landing his plane just like this," she said, then faltered. She frowned. "But maybe I'm remembering this."

"How can you *remember* this? It's happening right now!" When she didn't say anything more, I began to consider how the "gift" that Hannah had could be confusing. If she had Seen this already, then maybe what she was seeing now would feel like remembering.

"Hannah, is Seeing like dreaming?" I often dreamed vivid dreams, and sometimes had nightmares Gram helped me wake up from, and reassured me that they were just nightmares and they would not come back ever again. Sometimes they did, but I didn't tell her that. What would it be like, I wondered, to have a nightmare but wake up and know that it *was* going to come back as reality?

Hannah nodded. "When they happen at night, I can't tell if they're nightmares or Seeing." After a pause, she turned her head and looked at me. "I Saw you under the water, curled up on your side on the bottom of the lake under the ice."

"You mean, before it happened?"

She nodded again. "But I thought it was a nightmare and... I didn't tell Mom or Gram about it." She looked away from me, down the lake. "I'd forgotten all about the nightmare until it happened, and then it scared me and was so weird that I didn't say anything to Mom or Gram even then." She was still looking down the lake, thinking.

I looked, too, hoping for some action down there, but so far not much was happening.

"But it got scarier, not talking about it," Hannah continued, "and then I had the Seeing a few more times, just about little things, but they happened afterwards as I'd Seen them, and then I started talking to Mom and Gram about it."

"And then you Saw *us* drowning."

Another nod.

"Like, today? If we'd gone out in a canoe today?"

She looked at me again. "We were trying to get to an airplane that landed on the lake, Tessa. How many times has that happened recently?"

Far away, down the lake, we heard the sputter of the airplane's engine, a pause, then the sputter again, then a roar. We stared and stared to try to see what was happening. It looked like the airplane was getting closer... yes, it *was* getting closer. And it was pulling all of the canoes behind it! Jesse was out there getting pulled by an airplane, and I was missing it! All because of some vision of Hannah's that probably didn't mean a thing...

The white airplane sitting up on its silver floats grew nearer and nearer, with two canoes trailing off the left float, and two canoes and Lester Goodenough's kayak trailing off the other, all of them getting closer and closer, until I could see the V's of wake in the water behind them, then arms waving at the people on the dock, grins on the faces in the canoes. Something was different, though, and then I saw that Jesse's and Bobby's canoe was empty, and so was Lester Goodenough's kayak. Hannah noticed this, too, and she was up off the grass and jogging down the path to the shore before I even stirred.

The people on the dock had noticed the empty boats, too, and an alarmed buzzing was going around when Hannah and I walked down to join them. Gram didn't even notice us, she was staring out at the plane with her black eyebrows pulled together, her hands clasping near her throat.

"They're in the plane!" Earl Brightwater shouted.

The plane was roaring closer and closer to us, and there was someone waving to us from the right seat. The crowd on the dock surged forward, all of us trying to see into the plane. There were too many of us on the dock, and the far end of it began to settle and icy lakewater began to creep over the wooden planks toward my boots. The grownups realized what was happening and shooed us kids back up the dock though they were the heavy ones, and it didn't seem quite fair that most of them stayed out at the end of the dock to better see all the action.

The airplane engine cut off and suddenly it was absolutely silent except for the sound of the rippling water behind the plane as it glided forward to us.

"That's Jesse in there, isn't it?" "And Bobby?" Mothers' voices came out trembling and gaspy. Then Earl Brightwater rumbled, "Yep, and that's Lester in there in the back seat."

The silent airplane glided right up to the dock, hesitating only a few yards off the end. Earl Brightwater waved everybody back and picked up a tie-down rope in one hand and leaped from the dock onto the nearest silver float, grabbing onto a white wing strut. He leaned and gave a huge pull on the rope and slowly the airplane edged in to the dock. Another couple of dads stood by with more rope and there was a flurry of tying down and then the airplane doors popped open and suddenly everyone was talking loudly and there was some laughing and people started climbing out of the plane. There were

Jesse and Bobby, bundled in blankets, and Lester helping them onto the plane's silver float, moms and dads reaching out for them from the dock.

"We tipped over," I heard Jesse's voice. "The water was freezing!" His damp dark hair was mostly standing straight up and his brown eyes looked huge in his strangely pale face.

Moms and dads were hugging them from all sides. Earl Brightwater was thumping Lester Goodenough's back and making him lurch forward, and they both laughed. Farther up the dock, Hannah and I looked at each other, but we didn't say anything.

The canoes untied from the plane and everyone was climbing out onto the dock, which dipped dangerously lower in the water.

"Everyone move to shore!" Earl's voice boomed out and we all shuffled back to the rocky beach. Hannah had to grab my arm and drag me after her because all I could think of was getting a glimpse of the person in the other front seat of the plane. He was climbing out onto the silver float, he was jumping onto the dock and thanking the people who helped secure the plane. He was short and stocky, a bit bowlegged, in faded jeans and a patched and faded jacket. He had a cowboy hat pulled low on his brow, the hair sticking out from it black and white like Gram's. *My grandfather.*

~

I had to stay that night with Hannah, at her cabin. We lay awake for a while, not talking. But I knew she was awake too. I kept thinking over the jumble of the day's events. Jesse and Bobby tipping over in their canoe and Lester Goodenough almost instantly there to help them get over to the silver pontoons of the airplane, where *our grandfather* pulled them up out of the water and got blankets around them, then managed to get the engine started again. So it wasn't Hannah and me tipping over and drowning, but the boys just getting freezing cold wet, but they were okay. I couldn't stop thinking about that.

"Hannah," I finally said. "Sometimes something can change what you Saw was going to happen?"

No sound from Hannah. We were sharing her bed in her tiny room at the back of Auntie's cabin, with our heads on pillows at opposite ends of the bed (Hannah's idea: *So you don't bump me all night long, Tessa!*). I raised up on my right elbow to look down the bed at her. It was dark at ten at night in early October, but I could see her eyes were open.

"Unh hunh," she murmured.

"So, like something's going to happen..." I was too young to understand the argument about pre-destination and free will, the inevitable versus the accidental, but glimmers of it intrigued me. "But then one little thing happens, like someone has to run back to use the bathroom, and that one little thing could change everything?"

Hannah sighed into the dark. "It could be like that, Tessa. I just don't know."

I was sitting up now because I couldn't hold back the most horrible thought of all. "But Jesse and Bobby overturning... do you think that happened *because* of us? Because we weren't in the canoe to be the ones it happened to?"

Hannah sat up and looked at me. I could tell this wasn't a new thought; she'd been thinking this awful thought for a while herself.

"No," she said. "Or at least, we don't know, we can't know... Gram told me that it's not on my shoulders, if someone doesn't listen to the warning of a Seeing, or if someone *does* listen and still something bad happens. There's just no way of knowing, it's a... mystery."

That sounded like Gram all right.

I lay back down and pulled my blanket up, wishing I could understand even a tiny bit. I was so relieved that Jesse was fine. Like me, he had gone down into the lake, and like me he turned out fine, thanks to someone's help. I resolved to give him my little Viking pin passed down from great great grampa Vegard. He would like it.

"Tessa," Hannah's voice drifted down the length of the bed. "What do you think of Grampa?"

During the unloading of the floatplane, after Jesse and Bobby had been bundled past us by their parents, Gram had shooed Hannah and me off the end of the dock and told us to sit on the bank above the shore to wait for her. She had walked down to the plane and waited until Grampa had finished handing out boxes and bags to Lester Goodenough and a few other men still on the dock. Grampa had shut the back door of the plane and turned and gone real still— he'd been doing a lot of moving right up until that second, and then he just stopped—there was Gram standing right in front of him on the dock, kind of blocking his way. He wasn't much taller than she was, but he pulled his cowboy hat off his bushy black and white hair and bent his head down toward her as she talked at him, his head dropping lower and lower. They stayed like that for a few minutes, her doing most of the talking and him bending his head down to her.

I had wondered what they were talking about. Hannah had said she'd bet Grampa was thinking he'd like to get back in his plane since Gram was probably giving him an earful about why hadn't he been around for the past six years.

But then they'd walked side by side down the dock toward us, up the path, getting closer and closer, Grampa still holding his hat and Gram holding her head up high, the breeze ruffling her black hair with white threads running through it. I hadn't noticed 'til then that she was wearing her favorite kuspuk, the hooded spring green one dotted with the pink of fireweed, with the ruffle just below her knees.

Hannah and I scrambled to our feet when they came up to us.

"Hannah," Gram nodded at Hannah, and Grampa reached out for her hand and gave a long look into her eyes.

When Gram said my name, I stuck my hand right out and looked up to see him start smiling. His hand felt warm and dry and large as he shook my hand. His eyes were bright, even though they were as dark as Gram's and Auntie's and Hannah's. There was a brightness in them that jumped right out at me.

"Your grandfather's going to stay a couple of days with us," Gram had said softly, and then we had all walked up the hill to the village, not saying another word.

Back in the dark of Hannah's room, I said, "I like his eyes."

~

Grampa said he could stay for only a few days. He had to leave before the ice locked the lake and his plane with it. And it was true that each day it took longer for the sun to melt the skim of ice formed overnight by the cold seeping down from the mountains and the glacier just around the corner from the end of the lake. I stayed the nights at Hannah's house while Grampa stayed with Gram, and I felt kind of sad, getting kicked out and not getting to lie down on the rug in front of our fireplace and watch them sitting together talking every night. Jesse said they were probably doing other things too, but I thought it wouldn't matter, I'd be quiet and not in the way, and I just wished I had a little more time getting to know Grampa before he went.

During the days he did things around the village, like helping

Earl Brightwater finish building a hay barn before winter set in, and helping some of the guys fix up the solar panels on the main house roof, and helping Gram and Auntie make sure our rooftop watertanks with solar panels were ready for winter. He was always doing something. He was about half the size of Earl Brightwater, but he was wicked strong, as Jesse said, for his size. And he was always in motion.

But after dinner he sort of melted into Gram's big, comfy chair by the fireside—that was when Hannah and her brothers Willy and Bruce and I got to see him, at dinner and then for an hour or so until bedtime, and we were all quiet around the fire and sometimes Gram or Auntie told stories.

While Gram was still putting things away in the kitchen, I seized the moment and looked up at Grampa, all comfy quiet in the chair, and asked, "What's it like in the city, Grampa?"

His eyes opened wide and he looked down at me, not smiling like he usually did, but kind of solemn. "Well, now, little Ravenwing," he started, then stopped.

"It's a bad place, Tessa," Auntie said from the old wooden bench pulled up close to the fire, where she was sitting with toddler Bruce on her lap and Willy in front of her playing with some toy horses on the floor.

"Well, now, I wouldn't call it exactly bad," Grampa said. "But it's a hard place, not a place for young ones, that's for sure." *A hard place.* Earl Brightwater called it that, too. What did that mean? I was opening my mouth to ask, when Gram walked over to sit in the other chair by the fire, next to Grampa.

"Tessa, would you like to tell another Girl and Raven story?"

Everyone looked at me. Hannah sniggered a little.

"Once there was a girl who was best friends with Raven," I started right away. "And one day they were playing at the top of Mount Snow, right up on the ridge where the rock marker is that shows the very top, and the girl said, 'Oh, I wish I could fly!' and Raven said, 'I can help you.' And he flapped his wings one, two, three times, over her head and suddenly she found black feathers growing out of her shoulders and down her arms, and she saw that she had wings too!"

Grampa looked like he was enjoying it. He was settled back in Gram's favorite chair, firelight shining on his face, on the creases running to either side of his mouth and the lines on his forehead. He was smiling a little.

"So the girl flapped her new, big wings and rose up into the air next to Raven. She could fly! She soared straight down to the valley to the north"—I swung my arms around in the air, nearly hitting Hannah—"and she soared right over that little round lake all nestled into the green valley, but no one was there. Flap, flap, flap and she was back up over the top of Mount Snow and she looked down to the valley to the south, to our village and the lake, but no one was outside and it looked so boring. So she said to Raven, 'Let's go to the city!' And they flew higher and higher in the sky and there, far to the west, was the city, lots of...." Lots of what? What did it look like there? I didn't know. "Lots of people and lots of noise!" I did know that, from Earl Brightwater. "And the girl and Raven flew down and said hello to the people and asked them if there was a place where they could stay because they wanted to see the city—"

"All right, Tessa," Gram interrupted me. "That's enough for now. Thank you for that story."

Grampa cleared his throat. "I see that you're going to be a storyteller like your Gram and your Auntie."

"No doubt of that," Auntie said, standing up, holding Bruce on her hip. "All right, girls, let's get ready to head home for bed."

But it wasn't fair! I wanted to tell more of the story, and I wanted to see if Grampa would tell a story about the city. But Gram nodded at me, looking serious.

"Time to get ready for bed, Tessa."

Early the next morning he flew away in his plane, and it was many years before I saw him again.

3. August 2096–March 2100

Time began to run faster as I got older. It felt like the river flowing from the west end of our lake over a year: early childhood was like the wintertime water, dense and barely flowing, but then in spring it began to rush out, all in a hurry down the valley for the sea. It seemed like I was ten for a long time, and then suddenly I was twelve and everything was in a hurry.

My body was changing. I should have been prepared. Gram and Auntie Annie had never hidden their bodies from Hannah and me, had seemed comfortable with undressing and dressing in front of us. I understood the ample and saggy bosoms and thighs of mothers and grandmothers. But I was surprised by burgeoning sexuality. On the hottest summer days we'd sometimes splash in the creeks with our older cousins and I'd be startled by glimpses of gleaming skin, curving young breasts, dark hair suddenly in new places. I realized that all of this was coming my way and soon.

I didn't want it. At twelve I was the fastest kid in the village, faster than Jesse even. I was leggy and lithe and strong and I did not want to be slowed down by curves and gaining weight around my hips. I'd seen my Silloway cousin Jenna teased by the boys for having *nice boobs!* and I did not want nice boobs, thank you very much. I didn't want my hips to suddenly blossom like Hannah's did. I was okay with being female, but I didn't want to be too female.

Hannah sympathized. Auntie Annie had given her the menstruation talk when she was twelve, just as Gram gave it to me, focusing on how someday this meant we could have babies, but conveniently leaving out the *how*. I knew pretty much all that already, though, having grown up in a village with dogs and horses, and even once having seen bears do it. A stallion's cock was an amazing thing to behold, but I did not want in any way to consider its human equivalent. Hannah told me she knew at fourteen that no man was ever going to stick any part of his body in her body, ever. I agreed. Boys—well, Jesse mostly— were my best friends and that's the way it was always going to be, just buddies as usual.

But actually it no longer was *as usual*; I was becoming self-conscious as my body was changing. And by the time I was thirteen, I was noticing that Jesse's body was changing too. He was getting taller and broader, he had muscles much bigger than mine, he had a pungent, male sweat smell. He seemed proud of his low voice. It was all so weird and uncomfortable that I found excuses to not be with him as usual, and was alone a lot more.

Gram saw me spending more time alone and seemed to think this was a good time for me to work harder on being still and paying attention. *Focus is one of the most important tools for the healer*, she told me as she sent me off yet again to sit in my spot above the lake and meditate for an hour with my spirit helpers. *You are learning to still your thoughts and focus.*

Actually I was spending a lot of time there thinking about the future.

What was I going to do? Who was I going to be? Was I going to grow up to be the village healer someday when Gram retired from the role? I could not see myself staying in the village for my whole life. Gram herself had left for some years when she was young. Something was calling me out of the village too. Even at twelve I knew that there were things I needed to do and learn that I couldn't find in the village. I wanted to understand what Orion was, and what the resistance to Orion was. I needed to understand why my mother left for the city and the resistance, and why she never returned.

~

When I was fourteen and Jesse was fifteen, Emmitt and Marvin Silloway disappeared one night, leaving a note that said they had left for the city to join the resistance. Two weeks later Jesse's favorite uncle Lars left too.

This of course put the village in an uproar. No one had left in fourteen years, since my mother. The morning I heard that Lars Brightwater left, I found Jesse in the barn, brushing the horses. His eyes looked suspiciously red, like he'd just been crying, but I didn't mention it. I picked up a brush and started brushing, too.

Our favorite horse's name was Belle and she was a huge, muscled draft horse. I loved her warm, rich horse-smell and the way she heaved big satisfied sighs as we ran the brushes over her flanks. She let out a loud fart and started peeing a long stream, and Jesse and I both burst out laughing.

"I always feel better after I've been in here with the horses," he said as he turned away to set the brush down in the cabinet that held all of the horse accessories and tools. He began climbing the ladder to the hay loft, glancing over his shoulder at me, which felt like an invitation.

I set down my brush and followed him up the ladder.

His carving tools were in one corner of the loft—it was Jesse's space, his only private space in a crowded barn and house, and when he happened to have time free from school or chores, he would come up here and pick up a mask or traditional Tlingit box that he had been working on for months. But he didn't go into his corner today.

"It's kind of stormy in our house this morning." He settled back in the hay.

I sat next to him, staying upright, cautious and curious. I knew that Earl had a temper. He was usually loving and gentle, but he had a slow fuse and when it went, it went. Jesse had punched Bobby Kickbush's older brother Stan right off his feet a few weeks earlier when Stan teased Hannah about having "fits" (unfortunately Hannah had had a couple of Seeings during school hours), and Earl had roared at Jesse, *Ya don't solve any of the world's problems by punching people out!* and then stomped outside and punched a hole in the barn door, and grounded Jesse from any hunting trips for a month. Jesse didn't have Earl's temper, which was one thing I loved about him. A calm and steady quiet emanated from him always. But this morning there was sadness mixed in.

"He's upset about Lars going," I said finally, when Jesse didn't say anything more.

Jesse just nodded. And, of course, he was too. His uncle Lars was only twelve years older than Jesse and he was the one who had taught Jesse to hunt, and took him on hunting trips.

"Do you know if Lars went because of Marv and Emmitt? Like, was he going to try to get them to come back home?"

"He and Dad argued over that. Dad wanted to get in touch with Emmitt and Marv, find out if they had connected up with the resistance and were all right. Lars said to trust them and leave them alone, then Lars disappeared when he went with Dad on this last supply run. Now Dad's all mad and upset that something's happened to Lars."

Buttery summer sunlight streamed through the half-open window at the other end of the barn and gleamed on the top of Jesse's dark head. He picked up a piece of straw and held it up to the rays of sun and we watched it shine pure gold.

I had always wondered if Earl had contact with people in the resistance when he went into the city. Jesse thought that he did, from the bits and pieces he'd heard pass between his parents when they thought Jesse and his younger brothers were asleep. We did know that in recent years the city had gone from being *a hard place*, as Earl had called it, where, if you didn't fit in, you had to be extremely careful not to stand out and draw attention to yourself, to a place where it wasn't even safe to be seen. Earl's supply team stopped now at an outpost a few miles outside the city, rather than going all the way in. Earl and his team didn't go as often, either, and there were some things we were getting used to doing without, like batteries for lights and touch pads that we used in school instead of books, and for playing music and showing photos. Jesse had lately been tinkering on tiny solar chargers—he'd begun showing a prowess for working with machines, which was making him a highly valuable member of the village community—but they needed expensive parts that Earl hadn't been able to barter for.

But Jesse and I still didn't know much about the resistance. I was burning to know more. How were they fighting Orion? What had she known about Orion that made my mother leave home at the age of nineteen, alone, to join up? Perhaps Gram thought that by not talking about my mother, that would keep her away from our thoughts. But it did just the opposite: every day I wondered about her and longed to know about her and why she left.

"I don't tell the girl and Raven stories any more," I said softly, not even sure if Jesse remembered how I used to tell them all the time. "Because no matter what idea I have in my head when I start telling one, every single time it ends up with Raven showing the girl how to fly, and them going to the city together."

Jesse's dark eyes smiled a little, just at the corners. He remembered.

"Tessa," he said.

"What?"

"Just promise me that if you ever leave here, you'll tell me first."

That surprised me a little, but I nodded that I would.

Sudden child's crying—with a jag of fear and pain that pierced right through me—brought us both to our feet and starting down the ladder. It was Jesse's littlest brother Augie, only five years old, who'd come out in the barn looking for Jesse, and he was so small that Belle hadn't seen him and accidentally set her back right foot down on his little rubber boot. Fortunately the cedar shavings in her stall were soft and cushioning.

"Augie, man, you are always getting in trouble!" Jesse pushed Belle off of Augie's foot. "He reminds me of you, Tessa," he added.

He hefted Augie, now hiccupping between sobs, into the house against his shoulder. I followed close behind. Augie gripped Jesse's hair with both fists, his blond curls mingling with Jesse's thick black hair that came down to his collar. I was always surprised by how pale and golden Augie was in Jesse's dark family, but Jesse's Mom, Martha, liked to say that in him the Goodenough genes had finally won out, at least in appearance, against the Brightwater genes.

Earl had already left on some chore, but Martha was still in the kitchen and looked up from her baking, alarmed, when Jesse carried Augie in. She directed Jesse to put Augie in Earl's big chair closest to the woodstove, and she gently slid off the little red rubber boot, putting her hands on Augie's bare foot.

"What do you think, Tessa?" she asked after a moment.

I went down onto my knees next to her and put my hand on the little foot. It looked fine. Gram had taught me how to close my eyes and scan with my hands, feeling the energy field and then feeling through it. I did this now. The texture of the energy beneath my hands was warm and smooth and peaceful. I opened my eyes to see Augie's blue eyes fixed on me with great curiosity.

I smiled, and he smiled back. "How's that foot feel now, Augie?"

"Good!" was all he said.

"That's what I think too."

~

The rest of that year passed quickly. Bits and pieces of news of Marvin and Emmitt and Lars filtered back to us, some of it intended for the whole community and some of it not. I relied on Jesse to report to me what he'd overheard in the kitchen after his parents thought he and the younger boys were asleep. I passed this on to Hannah. She had taken Emmitt and Marvin's leaving hard, and I suspected that was because of things she had Seen. But I was afraid to ask her about our cousins in the city and what she knew.

Finally I did screw up my courage, when we were sitting on my cabin's front step in the warm sun of late afternoon while Auntie and

Gram were pulling the last loaves of fresh bread out of the oven box of our woodstove. I asked her what she knew of Emmitt and Marvin, and Hannah burst into tears.

"Nothing good! It's all pain and suffering!"

I put my arm around her shoulders, alarmed at this response, even though I'd been prepared for something rough. I was also worried about Auntie and Gram hearing her and rushing out and thinking that I'd caused this. Which I had.

Hannah surprised me. "I See us there, too, Tessa!" she sobbed. "I See us being fed into machines, with men standing next to them studying our brains while we're in them... I See you standing, crying, at a slit of a window that's in a prison..."

I felt a jolt of fear and prayed these were just bad dreams; she'd been confused by bad dreams before and thought they were Seeings. And what could I say? I tried to whisper comforting words to her, to remind her of what she had told me several times, that *one never knows, small things often happen to change the course of big things.*

This didn't help much, and Gram and Auntie came out then and looked reproachfully at me.

~

I began to find myself looking forward to my one and two hour long meditation times above the lake, and I think Gram was relieved to not have to be the enforcer any longer. Most of the time I was able to pull my mind away from the roil of internal and external changes and consider how the lake was both timeless and unchanging; I was learning that the seasonal changes were beautiful and sometimes breathtaking, but purely cosmetic. The lake and I began to bond.

And of course the ravens got to know me, because ravens themselves are always on the lookout for patterns. They learned my schedule. I began to suspect that the same ravens were stopping by to visit each time I did, keeping an eye on me, curious as always.

Early to mid summer was a busy time for them as the juveniles had fledged and began flying behind their parents, yelling loudly for food. Their high-pitched, raucous cries really were like yelling and made me laugh every time I heard them.

It's hard to tell ravens apart—you can just barely tell the males from the females by the longer, heavier bills of the males, and they're a little bigger overall, too—but over time I actually was able to get to know a few individuals. There was the female who was missing a couple of feathers from her right wing. One of the males had a scraggly tail, like he'd had a feather or two plucked out of it. They weren't a pair, but each of them always showed up with what I was pretty sure was a mate. Often a pair would land on a branch only a few feet from me, shuffle a little on the branch and then settle down into taking turns preening each other. Sometimes they would touch bills, and just sit there with their bills together. One or the other, or sometimes both together, would softly warble. Somehow they made me think of Jesse's parents. Recently I'd been in the kitchen with Jesse eating a snack, and Earl had tromped through the kitchen door to get something, and he grabbed Martha around the waist and sat down in the rocker with her in his lap and gave her a wet-sounding kiss. She had tittered and lightly smacked him with one hand, saying, "The *children*..." though you could tell that she was enjoying it immensely too. Jesse had flushed with embarrassment, but I was fascinated by the playfulness between them, and the underlying feeling of partnership. Something in me longed for this... someday.

A small stream ran down Mount Snow a few hundred yards east of my sitting spot. It was as if the mountain had a cloak that she'd pulled tight and there was a fold in it that the stream ran down through. The mountain hemlocks that clustered in that fold were thicker and taller than they were anywhere else around. I suspected that a number of the ravens had nests in there, and I couldn't resist ending my sitting sessions a little early in order to investigate... and sure enough, one day I found a raven's nest—it had to be a raven's next, it was so big!—built deep into a density of hemlock branches, high enough up to be safe from creatures on the ground, but still protected from the weather by the highest branches. It was built of sticks, aspen and cottonwood sticks I guessed, each stick broken carefully by a big beak, to just the right length. When I reached my fingers deep into the nest, I pulled out a handful of horsehair that looked the color of Belle. I remembered all the times Jesse and I had pulled horsehair from the curry brushes and sent it windward to the ravens, though we were sure they'd never notice it. Turns out, they did.

I stuffed the horsehair back into the nest and resolved to sneak back in the spring to see if a family would be in residence.

Jesse said to me one day, after I'd been telling him about how I'd gotten to know a few birds during my sitting time, "You're not sitting with the lake, Tessa. You're sitting with the ravens." He started calling me *Raven*.

~

When I was sixteen and Jesse was seventeen, we were the talk of the village after a snowshoe outing when we saw a yearling moose get caught in an avalanche down near the east end of the lake, and we saved it. Only his nose was left sticking out of the snow. We dug him out, just the two of us working as fast as we could, using our snowshoes as shovels. He didn't get to his feet right away after we'd cleared the snow off him; he just lay there, breathing hard and staring at us out of his rolling eyes. I sat close to him and tried to send him calm and warmth. Finally he staggered away, a little stunned, but fine.

"Tessa calmed it down," Jesse told everyone at the next story night in the main house when we were asked to tell the story.

"No, I didn't!"

"You did. I watched it listen to you."

People believe what they want to believe. The funny thing was, I had the clear impression afterwards that I had been listening to the moose, rather than the moose listening to me. He was cold and tired and wanted his mother. I totally understood.

By then—even in the face of cold and snow—winter had become my favorite season. It was the light I loved most. Because we were in the north, the long hour before sunrise and the long hour after sunset were the most beautiful times of all: the sky glowed blue, blue shot through with gold before sunrise, blue edging through amethyst and into purples after sunset, as night approached. Blue light. It echoed in the snow shadows during the day. Winter was the season of blue.

Winter also meant I didn't have to sit in the snow and meditate above the lake. Spending more time in the cabin was not a bad thing at all, in my mind, as long as I could look outside at my favorite light. The cabin was cozy and warm, with our woodstove and fireplace and solar hot water heater, and I could read for hours and Gram wouldn't complain about it. And the winter I was seventeen, I rediscovered my great great grampa Silloway's journals.

They always had been on Gram's bookshelves, along with a

couple of his books of poetry, and I had poked into them long ago when I was little, but was stymied by his cramped, pointy handwriting, and also by the fact that the journals also had the look of books of poetry. But one day in deep winter when I was seventeen and a half, I pulled out the journal with the cracked and faded blue cover and looked inside it, and a sentence stood by itself, printed, so it was easier to read—*The clouds made canyons in the sky, and we flew like birds through them.*

Gram had been out on some errand in the village, and I took the book over to the chair by our east window and started reading. I found that his handwriting really wasn't all that bad, once I persevered and began to get used to it.

He was writing about flying.

He wasn't the pilot, though. It was my great great grandmother Ellen Silloway who was the pilot. This of course hooked me, so I started from the beginning and in less than a week I'd read the entire journal. I didn't hide from Gram the fact that I was reading it—after all the book had always been right there in plain sight on the shelf— but something made me a bit furtive about spending so much time with it, so I read it in my room at night mostly.

Great great grampa Silloway wrote quite a bit about his wife, who was a high-ranking officer in the private security contractor named Minerva. There was extremely good and easy money to be made as a private security contractor midway through the Middle East war years, when there already had been one hundred years of fighting from Israel and Syria to Afghanistan and Pakistan, and it was pretty clear that it wasn't going to end soon. And according to my teachers at school, after two hundred years—nearing the turn to the twenty-second century—it was still going on.

So my great great grandparents had had careers with that company that helped protect the people of the world from the crazy suicide bombers and the deranged religious zealots who were trying to hasten the end of times with plots to poison whole populations. A noble organization to work for. It would seem.

And then, about three-quarters of the way through the journal, I found someone else's handwriting. It was much easier to read, tidy cursive writing that looked surprisingly like mine. I'd seen it in two other books on the shelves, written on the inside of the covers: *Dorie Ravenwing, her book.* My mother. The first date written in the journal in her handwriting was January 1, 2080. I'd been born in August of 2082. My mother had turned nineteen in 2080.

It was called Minerva in my great grandparents' time, she wrote. *But about twenty years ago they were investigated by Congress for war crimes, for carelessly killing civilians who got in their way when they were targeting the bad guys in Iraq, Syria, Sudan, Brazil, Myanmar, to name only a few of their war arenas. That was back when they still answered to Congress. More or less. A fine of a few million dollars was nothing to them! They got their hands slapped, recruited more retired military brass to sit on their board of directors, and then changed their name to Orion.*

My mother had written this just months before she left to join the resistance.

~

"I've got something to show you," I said to Jesse one evening as we lay in front of the fireplace in Gram's and my cabin, Jesse on his back with his eyes closed, and me on my stomach with my head resting on my arms so I could gaze at the color and flicker of the flames. I glanced over my shoulder and saw him open one eye.

"Yeah?" was all he said when I didn't start right up again. He'd had to spend a few hours chopping firewood and had slipped over to our place after dinner so he didn't get collared into another job. He was tired and sleepy and all stretched out.

I rolled over to a sit and pulled the book from under a cushion on the floor near me, holding it up in the air for Jesse to see.

"My great great grampa Silloway's journal."

"He's my great great grampa too." Jesse's eyes were closed again.

I kept forgetting that. Jesse's Gram on his father's side (she married a Brightwater) was the daughter of Dylan Silloway's son Chet, while my Gram was the daughter of Dylan's daughter Alice. So our grandmothers were first cousins. But I couldn't keep the family tree straight in my head, so I usually just forgot it.

"Right. *That's* why people leave our village, so they can marry people they aren't related to!"

Jesse frowned and sat up. "We aren't *that* related, Tess."

I started to give the comeback *Yeah, like we're going to get married,* but I stopped myself and reconsidered. Could he possibly have been implying that?

I swear this thought hadn't occurred to me until then. Suddenly I saw us with the eyes of someone, anyone, in the village and how easy it would be to expect Jesse and me to get married. Same age, distantly shared ancestors, but the Brightwaters and the Goodenoughs, and my grampa Chuck as well, had come in from outside villages, bringing in fresh blood. A Brightwater marrying a Ravenwing. Earl had teased me, just recently, about how enticing my mother had been when she was my age, and how at least one of Jesse's older uncles would have loved to have married her, but she left for the city before that could happen.

But... could they have slept together before she left the village, and I was their baby, and that's why she came back to the village to have me before heading back to the city to continue fighting with the resistance? In that case Jesse and I would be... first cousins. Incest!

But no, Gram told me that my mother had married someone in the city and was going back to him after she had me. And of course there were my pale gray eyes, which everyone said they'd never seen before in the village family trees of mostly brown eyes, punctuated with just a few rare blue ones in every generation that harked back to great great grampa Vegard the Viking, or to the blond haired blue-eyed Goodenough clan.

Jesse was looking at me, waiting for me to say something. Instead I just held up the tattered blue book.

"Great great grandmother Ellen Silloway was a pilot." I watched him for his reaction. "And she was a high-ranking official in Minerva, which became Orion."

Jesse sat up. "Our great great grandparents were working for Orion?" His rising voice cracked on that last word.

"Well, one of them was. But it was called Minerva back then, and they were doing good things, or seemed to be doing good things, in bad times."

"Minerva," he said. "How do you know it became Orion?"

"Well, that's where it gets really interesting." I opened the book to a page I had marked, my mother's January 1st entry, which I read to him.

Jesse kept shaking his head. So I read him bits from earlier in the journal, in our great great grampa Silloway's hand:

War is now continuous, and global. Few people are willing to risk traveling out of this country now. Our borders are closed. Militarization has happened slowly and insidiously [I had to look that word up] *so that most citizens aren't even aware that we now have an economy entirely dependent on our military spending. The only good jobs for our children are related to the military; our cultural heroes are all soldiers.*

I skipped the beginning, which was a New Year's Day. Dylan Silloway kept a journal the way I did, starting up hopefully and summarizing what he neglected to write about for a year or so, then after a few entries, he lapsed for another year. But he was a poet, and now that I was older, I loved the poetry that slipped into his journal writing. But I figured Jesse might get impatient with it, so I skipped the first couple of paragraphs describing the setting of the New Year's Eve party he and Ellen had attended in the city, considered Minerva's most important city on the continent. The party was held in a spacious apartment overlooking the bay and the mountains to the north stained crimson by the setting winter sun—beautiful—but I read instead from the fourth paragraph:

Something's not right here. So many smiles and self-deprecating jokes to put us little guys at ease, but there's a whole layer of something else just beneath the surface. We are being lied to, manipulated like little children by a father who claims to be acting in our best interests. Everything in me knows this. I'm going to stop playing their game and listen to my own heart.

"What the hell?" from Jesse. "Don't tell me, this guy was a mind reader."

"No, but he was an empath."

Jesse frowned at me again.

"Gram told me that," I said. "That's someone who picks up the feelings of the people around them." And I'd never admit to Jesse that that came naturally to me, too.

I kept reading:

I've decided to begin to ask the What If's. What if there is an agenda this company is keeping secret? What if Minerva is working to deliberately insinuate itself into this country's power structure? What if they are manipulating public opinion to ensure that the war continues, so that this country's economy is based more and more on the military, making our leaders more and more convinced that one long continuous "holy war" is the only answer to the problems of the world?

I looked at Jesse. He'd been staring into the fire as I read, frowning still. When I paused, he looked at me.

"Did he ask 'What if my wife knows what this sick organization is doing and is lying to me about it?'"

"No. He writes that she didn't know. At least at first. Then she began to suspect when he did, and they talked about how she could leave without her bosses knowing what she knew."

There was a pause. The fire crackled comfort and warmth, and its light was soft on Jesse's face. He was wide awake now.

"And they got away safely, didn't they?"

I nodded. "Along with a few friends."

"And your great grandmother Alice and my great grandfather Chet were little kids, or teenagers when they settled here?"

"And one other son I think. Sam maybe?" There was a family tree in another book on the bookshelves, but I wasn't going to bother hunting for it.

"So how'd they do it?" Jesse asked after a pause.

"Do what? Have Alice, Chet and Sam? Want me to explain the birds and the bees to you?"

He punched my foot, which actually hurt, but I wasn't going to let on. "No, Dumbhead, how did they get away from Minerva, which became Orion?"

I shut the book with a satisfying snap. "Our great great grandmother Ellen got sick. Or at least got a physician to certify that she was so sick she couldn't do her job anymore, and she quit."

"So Minerva never had a problem with some mostly useless people setting up a small village on a lake in the mountains."

"They managed to disappear." *Off the radar*, had been great great grampa Silloway's expression. *We've gone off the radar*, he'd written, *and our goal is to keep it that way for generations, or however long Minerva is in power.*

And they were successful. Only Minerva eventually became Orion, and became even more powerful.

~

Only a few nights later Earl returned from his regular supply run with the news that Marvin had been shot and killed in a resistance operation against Orion. I was walking on the path from the main meeting house, done with helping at a party for my cousin Jenna who was getting married to one of the older Kickbush boys in the spring. I was tired and ready for bed. Then I heard Jesse call my name.

He was jogging up the other path, from his home. He came right up to me and stopped, pulling off the rabbit-fur hat that he loved wearing in winter. His thick black hair fell over his eyes and he impatiently brushed it back. He was growing it long, wanted to wear it in a braid, warrior-style. I could see right away that something was wrong.

He told me about what he'd overheard his Dad say about Marvin. As he walked me up the path to my house, I asked him every question I could think of. He didn't know many answers. He only knew that Marv, Emmitt and Lars had joined the resistance army force in the city, whose job was infiltration and espionage, keeping the safe houses safe, and guerilla tactics.

"Marv was shot at the port." Jesse's voice was low and quiet. "He and Emmitt and Lars were all helping some grounders—that's resistance slang for the army guys—infiltrate a shipment going to one of the prisons, in the hopes of springing some grounders out of prison."

All I could see right then were Marv and Emmitt in their canoe, grinning at me, inviting me to join them, the big boys who I hero-worshipped. The canoe was moving down the lake, away from me, all on its own, disappearing. Marv was gone; Emmitt broken-hearted.

"Emmitt and Lars were with him." I was thinking of the grief, but maybe it had been comforting for Marvin if he was conscious at all between being shot and dying. Not comforting for Emmitt and Lars though. Except at least they knew what had happened to their beloved brother and friend. It was worse not knowing. I thought of my mother. No word, nothing, for years and years. That was the worst.

"Tessa," Jesse said at the door to my cabin, "I'm going to ski down the east valley to the bay tomorrow, if you want to come."

It had been a while since we'd gone to that valley together. It was one of his favorite places to hunt.

"Not hunting?" I asked.

He shook his head. "For some peace, to try to get my head on straight."

I longed to go.

~

The next day I skipped school to go with him (Jesse was done with school, and I was in my last year, as we traditionally were schooled in the village school until age eighteen). We pulled on our skis and poles and skied down the trail alongside the lake to the notch at the east end, and then to the big valley that wended its way through snowy mountain shoulders to the bay. We paused for a break when we reached the valley, listening to the wind and the calls of ravens on the wind and the smaller birds down amongst the trees, the nuthatches and chickadees and pine grossbeaks with their tuneful warble, pine siskins trilling as they tumbled in tight flocks through the air.

And in that valley we found some deep snow. There had been several snowfalls since anyone had been on the old trail that wound down to the bay, following the deep cut of the creek into the mountainside. The creek was frozen now, marked by the weaving line of gnarly old cottonwoods growing up from its banks. Their huge trunks were deep-seamed, weathered gray, and without the green ornament of leaves, their dark branches twisted in sharp angles against the distant snowslopes. They were my favorite trees, exotic since they only grow in sheltered and south-facing valleys, always next to water. They were hugely tall compared to other trees in our valley, but shallow-rooted in their unceasing quest for fresh mountain stream water. Jesse said their native name meant "drinks too much and falls over."

Jesse broke trail and I didn't mind, since he was stronger than me and didn't tire as quickly in the deep snow. It occurred to me that we'd have been much better off wearing our snowshoes, but both of us had hoped for some fast downhill skiing in the fresh powder, somewhere along the way.

We paused to catch our breath and looked down the valley at what was still ahead. We were about halfway to the bay and it was all gradual downhill—which meant this was going to be a long, slow uphill on the way back, but oh well. The sun peeked out from lifting dark gray snow clouds and set the snow to sparkling all around us. A breath of wind sighed through the gnarly branches of the cottonwoods and a chickadee gave its spring *phoebe* call from close-by, fooled by the warming sunlight. High up over the mountain ridges ravens were calling.

"I was thinking," Jesse said.

He'd pulled off his fur hat and his gloves and was rubbing his scalp, making his black hair fall into his eyes.

"Marv," he said. Then he sighed and said again, "Marv."

I reached out and touched his arm, my hand slipping on the fabric of his windbreaker. So I edged closer and just leaned against his shoulder as we stood side by side looking down the valley. Both of us cried some quiet tears for Marv, who was a third cousin to both Jesse and me—I think. In our village everyone was close, and that's what mattered.

Without saying anything more, we started skiing again.

An hour later, we were nearing the high bank above the bay. We talked in snatches as we pushed through the powder, revisiting the old question *Why do people from time to time move to our village, but they're never people from the city?* In every generation there had been a few who moved to our village from other villages, such as Jesse's great grandfather Buck Brightwater who came from a village even farther away than my grandfather Chuck Joseph's. Hannah's father had arrived *from the Navajo desert*, as Gram said, which I thought of as a foreign country until I read about the American southwest in school—-but he died in an avalanche while hunting when Hannah was only four, and her little brother Bruce not yet born, so we'd never had the chance to hear any stories he brought with him.

"Have you ever wondered if maybe our parents and all the other older people in the village are working hard to keep the city away from the village?" Jesse said over his shoulder.

"You mean like making sure no one comes in who can tell us about it?"

"Yeah."

"Well, my grandfather came in from the city, when he flew in and stayed with us."

"But he didn't talk about the city at all, did he? And then he left." *And he hasn't come back*, hung in the air between us.

And there was the other question that always haunted me—*why hadn't any women left our village for the city, except for my mother?* I hadn't ever spoken it, until now, to Jesse.

He stopped skiing and looked at me. "You really don't know the answer to that?"

"You'd better not give me any crap about women needing protection against bad men."

He smiled, despite himself. "More likely the bad men would need protection from you!"

Jesse was skiing again, so I hurried to catch up.

We'd reached the high bank above the bay. A mile of dark water spread out in front of us, dotted with white ice pancakes, a ripple here and there showing the tide at work. Directly across from us rose the mountains to the south, mantled in pure white. Rays of sunshine fanned downward, glinting on white shoulders and the darker folds of valleys. I took a deep breath, it was so beautiful. I knew that if I left it, I would always yearn for it. But I knew I would be leaving it before long.

"We'd better start heading back," Jesse said. "We took longer getting here than I thought we'd take, 'cause of the snow. And going back is going to be a climb."

"All that way just for one look," I said, still gazing to the south. "But it's worth it."

"It sure is." He was facing the water and the mountains too, taking them in. It was comforting to know that Jesse felt the same way about them.

~

Gram wasn't in our cabin when Jesse dropped me off on his way down the trail to his home. This didn't seem unusual as she often *did rounds*, as she called it, in the village in the afternoons. But as twilight fell and it got closer and closer to dinnertime, I began to wonder.

I hadn't told her I was skipping school to go with Jesse and I was beginning to feel guilty about that. Restless with guilt and growing unease about where Gram could be, I bundled up again and stepped out our door, thinking if I didn't find her at the main meeting house, maybe Earl and Martha Brightwater knew where she was.

Any clouds that had hung on in the afternoon had lifted and the sky was clear. The blue light had faded and now stars were so bright that the white summit ridges of Mount Snow and Ptarmigan gleamed like sheltering arms holding the bowl of our valley. The white snow on the lake was luminous with starlight. I stood just a moment to gaze up and open myself to the wonder of it all—the immensity of it, with me just a tiny speck able to see so far. We weren't fortunate enough in school to have a teacher who liked to talk about the universe, but I had read in a book that the starlight I was seeing right at that moment was actually thousands, millions of years old, it had taken that long to reach my eyes. And I wondered, as I'd done since I'd learned this fact, *what does it look like now?* If anything dramatic had happened out there within the last thousand or so years, we'd never know it. It hadn't yet caught up to us.

"Tessa! Tessa!" Hannah's voice pierced the dark. Something *had* happened; bad news was catching up to me. It had to be bad news for Hannah to be running uphill in the dark, calling my name.

"Come down to Brightwaters now!" she panted as she came up our path.

"Jesse?" I whispered. I think my heart had stopped beating.

"No, Augie." She stood in front of me, catching her breath.

At eight years of age, Augie was a major terror. He had the Goodenough genes for golden curls and bright blue eyes, but Martha had begun saying that everything else was pure intensified Brightwater. Augie was always getting himself in trouble. Jesse said he expected Augie to go through the lake ice like I did at the age of eight.

My heart gave a little jump in my chest. Was that what had happened?

Hannah told me what she knew as we jogged down to the Brightwater cabin. Augie and his best buddy, Dakota Evans, had somehow managed to take Dakota's Dad's snowgo—the only other one in our village besides Earl's, used only by hunters and for hauling sleds of supplies back from the city—out for an unsupervised ride when the main house generator was running for its monthly maintenance check. The sound had masked the startup roar of the snowgo.

The boys had rolled it over trying to climb the steep slope of Mount Snow's northwest ridge. It may have rolled over them both.

As Hannah spoke, I saw it as if I'd been there. How a big, loud machine that had been flying them over the snow suddenly had reared up over their heads, black against the deep blue sky, falling out of the sky onto them, crushing them into the snow.

Dakota wouldn't wake up. Augie had run back home for help and collapsed on the doorstep just as Jesse was arriving home from our ski.

Martha Brightwater had put Augie to bed since he couldn't speak after those few words he garbled to Jesse, and he was shaking so hard he couldn't stand up. Earl and Jesse raced out on Earl's snowgo to find Dakota. Gram and Auntie Annie had stopped by just then; Gram had had a feeling that she was needed. Auntie went home to send Hannah to get me.

"Have you Seen anything that would help?" I asked Hannah when we slowed down to negotiate an icy patch on the path.

She shook her head. "I haven't Seen anything about Augie or Dakota."

We reached the Brightwater cabin. Jesse must have been standing at their front window because the heavy cedarwood door opened for us as we came up to it, Jesse holding it for us, pale, his dark eyes gone far away.

"Dakota?" I asked him.

He just shook his head, not able to look at me. I felt such sorrow in him, helpless sorrow mingled with anger that there was nothing he and Earl could do to help when they found him. Hannah bustled on into the kitchen, but I stood there for a moment next to Jesse and put my hand on his shoulder for the second time that day. And again, we didn't need words.

Gram was sitting in the kitchen at the rough wood trestle table with Martha and Hannah. Martha was wiping tears away with one of Earl's big red bandanas, Gram sitting next to her, patting her shoulder. Gram nodded silently when I stepped in.

The silence in the Brightwater house felt so strange; the four boys had Earl's big energy—some of them more than others—so that the house always felt full and alive. This night it was silent. I gathered that Earl was still over at the Evans cabin while they came to terms with their son's death.

Only after Martha had put the kettle on, then put cups of hot tea in our hands, did Gram start speaking. She said she had done several healing scans over Augie, and she hadn't found any broken bones and was pretty sure he had no internal bleeding. She said she wasn't too worried yet, that he needed quiet and warmth and rest, and she'd be back in the morning to see how he was doing. But I could feel that Gram was worried, and working not to show it.

"Why don't you go in and sit with him for a minute, Tessa?" she asked me.

I stepped down the hall which took me past Jesse's room—he wasn't in there, and I wasn't sure where he'd gone—and then to Augie's, which he shared with his brother Davy, who I assumed was spending that night in the second oldest brother, Steve's, room. Like Jesse's room this one was small, its floor and ceiling and walls all of sweet-smelling wood, with one window.

I sat down in the chair by Augie's bed that Gram had left for me. "Hi, Augie," I said softly. "It's Tessa."

There was no response. His eyes were closed, his eyelashes, like his eyebrows, golden against his pale skin. I leaned forward and rested my right ear over his heart. It was beating, and he was breathing slowly, but I heard nothing else. He was so quiet.

I scanned him slowly with my hands just over his body, feeling his energy all the way from his head to his toes. I felt an odd stillness inside him, as if his humming body had come to a full stop and was considering not starting up ever again.

I decided to sit with him for a time. *Augie,* I spoke to him, heart to heart, *I'm here to see if I can help you feel better. But it really does depend on you. There's not all that much we can do for you if you don't want us to.*

I tried to picture him at his usual full tilt speed, charging down the hall of the main house at the end of a school day and the teachers not even bothering to yell at him, they were so used to his energy and had pretty much given up trying to get him to slow down and be quiet inside. But all I saw was Augie being held by Jesse that time the horse, Belle, had stepped on his little foot. Augie holding tight to Jesse's shoulder, his blond curls mingling with Jesse's straight black hair.

*Sometimes things go wrong inside us and there's no real knowing why...*I kept sending my thoughts into him, my heart to his heart. *Sometimes a little time helps, and sometimes someone comes along who can help the healing along a little. Gram and I can help if you want...*

I couldn't tell if he was listening or not, but it seemed right to just sit with him, breathing the same air he was breathing, hearing what he was hearing. Gram's and Martha's voices wove a quiet melody in the kitchen. Through the glass of his window, which faced the mountain, I faintly heard the long, lonely call of a wolf. I held my breath, listening. It came again, that long unwinding, descending cry. It almost seemed like that cry was coming from within Augie.

Right then I realized that all of those years, all of those times, when Gram told me to *pay attention,* really what she meant was— *Listen.* Be still and listen. I needed to be a listener.

When I was little and Gram had asked me if I knew why we told stories so often in our village, I had thought of stories as tales of adventure in response to a calling, as the crossing of thresholds, which all was true. But now I also understood that we told stories in order to learn how to listen.

Later Gram was quiet as we began walking the long hill toward home. I put my arm through hers, parka against parka. She paused, and sighed into the night.

"I'm having problems connecting with him," she said. "I'm worried about what I might be missing." Then she muttered, "I wish we had ultrasound here."

As we kept walking the snowpacked path, she explained what ultrasound was, how they had handheld scanners in the city that actually showed pictures of what was inside a body. I'd never heard her talk that way before about another medicine that might work better than her hands, with chants and prayer. It was alarming, wondering for the first time that Gram might not be able to help someone, and not only that, she wasn't able to know even what the problem was.

"What do you think, Tessa?" Gram finally asked me as we crested the hill and could see our cabin up ahead.

I was so surprised I didn't know how to reply. She wanted to know what I thought. It wasn't one of Gram's teaching quizzes or lessons where I had to go off and think for a few hours on something to get a glimmer of understanding. She was speaking as one healer to another.

I tried not to think too hard, but to find the understanding from my heart. That's what I was beginning to learn. Find the understanding in your heart. And it came from listening.

"You know," I said slowly, and watched my breath puff white in the dark winter air. "I think he's dying of a broken heart."

Gram gave me one quick look, then continued walking in silence. She began nodding to herself, then said softly, "I think you are right."

~

We went back the next morning. Again Gram peeled off to the kitchen with Martha and waved me on to Augie's room. No one else was home and quiet permeated the house.

"Hi again, Augie," I said as I sat down in the chair by the bed. "It's Tessa. I wanted to say hello and see how you were."

Again I leaned my head over his heart and listened. Still so quiet.

I sat like that, almost but not quite touching him, feeling what it might be like to not want to live. I sat there for a long, long time.

Tears ran down my face and dropped slowly onto Augie's sleep shirt over his heart. I began to feel where he was—he was giving up his soul. He was crossing over to a place where those he loved the most, who loved him the most, couldn't reach him.

I had never been there before, never had anyone die whom I'd loved so much that I wanted to die, too. I felt myself reeling back from the black gap that was slowly opening, getting wider and wider. What would it take to call Augie back? How could I ever think I could do it?

Gram was standing, silent, in the doorway. I stood up and walked over to her. At seventeen I was looking down at her, but it didn't feel that way at all.

Seeking healing is like seeking a blessing—I remembered Gram saying this when I was trying to figure out the mystery of how healing works. *And it's not you seeking a blessing, it's you somehow putting yourself into a blessing for someone or something else. You become part of that blessing. You can be the vehicle for the blessing.*

But I couldn't figure out how I could meet Augie where he was.

"I can't help him, Gram," I whispered.

She kept looking at me, not saying anything.

"I... I don't know what to do..." I stumbled along, trying to find the words. "He's gone so far away. I don't know enough, I just don't understand..."

Gram nodded. "Go ahead home, Tessa, and think and pray on it." She stepped into Augie's room and was sitting down on the chair as I left.

But I didn't go home. I walked the snowpacked path past home and up to my lookout place over the lake. I hadn't been there in some time, since it had been a bit cold for sitting, even on sunny days. But this morning the sun, halfway along Ptarmigan to our south, carried warmth now that it was late February. The lake lay sleeping under a thick white blanket.

A big sigh heaved out of me, as if my spirit was trying to go somewhere. I felt useless, completely failed as an apprentice healer. I could feel what was wrong in Augie, but I was so far from being able to help him.

I thought I'd been called to be a healer. But what could I possibly do?

"I give up," I said out loud to the snow, to the lake. "I give up."

I sat down in the snow, not caring about how cold I was going to be in a few minutes, and watched the lake with my mind in neutral. I heard a whuh-whuh-whuh of wings and looked up to see a raven wheeling overhead, looking down at me. A minute later he landed on a hemlock branch nearby. It was the raven with the scraggly tail. He fidgeted a little on the branch, looking around. Then his mate flapped down to join him. They nuzzled each other and I hoped they would begin singing.

A faint melody began somewhere, but it wasn't the raven pair. I looked around and didn't see anyone, not even a person snowshoeing or fishing on the lake. The thread of song got louder. It was inside me. I could begin to hear the words. It was a healing chant Gram had taught me a year or so earlier, one that I'd learned diligently but had not thought about much.

Sweep of stars in deep of space,
sweep of Earth around the Sun,
Ring of light around the Sun.
Ring of light around the Sun.

Raven circles on the wind,
over branching river fingers
And a man upon the water.
And a man upon the water.

Inside this man, the dust of stars,
His heart the sun, his blood the rivers
Universe inside an atom.
Universe inside an atom.

Sing in praise of curving light
Sing in thanks for rising Sun,
Journey inward and be whole,
Journey outward and be healed.

The tune was a minor key that evoked solemnity and mystery. It made me feel very small, but at the same time I could see so far. I felt the way I had felt the night before, looking up at the sky full of stars.

Knowing that one of the stars over my head actually was a galaxy—Andromeda—a human being could actually stand on earth and see, just with her eyes, a galaxy beyond ours. And then knowing that that was just one small galaxy in a vast sea of galaxies.

And every material in the human body had been given off by stars. What a wonder a human being was. What immensity was so far beyond us, and also so far deep inside us.

I got up and walked back down to our cabin. Gram and I met on the path I'd recently shoveled out to our cabin door. She stopped.

"Tessa, he needs you."

I took a deep breath. "You think I should go back?"

She just nodded. "Remember," she started, then stopped.

"I'm just the vehicle for the blessing." I finished for her. We stood there looking at each other for a moment.

"You know, I hate that word, 'vehicle,'" I said. "Could we think of it as something different? Something... maybe we could think of it as I am the song?"

She smiled.

I walked back down to the Brightwaters' home. I kept myself in the moment, no over-thinking, just in the moment with my senses so sharp I felt like I could hear the bears snoring in their winter dens, the ravens breathing as they flew overhead. I felt a tingle of expectation.

"Hi Augie, it's Tessa again," I said as I took the chair next to the bed. This time I didn't need to lean close to him; I could feel him letting me in as soon as I walked through the door.

I put both hands lightly on his closest arm and opened my heart, my mind, my soul to him, softly humming the tune to Gram's chant that I thought of as the "In and Out" because of the way it made my mind travel out, out, out and then in, in, in.

Images came swiftly to me—wonderful speed and wind in my face, trees whipping past, ravens and bald eagles in the air just off the bluff, the laughing face of Dakota, with his dark hair and dark eyes and round cheeks. I saw Dakota fishing from a fallen tree on the lakeshore, Dakota shrieking with laughter after jumping into the icy summer lake water, the light of a campfire shining on Dakota's face as he leaned in to roast something on a stick.

Then images went jagged at the edges, as if too painful to take in all at once—the darkness of the machine against the sky, falling on top of them, the body of Dakota, like a rag doll thrown in the snow. Not a mark on him, but so clearly broken. Dead.

So much grief washed over me that I gasped like a person going underwater.

Here was the broken heart. Here at the bottom of the lake. Here beyond all sound and touch and being.

No, not quite.

I held tighter to Augie's little arm and cast my spirit out to search for... the sun. What had I learned about the bond between Raven and the sun? I thought of the stories of how Raven brought the sun to the world. It finally made sense that it was a trickster who was able to do it.

Before there was anything—I began whispering the story to Augie, a story I knew he already knew—*before the great flood had covered the earth and receded, before the animals walked the earth or the trees covered the land or the birds flew between the trees, even before the fish and the whales and seals swam in the sea, an old man lived in a house on the bank of a river with his only child, a daughter...*

...at that time the whole world was dark. Inky, pitchy, all-consuming dark, blacker than a thousand stormy winter midnights, blacker than anything anywhere has been since.

The reason for all this blackness has to do with the old man in the house by the river, who had a box which contained a box which contained a box which contained an infinite number of boxes each nestled in a box slightly larger than itself until finally there was a box so small all it could contain was all the light in the universe.

It was a box as small as a heart. (I added that line.)

As I whispered the story of how Raven tricked the old man, how he became a tiny hemlock needle that the old man's daughter accidentally swallowed, how he transformed himself to a human being inside her, and was born as a strange-looking little boy who tricked the old man into opening the boxes—all the time I whispered the story to Augie, I could hear ravens calling outside. And the sun shone down.

Dancing gold upon the water. Flying just above it, a raven, black reflected on gold.

I saw myself—somehow transformed to a fish, a young silver salmon—swimming up through liquid gold, clear water running golden with light as I neared the surface and saw the world dance bright in the sunlight above me, just beyond the surface.

I brought the warmth and sunlight to Augie.

And we both broke through the surface into daylight.

"Augie," I whispered, "The song is in us. The song *is* us."

He stirred, slowly stretching his arms over his head, kicking his feet against the blanket cover. His eyelids fluttered, then his blue eyes looked at me. We gazed at each other for a long moment. Then he slowly smiled.

"Hey Tessa."

"Hey Augie. You won't believe how your Mom and Dad and Jesse and Steve and Davy have missed you. And me, too, and Gram and Hannah, and, well, everybody in the village."

He stretched again. Then I could see him remembering. I put my hand on his arm again.

"Some things we can't understand, at least for a while. Mysteries. But we keep going, and maybe someday we will. Dakota would want you to keep going, Augie."

After a moment he gave a little nod.

Then Martha was in the doorway, looking in, and crying, and running to hug him up into her arms, up off the bed. And Earl came through the door and hugged both of them up into his arms, laughing and crying all at the same time.

I moved off the bed to the safety of the chair, and was thinking about making an exit to the kitchen, when I heard footsteps running through the house, down the hall toward me, and Jesse came bursting in through Augie's door and into the room carrying energy like one of those midsummer winds that whirls up water over the lake. He barely looked at Augie and his parents, but reached down to pull me up, lifted me right off the chair and into his arms, against his chest, engulfing me so I could hardly breathe. But it felt so good, and so familiar.

Except for a quick hand on an arm or shoulder, we hadn't touched each other for years. We'd been careful not to touch each other in all the tumult of changing bodies and odd yearnings and fears. But when we'd been little, we'd curled up together in Jesse's bed, we'd taken naps against each other in the hay loft, we'd even punched each other a few times—well, that was more me punching Jesse; I don't think he ever hit me back. Then suddenly, his arms.

Jesse, at nearly nineteen, was almost as tall as Earl, though not big in the draft horse way that Earl was big. He had broad shoulders and arms so strong he could lift me right up into the air without an extra breath, but his muscles were long and lean. He'd grown up and I'd been living with him almost as much as I lived with Hannah, but somehow I hadn't really noticed.

"Raven," he breathed into my hair. "Thank you, thank you, thank you."

"Jesse," I whispered back. "Remember how you saved me when I was Augie's age?"

"All I did was get my Dad," he said, and smiled. "And my Dad saved you."

"Well, same here. All I did was...get Raven." It sounded strange, but, oh well.

We laughed and his arms tightened around me again, and I just took a deep breath and let myself come home, completely at home.

~

Snowclouds moved in and wrapped our mountains and village for a full week. On a couple of days it was snowing and blowing so hard that Gram recommended I not try to find my way to school. I was good with that. I sat in front of the fire and read, and when Gram napped, I switched books and read another journal of Dylan Silloway's that I had found. This was an earlier one describing his and Ellen's move to their new home in the far northwest corner of the continent, to the stronghold of the defense contractor then called Minerva. I found a lot more of my mother's handwriting in it.

On a blank page near the end of the book, I found these questions, in her handwriting:

- It happened so slowly that no one seemed to notice—When did our government become Orion, and Orion become our government?

- When was it decided that citizens were White and Christian, and anyone who wasn't White and Christian was pushed into a slum and couldn't vote?

(What's a *slum*? I wondered.)

Gram woke up, and under the guise of doing research for a history paper, I ransacked our cabin's bookshelves for books that would help me understand what my mother meant. One fat, faded and dog-eared book—someone's history book from at least four decades ago—gave me a little more than I'd learned in our village school. I'd wondered why Orion would make our corner of the continent, so far removed from the big cities of the East and South, its main base. At some point in the early grades I had learned about *The Traitor States*, Orion's term for what my teacher suggested we call *the missing states*, instead (and at first I'd thought they were *trader states*, and it took about a year or so for me to get that straightened out in my head). I had learned about how Washington, Oregon and California all joined the original Traitor State, Vermont, and so the entire nation lost its West Coast—except for Alaska.

But now I learned that sitting on the far northwest corner of the continent, at the opening of a ice-free polar sea, Alaska became the most important military base a country could possibly have. Plus it had unlimited clean water, and about the only other country in the world with that was Canada, next door. Refugees who had fled up the West Coast, fleeing rising sea floods, droughts and yearly summer wildfires burning through the canyons to the sea, leaving no safe space in between (so I guessed there wasn't much of value left in those western Traitor States), these refugees found themselves trapped again, but this time by a military government that declared them—well, most of them, the ones who weren't White and Christian—illegal aliens. Most were deported (it didn't say where to); some were tolerated as the non-citizen worker class.

But it was a slim paperback book, missing its cover, pushed underneath a dictionary on the top shelf, that got me thinking I knew why my mother would have left our safe, hidden village and joined the resistance. This was a book of stories, not myths but true stories, of what people had seen in the corners of this state home base of Orion. Whole forests of trees cut down so that roads, airports and rail-lines could be laid down, new cities laid out in grid patterns at intervals across the state. Bombs used to blast open deepwater ports all along the coast. Anything in their way was trampled down, crushed, tossed away without a second thought. Grizzly bears, wolverines, Dall sheep now joined the extinct polar bears, and nearly all of the salmon gone forever too, because of the increasingly polluted and warming seawater.

I walked over, carrying the book in my hand, to the window

overlooking our lake so Gram couldn't see my face. Inside I had the same feeling I had that day climbing Mount Snow, when I looked out over the mountain ridges for the first time and saw the inlet water in the distance, and the ranges of mountains beyond that. We were living in a tiny, protected corner... hidden, overlooked while so much around us was being destroyed. We were safe for the moment... but how likely was that to last? And was it right to stay where we were and not do anything to help fight the destruction?

Once I started thinking these thoughts, I couldn't think of anything else.

~

About a week later as we sat in our cabin and watched the fire, Gram said, "Tessa, God has blessed you with a powerful gift. You are able to cross thresholds, you're a go-between. You can be a song for healing. I won't be able to help you as a teacher much more, but I may be able to connect you to someone..."

My heart, and it felt like everything else inside me, squeezed tight. Gram had been thinking that all week as I had been thinking that I couldn't stay in our safe, hidden village. Now that I knew what was out there, what Orion was doing.

I had to tell Gram that I was going to leave for the city and the resistance. After my entire childhood being raised to pay attention and listen for the call, I wasn't going to learn how to be a healer, I was going to answer a different call and join the fighters instead. What a betrayal. It would kill Gram. But it would be even worse if I didn't tell her.

I left my chair and knelt down on the rug next to her. She turned her face from the fire to me. The firelight was soft on her face. She looked tired and sad, and she looked like she knew what I was going to say.

"Gram, I am going to be leaving soon to join the resistance."

She bent her head and looked down at her hands in her lap.

"It's something I know in my heart I have to do," I forced myself to go on. "But I know I will come back."

She was still looking down at her hands, her twined fingers whitening as they twisted together. She let out a long breath. I did too, feeling as if I'd stabbed her in the gut, and myself in the next second with the same knife. *God, if only she'd yell at me or even slap my face, that would be so much easier to take...*

"It's selfish to go, Tessa." Finally Gram raised her head and looked me in the eyes. "Think of all the people who depend on you—not just me and Jesse and Hannah and your Auntie, but the whole village."

"Gram, I'm going to go. But I also know that I'll come back."

"You were born with the gift to become a great healer with God's help, and your spirit helpers' help, for your village and perhaps beyond. You would turn your back on that and become a warrior instead?"

Now I couldn't look into her eyes. I bent my head and took a few breaths. It was almost as if I had to remember to breathe.

"Gram, I'm going to go. I will be back."

She shook her head. "No one knows that, Tessa. No one can know. What a loss."

There was nothing more we could say to each other that night. Sadness filled our cabin and weighed down so heavy on us both. I couldn't sleep at all that night, and I'm sure that, because of me, Gram couldn't either.

~

The next morning I skipped school again and found Jesse chopping wood outside the Brightwater barn. The snows were over and we were at the breaking point of winter, when it still felt like winter at night and before the sun rose, but once the sun came up over Ptarmigan to the south, it felt like spring. The sun was just rising when I came around the barn on the path packed in the snow by several pairs of Brightwater feet walking back and forth many times on chores.

Jesse was wearing only an old flannel shirt and jeans tucked into his work boots. He swung the ax easily down through the air to meet the wood with a deep *thunk!* and one big chunk opened into two small chunks that fell to the snow. He bent down and tossed them to a pile nearby. He saw me and set the ax down on the chopping stump, wiped his forehead with his right arm. He'd twisted a bandana into a narrow strand and tied it around his forehead, keeping back his shiny, black hair.

"Hey, Tessa, are you skipping school again?"

When I walked up to him, I had the sudden feeling that he wanted to put his arms around me, but was resisting. Part of me wanted his arms around me again, part of me wanted to hold back and be safe, part of me asked *safe from what?*

I had to clear my throat and I couldn't find the words at first, and then they came out rushed. "Jesse, I'm going to leave for the city soon."

His dark eyes were intense. "How can you go? You're the most important person in our village."

How could he say this? Did he really believe it? I certainly didn't, and I couldn't, wouldn't accept the load of responsibility this carried, even if it were true. But it wasn't!

"There are lots more important people in our village!" I nearly shouted at him. "Like your Dad, and Gram, and Hannah, who's Seeing more all the time. And you, too. In a few years, well, in a bunch of years, you'll be just like your Dad."

I meant that as a compliment. As the oldest of Earl's and Martha's sons, Jesse would take charge of the supply runs with the horses and wagons in the summers, with the snowgos and sleds in the winters, and while Jesse seemed to have inherited the artist's carving gift, he also had a gift for being able to fix machines, so that would make him even more important to everyone. He'd raise a big family, and always be the one watching out for all the village kids.

Jesse pulled off the bandana and used it to wipe his face. He stood there shaking his head.

"No, Tessa. I'm going to go with you."

He'd never spoken of leaving the village. Ever. Surprise must have shown all over my face, because he smiled and added, "Someone's got to be there to talk you out of hare-brained mission ideas that you surely will get."

We just looked at each other for a moment. I felt stunned. That he would offer... but I couldn't accept his offer. It was one thing for me to walk on out on my own, but I couldn't be the reason for Jesse leaving the village. I didn't want to be responsible for Jesse leaving.

He was good at reading my face. He put a hand, heavy, on my shoulder.

"Tessa, I'm going with you."

He turned to pick up his jacket that lay over a larger log nearby, slipped it on, and motioned for me to follow him. We walked around to the front of the barn, and I followed him in through the main doors that were open just enough for us to walk through. The rising sun shone in over our shoulders, touching everything to gold.

Jesse sat down on the pile of fresh hay just outside the horses' stalls, and beckoned me to sit down beside him.

"Have you told anyone yet?"

"I told Gram last night."

He looked at me steadily; I felt sympathy in the air between us.

"Yeah, that probably explains why I look like shit this morning," I said. "I didn't sleep a wink afterwards. And I'm pretty sure she didn't either."

"And she's going to let you go." It wasn't a question.

I wasn't yet eighteen, so in the eyes of our village I was not yet an adult, and therefore not completely free to make big decisions such as marrying or leaving school early. There weren't many big life choices to wrestle with in our village; for instance, having sex was fine as long as you understood the implications around it, and our elders all were careful about our education. Leaving the village was, needless to say, a big decision. By not interfering, Gram was showing me that she trusted my judgment, which meant that she believed I was capable of making the right choice (staying in our village) and was going to let me hold to my bad choice of leaving the village. It was on me.

Well, I could take it.

"Hello?" Jesse said. "Would you like to say some of that out loud?"

I couldn't help smiling, but the humor of it was gone in about a second. "She sees it as trusting me as an adult, and letting me make a bad decision."

"I'll bet she doesn't want you to go alone, though."

"We didn't talk about that." I frowned down at the straw that Jesse was twisting and twining with his long fingers.

"Tessa, I don't see you as the frail sex needing a man's protection."

"I know."

"I just think that anyone heading out needs a buddy, someone to help keep an eye out."

"I know."

"And we could be that for each other."

We talked then about how to get to the city. It was a good time of year for traveling because the snow was firm enough for easy walking in the night, and the daytime temperatures were beginning to go above freezing, so it wouldn't be too cold. We figured it would take us three days at the most. We were probably the fittest people in the village, so walking with packs for three days wasn't the challenge––the challenge was figuring out what to do when we got to the city. How did one join the resistance?

Then I had a scary thought. "And how will your Dad take it, you leaving with me?"

Earl wasn't likely to be supportive of either of us leaving the village. And yet... something told me that Earl wouldn't be all that surprised.

"Oh God," Jesse said, "there's no way I could tell my Dad."

"I think you need to tell him."

"Tessa..." He was about to tell me to take a hike and mind my own business, but he stopped. He was thinking on it. After a moment he said, "Are you willing to go with me to talk with my Dad about us leaving?"

I had to take a deep breath at the thought of it, but I said, "Yes, of course."

We walked back out of the barn, to where Jesse knew his Dad was, out mending the pasture fence. I followed Jesse, who was walking slowly, and I noticed, walking more and more slowly once we caught sight of his Dad in the distance. The set of Jesse's shoulders under his jacket told me that he was tensed up, knotted up inside, just as I had felt when I'd told Gram I was going to leave.

Earl paused and set down his tools when he saw us walk up. As Jesse told him that we were going to leave soon to join the resistance, Earl's face reddened from the throat up, the flush of red rushing right up around his eyes and to his glistening forehead. I braced myself for an explosion. But then he let his breath out in a long sigh and said, "I knew this moment was coming, just hoped it would be another few years."

Surprise spiked through the air between Jesse and me. We glanced at each other. Then I realized Earl was looking hard at me.

"You sure you can't wait another few years?" he asked. He was asking me, not Jesse.

I held steady under the beam of his gaze, then I nodded. "It's now. I know." That's all I could say.

But it seemed to make sense to Earl. He sighed again. "Just like your mother," he muttered. "When she knew something, she *knew*."

Now I stared at Earl, longing, no, feeling desperate, to hear more about my mother, but he turned to Jesse instead. "You think you know all about how to do it? Did Emmitt or Marvin talk to you before they left?"

Jesse shook his head. "No, Dad. We don't have a clue. No one's said a word to us."

Earl looked back at me. "What do you think your Gram will say, young Ravenwing?"

"We talked last night. She doesn't want me to go," I said slowly.

"Hmmmmm," Earl rumbled. "I'll bet it was like a knife in the heart, for her."

Exactly right. I bent my head. I couldn't bear to look at either of them right then.

"I'll go talk with her," Earl said slowly. He picked up his hammer and pliers, then he looked back at us. "Most important thing for the two of you is to know that you don't know jack about anything, so you got to listen to me when I tell you the things to look out for."

Jesse and I both nodded.

~

By early afternoon we had gathered our packs, a small tent, two sleeping bags, dried food that would be easy to carry. Because the bears were still hibernating, we wouldn't have to carry a bulky bearproof plastic canister for our food. We were ready. Earl described the route through the mountains for us, drawing with a stick a rough map in the hay dust on the floor of the barn. He told us where the trail branched off for the trading post south of the city and emphasized, stabbing the stick into the dust, that that was the way to go, for us not to try to go into the city by ourselves. He told us to ask for Emmitt and Lars at the trading post. At least one of them should be there.

"The most important thing to remember, besides your not knowing anything," Earl said, looking first at Jesse, and then at me, "is that you do not move until you've found one of them, who can help you go from there."

I nodded. Jesse, standing close on my left, nodded. That didn't seem too hard to do.

"Now, I gotta ask you not to say one word to anyone in the village about your leaving," Earl said. "Except of course your Gram, Tessa, and your Auntie and Hannah. Not one word. That's the way it has to be. When you come back—and I can't ask you to promise something you might not be able to promise, but I want you to do everything in your power to come back—then we can talk about all of it. But we can't yet. And I can't help you go to the city, except for drawing you a map and giving you advice."

After a pause, Jesse asked in a quiet voice, "Did you do that for Emmitt and Marvin?"

Earl nodded. "Lars went on his own, but then Lars is... Lars. Also Lars knew who to look for."

He must have felt my eyes on him, for he turned then and gave me a soft look. "Far as I know, your Mom left in the dead of night, not telling a soul, not even her mother."

Earl was still holding the stick in his hands, and he seemed to just realize that and turned and leaned it against the closest horse stall, then kicked the map out of the dust with his right foot.

I turned for the barn doors, to start walking home.

"Young Ravenwing," Earl said. I looked back. "That was good of you, knowing to tell your Gram. It's hurtin' her, but it sure helped that you told her. Just like I'm grateful to Jesse for telling me."

Jesse had turned to walk to the horses' stalls, but he stopped and looked at me too, and his eyes said, *Thank you.*

~

I still had to tell Hannah. I knew just where to find her at midafternoon. She'd be tidying up her classroom in the school wing of the main meeting house. This was her first year of teaching the youngest village kids, and she fussed and clucked about them like a happy hen. Of course I didn't want to run into my teacher, Mrs. Kickbush, having just skipped her class three times in the past week, and now proposing to quit it altogether. So I went cautiously up the path and slipped in a back door, quietly crossing through the main meeting room that was empty at this time of day, then around a corner and I was looking into Hannah's bright little room.

She looked happy as she sorted out different colors of crayons into metal cans, humming, her braids tied up on her head like a crown. I suddenly felt terrible about bringing such bad news to her, and she would definitely see it as bad news. But I also thought she wouldn't be surprised, either.

A wariness crept into her expression when she saw me slip through her door.

"Mrs. Kickbush asked me at lunch today if you were sick," she said, finishing with the small silver cans. Then she started in on picking up papers. "I said not that I knew of, but that at this point I was pretty sure you would be able to cure yourself."

"Hannah." I sat down on a little kid's chair and my knees nearly hit my chin.

She glanced over at me.

"Hannah, I'm leaving to join the resistance. Soon. Jesse wants to come with me."

She sat down on her chair behind her desk, so hard and quick that its legs screeched on the wooden floor. "Oh Tessa, how could you?"

"I've known for a long time that this was something I was going to do."

"Become a warrior, when you know you are being called to be a healer?!"

"I know that I need to go. Perhaps healing will be a part of it there."

"Well, what about everyone else you're leaving behind?" She hit her desk with the flat of her hand, a sharp smack. Probably what she'd like to do to my face. "What grief for Gram! Just because you *think* it's the right thing for you to do."

I bit my tongue so I didn't say something mean back to her. I knew I was hurting her, and I deserved whatever mean things she was going to throw at me.

"And all I've ever Seen of you," she went on, "Seen of any of us in the city, is killing and imprisonment and being wounded and crying our hearts out. Nothing good, ever! In the face of that, you still think you have a calling to go?!"

I just nodded. I didn't want to know what she'd Seen. She'd talked of prison before, and men and machines they put us into. I didn't want to think about that, but I still knew I was going.

She quickly stood up and walked to the one window in her room, a small window but with the best view of the lake from anywhere in the village.

"And then you bring this into my classroom, my favorite and happiest place, Tessa."

"I'm sorry. I wanted to tell you myself so you didn't overhear it being talked about."

"Oh, how thoughtful of you," in the most biting Hannah tone. She still kept her back to me.

I managed to extricate myself from the tiny chair, and I stood back up. "And I'm sorry, Hannah, for any pain I'm causing you. I need to go, but I'll do my very best to come back."

She said nothing more. I left with a heart so heavy I could barely walk.

At home Jesse was sitting in the living room with Gram. He stood up and walked over to me when I came in the door.

"I was afraid you'd left without me," he said softly.

"I was telling Hannah."

"Oh. I'm guessing that was pretty bad."

I just nodded, looking past him to Gram, who nodded slowly back, her face quite still.

Jesse put an arm lightly around my shoulders. "You're a brave soul, Raven, but you look all done in. Why don't you lie down and get some sleep."

"And you're going to stay here keeping watch so I don't sneak away?"

Jesse just smiled.

~

I slept hard for a couple of hours and felt much better. Jesse was gone when I came out of my room. Gram said he'd gone home to his house for dinner, but that he'd be back afterward.

Washing up after our light supper, I stood at the window above the sink and watched the setting sun light up the east end of our valley. The sun was so low in the west that our cabin and all the valley were in shadow, but the snow of the east end of the lake glowed gold. The sharp rock walls of the small gorge beyond, that the river ran though, even they looked soft in the gold light. Suddenly it was spring, no longer winter. I thought of all the times, in every season, I'd walked, skied, canoed down there at that end of the lake.

How could I leave it?

Gram was there at my right elbow, leaning against the sink and looking out at the lake.

"Tessa," she said softly, "I want you to know that no matter what, I love you. I will pray for you every day. I'll be waiting for you."

I had no voice, so I just leaned over and put my cheek down on her shoulder. She reached her arm around me and we stood like that

94

for a long moment.

Later, when we sat in front of the fire with cups of tea, I asked her if she could tell me a little about when she left the village to live with her granny Ida's family far to the south.

When I was eighteen, she said, *I was a lot like you, in that I knew what I was going to do and I didn't like anyone to tell me otherwise...*

Jesse walked in the door then, heard that sentence and smiled. He lay down on his stomach on the rug at our feet and watched the fire.

But my life had changed that year, Gram went on, *because I'd become very sick, and nearly died, and in a sense had lost my way.*

I had not known this. I was bursting with questions, but held them back because I could see that Gram was in storytelling mode, and nothing should interrupt a story.

My Granny Ida thought it might be good for me to spend some time with her relatives in the Tlingit village she grew up in, far south along the coast. My mother and father agreed, though they were afraid I'd love it so much by the sea that I wouldn't come back home to the lake. Grampa Vegard and Granny Silloway also thought it was a good idea. Grampa Silloway didn't say much, as usual, but he smiled at me and said that leaving for a time was definitely the right thing for me to do.

But my parents weren't happy to see me go. I was their only child, though I'm sure at that point they were ready for a break from me. The sickness had brought me to a stop, but before that I had had the same energy that you have, Tessa... Gram paused, and looked at me.

I saw Jesse smile again. I nudged his shoulder, gently, with my foot.

So I sailed with a friend of Grampa Vegard's to Granny Ida's Ravenwing clan in a village bigger than ours on a peninsula far to the south, but it looked so much like here, with the mountains marching, so green, right into the sea. It was less snowy there, much rainier than here. The trees were taller than ours, cedar growing everywhere and the glorious Sitka spruce.

I lived with Granny Ida's sister Hattie and her husband. Hattie was the village healer. She was kind but stern, a taskmaster. I lived with her for two years, and she taught me how to be still and find the patterns. How to feel when the spirit world drew close. How to listen. Oh, there is so much that we can hope to learn, and try to learn!

She looked at me and I felt sadness, but no anger. *This is how things are,* I heard her voice inside my head, *and we live, and learn, as best we can.*

"Well, that's all the storytelling for tonight," she said, and slowly stood up from her chair. "I'm off to bed."

Jesse sat up and we both thanked her for her story. I watched her slowly move across the living room, pause in the doorway to her room and look back at me. I blew her a kiss and she smiled.

I sat down on the rug next to Jesse, but not touching. We sat there and watched the fire for a few minutes.

"Let's go tonight," I said softly. It felt right. And I couldn't bear any more goodbyes.

Jesse looked at me, and then nodded.

4. March 2100

When I was little and Gram let me climb Mount Snow by myself, she called it *walking the mountain*. The first night that Jesse and I followed the trail, under the moon and the stars, I kept thinking to myself *we are walking with the mountains*. They had a presence. Wearing their winter cloaks of snow still, they were quiet but they felt alive, as if they might begin whispering to us. I kept watching them, waiting for that moment.

Jesse was quiet as he walked ahead of me. He had on a home-knit wool cap, like I did, pulled low on his brow, then his dark, bulky jacket and overpants. He was giving off the feeling of seeing something through, calm and resolved, while I felt like skipping and singing. I was careful not to do that, or chatter, because I was grateful for his calm and resolve, for his reassuring presence. It *was* better traveling through the mountains with someone, rather than alone. Especially in the dead of the night as we walked through a narrow, dark valley and heard wolves begin calling on the distant—but it didn't feel distant enough right then—mountain ridge to the north.

Jesse stopped, listening.

I stopped too, trying not to say anything. Then I had to ask, "Do you have a gun?"

"No." He turned and looked down at me. "Dad and I talked for a while about that. He thought it was better for us to go without one." A shadow of a smile passed across his face. "I do have a knife."

"Oh great, a wolf would have to come awfully close for a knife to help us."

"I don't think they'll bother us. They have plenty of other things to eat right now."

Just keep projecting calm, I thought at him. *As long as you feel calm, I'll feel calm.*

But we didn't hear wolves again that night, and the fear dropped away, and I felt happy. I had thought for years about following this trail through the mountains, and finally here I was, walking the snow-packed trail. Earl and his team had done a resupply run after the last storm, and their snowgos had packed the snow so well there was no need even for snowshoes. If I hadn't had a pack on my back, I would have been jogging. The night air was crisp and just cold enough to keep us walking, but not bitter cold, now that it was early March and spring was sending its feelers out, even here in the mountains. Under the sun the trail would soften, especially in the open, south-facing places, so that was a good reason to walk at night. The other reason was to not be seen, but I wasn't quite sure who we were trying not to be seen by. Jesse said from what he'd overheard at home over the years, Orion stayed in the city. But Orion did have devices called drones that they flew remotely to keep an eye out for anything unusual.

I wasn't going to worry about things I didn't yet understand. I was going to enjoy *walking with the mountains*.

Then I noticed the mountain peaks were getting a little brighter. Behind us, in the east, the clear sky began paling, sliding into the shades of turquoise I loved so much. Sunrise was coming.

"Time to find a place to camp," Jesse said.

Choosing a spot didn't take long. The snow had melted off a rocky ledge next to the trail, which meant we could leave the trail without making tracks, scrambling over the rocks to a swath of hemlocks that opened here and there into little snow glades, perfect for sheltering our tent. I wasn't much help since I'd never put up a tent, but Jesse didn't seem to mind doing it himself while I collected clean snow in a tin pot to boil for drinking water.

By the time the sun inched up over the ridge, we had our packs stowed in the tent and a pot of melting snow on the small burner Jesse had carried in his pack, along with a cylinder of gas to fuel it. I sat back on my heels on the cold rock, watching the white mountain peaks all around us glow gold in the rising sun. The hemlocks smelled deep green. The air smelled like snow, with an occasional whiff of gas from the stove. Ravens called as they woke up and started their breakfast foraging. They'd be checking us out soon.

We didn't talk much as we drank our tea and ate oatmeal, and Jesse ate three of Martha's precious fruit and nut bars (assuring me that he'd saved me a couple). I was realizing how tired I was, not just from the night's hike, but also from the preceding two days of so much suddenly happening to change my life, and hardly any sleep with it.

"You look done in, Raven," Jesse said. "Why don't you go to bed. I'll clean up."

The tent fabric was the color of spring birch leaves, gold-green, and it was lit by the rays of the rising sun so that I felt like I'd crawled into a green nest. My sleeping bag was warm, with a foam pad under it to insulate me from the snow under the tent floor. It was a lovely place for sleeping, and I was exhausted, but I couldn't fall asleep because it all was so strange. Sleeping in a tent, in the daytime, with Jesse's sleeping bag only an arm's reach away. Sleeping with Jesse. That was what was keeping me awake. *They're sleeping together,* Hannah had said about our cousin Jenna and Brad Kickbush, meaning that they were having sex, and really sleeping didn't figure into it at all. I was seventeen and I knew these things. But I myself didn't want to have sex with anyone yet. At least I was pretty sure I didn't want to. I couldn't imagine having sex with anyone but Jesse, who was the only person I trusted enough to have sex with, but at the same time I couldn't imagine the upheaval that would be, not just physically but also in... everything.

I jumped in my sleeping bag at the sound of Jesse unzipping the tent, which made him laugh.

I dove deeper into my bag and found an excuse, "I'm so tired, I'm twitching."

"Just go to sleep, Tessa," he said, zipping it back up behind him and then pulling off his jacket and bunching it up to use for a pillow. "You're safe with me."

And also *safe from me?* I wondered. Even deep in my bag I could see that he was on his back on his sleeping bag, unzipping his pants. I couldn't bear it and rolled over, facing the green glowing wall of the tent and prayed for sleep. But I couldn't fall asleep with Jesse there, so close. I could hear the rustle of him settling into his sleeping bag, the soft sound of him breathing. My whole body was tensed at the thought of him so close, within reach, nearly naked or maybe completely naked.

Something was welling up inside me, rising up through my chest and into my throat, and I tried to choke it back, a gasp, a sob, a laugh all in one that sounded so strange that Jesse said, "Tessa?"

"I can't sleep!" I wailed into my sleeping bag. Better wailing than hysterical laughter, or screaming.

"It's okay. You're probably overtired." I heard the rustle of him moving closer in his sleeping bag. "I'll tell you a bedtime story, okay?"

I still couldn't roll over to face him, but I said, "Okay."

Bluejay was a healer, a medicine man, Jesse murmured. *And Bluejay fell so in love with a beautiful girl in a nearby village, and she with him. Their hearts were one, and they wanted to marry, but her father didn't think Bluejay was good enough for her and forbid it and kept them apart.*

A raven called just then from very close, probably perched at the top of the hemlocks just outside our tent. *Haw, haw, haw,* like he was commenting on the story, and really he didn't care very much for jays.

She fell sick and no one came to ask Bluejay to help, Jesse went on, *and she died. When he finally heard, he came anyway, to see her once more as she was lying on the burial scaffold, covered with blankets and beautiful things. He loved her so much he was willing to give up half his soul to bring her back to life, so he carried her in his canoe up the river, singing his whisper song, called a tam'mut, which means a longing for something you know you never can have.*

I rolled over to face him. He was telling the story with his eyes closed, lying on his back, just inches away. The morning sunlight through the fabric of the tent glowed golden on his face.

And as Bluejay goes, he sings to her, and she comes back to life slowly. After a few days of this, she's awake, and he breathes into her and leads her to his home where they live as husband and wife, so happy. But he tells her that half his life is inside her, and she can't go away from him now or she'll die and he won't be able to get her back next time.

I kept staring at his face in the soft light. His eyes stayed closed.

But someone tells her father she's with Bluejay, and he comes and gets her and takes her away, even though she doesn't want to go, and she tells him they're married now, but still she goes with her father. And she dies before she gets back to her old home. The father sends gift after gift to Bluejay, begging him to come and heal her again, but Bluejay tells him gifts are meaningless when it comes to a life. How stupid of her father to think he can buy her back? But Bluejay couldn't help anyway because he'd given up half his soul and there was hardly anything left. So Bluejay called all the healers to him and told them from now on, no giving up souls to save people from death.

"What a beautiful story," I whispered after he'd been quiet for a moment. "Beautiful, but sad. Where did that story come from, Jesse?"

"One of my aunties often told it to me when I was little. Not the auntie our teacher." He opened his eyes and turned his head to look at me. His brown eyes were lit by the gold-green light to a warm brown, the color of the wood in the barn in the morning sun.

"It's a warning story, Tessa. Maybe a warning for you. You're so quick to jump in to everything... Makes me worry."

How wonderful to have someone care enough to worry. I inched my body in my sleeping bag a little closer to him, so my head just barely touched his shoulder. This felt so good, so right. My whole body was relaxing.

"Don't worry about me, Jesse."

His breath was warm on my cheek and smelled of the minty honey we'd put in our tea. He rested his arm around my shoulders and I felt safe and comfortable, and finally sleepy.

"Got your back, Raven. Always will."

"You saved my life once already," I told him. "I'll never forget."

My muscles softened and sleep began to cover me, gentle as a down coverlet. But just before letting it cover me, I felt a sudden urge to reach out my arms, to reach for a kiss that would surely lead to a lot more, then realized I was inside Jesse's head, this was what he was yearning to do, and there was one moment where I was poised on the brink—should I? did I dare?—No. It was too much. I hit overload. I let myself slip backward, into sleep, and the safety of the known and the familiar. *Please let's keep things as they are...*

I heard Jesse's sigh and soft words, "'Night, Raven," but I was too far into sleep to be able to reply.

~

Two nights later we walked out of a valley to stand on a ridge and see the nearly full moon hanging above the sea in the west. And the city, less than ten miles away, at our feet, what I'd longed to see for years, but it was hard to see it clearly in the dark. So many lights––horizontal strings and grids of them, and vertical lines of lights in the blocky shapes of buildings that lay straight ahead and about a thousand feet below us, over the middle part of the peninsula. The tallest blocks and spires, also studded with lights, rose out of the city's northeast quadrant to our right. A faint but steady hum wavered through the air, the sound of the city.

So many lights. I could see now why the sky at night glowed to the west when I looked up from our village. I was finally seeing it, Orion's city, Fayerport.

"Well, here we are," Jesse said.

I was tired and footsore and hungry, and about to give him a glare for being obvious and idiotic, when it occurred to me that perhaps we *weren't* quite where we were supposed to be. Earl had said we would come out south of the city. We weren't south at all; where we were standing seemed about smack at the center of the city.

"Um, do you think there's a chance we missed that turn your Dad was talking about?"

The night had been cloudy and dark up until the moment of our stepping out of the mountains. We'd dropped our pace, trying to make extra sure that we were staying on the trail that kept disappearing in the gloom. My night vision seemed to be a little better than Jesse's, so I had taken the lead in those sketchy parts. It was kind of like finding a star by looking at it only out of the corner of your eyes.

With hindsight I could think of at least three places where I might have led us wrong, but I wasn't going to admit this to Jesse. Not yet, anyway.

Jesse let out his breath. "Fuck. I was trusting you to not miss it, Tessa."

"Hey, I was doing the absolute best I could!"

There was a pause in which each of us was holding back from saying more. The hum of the city grew clearer, punctuated by odd percussives. I couldn't recognize one sound.

Jesse rubbed his eyes with his fists. Finally he said, "I really don't want to turn around and retrace our steps over the past twelve miles."

"Me either."

"The path's pretty clear up ahead," he pointed.

"Let's keep going." It was my suggestion, but he seemed to want to do it, too.

He stood there silent for another moment. We were both tired. We'd walked for ten or eleven hours each night for three nights and we hadn't slept as much as we needed to during the two days. Even that first day when I finally fell into such a deep sleep, I didn't sleep for long enough. It was impossible to sleep for very long with the sun so bright outside our tent and so many birds to listen to. And so much tension crowded the air of the tent—both of us so intensely aware that we weren't the little kids who used to nap together in the hay loft—that it was almost impossible to breathe, let alone sleep.

The second day on the trail Jesse had made excuses to stay outside the tent until I was asleep and just a lump in my sleeping bag (hopefully not snoring). That had helped. A little.

If we'd been able to think more clearly, we would have realized that we were not at our best, and it would have been wise to retreat even just a mile or two to find cover so we could try to sleep through one more day, and then regroup.

"I'll bet we're okay," Jesse finally said. "I'll bet this trail leads down to the trading post Dad described."

"Let's keep going," I said again.

We did.

The snowpacked path was easy enough to follow as it wended through last year's bare-but-still-thorny devil's club as high as my head, and grasses, tall and rustling dry as they stuck out of what was left of winter's snow. The air filled with the dense, rich fragrance of moist earth emerging on south-facing banks.

"Bears might be out already down here," Jesse commented in front of me, pointing to the tunnel of alders the path was headed for. "Start your usual chatter, Tessa."

But I couldn't think of anything to say. Now that we were almost there, I was in the grip of doubts. Had we missed that turn? What if we couldn't meet up with anyone we knew? How did one ask questions about finding the resistance in a city where if you said the wrong thing you got shot? I hadn't doubted myself very often so far in my life; I didn't like feeling this way.

Jesse didn't follow up with any teasing remark about how could I be quiet for probably the first time in my life, right when he needed me to make noise. I guessed that he was thinking the same tired and discouraged thoughts that I was.

But we didn't see any bears. The path broke out of the alders to run more steeply downhill into a ravine—hard when your legs were tired and you had a pack on your back—and I fell back a little, which was also unusual for me.

One shoulder of the ravine drew close on our right, so close that we couldn't see around it. Up ahead the path kept dropping down, but high banks rose up along its sides. Jesse waited for me at a structure that rose over the path just beyond him.

In the ravine still night-dark, I couldn't quite see what it was. A square frame maybe three times as high as Jesse was tall, the span of the sides and its depth perhaps twice its height. Metal faintly gleamed. I'd read about bridges, though I'd always pictured them as much bigger, crossing big rivers or wide valleys. I took a step past him, so curious, wanting to touch it, when Jesse reached for my arm.

"I hear something," was all he said.

A high-pitched humming sound, more a vibration than a sound floated on the air. It seemed to come from nowhere, and from everywhere. As I listened, it grew a little louder. I'd never heard it before, but I didn't like it.

"I'm going to climb up for a look," Jesse said. He dropped his pack and scrambled up the bank to the left of the bridge, a bank which was mostly moss, with only a few old snow patches. I dropped my pack and followed him. The odd high-pitched vibration grew louder and louder as we reached the top. Fear clutched in my gut.

"Stay back, Tessa," he said. I think that's what he said. He waved his hand to keep me back. My every instinct right then *was* to keep back as that sound was getting so loud it was just about to drive me insane. I wanted to turn and run away down the bank. But Jesse took a few more steps forward, away from me.

It was the voice of a machine, not the roaring of Grampa's airplane engine but a machine sound at the highest pitch of the sound spectrum, vibrating, singing, piercing, piercing, piercing... And then suddenly in one second it sprang onto us from around the shoulder of the ravine in a blast of light and sound and motion, and there wasn't even time to think *Holy shit, we truly are fucked now.*

I froze. I saw nothing but Jesse, suddenly caught in the light, then Jesse thrown high into the air, his arms spinning, his mouth open, but any sound he made was only the tiniest drop in the huge roar of sound that filled the air, and us, and every mound of moss and melted out dirt and patch of snow for miles. His body hit the top of the huge thing that bore down on us, he spun upward again and disappeared on the other side of it.

I screamed and screamed at the top of my lungs but the sound was sucked out of me.

I screamed until I couldn't breathe. And the colossus of the machine roaring, roaring, still roaring by me, sucked all of the air out of me, pulling me closer and closer. It had taken Jesse and now it was taking me. My legs began vibrating as ripples of suction pulled at me.

Suddenly something hit me from above. Pressed my arms into my sides, useless, lifted my feet and legs off the ground, my knees slamming into my stomach. Tessa, Young Ravenwing as Earl called me, Raven as Jesse called me, I wasn't any of those things anymore. I was just a ball being pulled into the blasting roar.

Then I was above it, and rising. The roar faded below me.

The dropping sensation in my stomach told me I was still rising. Above me a quiet humming pulsed in the air.

A voice said, "It's okay now, you're going to be all right. We've got you." A woman's voice, a kind voice.

A square black doorway was level with me. But that's all it was—just a black doorway in the dim gray sky, nothing above it, below it or around it. If I'd cared right then, I would have thought it was the most amazing thing I'd ever seen in my life—just a doorway in the sky.

Raven pushing against the sky... *He pushed his mind through and pulled his body after.*

A person emerged from the doorway, reaching out for me, blackness beyond her. I saw that I was wrapped in a net and the person, the woman who had spoken, I guessed, was reaching out for the cable that my net was attached to, swinging me closer to the doorway.

I was through it. Whatever I was in was so dark I couldn't really see it.

The woman's voice gave the command, "Go!" We jumped forward so quickly that my stomach lurched. In the net, without the use of my arms, I toppled over and hit my head on something and was glad to go unconscious.

II. Warrior

As in so many myths about the righting of the balance of life, the overture myth tells of the returning of articles and beings that have been misplaced. Things have gotten on the wrong side of the boundary; there is a mislocation of power— power in the wrong place—which is dangerous to pluralistic harmony.
—Sean Kane, *Wisdom Of The Mythtellers*

5. June 2100–February 2104

From high in the air, small mountain lakes look like eyes, lines of mountains become wrinkles in weatherbeaten brown skin, rivulets of seawater run through mud channels like the patterns of veins in the back of the eyes when bright light shines straight in. As I fly the jopter, gazing down on the world to see these things, boundaries blur within me. I feel like I'm inside Gram's *Sweep of stars in deep of space* song, and then the tears come, the longing for Gram, for home, for Jesse.

Gram is gone, home is gone, Jesse is gone. Because of me.

According to Quinn, the woman who pulled me through the door of the jopter, I have lived for three months without them. If you could call the past three months of my life living.

The thought of Jesse's body left there on the bank—Quinn said they couldn't stay one second more in the Orion hot spot where we were, they shouldn't even have stopped to pick me up, they had to leave—no one to claim and bury Jesse, no one to sing for his spirit on its journey to join his ancestors, to memorialize his short life—this is as terrible as the thought of how he was killed.

I had helped bring Augie back to his life, to Earl and Martha and his brothers, and now I had torn Jesse from them. Their first-born son and beloved brother. Jesse, whose heart was as big as Mount Snow, as deep as the lake, who should have lived all his life there, loving and taking care of the people of the village. Jesse never would have died if it weren't for me. He had come to the city only to keep me safe. Look where it got him.

Now I understood how Augie had felt that long night and day that he lay in bed without moving. I had no reason to live. It wasn't right that I was the one still living. I couldn't go home without Jesse.

"Raven, you're too low." Quinn's voice in my headset, using my call-name, startled me and I automatically wiped at my face with my jumpsuit sleeve.

Three thousand feet above ground level was the required height for a jopter to remain undetected to the human ear. Since we were "cloaked," we were invisible, blending into the sky and the mountains and everything around us that reflected off our ingenious metallic coating, though we were visible on radar to other jopters within a two mile radius. Any other jopters around us would be Orion jopters, since Quinn already knew where all of our resistance jopters were around the city of Fayerport and for miles in every direction.

But today we were in an area considered reasonably safe from Orion, where we had been coming for weeks for my jopter training. Certainly no one was here in this broken, forsaken valley of scree and shale, glinting hard and cold even under the summer sun. I had been distracted by my thoughts and had flown us up this narrow valley between jagged rock mountains, and Quinn had been waiting to see what I would do. I wasn't doing very well. We were safe from Orion, maybe, but not from the terrain around us.

I increased our engine rpm's and began a gentle turn. Plenty of room still to maneuver away from rocky ledges and a cluster of mountain goats who no doubt were puzzled by the whine and hum of our invisible jopter. I could easily fly us out of this broken rock valley and Quinn was going to watch me do it, and it would be just fine as long as nothing went wrong...

And then the engine coughed. A shudder ran through the jopter and through my body. *Oh shit...* I backed off the rpms's slightly, though that couldn't have been the problem.

The whine of the jopter rose oddly and then faded. Another shake and shudder.

"I've got the controls," Quinn's voice spoke, calm but with an edge, over my headset.

I let go of the stick and moved back in my seat, watching her on my right. About ten years my elder, always cool and competent, a respected Captain in the resistance air force—the one who had given the command to move in and net me when she and her duty crew were flying over the train that hit Jesse—Quinn was moving more quickly than usual right now, tapping on the computer screens between us, scanning numbers.

"Fuck," was all she said.

I'd never heard Quinn swear before, and that was against the backdrop of considerable swearing at Fortress base, my new home.

"We've got to set down now," she said over the headset, "while we still have control. I'm executing a forced landing in a jopter, Raven, so pay attention in case this shit luck ever happens to you when you're alone." *Provided, of course, you survive this*—I heard those words too.

I looked out my window. A forced landing here... on three sides of us cliff walls of crumbling shale rock, brittle and shiny, the white thread of a waterfall tucked in at the farthest reaches of the valley, down below us a small creek meandered through broken rock and bushy alders—bear country—to make its way out to the greener world we'd left behind.

Another one of my big fuckups. This was undoubtedly going to wash me out of pilot training, and flying was the only thing in my life that was keeping me alive.

I hoped we did stay alive through this, for Quinn's sake. I really wasn't afraid for myself; I'd told Quinn when we first started my flight instruction that I was pretty sure I would never feel fear again, that I had used up my whole life's fear factor in that second when the train had hit Jesse. I was surrounded now by a numb outer shell that I expected would remain for the rest of my days.

But God, I didn't want to be the reason for a wrecked jopter and someone else dead.

Fortunately the broken talus and the alder stands below us let up here and there, and I glimpsed level ground, just enough room for a two-seater jopter. Quinn was maneuvering us over one of those places, her hands deft and light on the controls. It seemed we had enough engine power for a fairly normal though quick descent. This was good. Without our engine, just relying on our rotors, would have meant more of a crash than a landing, a wrecked jopter, and if my legs weren't broken I might as well start hiking out the valley and head north and never come back.

One hundred feet AGL, completely committed now, eighty, sixty, forty...

"Brace yourself," Quinn said, calm and cool. "But I don't think it's going to be bad."

I just sat there watching her, and through her window, the alders and broken rock rising up to meet us. We touched down with only a bump. She turned off the engine. We took off our headsets and she looked at me. Her short fair hair was tousled and standing mostly upright, the set of her mouth and chin was serious, but her blue eyes looked kind.

"I'm sorry," I said. "I totally fucked up. I'll walk away right now and never come back if that helps."

She smiled. "Well, it was only partly your fault. As your flight instructor I take all of the responsibility. Our APU going out on us here, when we were too low over bad terrain, is the worst shit luck I've had in a long while."

I took a long breath.

"And it gets a bit worse," Quinn added. "We have no radio communication in this crappy valley."

She opened her door and I felt cool mountain air on my face.

"So I guess we are walking after all?"

"Well, walking until we are out of this hole and I can use the handheld."

I opened my door and smelled mountain stone and shale and the spicy scent of alders. The creek burbled and splashed over rocks. This wasn't a forsaken valley after all. From just up the thread of alders over the water, a white-throated sparrow sang his *old-sam-peabody-peabody-peabody* song. I closed my eyes and felt alive for the first time in three months.

"Tessa, are you all right?" Quinn was standing in front of me. She'd gone out her door and walked around the jopter while I was sitting with my eyes closed. I don't think she'd ever used my first name before, and I realized I didn't know hers. We were in the world of military call-names, distancing us from each other and ourselves as well.

I was distanced all right. I wasn't Tessa anymore, not without Jesse, Gram, my home lake. I was a call-name now—Raven. And life inside Fortress base—a barracks and jopterport carved out of the inside of a mountain, a life entirely enclosed by dark rock—was like being on a spaceship in deep hostile space. It couldn't be called living. I was starved for fresh air and sun and the sound of water and birds. Even alder leaves looked beautiful.

"You're going to need to do some talking before I approve you going ahead in flight training," Quinn said, standing there on dusty shale, hands on her hips, looking up at me as I still sat in my seat. "And it looks like we'll have plenty of time for talking."

We pulled on our backpacks and Quinn locked up the jopter, looking around and remarking that it seemed a safe enough place to leave it as someone would have to be directly overhead and looking down to see it.

"Too bad they can't stay cloaked when they're turned off," I said, then almost laughed at the thought of how you could lose your jopter that way, lock it up and walk away and *hey, where'd it go?*

I hadn't laughed in three months. The moment passed quickly though.

"The trick is knowing how to disable the alarm system when you turn the jopter off," Quinn was saying over her shoulder as she started walking. "That's the first time, when it's shall we say, requisitioned, from Orion. If you don't have the code, and switch it off, it sends out a radio beacon signal that Orion picks up so fast that you're—"

She paused, searching for a word.

"Fucked," I said.

"Right."

"So that's the special skill needed when someone steals an Orion jopter," I speculated, "besides of course being good at stealing something so big and loud." Recently I'd overheard several "jopter requisitioning" stories in the Fortress base mess hall.

"Right."

The footing was tricky as we made our way over the slippery, broken shale, but walking along the creek through leafy alders much higher than our heads appealed even less. But my bear sense told me that this wasn't the type of valley a bear would hang around in. Not much to eat here.

Yet it sure as hell beat the sterility of Fortress, home of the air force branch of the resistance, only thirty miles northeast of the city of Fayerport, but hidden inside a mountain, home of two dozen jopters, all requisitioned from Orion over the past few years. I'd woken up in sick bay at Fortress base later on the day I'd been rescued. I'd screamed again when Quinn had told me that they couldn't stay to look for Jesse. They'd sedated me for days, or it could even have been weeks. I'm sure they had no idea what to do with me, half-prisoner, half-rescue, half-alive. But Quinn had given me something to live for when she had told me that she'd teach me how to fly jopters if I wanted to become an aviator.

The clouds made canyons in the sky, and we flew like birds through them.

It was the only thing that could have enticed me back to the land of the living.

"Raven," Quinn said as she picked her way over the shale and stepped on a thin piece that gave a loud snap when she put her weight on it. "You need to start talking. For three months I've refrained from pushing you to talk about yourself, but it's time. I need to know what you're thinking, what you're feeling. You seemed stable enough to start flight training, but right now I'm not so convinced."

You had better be honest, I could hear Gram saying. *If you try to hide something, it always finds a way out...*

What had I told Quinn so far about myself? I pondered as I stepped carefully over the shale, two paces to her left. I hadn't told her much. All she knew was that I came from a tiny village deep in the mountains, that I'd grown up wanting to join the resistance, that Jesse had been my best friend in all the world and had been with me because he hadn't wanted me to come to the city alone. She also knew that my great great Gram had been a pilot and high-ranking in the Orion air force before it was Orion, before disappearing with my great great Grampa and with Granny Ida and Grampa Vegard into the mountains. I had told this story to Lieutenant Hoban, chief officer at Fortress base, when he'd interviewed me as a potential resistance aviator and kept asking how I had known about Orion and the resistance, growing up so isolated, deep in the mountains. He loved the story and called Quinn in to his office to hear it too.

I'd mentioned having a mother who had left home at nineteen to join the resistance in the city, came back to have me, then left again and never returned. That was all I said on that.

These few external things Quinn knew, but I could see now how little that was. I'd said nothing about what was inside me, how I'd been raised by Gram, the lake and the ravens. How I'd grown up pulled between wanting to learn to be a healer, and wanting to fight for the resistance against Orion. How I had left the path of the healer against Gram's advice and chosen to be a soldier. How I couldn't go back now, not to the village, not to the path of the healer. Not ever.

Quinn and I both stopped walking. We'd come to a low cliff. On our right creek water fell through the air for maybe fifty feet before splashing into a foamy pool below. Quinn motioned with her left hand to the scree slope on our left, and I paused to give her a little space, then followed her onto the rocky bits that slid several feet downward with every step we took. I'd been on scree slopes before with Jesse and had learned that the easiest way down was not to hold back, but to let go and jog down, sliding with the stones. The sound of someone on a scree slope always made me think of the hushed sound of falling rain on our cabin roof.

Careful to stay several body-lengths off to the left, I quickly passed Quinn. Out of the corner of my eye I saw her change her body angle a little, cautious, beginning to jog on the shale like I was doing.

She caught up with me at the bottom of the slope, on another talus heap.

"You're pretty comfortable on rock, Raven."

I found myself smiling. "I climbed a mountain all on my own at the age of ten. Mountains are my home."

She didn't start walking again, just kept looking at me. "You know, I've played an awful lot of poker during the boring off-duty times at Fortress, and I've never—" She pointed her left index finger at me, at about heart level—"never seen anyone hold their hand closer to their chest than you do."

"What's poker?"

She laughed. "Christ, most of the time I have no idea what to do with you! You've lived at Fortress for three months and you don't know what poker is?"

I just shook my head. No sense trying to explain to her that I hadn't looked around the barracks yet. I knew where my room was, the mess hall, the flight room, the cavernous in the mountain jopter hanger. I was always where I was supposed to be, and if I had extra time I was sleeping in my room. Sleep was my coping mechanism, while flying gave me a tiny bit of hope.

"If you were to learn, you'd probably be so good no one would ever want to play you."

We were walking again, side by side. I was realizing that while I was comfortable in the mountains, I was getting tired from just a short walk. All that sleeping, not a lot of eating, and no physical exercise and I had lost not just weight but also my natural physical toughness.

"How do people stay fit at Fortress?" I asked.

"There's a workout room," Quinn said. "I guess you don't know what that is either?"

I shook my head. She described a big room filled with machines that people used for weight lifting and rowing and running so that they could stay in shape, and at one end of it was an enclosed ball court where people smacked balls against the walls and sometimes each other, all very collegial. She recommended that I try it.

"Now, start talking, Raven." She shot me a quick look. The going was smoother now; we had walked out into a wide swath of grasses that reminded me of the Brightwaters' fields. There was more sky over our heads as the rocky mountain shoulders receded. I took deep breaths of green meadow air.

I tried to talk. I told Quinn about our village and the lake and being raised by Gram and having second and third and fourth cousins all around me as I grew up. She asked many questions about what school was like in a tiny village, and were there church services, and what did people do for entertainment? I answered her as best I could. I told her that I had a Grampa who lived in the city and flew a float plane, and once he'd come to visit and had landed on our lake, but had flown away just before winter ice had locked the lake and he'd never come back, and I'd never had a chance to even sit in his plane.

I didn't tell her about Hannah's gift of Seeing. I didn't tell her that I had been training to be a healer. Or about the empath gift that ran through our family as well. I was honest... to a point. There just were some things I was leaving out.

We took a water break, filling our bottles from the creek still running beside us, turning on the UV lights in their caps and standing there shaking the water around in the bottles for twenty seconds. I heard another white throated sparrow. The water was wonderful, cold, with the mineral taste that comes from flowing over ice and young rock breaking down into screes and shale and glacier dust. I closed my eyes and said a silent prayer of thanks.

And with no warning at all, tears filled my eyes to overflowing. I was helpless against them; I turned away from Quinn, wiping my face, hoping she hadn't noticed, but of course she had. *As a flight instructor, it's my job to notice everything,* I had heard her say in the cockpit numerous times already.

"Raven," she said, "there are things you are holding back, but that's okay for now. I get that. But can you tell me where your heart is right now?"

My heart was torn, shredded. Was it even still there? Yes, because of the ache I felt in my chest when I thought of Gram and the lake—*home*—and I couldn't even bear to think of Jesse for fear that it would bleed out completely.

It took me a couple of minutes to finally say, "I'm not sure it will ever be healed."

"Jesse?" Quinn quietly asked.

Jesse, the guy you didn't stop for, the body you wouldn't recover, the half of me that's gone and can never be mourned properly... I just nodded.

She touched my arm. "It will take a while, Tessa, and don't let anyone ever tell you that you'll *get over* Jesse, but you can learn to live again, carrying the loss, letting it transform to something that nourishes you, and that you bring to others."

Hearing her say this surprised me so—this didn't seem to fit her decisive, tough, even rather gruff exterior—I just stood there staring at her.

She dropped her arm and shook her head. Her mouth moved, not in a smile, but more wistful, sad.

"These are hard times," she said. "You'll find that most of us at Fortress have lost family or people we've loved deeply. We're all kind of battered in that way. You actually are going to fit right in, if you let yourself."

A breath of wind moved through the outer reaches of the valley. The grasses around our knees stirred, and suddenly I heard a raven call from high up, calling on the wind.

I looked back at Quinn and nodded. "I want to stay. I want to fly jopters."

She hefted her backpack and slipped her arms through its straps; I did the same.

"You're going to be a good pilot, Tessa," she said, "as long as you remember that you can bring nothing into the cockpit but your full concentration. Nothing else but flying. You have to *be* fully in the cockpit."

As we walked through that last stretch of the valley, through the grasses, past occasional young aspen thickets, then under a long, leafy line of young cottonwoods that had found and embraced the creek, I drew Quinn into talking about her own childhood in the city of Fayerport, and asked her to tell me how she had come to join the resistance.

"My sister and three brothers all signed on as Orion officers, which meant that they went to Orion colleges for free, even with a stipend for books and clothes," she said. "That's how Orion recruits. They're the only show in town, hell, in this messed up nation we live in. You're either with them or you're a nobody with no options at all."

It was what my great great grampa Dylan Silloway had written in his journal.

"I managed to slip away, to disappear one night." A small furrow appeared between her pale eyebrows; her mouth tightened. "I miss them. My brothers and sister. And my parents. But this was my choice—really, I knew I couldn't have done anything else. I couldn't join, and I couldn't stand by and let Orion do what they are doing."

She stopped and took off her pack, pulled out her radio and checked again for a signal. Still nothing.

"Soon," she said as she pulled the pack back on. "We're almost out of the valley. Next time we stop we'll have a signal."

As I walked I listened to the cottonwood leaves rustling in the breeze. It was a sound that made me almost happy.

Quinn was still on the train of thought I had coaxed her onto. "Of course Orion only recruits citizens in good standing," she said.

I nodded, thinking of that tattered paperback book I'd read back home.

She looked over at me. "You understand how xenophobic this nation is?"

"Zen, zen..." I was having trouble with the word.

"Xenophobic. It means *fear of foreigners*. The Homeland is for whites who wave the U.S. flag and speak English without an accent, and are Christian. If you look native, you're very careful about showing your face on the streets. And of course people from some countries—the Middle East, Africa, Mexico, for starters—aren't even allowed across the borders to come in."

"But other countries are seen as okay?" I asked. I was thinking back to sitting in the village classroom and getting lectured for talking, but this would have made me shut up and listen. I'd never heard the word *xenophobic* in school.

"Japanese or other East Asians—you'd have to be very careful to be as patriotic as possible. You'd join Orion and be a gung-ho citizen and fly the flag outside your house every Sunday and go to church and learn how to drop the accent." She looked at me again. "You yourself could get by. If you hid your hair, you wouldn't look native."

How much I didn't know. Some things, though, I didn't want to know. I didn't think I would ever actually live in the city, though that was where Emmitt and Lars were, with the—what was the army branch of the resistance called? *Grounders*. And then I came to a thought I'd been trying to avoid for quite some time: If I was going to stay with the resistance and not ever go back home, at least I should find Emmitt and Lars and tell them about Jesse. That thought took my breath away. I had to pause and bend over and pull in a couple of deep breaths.

Quinn of course noticed. "Are you okay?"

I stood up and resumed walking. "Just a little faint for a second."

"You should start working out regularly. Make that a resolution, along with the one about bringing nothing but your focus into the cockpit with you."

I looked over at her, "Yes, ma'am." I tried to sound cheerful, but inside I was cringing over what a coward I was, a despicable, low coward who would never be able to face up to the blood of her dearest friend on her hands.

I can't ever go home, I can't ever face any of my loved ones again, I thought, *but I will be the best damn pilot they have ever seen.*

~

Two weeks after our forced landing, and rescue by another jopter who dropped off mechanics to repair and return ours, I was ready to solo. Quinn was busy in the air with a surveillance crew, but not too busy, she said, to be able to talk with me over our secure radio channel. *To be available in case you get your ass in trouble again,* I distinctly heard in her voice. I used cheerful enthusiasm and the fact that she was slightly preoccupied to cover for my plan of heading a bit farther into the mountains than she probably would have allowed me to go, if she had known.

It felt strange to climb into the jopter, shut my door and start preflight, and be the only one in the cockpit. I felt proud to finally be on my own, with a quiver of excitement mixed in. But no fear. I was ready.

I spoke to Fortress Flight Control over the radio. They advised there was no traffic in the area, the doors were clear, and I could depart when ready. Looking carefully to either side of my cockpit bubble, I increased power just enough to lift four feet off the paved floor of the cavern. Levi, one of the linemen who was about my age and about as new to Fortress as I was, lifted his hand, thumb up, and grinned. I waved back, then lightly touched the stick between my knees and slowly began rotating to the left, away from the other jopters, still just a few feet above the floor. I hovered along and watched directly ahead as the two panels of the huge metal outer door began sliding open, wider and wider, opening onto the world outside—snow-streaked mountains in the distance dappled with sunlight moving through swift clouds, green grasses on the slope just outside the door.

I edged the jopter out through the doors and hovered a few feet above the short grasses and mountain moss. A parkie squirrel bolted for the safety of his burrow in the rocks about twenty yards away.

"Four Three Tango is clear," I said into my microphone, using my jopter's ident. "Cloaking on." I threw the switch on a console above my head that made my jopter invisible. Then I moved my hand on the stick and I shot straight up.

My stomach dropped away with the mountainside. I felt dizzy with the rush of speed and felt myself smiling wider and wider.

"Flight plan?" Quinn's voice in my ears only slightly dampened the joy of the moment.

"All filed," I said, and hoped she didn't want particulars.

There was a tiny pause, then she said, "Okay, Raven, just check in with me on this channel in, say, thirty minutes."

"Will do."

I didn't need to use a map. I reached an altitude of five thousand feet and flew up the valley that continued east of Fortress. I was flying into a gentle east breeze that was making it a crystal clear day. In the past three months I'd learned that there was usually a "haze" over the city that reached into the first lines of mountains to the east, that spread north over the plain that had once been forested but now was cleared for miles and miles of industrial parks, and then more cities on the other side of that. The "haze" was really pollution, particulate from the whole huge aggregate of humming machines around Fayerport. And people said that this was actually much better than anywhere else in America, and America was much better off than most of the rest of the world. Someone said that ninety-nine percent of the people in the entire world had grown up never having seen the stars at night.

Today the sky was clear and deep summer blue. Only the tallest mountains, those above four thousand feet, still had snow streaks, some of them striped almost like zebras, bright white snow stripes against dark almost-black rock. Below me the jagged rock fell away into emerald green valleys, and the sun's rays glanced off glittering lakes.

After a few minutes I found a valley lined up just the way I wanted to go—south—so I turned and followed it, dropping down to four thousand feet for the challenge, and because it was a calm day and there was plenty of smooth air for clearing the mountain ridges, or going around them. I kept flying south. I didn't need a map.

It wasn't long before the rocky bulk of Mount Snow loomed ahead. Its upper half was all kinds of rock—scree, shale, huge boulders, old bedrock thrust skyward—but below that, from its waist to its feet, was lush green. I flew over the small lake in the empty emerald valley on its north side, then over the summit of the mountain. You could say I was *homing*.

I circled the summit rock cairn, realizing that if someone were up there, like I'd been up there that day I climbed the mountain, they would hear the jopter's loud humming and whine, but not be able to see anything since I was cloaked. But no one was there.

I stayed at four thousand feet so that no one in the village could hear me. The valley, the lake, my home all spread below. I looked with the golden rays of sun straight down on the lake, down through the water. The rocky lake floor fell away quickly; the middle of the lake did look bottomless from the air. My eyes found Gram's cabin, looked for the curl of smoke from the chimney, but there was none. It was nearly noon. Perhaps she was sitting outside on the front step in the sun, eating lunch.

My heart gave a painful squeeze and tears filled my eyes. *Gram, I'm here watching you. I wish we could talk...*

I miss you, kept running through my mind. *I miss you, oh, I miss you...* Gram, the lake, Jesse.

"How's it going, Raven?" Quinn's voice filled my headphones. She had the most amazing knack of reading me, and she didn't even have to be with me in the cockpit.

I quickly brushed tears off my cheeks, glanced at my watch. Damn, I'd missed calling her at thirty minutes out.

"I'm in the cockpit," I blurted on the radio. "Completely present." And sounding idiotic.

A pause. "Well, that's a good thing," she said in her driest tone.

"Wherever you are, if you haven't done it already, it's time for you to head back in."

"Will do."

I circled back for one more slow trip down the lake, over the village, looking down to absorb as much of it as I possibly could. To hold it in my heart forever.

To think that they didn't even know I was there, couldn't hear me, couldn't see me. I felt like a ghost.

~

I flew jopters out of the base in the mountain all fall, winter, spring and into the next summer. I stopped using the sleeping pills I'd managed to keep getting from sick bay, and the nightmares and sleeplessness started up, but still it was worth it to have the increased energy and focus for flying. I became a familiar face in the workout room and learned how to play poker (though I wasn't nearly as good at it as Quinn thought I would be). I hung out occasionally with Levi and a few other guys on the maintenance crew. I sat down in the mess hall with some of the other pilots, several of them women in their early stages of jopter training, who wanted me to tell them stories from my "early flying days."

I was doing the grunt work, low-risk surveillance along the edges of the city, and supplies transport from our base to other resistance bases within a one-hour flight radius. It was the ideal way to rack up the hours in the jopter, learn how to fly it in wind and rain and snow, sometimes just for fun flying high to see how high I had to go in order to pop up out of the usual Fayerport "haze." And I'd learned what to do when the nav warning system kicked out a flashing warning that I was "hot," which meant that I was showing up on the scope of an Orion jopter, equally camouflaged out there somewhere, and I had better do something about it and fast.

I often flew with Quinn as her co-pilot, and sometimes she flew with me as my co-pilot, which brought enjoyment to tedious routine. I was at the controls with Quinn in the right seat when I had my first experience of having to take evasive action against Orion weaponry aimed at my jopter.

When the alarm system on the control panel went off, she coolly looked over at me and said, "Okay, pilot, what do you do now?"

I didn't bother to speak, but automatically launched into the procedures I'd mentally rehearsed dozens of times: press the stick into my right knee to send us into a descending hard starboard turn that might be all we needed to get off the Orion jopter's scope.

No... the red light still flashed. Still less than two miles, so he was descending with me.

Step two was slamming forward at full speed, dead ahead. We'd been up high to begin with—this is why we usually flew at altitudes of eight or ten thousand feet, to have a little extra altitude to give away in an emergency—so I was able to throw in another sharp descent as we sped due west, gravity helping us to more speed, edging our airspeed into the danger range.

But we managed to break contact.

"Yes!" I hissed and leveled out, still speeding west, but beginning a slow climb back to cruising altitude.

Only then did I glance over at Quinn and saw the yellowish-green cast to her face. I think she'd been staring at me for a few seconds.

"Shit, Raven, who taught you how to do that?"

I smiled. "You did." I held out my right fist for her to bump it.

"Scared at all?"

I shook my head. I was feeling alive, really completely alive for the first time in over a year. I thought again of a mess hall conversation I'd overheard a few days earlier, someone talking about a buddy who was flying kestrel jets out of a base far south, along the coast. They needed pilots down there but it was hard to find pilots who wanted to fly jets with ancient computer systems against Orion jets with the best technology that money could buy. And of course this was also the reason they kept needing new pilots, since three or four kestrels were shot out of the sky for every Orion jet shot down. You had to be very good to fly a kestrel and stay alive.

"Quinn," I said. "Do you suppose I could fly kestrels?"

She didn't hesitate. "Yes, I suppose you could. I'm guessing it's not a suicide wish, though, but that jopters aren't quite fast enough for you?"

That was it exactly.

~

A month later I had a ride on a resistance transport down to Whitewater Bay, about an hour's flight south, down the coast from Fayerport. I had turned nineteen two days earlier. It had been sixteen months since Jesse and I had left home, but it felt more like three or four years. No, it was much more that. The person I had been back home in the village was gone along with Jesse. Now when I looked in a mirror I saw a young woman with pale gray eyes, serious and reserved. You could see, as Quinn said, there were things I was holding back. Except for my thick black hair, you couldn't tell I had any Tlingit blood in me, my skin had been out of the sun for so long. I pulled on the standard issue resistance jumpsuit every morning, tied my boots, walked down halls inside a mountain *again* since Whitewater Bay was built inside a mountain just like Fortress base; again I felt like I was on a spaceship headed to outer space, completely separated from the sounds and smells and feels of the real world.

The nightmares were getting worse rather than better; I often woke up screaming. Sometimes I dreamed that Jesse and I were back on the trail, hiking out of the mountains to the city, and he had gone ahead of me, but when I came out in the open I couldn't find him. I would call and call for him but mocking silence pressed down on me from all sides—the mountains, the sky, the dirt beneath my feet. *He's gone, he's gone, he's gone...* Or I would dream that we were out on the lake in a canoe and I stupidly insisted that I could stand up and walk the length of the canoe, and I tipped us over and he fell in off one side, and I off the other, and I struggled around the canoe in the icy water but couldn't find him. I tried diving down in the water but it was black and I knew there was no bottom below me, it was an infinite, black depth that terrified me and I wasn't brave enough to go deep enough to try to find him. *He's gone, he's gone, he's gone...* Or worst of all was the dream I had had twice of being on the trail, behind Jesse, and knowing I had almost caught up to him, but suddenly I heard him start to scream, horrible screams of agonized pain, and I knew he was being mauled by a bear, but I couldn't get my feet to take me another step to help him, but he was screaming to me, "Tessa, Tessa, run! Run away!" In the agony of being eaten by a bear, all he wanted was for me to run to safety.

When I arrived at Whitewater Bay I felt sorry for whoever had to bunk with me.

My roommate became a close friend, though, and by my third year there she was more like a sister than a friend. Her name was Sharon Matthew and she came from a native Haida family of many generations and many branches, all around Whitewater Bay. I told her as many of Gram's stories as I could remember; she loved hearing the more recent story about how my great great grandparents left Minerva-to-be-Orion and helped make a village in the mountains. And she told me the story, The Woman Who Married The Bear.

Whenever I woke up screaming with nightmares, it was Sharon's quiet voice in the dark that brought me back to the world of the living.

The princess of the tribe is picking salmonberries. It is not a task she enjoys very much—she, a princess, one of the high family, gathering berries in the woods along with the other village girls... She's stuck up, this high-born girl, not happy to be out in the woods doing a chore with the girls who aren't of royal blood. She's a complainer. She steps right into some bear shit that *just happens to be lying in the trail.* And then, of course, she really gets mad and raises her voice with some nasty words for the bear that was so thoughtless.

Sharon and I would begin giggling like little girls over this. We could relate, not to the princess part but to the bear shit part.

I always feel like I'm stepping in shit! she'd side-comment. I'd agree that it was the same for me, but she had it worse, working on the flight line, getting barked at all the time by the nasty Sargent who seemed to think women had no call to be working on machines as complicated as kestrel jets.

No, Tessa, she'd say, *you have it worse! I can't imagine trying to fly a jet while getting yelled at over the radio for forgetting to pull in the flaps.*

Well, I'd answer, *it was just that one time.* Though there were plenty of other mistakes I got yelled at for over the radio.

And so the complainer had to learn a lesson. The high-born princess with bear shit on her shoe fell behind all the other girls when it was time to head home, because her basket strap kept mysteriously breaking. And suddenly two handsome young men showed up to help her, and she was so enchanted by their lively conversation and laughter that she didn't realize that they were leading her back up into the mountains, not down to the beach where the canoe waited. They actually were bears, leading her to their home. Ah, this was the spirit world.

~

Living inside the mountain at Whitewater Bay, we were living hard lessons of how to fly tiny jets or, in Sharon's case, how to keep them in good flying condition. The kestrel was single-seater, which explained the yelling over the radio, heard by many ears. Fortunately, after the first few weeks, there wasn't too much more of this directed at me. And they were wonderful jets. My flight instructor, Captain Braytan, called them *hundred year old pieces of shit, though they do fly well.* He hated the fact that their nav systems were the old back-up systems used one hundred years ago. But the resistance forces at Whitewater Bay didn't have the funds for high tech jets, and we'd found that the kestrels' extremely low tech nav systems were hard for Orion radar to detect, hence the value of flying with archaic technology. The kestrels weren't cloaked, but neither were the Orion jets. Sharon claimed this was because at the speeds they flew, no one would ever be quick enough to avoid another one in the air, and they'd all be flying into one another. It made some sense.

Any technology still did—and always would—baffle me, so I was happy with kestrels.

And, in the air, I actually was happy. My brain had to stay busy with flying the plane, so there was no room for remembering nightmares, even less room for thoughts of the past. Quinn would have been proud of my cockpit concentration. Being in the air felt like being at home, especially in the fast-moving kestrel that was so maneuverable that it seemed like an extension of my mind. I felt like I'd been born for it. I was a raven, after all.

When I first arrived at Whitewater Bay, most of our missions were recons for the resistance navy who sailed below us through the myriad tiny islands along the coast, harassing and occasionally intercepting Orion shipping, blowing up anything of Orion's, if they couldn't steal it first. Our base was camouflaged into the mountainside with a cavernous hangar, like Fortress base, but we had a short runway between the hangar and the outside doors that opened at the edge of a cliff. The little kestrels were lightweight and built for short takeoffs and landings, and our runway was augmented with a catapult for takeoffs and with hooks to grab the landing cable hanging down from our tails when we landed at stall speed. It was challenging.

Needless to say, those first few weeks of learning takeoffs and landings were extremely exciting. I wished I could send Quinn a message: *Definitely feeling scared now...*

The high tech Orion jets—two-seaters to our one-seater kestrels—needed real runways, paved runways more than a mile long, which was a distinct disadvantage along a coast of over a thousand miles of mountains rising straight up out of the sea, with tiny forested islands that, if cleared and paved, would be totally exposed air bases. But Orion adapted their jets and then began flying them off ancient but still functioning aircraft carriers, hidden, so they thought, amongst the islands of the coast, and things at Whitewater Bay changed.

We began flying more and more combat missions. And we lost increasing numbers of pilots and jets because though our little kestrels were so maneuverable, Orion's jets had far better weaponry, were faster and had longer ranges. They were new jets, dependable jets, with perfectly working systems. Our kestrels were becoming harder and harder to get back into the air, despite the skills of Sharon Matthew and her crew. We had fewer planes at the end of each month, and fewer pilots too.

And so I became a warrior. I was given a combat ensignia to sew onto the left shoulder of my flightsuit, and I continued with my call-name Raven. Bigger guns were welded onto my kestrel and I spent several hours each week learning the best way to use them. *I'm just shooting down enemy jets*, I told myself. *I'm helping my fellow pilots and the resistance.*

It turned out that I was very good at it.

By the time I turned twenty-one, I was the "Kill" leader at our base. The nightmares were escalating. In the cockpit waves of nausea washed over me as I shot Orion jets out of the sky. You'd think I'd recognize that something in the very core of my body was sending me a message, but I tuned it out. I stopped eating and kept on flying.

I was becoming known as a crazy ass pilot, and Captain Braytan pulled me aside to give me a little talk about how I needed to protect myself as well as my wingmates—*Yer scarin' me a bit out there, Raven.* I assured him that I wouldn't take unnecessary risks, I assured myself I knew what I was doing. But I really didn't know what I was doing. Something dark was growing inside me, bigger and bigger with each "Kill" marked on the board by my name.

~

Mission Fiery Chariot, two months in the planning, launched on a dark night in mid February in my third year at Whitewater Bay. Six of us were going to fly formation from the base due south along the coast to where the latest intelligence told us an Orion aircraft carrier was lurking. We would almost certainly be outnumbered by Orion jets, but if we each did our part, one of us should be able to break away and fire a missile into the carrier. The unofficial word was that the resistance was getting desperate, so many jets and ships were being lost to Orion jets flown off the aircraft carrier. Every one of us who flew that night volunteered, knowing that chances were better than ever that we might not come back.

I stepped into the hangar with my stomach in a knot. I pulled on my headset to protect my ears from the whine of engines spooling up. Sharon Matthew was standing next to my kestrel, waiting for me.

Her ears were already muffed up and ready for the howl of kestrel engines on takeoff, but we'd had plenty of occasions to practice lip-reading in the hangar.

See you, her mouth said. *Be good!*

I made myself smile and give her a little wave, and hoped I didn't look like I was just about to throw up.

My kestrel and I were the last ones to shoot out the hangar doors into absolute blackness. Orders were for a left turn, heading 280, quick climb to altitude three thousand feet. This would take us to the channel where we'd go into formation. Half of the instruments on my control panel were in-op, but I knew the channcl, the mountains and the coastline so well I could fly blind. Well, maybe not quite. The good thing about this night was there was snow on the ground; all I needed to remember was that dim white was earth in between the black of sea and sky.

Up ahead burned the steady red and green wingtip nav lights of the five other kestrels. I came up on them from behind and below, per orders.

"A little slow due to puttin' on yer makeup, Raven?" Captain Braytan's voice drawled over the radio, followed by a couple of snorts of laughter from other jets.

I was the only female flying on the mission, and used to it. I slipped into my wingman spot just off the starboard red light of Steck's jet and clicked on my mike. "If that isn't sexual harassment, I don't know what is."

A few more laughs, then Brayt's voice again, "Radio silence now, please."

And there I was, back in the classroom overlooking the lake, having just had Jesse whisper something to me and in the process of whispering back, I was the one who was caught by our teacher, his aunt, Mrs. Kickbush. *Tessa, that is the last time I am going to tell you not to talk in class!*

There wasn't anything to do for ten minutes, besides keep quiet. Just fly straight and level and keep an eye on Steck's starboard light about twenty yards off my left wingtip. I couldn't bear to think of home, and Jesse, right then.

Instead I thought of Sharon's story of the princess and the bear.

She did not recognize these men, but found them most handsome, especially the man who seemed to be the leader. She failed to note that the trail was not going down to the canoe but away into the mountain. They followed a very good trail, and she went along, laughing all the time.

First she was oblivious. Then there was quite a change. The spoiled little princess with bear shit on her shoe suddenly found herself inside a mountain, seeing the people around her assume their bear forms by pulling on bear skins when they stepped outside. Nothing was as it seemed. She'd crossed a threshold and it didn't look good for her, until she made an unexpected friend, Mouse Woman, whom she had helped with a small gesture. Mouse Woman gave her some very good advice:

Mouse Woman, in return, tells the princess to put pieces of her copper bracelet on the latrine after she has used it. Then the bears will think she is a naxnox *one of the supernaturals. They treat her better after that...*

Sharon Matthew and I had laughed over this, too. *More shit!* But the princess had been accepted by the bears, and even given as bride to the handsome son of the Bear chief whom she'd been favorably impressed with as he led her to the mountain. In the winter when they all went to hibernate, she realized she was very near her old village. But she was pregnant with twin sons, and she had begun to love her bear husband who was kind and loving. Yet she missed her village. And her brother was coming, with the other hunters from the village, to kill her bear husband for food.

You couldn't be much more caught between two worlds.

Her bear husband knew he would be killed soon by his brother-in-law, and he instructed his bear cub twin sons (suddenly born and grown very quickly, and so clever) as much as he could before his time came. He gave his wife, the spoiled princess, instruction too:

...listen as I sing my dirge song. This you must remember and take it to your father. He will use it. My cloak he shall don as his dancing garment. His crest shall be the Prince of Bears.

The saddened princess went back to her village after the bear's noble death, after he gave himself to the hunters so the people would have food in the winter, as well as giving them his song, his cloak and his crest. But her twin sons were always restless and eventually they returned to live with the bear people.

It occurred to me for the first time, sitting there in my jet, how much the princess had lost by the end of the story. She'd lost her husband, and also her children. She had returned to her home, but she had lost all that she loved in the other world of the spirits. Such heavy penalties she paid! And she hadn't been called, she hadn't woken up one morning and said *I'm going to set off on a journey and see some things.* No, she'd been pulled out of her world into the bear or spirit world. But it had been her bad behavior that had done it—that was the call, in fact—her stuckup behavior had called to the bears: *here is an imbalance that needs to be corrected!*

I paused in my thoughts and did a quick scan of the black around, above, below me. The pilot's scan of the dark. Far ahead ghostly shapes of white mountains marched off to the east; to my right, to the west, lay the black sea. No lights in the sky except those of my comrades on my left. In front of me the simple kestrel instrument panel didn't even have a radar scope. It wouldn't have helped much, anyway.

Sharon and I got a kick out of the fact that like the princess, we were living inside a mountain, pulled out of the real world, but we weren't proud princesses (well, Steck would argue that—at a rare party, while drunk (he was drunk, not me) he'd pinned me to the wall and tried to kiss me and I'd punched him, and he'd called me an ice princess, but afterwards we joked about it). Yet I felt a grave imbalance weighing down my heart, and a darkness growing inside me. How far I had journeyed from my village, not just with my feet, but in my heart and soul! I had stepped out of one world and into another. I had left all those I loved behind; I even had left myself behind.

Sitting there in the cockpit, contemplating how much damage I could do with my jet and two activated missiles, I was about as far from a healer as one could get.

Unless you thought of healing as a swift scalpel cut to remove the cancerous and deadly growth so life could take hold again. Perhaps I had been called as a healer to that very moment. Perhaps taking out the Orion aircraft carrier would be healing for many people.

Still, deep down I knew it wasn't for me to do.

Taking up weapons is not the answer, Gram would say. I was pretty sure she had been right all along. A lot of people had died because I had insisted on leaving home to become a warrior, and how many more in the many, many years before?

"Incoming!" Brayt's voice crackled in my ears. "Break formation. Good luck!"

Orion had found us. Whether or not I was ready, it was show time.

I broke hard to the right in a climbing roll, going for the altitude advantage. Several voices garbled in my ears as my kestrel swung over the apex of the climb—*Tallie, he's on your tail!... Break left!... Shit, I've been hit!*

An explosion of sound and fire lit the night and buffeted right through my jet to my stomach. I was pretty sure that was Steck who'd been hit. *No!!* But it had been quick, the kind of death we pilots prayed for, knowing there were many other ways that involved lengthy and awful suffering if we ended up in Orion's hands.

I craned my head to look up and out the canopy, to scan the sky for the telltale red flashing strobes of the Orion fighter jets. The idiots always flew with so many flashing lights you'd think they were trying to help us out, us without working radar. They spent their whole time in the cockpit looking through computer screens, while we spent ours looking out at them. I was always a split second ahead of them because of that.

No one was above me. I settled onto the tail of the Orion jet just below me, the one who I was pretty sure had just blown up Steck. He was in my sights. I squeezed off a round and pulled another hard roll to the right, knowing I'd hit him and he was about to blow up in my face.

Swinging around again, with the Orion fireball lighting up the inside of my cockpit, I was almost face to face with another Orion jet who screamed by me at mach-whatever, so fast he couldn't shoot me.

I rocked in his wake. *Asshole*, I thought, *you are next...*

He had the speed, but I had the maneuverability. He was swinging back through the sky for me, but I wasn't going to be where he expected me to be.

I climbed full throttle again, wheeling left, coming out of my turn so we'd be face to face again. With all his speed, he'd be slow to get his shot off. I had the advantage.

But he wasn't there. I craned my head all around, looking out my canopy. Where was everybody?

But ten thousand feet below I saw lights on the water. The aircraft carrier. *That* was my target.

My right hand moved on its own to flick open the lid that protected my missile launch switch. I was going to swoop in fast and low for maximum destruction. A voice in the back of my mind—it sure sounded a lot like Gram—said, *There are men and women down there who are just like you, with loved ones waiting for them to come home. Are you sure you want to do this?*

Yes, I answered. *I signed on for this!*

But I hesitated, just for a second.

Red strobe lights arced up from under me, right across my nose. Too close to fire at me, too quick for me to fire at them.

But there was a jet behind me, farther away, that fired the shot that took off the right vertical stabilizer of my Kestrel's twin tail.

No explosion though. Maybe I could still hit my target? But without half its tail my jet was spiraling straight down. Falling from the black sky to the black sea.

I had a parachute on but wouldn't use it. There was no hope for a resistance rescue, even if I miraculously survived the plunge into the icy sea.

And I finally knew that I didn't want to survive it, felt I no longer had a right to live. Too many people had died by my hands.

Falling from the black sky to the black sea. *Raven falling ... Turning round to the right he went down through the clouds and struck water...*

Faces shaped in the darkness, in my cockpit. Gram, Jesse, Hannah, Sharon, Quinn. Each looked deep into my eyes. *I think I chose wrong after all,* I said to them. *I really have no right to live. I'm sorry.*

6. February 2104

Apparently I ejected.

There was the oddest blank, an absence of time, inside me. I remember sitting in my jet falling through blackness toward the sea, *Raven falling*. I was not going to eject. It was clear that I had fucked up as much as I possibly could with the gifts I'd been given, and I did not, by any stretch of the imagination, deserve a second or third chance. I had said my goodbyes.

And then nothing.

And here I was in a tiny white-walled room, overhead lights piercing pain into my concussed brain, aching all over, wrapped in something warm and dry but my hair was wet, and the whole room was moving up and down—this clearly was not the afterlife. I shut my eyes tight.

"We saw your jet get hit," a gentle male voice said. "At the last possible second your canopy blew off and we saw your dark chute— because we were looking for it, we saw it." The voice paused; I heard a clink-clink of metal on metal, and beneath that a low rumble of engines. I kept my eyes closed against the painful lights, not caring who was speaking.

"Orion wasn't paying attention to any of you once they hit your jets and sent you seaward... We sent our diver out for you. He was able to recover you as soon as you hit the sea." The voice faltered, then said, "I'm sorry we weren't able to save anyone else."

I kept my eyes shut, felt tears well up in them and slide down my cheeks. The room kept lifting and falling, and I realized I was on a ship. And that's also when it became clear that I would never be a sailor.

~

I was on the resistance ship *Tacoma*, which, fortunately for me, was headed for resupply at a small coastal city only two days north of where my jet had gone down. I was so seasick that I couldn't even keep water down, so the kind medic—when I did look at him I saw that he could not have been any older than me, and he had bright blue eyes and a shy smile—put an IV in my arm, saying that as one of their most spectacular rescues ever, I wasn't going to be allowed to die from seasickness before he got me to shore.

I wasn't sure I wanted to get to shore. I had been ready to die. Most of my flying friends had died. Steck, Tallie, Hotch, Bogie... Captain Braytan, oh God, had he gone down too? I held out hope that he had been the one to break away and take out Orion's aircraft carrier. But if that had happened, there would have been a terrific explosion and this ship might not have survived that.

"The aircraft carrier," I tried to say to the doctor, finding my tongue thick and sluggish in my mouth. "Did we blow it up?"

He shook his head sadly.

Shit. Not one of us did it. That meant that Captain Braytan went down, too. Sadness welled up inside me and spilled over, out of my eyes, tears running down my face. Everyone gone, and Sharon Matthew—would I ever see her again?

"I'm going to give you something for the nausea," the doctor said, "and it might make you sleepy."

"Oh thank God," I said. Another time blank, and this one I was so grateful for.

~

I woke up thinking about Jesse. Long ago—it must have been around the time when news of Marv's death reached us—Jesse and I had a conversation about the afterlife. I'd asked him what the Catholic priest in our village taught, and he told me about the good people, Christians, going to heaven, and bad people going to hell, and then he paused and thought a bit and said there was also some sort of in-between for people like me who couldn't quite make up their minds. Then he laughed and said he didn't believe any of it. What Jesse believed was what his great auntie Celeste, a Brightwater auntie of Earl's, taught him when he was very little. In Tlingit tradition the resting place of those who die is called *Dakanku*, or The Land Beyond, but they aren't far away at all from their families: they are still alive in spirit, continuing to live much as they had lived in the body, quite close by. Jesse thought the idea of The Land Beyond made a lot of sense, and I did too, having learned from Gram that the spirits of not just people, but also animals, continued to live all around us even after their bodies had died. But there were older stories of another place, *Keewa.aa*, The Place Above, where the warriors' spirits went. Jesse's great auntie told him that when we looked up at the northern lights high in the sky, we were seeing the warriors dancing, for they had become the people of *Keewa.aa*. And

Jesse really liked the idea of warriors dancing in the sky with the northern lights. He said that's where he wanted to go.

Remembering that conversation brought me no comfort; it felt like he had gone there, into the sky, beyond the sky. A warrior dancing. He felt immeasurably far away.

~

My stomach stabilized enough in my last hour on the ship that I was able to stand on deck and watch the sea quietly slide past, thanking Raven and all my spirit helpers that now we were in calm, sheltered waters, with steep forested mountain slopes drawing close on either side of us and a small city named Glacierport at the head of the bay coming nearer and nearer. There were no tall glass towers here, none of Fayerport's showy spires and arches; it looked like an unpretentious, hardworking city supported by the resources of fish and timber.

I would just be passing through; but I had no idea what I would be doing, where I would be heading. Directionless and empty, that was me. Except I wasn't empty at all—I was filled with the murmurs and rustlings of people I had loved and lost. Their faces, voices. It would be easier if I was empty, but as the survivor it seemed that my job now was to carry them all along with me. *This is what carrying on means*, I thought.

The young medic paused next to me on the deck, leaning on the rail. He was no taller than me and with such a round childlike face, and yet there was something in it that said he'd lived a lot already. As we watched the city grow closer, he told me that long before the air force began surveilling and fighting, and even earlier than the ground movement, resistance sailors were cruising up and down the coast to intercept, capture, destroy whatever they could of Orion's. I listened to his voice under the hum of the ship's engine and the quiet rush of the water past us.

"We think of ourselves as modern day Vikings. That's our symbol, a Viking ship."

"Wait a minute...it's your symbol? What is it exactly?"

"A stylized Viking ship, you know, with the curved prow and the curving sail above."

"I inherited a pin like that from my great great grampa Vegard the Viking," I said slowly. That was the pin I had given to Jesse after he survived falling into the lake; it made me feel a little better about the fact that it should have been me. I wondered if Vegard might have had something to do with the resistance on the sea.

The *Tacoma* slipped into the small city harbor. I stood there at the ship's railing with no idea what I was headed toward. I only knew that I was not going back to Whitewater Bay—there was no way I could get back into a kestrel cockpit and do more killing.

I arrived on terra firma with nothing but the clothes on my back, and even most of those were borrowed. I was grateful to keep the leather boots and the canvas worn-to-smooth pants I'd been issued as part of my uniform at Whitewater Bay, but I had to give up the jacket which clearly identified me as air force. The resistance sailors gifted me a light flannel shirt and a warm, plain brown jacket, which I was extremely grateful for.

The medic and a couple of sailors led me off the ship, down a long wooden dock that led to a low building, shedlike, between water and land, with more doors than windows. Behind us a crane swung and creaked and began offloading fish—the *Tacoma*'s cover, I gathered. It was just a fishing boat, and the people who saved my life were just fishermen, nothing more.

"I shouldn't have even told you as much as I did," the young medic said quietly as we walked down the dock. "The less anyone knows, the better for all of us, in case any of us is picked up and questioned. Orion's running the show, even in a little place like this."

He led me through some corridors in what he called *the cannery*, and then into a loading bay, and motioned to me to get into an aircar that already had a driver in the front seat, waiting for us. There had been an aircar at Whitewater Bay that I had always wanted to get my hands on, to see what it could do. Unfortunately here, after I climbed in, the medic gently tied a bandana over my eyes, saying he was sorry but that was the way it had to be.

We hovered out of the building and then only for another minute or two, remaining level, so I figured we just went a short way down a city street. Touchdown was so smooth I barely felt it. The medic gently took my arm and guided me out of the vehicle and over smooth pavement, and through a door, and then he undid the bandana and I saw that I was in another low-ceilinged corridor. I thanked him when he turned away and headed for the door we'd come through.

"Please thank everyone again for me," I added. "I am grateful to you all for saving my life." Gram had taught me that gratitude was the next most important quality to cultivate after love and honesty. Even if you don't exactly feel it. *Sometimes it just takes time.*

A tall woman stepped out of a nearby doorway and motioned to me to come to her. She looked like she could have been Quinn's older sister, though from what Quinn had told me that day I'd nearly crashed the jopter, it sounded like no one else in her family would ever have joined the resistance. She led me into a small office and said I could call her Halliday, but it wasn't her real name—she hoped I understood the need for secrecy. I gave her my name as Raven.

"What are your skills, Raven?" she asked me after I'd sat down on a metal chair on the other side of her messy desk.

Flying was the only thing that came to mind, but I knew I would never return to using jets or jopters to kill people.

She shook her head when I asked her if there were any flying jobs with the resistance that didn't involve combat. "Not down here, anyway," she amended it. "Since you say you can't handle the sea, I'm going to send you to Fayerport. You might find something there with the grounders."

She handed me a big pair of scissors. "Cut your hair short. There's a bathroom just down the hall. Try to do it yourself, and try not to make a mess." Then her face softened just a bit, reminding me again of Quinn. "If you really need help, I'll come, but I do have a lot of work to do here."

I did it myself. My heavy black shining hair—they'd let me take a quick shower to wash off the sea salt when I was on the *Tacoma* and there had been a small bottle of shampoo in the shower, and it had felt so good—but it was okay, I didn't mind too much. I cut it all off just below my shoulders, and then I cut it again. I was careful to throw it all into the trash bucket and to wipe every stray strand out of the sink. My head felt light and free.

When I walked back into Halliday's office, she gave me a small smile and a nod of approval. She called in a girl with curly blonde hair and bright green eyes, who sat me in a corner of the room and took an image of me, disappeared down the hall for a few minutes, then returned with a card that she handed to Halliday, who took it, smiled wider and reached across her desk to hand it to me.

"Your new identity, Raven. Now your name is Ellen Gray."

Ellen. Gram's name. Somehow that was right. I barely

recognized myself in the small photo: wide gray eyes, pale skin, cropped and slightly spikey dark hair, just slightly more female than male. My instincts told me that a little ambiguity was a good thing if I was headed to Fayerport. *It's a hard place*, I could hear Earl's voice; well, the time had come.

Halliday gave me instructions for where to go when I arrived in the big city, who to contact. Again I was only told as much as I absolutely needed to know, and nothing more. I was bursting with questions, but Halliday just shook her head. She wished me luck, and handed me a water bottle and a sandwich, which I stuck in my jacket pockets and was grateful for.

I was blindfolded again, but again only briefly, and helped back into the aircar.

"There's two of us here with you," a man's voice said from my left, rough-edged but kind, "taking you to the train station. We'll be going with you to Fayerport. I'll tell you when you can take off that bandana, at the station. Just five minutes is all."

No one said anything else after that. I sat blinded, hearing the whir of the aircar through the air—we were higher this time—and city sounds below and around us. Beeping signals, perhaps for the aircars, metallic whirring, the rising and falling wail of a siren, all of it putting me on edge as I couldn't put out of my mind the fact that we were headed toward a *train*, the thing that had killed Jesse. My stomach clenched tight and I began to feel waves of nausea.

We settled to the earth and I took off the bandana when I was told to, and looked at the two men on my left. The one closest to me looked just a little older than me, tall and thin with curly brown hair, a long narrow face, lively dark eyes; the other, the driver, was stocky and much older with white running through his brown hair. I wondered if they were grounders in the resistance, but sensed that I shouldn't ask questions. If they were grounders, I figured they wouldn't tell me. Halliday had explained to me that they would help me change trains at the Fayerport rail station. My identcard—it was a worker third class permit—would get me on the worker train to the projects (*what are projects?*). She told me where to get off and who to look for, and said that was all I needed to know. *I need to know a shitload more!* I'd wanted to yell, but I had learned some restraint since leaving home.

"Is there any way I can get to Fayerport without going on a...

train?" I asked the older man before I exited the air car.

He looked a little surprised, then shook his head. "You can call me Mack," he said, and pointed to the tall, young guy. "And you can call him Davis."

Both men had leather satchels slung over their shoulders, courier-style. I followed them across an open stretch of black pavement, skirting a few puddles, glad for the warmth of my jacket. The early afternoon air was damp and chill and smelled of the sea. We were headed toward a tall building of steel and glass, and as we walked we mingled with a flow of other people dressed like us, all heading in the same direction.

Uniformed soldiers stood at the two wide entryways of steel and glass. I had never before been this close to Orion soldiers. Harsh neon-bright overhead lights glinted on the Orion insignia of three silver stars just below the collar of their black uniforms. They wore black caps pulled low on their brows, their boots were shiny black, they carried big guns holstered over their shoulders. They looked bored, but they were watching as each person ahead of me pressed their identcards to scanners in the entrance walls.

Your name is Ellen Gray and you were born and raised in a village east of here, Halliday had told me. *You came to Glacierport last June and were hired at the cannery. You decided you wanted to find work in the city, and your employer attests that you were a satisfactory worker. There is enough credit on your card, after your trip today, for you to travel from the projects to Fayerport several times.*

I was reciting this to myself as I walked up to the entrance, not looking at the soldiers, and held my card up to one of the scanners. A red light turned green, but I must have been a little slow, because I was bumped by someone behind me. Davis beckoned me forward, through the tall metal doors, into a cavernous hall. Footsteps on the cement floor echoed, as did the quiet murmur of voices. Gray light of the overcast day outside the vast expanse of glass was brightened by yellow-glowing ceiling lights. Huge flags hung at either end of the building, all black with gold stars that gleamed in the light, the Orion stars. I followed Mack and Davis through the huge space, guessing there were more than a hundred people around us, all headed in the same direction we were headed—through several more tall metal doors that let in the rain and sea damp air.

We stood on a wide platform with a low roof over our heads. I looked straight out over parallel lines and couldn't stop the images in my mind of the bank Jesse and I had climbed up, the tracks for the train that we hadn't recognized.

And then I heard it. The air filled with that high-pitched metallic singing sound, growing louder and louder. My heart felt like it was going to jump out of my chest. I leaned forward, put my head between my knees to try to keep from blacking out, with my hands over my ears to try to keep the sound out. No good...

I was on the cold floor of the platform, and the platform was shaking, and Davis was crouched next to me, frowning, his lips saying something, but all sound was swallowed by the singing roar. Feet, knees, legs eddied around us as people actually moved forward, toward what was coming... *the train*. A few faces glanced down at me, curious, but most of the people just moved forward, paying no attention.

Who cared about going to Fayerport? Even vomiting for days on a ship beat this. I decided to make my escape from the station, and made it to my knees, but Davis was pulling on my arm, and then with a long, loud *Hissss*, the sound stopped. The train was in front of us. I got to my feet and let him lead me forward. We joined Mack at the nearest door of the tall metallic tube with a four foot high seam of glass down its middle. Each person who went through the door pressed their card to a scanner; so did I, and I boarded the train.

I followed my male companions down an aisle, awful fluorescent light overhead, rows of padded bench seats to either side of us. People were rapidly filling the seats. Mack paused at an empty bench and ushered me in, giving me the window seat. He and Davis both stowed their satchels in a bin above the seat.

"Are you feeling all right?" Davis asked me, sitting down between me and Mack.

I nodded, but I didn't know what to say. "I had a bad experience with a...train... a couple of years ago," was what finally came out.

I didn't need to say anything more; they seemed satisfied, not caring too much except that I was going to make it to Fayerport after all. Hopefully.

Whistles blew and then a moment later the train began moving, so slowly that there was no sensation of motion, just the other metal tracks and the fences around the station beginning to slide by my window. The train had reversed direction as if by magic. Then I realized that it wasn't attached to the rails; it must be floating just over them, the ride smoother than an aircar's. The speed built and built as we emerged from the station, the tall fence on the other side of the track began blurring, then city buildings and trees beyond the fence blurred until I got dizzy and needed to look away into the distance. There were the mountains. There was an entire mountain range, hundreds of miles long and wide, between us and Fayerport, and because the mountains came right down into the sea along most of the coast, we would be heading north, into the mountains, before we could turn west again. At least I could sit and watch the mountains.

And then we went into a tunnel.

"Only a couple of tunnels between here and there," Davis said from my left. He must have been watching out the window too. "It's about a two hour ride."

I thanked him for the information and saw that he and Mack had both pulled sandwiches out of their pockets and had started eating. I realized I was hungry too; I pulled out the sandwich Halliday had given me, wondering how long it had been since I'd had a meal. I couldn't remember.

A woman wheeled a cart down the aisle, stopping whenever hailed, swiping cards and pushing a button on a machine to fill cups, which she handed out. The wonderful smell of coffee filled the air. Mack bought three cups and Davis took one, and handed me one. I sipped and remembered the last time I had had coffee was breakfast——just coffee for me—of the morning of our failed mission, sitting next to Sharon in the mess hall. I paused and held my cup up just for a second to her: *I miss you. Please know I'm all right. Hopefully I'll see you again.*

I spent most of the time looking out my window. The tracks ran through the mountain valleys, with the occasional plunge into the black of a tunnel, then we'd pop out, emerging into the startling daylight, just as I'd emerged, flying, out of both Fortress base and Whitewater Bay. I craned my neck to catch dramatic glimpses of snow-powdered rock high up, as heavy gray clouds snagged on mountains taller than four thousand feet. It would be winter here for some time more. It was beautiful.

I remembered seeing the tracks from the air when I was flying jopters east out of Fortress base, but I'd only occasionally glimpsed trains on them. From all the flying I had done, I could close my eyes and see the land as it looked from the air, the narrow and deep mountain valleys, still in winter white, but frozen creeks getting ready to burst out of their ice. We would run not even thirty miles to the north of my home village and the lake. I could feel home pulling at my heart, but with such a feeling of loss. I couldn't go back, not without Jesse, and since Jesse was gone, well, I was headed back to Fayerport with no idea what I would do next, and no sense of anticipation. It didn't really matter what I did, but I knew deep in my soul that I must not take another life. I'd been given a second chance, whether I wanted it or not, and I was resolved to not fuck up this time.

~

There were only two rail lines in and out of Fayerport—convenient in terms of checkpoints—the north-south route crossed a long bridge over the north bay, connecting Fayerport to its jetport and industrial center, and then to the sister cities of Augusta and Chellis about one hundred miles to the north, and several more smaller cities a few hundred miles farther north of them. We were approaching Fayerport along the east-west line through the mountain range. The big river that ran alongside us through the valley, Fayerport's main water supply from the mountains, was mostly ice-packed.

"You have a weapon?" Mack asked quietly, leaning across Davis, who appeared to be asleep. As tall as Jesse, he was leaning his head back against the top of the seatback, eyes closed. When I was young, I easily would have known if he was asleep or not just from how he felt—I would have picked that up right away. Now I couldn't. That had disappeared when I had become a warrior. *The price you pay*, Gram would have said.

I shook my head. "No weapon."

A pause, then Mack asked, "You want one? After you get off the train, I mean."

I shook my head again.

Another pause while he settled back and kept looking past Davis out my window.

"Well, maybe just as well," he commented. "Lots of times people carrying weapons don't know much about how to use them, end up havin' 'em used against them instead."

140

There didn't seem to be a reply necessary, so I watched out the window as the valley opened up and we caught the first glimpse of Fayerport's north bay in the distance. A mountain shoulder still hid the city, but soon we'd see it—what was known as *downtown*, the busy port, the hundreds of tall glass buildings where Orion headquarters was.

"Could be okay," Mack started up again, and I wondered if he was talkative because he might be worried about me. "You carry yourself right for a female who isn't carrying a weapon, if you know what I mean."

I didn't have the faintest idea what he meant, and after I didn't say anything, he went on,

"It's a don't-fuck-with-me walk. A good thing for a female to have. Here anyway."

Davis smiled, though his eyes were still closed. Not asleep.

It's a hard place, both Earl and my grampa had said long ago, *It's not a place for you.*

It was going to be my place. Though what concerned me more at that moment was that these guys had been assessing how I walked, back at the safe house near the cannery. And did I really have a don't-fuck-with-me walk? I liked the idea of it anyway.

The train rounded the last mountain shoulder and there was the city, only about ten miles ahead of us. It gleamed with dramatic gold light as weak rays of the February midafternoon sun shone through clearing clouds to the west. Rows of towers lined the bay, impossibly high, many topped with spires or enormous globes that caught the light and looked like miniature suns... it was all vertical, set beside the horizontal bay that also shimmered gold and didn't look anything like seawater. The towers looked taller and taller as we drew closer. I'd never seen it from the ground—except the glimpse Jesse and I had had from far away on the mountainside. I'd only looked down on it from high above a few times, furtively flying my cloaked jopter at relatively safe altitudes to clear the city airspace. It had been a stunning sight from the air, but from the ground it was immense beyond my imagination.

"How could there be so many people here?!" The question burst out of me; but surely it was a safe question to ask, nothing to do with Orion or the resistance.

Davis, who'd been looking out the window too, gave me a quick

141

glance, then chuckled. "Where'd you grow up, some little bush village?"

"Yes, as a matter of fact."

"Well." He seemed to think for a second. "There's plenty of water here, isn't there."

I was stunned. "That's it? That's why people are here?"

"Those who could get here."

Back in history class, Jesse's auntie Mrs. Kickbush droning on about water... there was too much water (the rising seas) and too little water (the terrible heat and droughts in most of the rest of the world that wasn't underwater). There had been global waves of refugees, turned away at every border. The lucky ones got into northern North America, Scandinavia, Greenland and Iceland and resettled, but you had to have connections and money, and in the United States you had to be white and Christian in order to be allowed over the border. Of course people always tried to get in illegally; many died trying, but some made it.

"What about the people who were already here?" I asked. "They're still here, right?" Thinking of the Brightwaters and the Kickbushes and great great granny Ida's Ravenwing clan, all of the indigenous population. They were in villages, but many must also be in the city.

"You mean the natives?" The train was slowing as we approached the city. "They're still here but not in any of the buildings you're looking at. Those still here got resettled, to the projects, south of the city."

The projects. That's where I was headed.

"What's a project?" I asked Davis.

He looked thoughtful. "I guess it's a carry-over name from last century when it was an idea the government had to provide housing and services to the middle class workers of the city, built just south of the city on the rail line." He was looking past me out my window.

The city loomed larger and larger; the train began rising on elevated track so that now I was looking down on corridors between buildings and aircars zipping around in every direction.

"Then the services and the middle class both disappeared," he continued in a soft voice, "and what was left was a pretty crappy place to live, and not much else."

I looked at him. "That's where I'm headed."

His dark eyebrows lifted then fell, like a shrug. "You'll be fine. Don't doubt, don't show any sign of fear."

"Don't fuck with me," I said when he stopped.

His thin lips gave a quick twitch of a smile. "Exactly."

The train slowed more and more until we were creeping forward, then we stopped. I guessed it was the checkpoint. Mack and Davis both pulled their identcards out of pockets, and I did, too, hearing Halliday's voice again—*don't ever let this card out of your sight, sleep with it against your skin.*

Tiny screens clicked open along the seatback in front of us, lights winking in them. I was mesmerized.

"Hold up your card next to your face," Davis said to me without turning his head.

I did, as he and Mack already were doing. Lights blinked inside the screens for several seconds, then winked off and the screens closed. The train began moving forward very slowly.

"That was your first checkpoint?" Mack asked me.

"Yes."

"Well, you've had your card and face scanned and now you're in the system."

"Welcome to Fayerport," Davis said.

~

The train stopped a few minutes later and people stood up; Mack and Davis pulled their satchels out of storage above us. I followed them down the aisle and out the nearest door, onto a platform much like the one we'd left at Glacierport. But it was a much bigger building that rose up in front of us. Crowds of people moved quickly, not looking left or right, no one looking at anyone else. A metallic-sounding woman's voice carried through the air above us, monotoned, naming places and times, apparently information people needed in order to know where they were going, and when, but these people didn't seem to listen, didn't need to know it. They already knew it, I guessed. I was suddenly grateful for Mack and Davis next to me.

I followed them through huge metal and glass revolving doors into a building twice as high and long as Glacierport's terminal. Same bright ceiling lights above; the black star-studded Orion flags. Halliday had said my card had credit for several trips back and forth on the Fayerport trains, but I planned to never be back here again.

Not if I could help it.

"I'm here once, twice a week for part of the day," Davis said quietly to me under the louder murmur of footsteps and voices and automated announcements. "You'd find me at the tech shop at the end of the terminal."

I glanced up at him, not quite sure what he was telling me. But I liked his eyes; they reminded me of Grampa's.

"Should you need a port in the storm," he said.

"Thanks," I said. "But I'm not sure I'm ever going to be back this way again."

He did that quick eyebrow shrug and looked straight ahead again, and I followed him and Mack through the building and out another set of doors to the other side. Another platform. A train waiting.

"Here you go," Mack said. "Hop on. You know where you're going, I guess."

I nodded. Well, I was pretty sure I remembered the place name Halliday had given me.

A whistle blew. Mack turned away, back toward the terminal. I looked at Davis, whose eyes gave me a smile.

"Do you know anyone in the city named Emmitt?" I couldn't resist asking him.

He shook his head, looked curious.

"He's a cousin... I want to try to find him." But then I realized that Emmitt probably didn't even go by that name. Oh well. On an impulse, I reached out my hand. He clasped it with his large and warm hand, and I felt much better suddenly. Like I knew what I was doing, where I was going.

"Go ahead then," he said, nodding toward the train. Lights were flashing along the nearest door. I quickly walked to it, pressed my card against the scanner, and stepped on board.

The train began moving almost right away, and I glanced down the car to find a place to sit. There was an empty seat at the back and I made my way down the aisle to it. The car wasn't as full as the one we'd been on out of Glacierport, but there was a similar mix of men and women—not a sign of a child—dressed like I was in plain pants and jackets, working clothes, probably people heading home to the projects from their work in the city. It was midafternoon, and I guessed that the later trains would be more crowded.

I sat down by the window at the back of the car and watched the city. The train was moving slowly, so I had plenty of time to look around. The narrow towers of buildings were so tall that I had to crane my neck to see their tops. The sun was closer to setting, there was a tint of red in its light now, and this glinted off vast expanses of glass and off the bay that I caught glimpses of between buildings. In a way, it all was beautiful.

If I looked north, down the rows of buildings, I could see huge ships docked, with cranes as tall as the smaller towers reaching out over them, lifting metal boxes into the air, swinging them from the ships to the docks. Shipping containers—I knew that word from somewhere— bringing supplies to the city.

We began to curve left, to the south, still elevated so that I could look down into what seemed like canyons between rows of buildings. Lights began to wink on down there where it was rapidly becoming darker. The lights of aircars flickered at various altitudes below me. A large open space—a park, I guessed, having read about city parks in some social studies class at school—opened up below, a big break in the buildings, and I looked across it in the direction of the bay and saw the strangest thing: lines of glowing neon green, roughly a square, with several buildings on the inside, already lit up though it wasn't dark out there at the edge of the bay. After staring for a long moment I figured that the green was some sort of wall... but how did it glow like that? Something in me shuddered; perhaps it was a premonition. Whatever it was, there was fear in it, and pain.

This city can be so beautiful, my great great grampa Silloway had written in his journal, *but underneath is fear and pain.* That was from his journal entry on January 1, 2010, when he was thirty years old, and his wife Ellen was still working for Minerva, before it became Orion. He had been describing the party he and Ellen had been invited to, in a sumptuous apartment at the top of one of the downtown buildings that looked over the bay. He wrote that the midwinter setting sun had stained the bay and the mountains to the north a deep crimson, like blood. I had skipped the descriptive parts when I read Jesse some of this journal entry, stuck to what Dylan Silloway had written about Minerva having already changed its name once, paying a fine, and continuing on with its business of developing and exporting weapons, training mercenary armies all over the world, and then defending America against them.

Earlier in his diary great great grampa Silloway had written that the city was small as far as cities went, only about three hundred thousand people spread across the peninsula, in big neighborhoods, with most of the businesses downtown. It was the biggest city in the north in those days, early in the twenty-first century. Now surely the population had tripled, quadrupled maybe; certainly the buildings had grown that much taller, and apparently a lot of people now lived in the towering buildings downtown with their beautiful views of the mountains in every direction, and across the bay to the other huge cities to the north. Water, and of course good Orion jobs, that's what had been drawing people north for the past ninety or so years.

Now I was here.

All I knew was that I wasn't going to kill anyone else, ever again... I wasn't going to get on a train again, if I could help it... I was headed to the projects to meet a woman named Cat... and I wanted to find my cousin Emmitt, even if it meant I had to tell him about Jesse.

Earl had said Emmitt was working at a safe house in the foothills well south of the city, and I was headed south of the city, so at least I was headed in the right direction. I needed to explain to him, to Lars if he was still in the city, to my whole family, how Jesse had died. As unbearable as that would be; I had to do it.

The mechanical-sounding woman's voice floated over our heads again, but I couldn't quite understand what she was saying. I guessed it was the warning for the next stop, and I felt a cramp of fear again——how was I going to know when to get off the train if I couldn't understand? I took a couple of slow, deep breaths and glanced across the aisle and saw the person at the window across from me tap at the screen in the seatback in front of her, and what looked like a map materialized under her fingertips. I did the same thing to the screen in front of me—half of me fearing it was going to set off some sort of alarm—and got a map of the train route. There was the name of my stop, Easthaven, about three-quarters of the way down the line. It was shared with Westhaven. Northhaven was the stop before it, and Southhaven was the stop after it. *Orion isn't very imaginative with names.* I relaxed a little and looked out the window again.

The stunning glass towers of downtown fell behind us as the train headed south. After the first stop we began descending until we were running at ground level, but not nearly as fast as the train from Glacierport had run. I looked out at the mountain range to the east, through the window across the aisle from me, and was hugely relieved that the train I was on was running much farther out on the peninsula than the train that had come upon Jesse and me. We stopped, and started, stopped and started, people getting off at each stop with only an occasional person getting on to go farther south. Outside my window low gray buildings slid past, the tallest no more than ten stories high, and there were more trees and occasionally a creek that we crossed over on a small bridge. I saw some aircars zipping along at our level, or a bit higher, but the farther we got from the city, the fewer I saw. Now most everything was on the ground— there were more and more of those fat-tired ATVs, some pulling fat-tired carts, and a lot of people just walking on paths beyond the rails.

Then it was my stop. I followed a clutch of others off the train and onto a platform, past a large white sign with black letters that read *Easthaven*. The station building was quite a bit different from Fayerport's, and even Glacierport's. It was just one room, low-ceilinged and dark, grime and scraps of paper on the concrete floor. Behind me the train started up again with a pulsing high-pitched whine which instantly made my heart thud in my chest, my mouth go dry, my feet twitch with wanting to sprint away. *No more trains,* I vowed. *I'm not coming back here.*

I walked quickly through the dingy station to the other side, to the flight of wide concrete steps that led down to a square of some sort, packed snow with mud showing through here and there, bordered by low buildings. I stopped at the top of the steps and looked east, toward the mountain range that Jesse and I had walked out of in what felt like an eternity ago. Halliday had said I was headed to a neighborhood about a mile's walk from the train station to the east, uphill. I looked up the snowy hillside and saw rows of metal boxes, shipping containers, I realized, just like the ones I had seen being lifted onto the city docks. People lived in shipping containers? I guessed I was going to find out. Several ATV paths led that way through the low buildings and some warehouses, and up a snow-packed track through a birch and spruce forest. I started walking, glad to be away from the train and moving on my own.

You're looking for a woman named Cat, about your height and build and age, red hair and blue eyes, but probably she's wearing a blonde wig, Halliday had said. *Once you're there it's okay to ask for her by that name, but don't say anything to anyone until you're there. When you meet her, tell her you're nearing home.*

The buildings and village bustle dropped behind as I followed a snow-packed path uphill. My breath came quicker and I felt ashamed at how much conditioning I'd lost. I paused when the path reached the forest, and just stood there for a few minutes breathing in the scents of pine and mud and winter-dry grass that had melted out for a few hours under the day's sun, and now were freezing again. The light was fading fast. I started walking again, thinking it would be good to get to *the project*—the rows of containers on the hillside— before full dark.

Soon I came out of the forest and was climbing up the slope to the first row of metal containers terraced into the hillside. From what I could see in the deepening twilight, I guessed there might have been fifty or sixty of them, about a dozen per long row, with alder shrubs and a few small trees growing on the short, steep slopes between the rows. The roofs of every unit were in three sections: one of them sloped, black with solar film; the middle section was flat, punctuated by a stovepipe; and then each roof held a water tank like the ones we used in our village on the buildings highest up from the lake. The steel walls had been cut for doors and windows, and I recognized the tiny extra closet-type structures that stood beside each unit as outhouses, a familiar sight to me, though most of us at the lake had small but warm indoor bathrooms in our cabins.

Something prompted me to continue up the ATV track that kept climbing the hillside north of the rows of buildings. Interior lights began coming on, making small glowing rectangles in the lines of much larger metal rectangles. Someone opened a door in one unit, and warm light spilled out onto the dirty snow pathway out front of it. I smelled woodsmoke in the air, and caught a hint of cooking food too. I heard quiet voices and turned to look back to see people below me, emerging from the forest path that I'd just come up, headed for their homes. Small lights winked on along the paths, just a foot or so above the ground—solar powered, I guessed—sufficient for seeing where one was walking in the dark.

I stopped when I got to the top row, and then I found myself following the little lights that illuminated the path running down this line of shipping containers. Some curtains were pulled now in the

148

lighted windows, but some weren't, and I couldn't resist taking quick looks in as I walked past. People moved about inside, I glimpsed tables and chairs, a rough wooden cupboard in one, a bed with a dog on it in another. Lights, woodstoves, cooking food, I suddenly missed home. I found myself yearning for even just a shipping container I could call home.

But how was I going to find a woman named Cat in a community of maybe two hundred people? I tried to remember what else Halliday told me about her: She worked as a grounder; she was part of the underground railroad that helped move resistance workers around right under Orion's nose, so to speak. Though how that was going to help me, I did not know...

"Hello," a woman's voice said quietly behind me. "My name is Cat. Can I help you?"

I quickly turned and saw a woman about my size, as Halliday had described, rays of light from an uncurtained window shining on her cropped red hair. Growing up with Gram, and with Hannah, I didn't believe much in coincidences: mystery yes, coincidences not so much. I figured my ancestors must be looking out for me, at least for the moment.

"I'm Tessa Ravenwing," I said. "And I'm nearing home."

She smiled. "Well, Tessa Ravenwing, why don't you come home with me for dinner, and you can see if you want to stay."

She led me down the snowy path to the end unit.

"Home," she said, unlocking the door and waving me in ahead of her. "Just one neighbor on the north side, so it really does feel kind of like a little house on its own."

I had an impression of cool, dark stillness. She stepped past me to click on a lamp, quietly continuing to talk—she'd moved in three months ago, the lucky lottery winner after old Sam Brown finally died of cancer, with no family or close friends, and his unit became available. She'd lived on the first level, with neighbors on three sides and the forest up close in front of her door, for four years and now she still couldn't believe the view from the top level.

"Plus there's a nice sitting spot a little higher up at the edge of the upper forest." She set down a small knapsack she'd been carrying and walked around the little room, pulling curtains. "There is nothing more restorative than sitting and gazing out at the sea."

Anyone who talked of sitting and gazing at the sea, and used the word *restorative*, was someone I wanted to get to know better. I took a long breath and let it out, relaxing for the first time in a long while. I felt so tired, so in need of restoration. Cat smiled and motioned toward a plush armchair near a woodstove, and I gratefully sank down into it.

She busied herself starting a fire in the stove, using kindling from a basket beside it as I had grown up doing. I looked around the long, narrow room which she had brightened and warmed with colorful rag and wool rugs on the floors and even over the steel walls. Bright green curtains kept out the dark beyond the windows, and there were two other soft chairs almost as comfortable looking as the one I was in, with small tables made out of stumps next to them. A tiny prefab kitchenette stood halfway down the room, opposite the door, with a sink, a small counter, and a two-burner gas stove with a refrigerator below it. Beyond it stood a small table with two chairs, and beyond that was a curtain that I guessed made a tiny bedroom out of the other end of the unit.

"The bedroom's actually kind of nice," Cat said after puffing a few breaths into the small woodstove. "It's got three windows, and they even open, with screens in them. There's room to put a second mattress on the floor, if you'd like to stay here."

I took another deep breath and thought the word *restoration*. Perhaps this could be home for a little while, where I could regroup, figure out where I was headed next? Cat blew on the fire again. A spurt of flame inside the stove lit up her face—porcelain skin, fine features, something intent or serious or even sad there. I heard the wonderful sound of crackling kindling and knew that in just a few minutes we'd be feeling the radiating warmth. Cat stood up and took a step to the kitchenette, saying she was going to heat up some soup for us.

That's when I saw the two wooden shelves holding rows of books in the corner just beyond my chair. I got up and began touching them, real books that you could hold in your hands. It was quite an assortment—ancient science fiction paperbacks by Isaac Asimov and Arthur C. Clarke, even older than my great great grandparents, their covers worn to fabric and their pages yellowed and brittle; several novels I remembered from my childhood; some history books on the calamitous climate change years in the 2020's; books in what I was pretty sure was Spanish, including some by a poet named Neruda. I kept running my fingers over the old leather of these books, and smelling them.

Cat smiled at me across the room. "You're a reader."

"Oh, I've missed books! I grew up with them. Where did you get these?"

"Billy." She nodded past me, to the end of the room that was almost completely covered with a tall wool blanket of bright green and yellow geometric designs. "He's in the unit next door. His end door opens up facing us, and this door at your end opens up facing his unit, and in the summer we're going to make a patio between us and invite friends over. He says he can't wait to string up some festive lights and build a firepit."

"And he loves books."

"Well, his taste runs a bit more toward tech manuals, but he knows where to find books for me."

Cat beckoned me over to the little kitchen table, where she'd set down two steaming soup bowls and half a loaf of crusty bread. I was suddenly ravenous, and sorry that I had nothing with me to share with her. When I apologized for literally arriving on her doorstep, hungry and destitute, she just smiled and shook her head.

"I gather you've come from Glacierport."

I nodded. "A woman called Halliday gave me my identity card and sent me up here on the train with two men named Mack and Davis."

"I know them all," Cat said. "We work together from time to time... part of the railroad for resistance fighters. How did you end up in Glacierport?"

I sipped my soup—rich and filling lentil—and tried to think of how to explain myself to her. "A navy ship saved my life—I was a pilot, shot down over the sea—but on the ship I was so seasick, it was pretty clear that I wasn't a candidate for the navy. And I can't go back to fighter jets now..." It really didn't make any sense. The resistance had saved me, at some risk to many people, and helped me get to Cat and what felt like a safe place, but I wasn't a fighter any more. What could I do?

Cat reached across the table and touched my hand. "Tessa, it's fine. You're going to be fine here, and you'll figure out what your role is. But I need to tell you something. There's a gift that I have, that I was born with, that really doesn't feel like a gift at all... but I can't help it." Her blue eyes looked so sad, almost as if she were about to cry. "I'm telepathic."

I heard Gram's voice in my head right then as clearly as if she were sitting at the table with us: *Gifts run through our family, gifts that are—well, a bit out of the ordinary.* Just after I had helped heal that young raven, she had talked to me about the important thing being that we use the gifts as blessings.

I gave a long sigh, thinking that I had forgotten so much.

Cat's laugh surprised me. "Usually people are horrified," she said.

"Oh no, not me." I suddenly laughed too. "You should meet my family. We have a long history of empaths, for starters." And I thought of Hannah, telling me that her gift seemed like nothing but a curse, and how she struggled every day to live with it.

Cat looked sad again. She knew what I was thinking. It may sound a little surprising, but I didn't mind at all. She felt like family.

"I wish you could meet my Gram," I told her.

She nodded. "Maybe some day I can."

And so began my life in the projects.

7. March 2104–April 2111

It turned out that Billy, next door, was nearly a giant—well, at least several inches taller than Jesse and an extra forty pounds or so as well—and he had red hair like Cat, and he was only twenty years old. He'd escaped from Orion's big western city named Las Vegas, far to the south, and made his way to the coast, and then to Fayerport by sea with a few friends who enlisted in the resistance navy. But Billy was a technology wizard and spent much of his time in his unit working on what he called a laptop computer, which he ran off his solar supply. He made forays into the city every few weeks, and we quickly came to an agreement that I would cook for him if he would supply me with books, which he bartered for.

Cat's own story was a sad one. She had grown up in Fayerport, the child of card-carrying Orion officials who quickly realized their daughter had special abilities. They kept her abilities a secret all through her childhood. *Our secret, fun game... no one can know.* But when Cat was eighteen she discovered that her parents were talking with an Orion scientist about her, negotiating with him, persuading themselves that he would treat her well if they sent her to him for vital research Orion said they were doing.

"It's pretty hard to keep a secret from a mind-reader," she said the morning after I arrived, as we sat side by side on the dried out log up above her unit—the nice sitting spot. For restoration. "You can see why I haven't had many intimate relationships so far in my life. Though, to reassure you, I am quite good now at blocking."

Cat had run away from home after realizing what her parents were thinking of doing to her. She knew about the resistance and she knew the address of a safe house at the outskirts of the city, thanks to crossing paths with resistance when she was in crowds with her parents. She left without taking anything with her and after a long day of walking, and a ride with two men in a produce truck who had thoughts about her that nearly made her jump out of window as it sped along, she knocked on the door of the safe house. She didn't know what to say, so she just said, *I'm supposed to be here.*

They'd sent her to the projects south of the city, to Easthaven, and she'd started working as a grounder, commuting to the city weekdays with the city workers who went in and out of the city from the projects every day. She guessed there were a number of other grounders living in Easthaven, but as the resistance operated on need-to-know-only for the sake of everyone's security, she didn't know more than two other grounders in the project. She had a contact in the resistance named Baker, in downtown Fayerport, whom she reported to regularly.

"I spend a lot of my time in the train terminal," she said. "That's how I know Mack and Davis. They're both good men. Mack's been bringing people up and down that train line for longer than I've been there. I don't know Davis as well."

"What's your job at the terminal?" I asked her, trying to remember spy lingo—was it *what's your cover?*

She smiled. "I work in the Information Booth."

A few minutes later Cat left me there on the log, encouraging me to try it as a meditation spot, after I'd told her about how I'd spent hours at the lake under Gram's tutelage. My jacket was warm and Cat had given me a home-knit wool cap, and we'd brought a blanket for sitting on, so I was comfortable. I wanted to give it a try, but home and the lake and meditating and Gram—and Tessa herself—were all so far away it almost didn't even make sense to give it a try.

Gazing straight ahead I felt as if I were in a low-flying jopter, I was that high up on the hillside. Below the rows of shipping containers, and then the spruce forest, sprawled low business buildings and warehouses, then the project of Westhaven on the other side of the small train station, all of it the detritus far to the south of the gleaming towers of the city's downtown. But I didn't pay it much notice. Instead my eyes were drawn straight out to the west, to the sea. There it was, beginning to shimmer under the rising sun, stretching on and on and on, unbroken by any land to the west, at least for a couple of thousand miles. It made me want to fly again, so I could soar over it and keep going and never stop.

White mountains rose to my right, far to the north beyond the bay and beyond Fayerport's sister cities. And more snowy mountains rose to my left, on the other side of the long, south bay that Jesse and I had skied to during my last winter at home. The east range of mountains was at my back, between me and home. I couldn't go back yet, but I yearned to fly over the sea.

~

I meditated there on the log each day that week, though at first all I could think of was how far away I was from the lake, from Gram, from myself. I'd pretty well fucked up as a healer. Yet, gazing out at the sea, it felt like something was calling to me. After what I had done as a fighter, I didn't believe I could ever really have a second chance... but it seemed like perhaps I should at least try to live the rest of my life as if I were trying for it.

I tried explaining this one evening to Cat as we sat in the comfortable chairs on either side of her woodstove, with books in our laps, but really we were talking, not reading. I tried again to explain what the lake had meant to me, how Gram had talked about not just me getting to know the lake, but the lake getting to know me, but to my ears it sounded like lame rambling; I must sound like some sort of nut, and how could she possibly want me to stay with her, to live with her for a time?

Cat leaned forward in her chair, her blue eyes intense. "Tessa, you don't get it. You are the first person I've found who doesn't think *I'm* a nut, who understands me. I would love to have you stay here with me for as long as you want... if you will?"

Tears filled my own eyes as I nodded, unable to speak for a moment I was so overcome by gratitude.

And as the days went by, the nightmares that had been my constant companion for nearly four years began to ease. I still had them, but I also began dreaming of home. The smells, the feels, the images of home began to enfold me as I slept, like warm and loving arms. Home was here, the lake was here, and that was a comfort. Gram had scooted me out the door how many times, so I could sit and become a part of the lake, to become completely there. *You are letting that place go all the way deep inside you, so that it is always there for you to call on when you need it.*

And now, somehow, it was here. Despite everything I had done, and everything I had not done, it was here.

When I woke in the night to the whispers of people that I had murdered with my jet and my missiles—I thought of the lake. In my meditating in the mornings on the log above Cat's unit, I began picturing myself sitting in my old spot. I found a glimmer that might have been hope. Perhaps a day would come when I might be able to make reparations. *Might blessing, somehow, glimmer out of all this darkness...*

I had a dream of Jesse that wasn't a nightmare, but instead a penetrating of warmth and nearness and comfort. When I awoke from it, I sobbed with gratitude. Perhaps, from the spirit world, he was forgiving me.

In another dream I was back in early childhood, dancing with Hannah and Jesse and a few other kids in the first heavy snowfall of winter, catching snowflakes on our tongues... the snowflakes turned into snowy owls... one perched on my shoulder and I walked home with him to Gram, who laughed and invited us in to sit next to her by the fire.

Another time Jesse and I were out in a canoe, just sitting quiet on the water smack at the center of the lake, and as we looked down through the sunlit water we saw far, far below a huge fish that looked up at us and then circled upward to us, closer and closer, becoming huger and huger, until he was just beneath the surface looking up at us with wise eyes... it seemed that he was about to say something, but he didn't, he just looked at us and he smiled.

~

Sometimes at sunrise—on the clear days—meditating on the log, I caught a flash of light out on the water, maybe a mile out from shore. It was like a star—it seemed that something was out there, stationary as the sea quietly moved past, if I didn't look at it directly. Of course this was like me as a child getting distracted at the lake and imagining what it would look like if I made all of the water disappear; I could hear Gram's voice saying, *Focus is one of the most important tools for the healer. Tessa, you need to learn to still your thoughts and focus!*

Oh well.

On a Sunday, when Cat didn't have to leave early in the morning to take the train in to the city, she came up with me to the "sitting place" as we were calling it, and I asked her if she had ever noticed the glint of light on the sea.

"It's the old airport tower," she said right away. "There are just a couple of windows left in the entire tower, and they catch the sun."

And then I remembered seeing it once from my cloaked jopter as I flew high past the peninsula: a round metal tower with most of its windows long gone, sticking up out of the gentle waves a mile or so offshore. Cat explained that one of the old terminal buildings still stood, too, just under the water. It was a little closer to shore, close enough to the new shoreline to be deemed not hazardous to shipping, which kept farther out in lanes that led in to the deep bay north of the city. Too expensive to dismantle underwater, or blow up, so it was left there, marked on maps—a manmade reef breaking the surface to glint silver amongst wave foam at low tide.

That was all that was left of the huge city airport that had gone under the rising sea in 2028.

Never having seen an airport, I wondered what one was like. How did it work? Cat knew because as a child she had flown several times out of the rebuilt airport on the bluff across the bay from downtown Fayerport. As we sat on the log, Cat described airport terminals—how people walked through high-ceilinged, windowed concourses, starting with ticket counters where boarding passes spit out of machines, then to gates where you sat in seats, waiting for your jet, and sometimes there was art to look at to help pass the time, huge murals on the walls or stone sculptures of bears on their hind legs, growling.

Sometimes the bears weren't stone, but were actual bears, dead and stuffed.

Dead bears? Stuffed with what? Why on earth would anyone do that?

People do strange things, Tessa...

People walked on and off jets through telescoping tunnels, and baggage was carted into and out of the building's bowels, sorted through conveyor belts.

And there was the intriguing image of an entire airport gone underwater. Besides the control tower, a whole building was still down there, lurking under the waves... I pictured fish swimming in and out through doorways that travelers once used... sea anemones attached to ticket counters... crabs strolling through Baggage Claim... seals and orcas cavorting past murals of themselves on the tall walls now rising out of the sandy ocean floor. Stuffed bears growling bubbles of salt water. It was theirs now.

Talk about meditation time distractions.

~

In mid March the ground in the woods was still frozen, but the last of the snow on the hillside had melted and the mud was drying. I decided that one thing I could do in exchange for my room and board with Cat was to start a garden. But I needed Billy's help.

"It's oooopen!" came his cheerful call when I used Cat's (and now my) code knock—knock, knock, knock-KNOCK-knock!—on his door.

I looked in and saw him hunched at his small table, tapping on the metal keyboard beneath the small, lighted screen. Everything looked small around Billy. Good thing he didn't have a roommate, I thought.

"Hey Tessa," he said, still looking at his screen.

"Hey Billy. Can I come in for a minute?"

"Sure, anytime. Let me just finish this."

I sat down in the other chair and watched him, deep in thought, humming a little, looking like he was trying to figure out something complex. He shut his eyes for a minute—he had Cat's exact shade of red hair, but Billy's eyes were hazel, a wonderful rich combination of green and brown that reminded me of sunwarmed moss—he hummed one long note, then opened his eyes and said, "Bazinga! Got it."

After another burst of tapping on his keyboard, he snapped it all shut.

"Billy, can I ask you something?"

He grinned. "Well, you can *ask*."

"Are you working for the resistance? Are you a grounder?"

He tipped back in his chair, one hand on the table. "Well, that's not exactly the kind of question that gets asked around here, if you know what I mean."

"There are some grounders here, living in the projects, but that's their cover, just normal workers commuting back and forth to the city?"

"Right. Or maybe working in a shop down by our little station. How about you, Tessa?" he asked. "Are you nearing home?"

I finally got that that was the code for resistance to be able to recognize resistance—*Are you nearing home*? "Well, I was a pilot."

"No shit! What'd you fly?"

"Jopters and little jets called kestrels."

"The resistance has jopters?"

"Repo jopters we called them. You know, as in pre-owned?"

Billy laughed. "Oh man, stolen from Orion!"

"Yeah, some people I worked with were really good at it."

"Bet it was an art."

"Actually it was a real technical problem. They had to immediately disable a couple of systems so as not to trigger built-in alarms." I thought about it for a moment. "Actually, I bet that's the exact kind of thing you'd be good at."

"Hmmmmm." Billy looked thoughtful, then he seemed to think

back to my original question. "I do tech stuff for the resistance. I've been able to hack into some low-level Orion channels, and learning more every day," he said slowly. "I go in a couple of times a week to hand off intel, usually the downtown train station."

"Oh, so you must know Mack and Davis too."

Billy nodded. "I work with Davis mostly. I do the work and he pretends it's his. Nice guy, and smart in his own way, but not super smart with computers."

"Say hi from me. Tell him I'm your neighbor now."

Billy shook his head. "Can't pass stuff like that around. Not safe. Say Davis got picked up by Orion... they'd have all of his contacts real quick. That's why we don't give real names or real places."

I must have looked skeptical, because Billy gave me an intent look. "They've got drugs and machines they use all the time on people, they could get anything they wanted out of you."

We sat there in silence for a moment. As if to underscore that last remark, an Orion jopter flew low over Easthaven, the low hum woven with the high-pitched whine of the APU, a sound I'd hardly noticed from the inside while flying, but I didn't like hearing from the outside. I'd only been living in the projects for a month and it seemed like Orion jopters flew low—invisible because of their cloaking, so that they were seeing us but we couldn't see them—over our heads nearly every day. I wondered if it was intimidation tactics.

Billy let his chair down and leaned his elbows on the table, still looking at me.

"So, did you just come by to chat?"

"Actually, I was wondering if you wanted to help me start a vegetable garden. If you help me, I promise you wonderful fresh produce for the next seven months."

I loved Billy's wide grin. He already felt like a kid brother. Cat said he moved in to the project about a year ago and she was even happier about being his neighbor than she was about the great view from her new unit. *He's a little different, like us, Tessa,* she said, but she wouldn't say any more than that. Just that she knew Billy and I would really hit it off as friends.

Billy had a bunch of connections, and people who owed him for computer favors he'd done for them. He knew where to find lumber for building us garden boxes so that we didn't have to struggle with thin, poor soil and weeds; we planned to build the boxes right into the sloping ground in front of our units. And he explained to me that we had an unlimited supply of exceptionally good compost: every composting toilet in the project was emptied twice a year and "zapped" with UV light down at the maintenance sheds and composted for some time so that it was—*well, you know*, Billy said, *not all yucky to handle!*—and the compost was free for gardens. A small hardware shop in town sold garden tools and seeds, but Billy had done work for the owner so he wouldn't charge us. We were all set.

I had been a dutiful but not very enthusiastic gardener as a child; mostly I did what Gram asked me to do for her, and gardening for her involved growing more healing herbs than vegetables. Now I felt a deep need to put my hands in the rich earth and make things grow out of it. It was as healing as anything could ever be.

~

That spring I also began to learn how to cook. *Began to learn* is the correct phrase because I realized that it would be an endeavor of at least a decade or so. Some of my attempts came off better than others. But Billy and Cat were both enthusiastic eaters, and Cat told me that just having someone put a hot meal on the table when she walked in the door in the evening meant more to her than she could ever say. I walked down, out of the project and through the forest to the settlement of Easthaven almost every day and got to know the few shops that sold food there. Cat and Billy and I pooled our credits (though mine on the card that Halliday had given me only lasted a few months); I learned how to bargain, and I got to know a few shopkeepers who knew Billy and would give me significant discounts as Billy's friend. I began to feel like I was making a contribution, which was a great relief.

And in my spare time I read and read. I read every book on Cat's shelves—except the ones in Spanish, and I hoped that I would be able to find someone in the project, at some point, who could teach me Spanish since so many people around us were speaking it—and then Billy began bringing me more books from the city. I had been starving for them without realizing it. I had taken for granted the two hundred or more books that I had grown up with, and I vowed I would never take books for granted again. I read whenever I could, voraciously, gratefully, enthusiastically. Adventure tales, history, biography, mysteries, novels, two hundred year old science fiction that still was way-out-there-science fiction—I was amazed when Billy told me that there still were no humans on Mars, there was no speed of light space travel yet, no money had been spent on space research and development for over a hundred years. It was all going toward wars.

We met the woman who lived in the unit directly below Cat's on the sunny Sunday when Billy, Cat and I assembled the garden boxes at the top of the bank between our units.

"What are y'all doing, building coffins?" a woman's voice hollered up at us, and we looked down to see a tiny woman, white in her hair, hands on generous hips, staring up at us from her yard. I had seen her before at the weekly *citizen group* all of the project residents had to attend. It was run by Orion officials and we called it, more accurately, *indoctrination group*. In addition to revised world history, we also were taught English and Christianity.

"Yep!" Billy called out cheerfully, but Cat and I scrambled down the path that ran to the side of our units to introduce ourselves to her.

Her name was Sadie. She was so small that the top of her head barely came up to my collarbone, and she was stout to the point of straining the seams of her colorful cotton shirt and skirt. The skin of her face and arms was brown and wrinkled, with the deepest wrinkles being the laugh lines etched next to her eyes.

After that, as green sprouted up and then began bursting out of our boxes, Sadie came up almost every day to chat and sit in the sun and watch things grow, as she liked to say. Cat and I walked with her to our weekly indoctrination sessions at the office building in the forest below the project, and we usually sat in the back row and whispered comments as the speaker droned on about Orion's military successes. Sadie was our first guest on our patio that Billy started building as soon as he finished the garden boxes, and she was the one who found the strings of tiny lights shaped like red chili peppers that we strung from Billy's unit to ours, right over the patio.

"Reminds me of home," she commented when Billy turned the lights on, as we sat on chairs we'd pulled outside onto the cool stone.

Sadie had been born in Mexico but as an infant had been smuggled across its northern border by her parents as they escaped another *failed state*, like so many in South America, Africa and the Middle East. Life hadn't been much better in California (Traitor State), but they had had their own small farm where they grew much of their food, and they were far enough into the mountains that they had access to water, unlike much of the rest of California, where violence was driven by *water desperation*, as she called it.

There was clean air, too, in the mountains where Sadie grew up. In fact her childhood home sounded a lot like our village at the lake, and as summer went on, Sadie and I talked about our home places, *our soul places* as she called them. One afternoon when I helped her sort healing herbs in her kitchen—we had devoted one box to various herbs and Sadie seemed to know as much as Gram in this arena—I told her about growing up without a mother, and Sadie stepped around the small table to stand directly in front of me, short as Gram, but somehow big at the same time.

"Tessa, you must know by now that there are all kinds of mothers," she said, staring intently up at me with her dark eyes. "Many of us had mothers who were physically there but, at the same time, not there. They weren't able to mother, perhaps because they hadn't been mothered themselves so they didn't really know how to be mothers, or they'd had violence done on them as children and so, in a sense, were still locked into being children. The important thing is that in a community—what we may be able to build here, slowly but surely, and what you had at your lake—in such a community you have *todas las madres*, the many mothers. Right? You had your Gram, your Auntie, probably a teacher at your little school?"

I nodded. Yes, it was true.

Sadie nodded, and smiled. "And someday you may be a mother, not just to your own children, but to others as well. *That* is how we raise our children."

That summer Sadie became one of my *madres*. While we worked, we talked about things like the fallow times in a woman's life, when for whatever reason—and it could be any number of things, from loss of work or love, or relationships holding her down—she found herself not herself, but dried up inside or burnt out, or feeling deadened. Feeling like she squandered her gifts or her soul. And what to do? Sadie nodded when I told her about all the time I'd spent sitting and meditating at the lake, following Gram's advice, and how I was beginning to do that again here in Easthaven project, looking out at the sea.

"That's exactly right," Sadie said. "When you realize you are in such a time in your life, and we *all* have those times in our lives, you shouldn't keep going. You stop, you listen inside as well as outside. And if you do listen, you will hear, and you will find that woman you are is still there. You can reconnect."

~

Sadie had wanted for several years to start up a small health clinic to help serve the needs of the people in Easthaven project, and if it was successful, become a model for other clinics to spring up in the other projects.

"But I need youth and energy," she said to us as we all sat eating dinner at Cat's table that we'd dragged out onto the patio, on such a warm summer evening. "That's where you three come in."

"Not me!" Billy said immediately, and stuffed another heaping forkful of enchilada into his mouth (Sadie had been teaching me how to cook some of her favorite dishes, too).

"Ah ha, young man," Sadie leaned forward to give him one of her piercing looks, "not so fast. You have the connections."

Billy groaned, though managed to swallow.

Cat said she'd just been given the okay to cut back her commute to the city to three days a week, so she had more time she could give to help Sadie.

"I would love to help you," Cat said. "There's such a need here. Sick, unvaccinated children, pregnant women not getting the right diet, some of them losing their babies..." She looked sad suddenly.

Sadie and I, on either side of Cat, both reached out and patted her back. I thought of Hannah again, and how hard it must be to live with the burdens they'd been given.

There was a pause, and I realized both Sadie and Cat were looking at me.

"My Gram was a healer," I said softly. The late summer sun was just beginning to set into the sea, turning it to molten gold with crimson gleams, and the sea was a giant mirror reflecting on the hillside, on the rocky tops of the mountain range behind us, on our faces.

I had never talked of growing up in the healing tradition, but at that moment I found that I could talk of it. In the past tense. The gift was gone, but perhaps there were things I had learned from Gram that I could bring forward now to help others. I felt such a strange mixture of relief, but also sadness over what I might not be able to bring, that once I could have, as I talked with Billy and Sadie and Cat there on the patio that Billy had made for us.

Sadie patted my hand, her face soft in the wonderful sunset light. "Whatever you can bring to it is good, and a good thing it will be to do, for so many who need it."

~

There happened to be an empty unit in Sadie's row, only two down from her. Actually it wasn't officially empty, but the complicated logistics of who had been living there, and who moved out to make it empty for our purpose were all kind of confused in my mind. Brothers named Pedro and Manuelito were living in the unit next door to Sadie, and they had something to do with it. They believed as fervently as Sadie about starting a community health clinic and they helped find furniture for it—a couple of tables, a lot of chairs, three beds to be put at one curtained-off end—and worked with Billy to scrounge our first medical supplies.

The first big breakthrough came when Billy thought to ask Mack and Davis about smuggling vaccines on their regular runs up from Glacierport. They could do it and they were glad to help, and they thought they would occasionally be able to smuggle up other drugs such as antibiotics. The next breakthrough was finding a doctor—a friend of Sadie's down on the first row of the project had been a physician in California before becoming a refugee. He hadn't practiced medicine in some time but thought he could help at least for a few months, to get the clinic started. *He's been very depressed for a year,* Sadie told me, *since losing his wife to cancer. He needs to get out and help others!* Sadie meanwhile turned her kitchen into a dispensary for preparing herbal medicines, and I spent many afternoons helping her make salves, ointments and tinctures.

Word quickly spread up and down the rows of shipping containers, and by early September the clinic—behind a freshly painted bright red door (Billy's idea)—had its grand opening. Cat, Sadie and I worked all day long helping Doc Manuel give vaccinations. Pertussis, tetanus, typhoid, borrelia... no adults in the project ever had been vaccinated, either, so we started with adults who were willing and grateful and didn't mind the needles at all, which Doc said was the best way to get a little practice before sticking needles in children. Even then, Cat and I couldn't face vaccinating children, and Sadie and Doc had to do it. During our lunch break on that first day, he tried to frown at us as he announced it was all right, but by early October, when it would be time to give the influenza vaccine, if we could get it, *All hands needed on deck!*

"You say you lost your healing gift," Cat said quietly to me after Doc and Sadie went back to work, and we stayed behind the scenes, sorting vaccine vials and unpacking syringes for them. "But you're an empath, Tessa, through and through."

Well, perhaps I hadn't completely lost that, or perhaps it was returning. As hard as it was, I realized that I also was taking some measure of satisfaction from taking on physical pain others around me were feeling, because at some deep level in my soul I felt that I deserved to feel this pain, after the pain and death I myself had inflicted over the past few years. *And it seems right that I should pay for it for the rest of my life.*

"I don't think it's gone, Tessa," Cat said quietly. "It's too valuable a gift to the people all around you. Don't give up on it yet."

That was the first day at the clinic.

After that, life became very busy, what with daily clinic staffing and taking turns being on call for after-hour emergencies—in the first week we had a midnight childbirth, an eight year old with a broken arm, and a stabbing wound from an early hours fight at the train station—added to the indoctrination sessions, gardening and cooking and reading and a few hours of Spanish each week with Sadie. The Spanish wasn't just so I could read Neruda. More than half of the people in our project were Spanish speaking, most of them refugees who'd managed to make it over the border from Mexico to the southwest and then make their way north. Understanding Spanish was crucial to being able to help most of the people who came through the clinic door, and it was much more comprehensively an understanding of a whole culture. Billy joined me in the Spanish lessons with Sadie, though he kept complaining that he was hardly getting any time any more to sit in front of his laptop in peace and quiet.

~

On a cool day in late September with flocks of geese crying overhead, Cat and I were organizing small glass jars of salves and ointments on the clinic shelves when the red door opened. A short woman bundled in a poncho over bulky wool pants and a jacket stood there looking at us. I felt a wave of tiredness, of weary loss, wash over me as I looked at her. She felt like someone who had come a long way, through a lot. Hopes raised, and then dashed; *weary unto death,* as Gram sometimes said. It occurred to me that I had just felt myself walk through the door. But that couldn't be right!

She pushed back her hood; she brushed back her black braids with a quick gesture I knew so well. It was Hannah.

"Oh my God, Hannah," I said, but I couldn't move off the stool I was sitting on. The sadness, the loss, all of it intensified as I looked at her face: I saw Gram sobbing at our kitchen table, wondering where I was, and Earl and Martha crying for Jesse, and Jesse's brothers grieving and aimless.

I began sobbing and couldn't stop, just barely choked out through the sobs, "We're so far from home, so far!"

"Tessa," she said, and then smiled. "I thought the expression I was supposed to use was *nearing home.*"

She walked in from the door, right up to my stool, and put her arms around me. We cried together for a moment.

"How'd you get here? How *are* you?" I finally managed to ask, lifting my head so I could look into her face.

She sighed and leaned her head, for just a second, on my shoulder. "I'm tired. It *has* been a long way."

Cat materialized off my other shoulder. "Hannah."

Hannah raised her head to look at Cat, and I swear that in that first second they recognized each other as kindred spirits. Completely different personalities, but kindred spirits.

"This is Cat," I said to Hannah as I let go of her. "She's my best friend here." I added, rather inanely, "She's a mindreader, but it doesn't matter."

Cat said to Hannah, "Don't mind her."

Hannah burst out laughing—something I hadn't seen since childhood—which brought Cat to laughing, and finally, after wiping my face vigorously with my sleeves, I started laughing too.

When we'd recovered, Cat brought a stool for Hannah to sit down on, close to us, then she made us all cups of tea, using milk and sugar from Doc's stash in the kitchenette refrigerator.

"I don't think he'll miss it," she said softly when she handed us our mugs, "and besides, this is a special occasion."

She sat back down on her stool and looked at Hannah. "You came here, you found us, because you were called." Their eyes held for a moment. "And it was such a strong calling!" Cat breathed, shaking her head in wonderment.

Hannah nodded. "Every day, every night for weeks. Finally I came." She told us about how Earl Brightwater had brought her out, hidden, in his wagon on his regular supply run. How she'd spent a few days at the safe house in the south of the city. But neither Emmitt nor Lars were there, and no one there knew where they were now, only that they had left about a year ago.

We sat quietly for a moment, sipping. I tried not to stare at Hannah, but I kept thinking she looked different, older. Well, she *was* older. So was I. What of the past four years showed on my own face when she looked at me?

"Hannah," I said softly. I could barely say the words. "When you left... how was Gram? And Earl? And your mom?"

She looked at me and paused before answering, "Well, no one knew where you and Jesse had gone to, and no word from either of you for almost four years has been pretty hard. I've Seen some things over the years...but when it's you I'm seeing, Tessa, I never quite know what to believe. It just seemed so strange I thought it was dreaming and not Seeing. Is Jesse here too?"

I couldn't bear to look at her any longer; I just put my head down on my knees to muffle the overpowering sobs.

"Jesse's gone!" I tried to say. "He's dead. It's all my fault!"

"Dead!" I heard Hannah exclaim. "Dead? No, that can't be..." her voice trailed off. Then she said slowly, "It's strange. Maybe those were dreams about him, instead of Seeings. It just seemed so strange to me that Jesse would have taken to the sea."

I lifted my head and wiped my face again with my sleeve and looked at her. "Taken to the sea! What do you mean?"

"Well, I've Seen Jesse a couple of times, on a ship. But you weren't with him, which was strange, and it also surprised me that he would be sailing a ship, so I couldn't quite believe that those were Seeings."

Finally I was able to tell Hannah about how Jesse and I had come out of the mountains in the dark before dawn, how we'd missed the important turn in the dark, how the train had come around the bend and hit Jesse, how the resistance had picked me up and wouldn't go back for Jesse's body.

"You don't suppose, Tessa," Hannah said slowly, and I could feel her feeling for the right words, "you don't suppose that he could have survived being hit and maybe got away..."

"Nooooooo!" My voice rose shriller and shriller until it broke. It took a long minute before I could speak again. "Oh, God, Hannah, if only! But no one could have survived that!"

"Shhhh," she said. "Okay, okay. Well, we're here together now."

I sat up and wiped my face again. "But how *did* you find me?"

"Tessa, I Saw you here three or four times, I kept seeing the name *Easthaven*, as it's on the sign down at the station. I knew I had to come. Somehow I'm supposed to be here with you."

Cat leaned over and hugged Hannah. "Thank you. Thank you so much for finding Tessa. We have plenty of room for you at my place and would love you to stay."

Hannah looked more than a bit pleased with herself. But that was okay. I, too, was grateful with all my heart that she had come.

~

Hannah moved in with Cat and me. Our bedroom end of Cat's shipping container had been a bit cramped to begin with, but Billy made us a bunkbed which Hannah and I shared. I had the top bunk, with only about eighteen inches of clearance between my head and the container roof, and Hannah had the bottom bunk with maybe six inches more clearance, but she said that since I was the athletic one, I had better take the top bunk. I didn't mind too much because the unit's end window looking out on the forest slope to the south of the project, was only a few inches away from my head when I lay in my bunk. I could look through the fine mesh screen in the window and watch the stars—we were just far enough south of the city lights to be able to see the stars—on clear nights.

Fortunately my nightmares had mostly stopped. Interestingly enough, it was Hannah who slept restlessly for weeks; some of it may have been the aftermath of her journey alone, so far from home, and she also admitted that some of it was because it was hard adjusting to the noise of people all around her, and not having anywhere to go to get away from it. Cat and I showed her the sitting spot on the log at the edge of the forest above our container, and we took turns using it.

Hannah, of course, was a natural for the clinic. And best of all, she was really good at sticking needles into small children, so Cat and I were off the hook there (she said it wasn't because she didn't mind— —*it's just that like with anything else, you make up your mind ahead of time to do it, and then you just do it!*). The clinic was quickly becoming the focus of our lives, but we weren't always busy: there were many quiet moments when we were either waiting for people to show up, or sitting next to people in the hospital bed end of the unit, waiting for them to get better. We had some strange and wonderful conversations during those times.

Just a few days after Hannah arrived, she was sitting with a young teenage boy who'd scored a designer drug off an older boy and had nearly died from an overdose—this wasn't all that unusual in the projects, we were learning—and I couldn't sleep, so I walked down from Cat's unit and offered to take Hannah's shift. She was grateful, but said she'd just had some strong coffee, and expected she'd be awake for a few more hours, so we sat there and quietly began talking of home. We hadn't had the time yet for Hannah to give me all of the news, after of course going over everything she could tell me about Gram and her mother and brothers, and Jesse's family. Old Tucky Lotts had died, which wasn't a great surprise, though it had been an interesting death—he took a canoe out for the first time in thirty years, to go fishing, and fell out of it at the far end of the lake and drowned (*pretty much everyone thinks that was Tucky's way of putting an end to it,* Hannah said, *which is kind of sad, but you have to give him credit for initiative!*). Jesse's auntie, my teacher Mrs. Kickbush, had at the amazing age of forty-six, just had another baby, which had the same birthday as her grandson, firstborn of her son Brad, who'd married our cousin Jenna. Oh and Auntie Annie, Hannah's mother, had thrown windows open all winter long to help her hot flashes, and drove everyone nuts. *And remember Jesse's little brother Augie?* Hannah asked, starting to laugh. *Well, he was out ice fishing with Earl and fell through the ice almost exactly where you did when you were little, and Earl saved him just like he saved you!* We sat there in the peaceful dark just shaking our heads over how strange life could be.

"Hannah," I said softly. "I long to go back."

"Then why don't you?" She was sitting quietly, almost blending into the dim light, her eyes large and black, her braids wound around her head as they were when I'd last seen her, in the schoolroom, back home.

I finally gave a long sigh. "I've been such a coward. I was so afraid to have to tell everyone about Jesse."

"They still think he's alive," she said finally. "Maybe it's better this way."

That was, as they sometimes said at Fortress base, putting a positive spin on it. It was kind of her, and I'll admit, not what I expected her to say.

"Is that the only reason?" she asked. "The only reason you're staying here?"

Maybe it wasn't. Maybe there was more. There was the feeling I got when I sat and meditated each morning with my eyes on the sea... something out there, maybe still something for me to do.

Finally I looked back at Hannah. "Sometimes I feel like there's something for me, for us, still to do here."

She nodded. "That's why I came out. I feel it, too."

~

By early November the mountains wore their winter white cloaks of snow. We'd harvested all of our veggies but left some kale covered so that we'd have greens for as long as possible. Each day was colder than the day before; the ground had frozen solid and the little stream that ran down the hillside just south of us had iced over. Insulated windows were a luxury not found in the projects, so we all had to work to stay warm—people were willing to eat less in order to be able to buy warm clothing , thick curtains were essential, and rugs for the floor and walls made the difference between cold and comfortable, and on the weekends everyone participated in bringing in firewood from the forests above and below us.

I had more physical energy than Cat or Hannah, so I enjoyed bundling up and joining the mostly male work parties wielding saws and axes. I didn't do much axe wielding, but I was good at dragging smaller trees and foraging for good kindling. I often worked near Billy, and this is how I discovered that he was gifted like Cat and Hannah, but in a surprising way. On the second Sunday in November, I quietly walked up from below to join him where he was working in a grove of old cedars, though he was just standing under a tree, looking at it, and then I watched a huge, ferny branch break off and crash to the ground, and then another, and then another... but there was no one else around, just Billy standing there looking up at the tree. I must have made a sound, because he whirled around and looked surprised to see me.

"Uh, Tessa, it's not what it looks like..." he started to say, but just then we heard an enormous crackling that ended in a vibrating thud in the woods above us, and men's voices shouting.

Billy spun back in that direction, muttering, "Fuck! I'm in the wrong place again!"

He started running uphill, in the direction of the shouting. I followed him, confused on just about every front, but it sounded like there had been an accident above us and people were calling for help.

We bashed through thick stands of browning devil's club, its thorns tearing at our jackets and pants. I had a stich in my side and could hear Billy breathing hard just ahead of me. Weak sunlight filtered through the spruce and cedar forest, brightening up ahead in a small clearing where a lot of people milled about. Two huge cedars were down—I guessed they'd come down together—and I wondered what the fuss was about, and then saw two men lying under the trees, not moving. A big bow saw that they had been using lay nearby, at the base of a freshly torn tree stump. I'd heard of trees getting hung up in other trees, or sometimes coming down wrong; Billy had talked about how logging was the most dangerous job of all. We were in it now.

Billy dashed to the group of men standing next to the bodies, several of them kneeling, more of them standing and gesturing, arguing over what to do. An ATV with a cart careening around behind it roared up a track just to the north, a much faster way in than the woods-bashing that Billy and I had just done. More shouting and gesturing from the knot of men next to the trees. Then Billy yelled, "Come on! help me!"

He squatted next to one of the trees, a few others joined him, the tree began moving. Another man—I recognized Pedro, Sadie's neighbor—crouched down next to Billy and pulled one of the bodies out from under, and someone else was pulling on the other. They pulled them by their jackets, out from under from the trees which thudded back down as soon as they were clear.

"Jesus Christ, how the *fuck* did you do that?" somebody said to Billy.

Pedro and two others gently lifted the limp bodies of the men, first one, and then the other, into the back of the cart behind the ATV.

The whole time I just stood there, staring. What could I do? My body was frozen; my mind went back to my last winter home, when Augie had that snowgo accident, when his buddy—what was his name?—was crushed by the machine, when Jesse and Earl had raced off to find him, and then found him dead. Dakota, that was his name. Little Dakota, Augie's best friend in all the world. How horrible that had been for Jesse...

"Tessa!" Billy yelled over his shoulder at me. "Go with them! Jump out at Cat's and get her and Hannah down to the clinic!"

I ran to the ATV. Pedro had climbed into the cart and was cradling one of the bodies, *oh damn, it's Manuelito...*

Billy picked me up and set me down behind the guy reving up the engine, and I managed to grab on tight to his jacket as he gunned it and we lurched forward. The track was so narrow on the way downhill that branches whipped our faces. Then the woods gave way up ahead; I saw Cat's unit at the end of the top row. The ATV driver slowed down when we came up on it and I jumped off and skidded on the path, managed to make it to the door, which was opened by Cat who calmly told me that Hannah was already at the clinic and she was ready to go with me. We didn't bother with the path, but stumbled and slid past the empty veggie boxes and down the bank, around Sadie's house, and arrived at the clinic as Pedro and the ATV driver were carrying in Manuelito, eyes closed, face shocking pale, arms dangling down limp.

Doc Manuel was there in the clinic, thank God. He and Hannah calmly directed each man to be placed on a table, and he went to work calmly and thoroughly, cutting away their clothes and checking them all over for injuries. I listened to Doc's quiet stream of talk—*thank God no major head injuries... but definitely broken bones... see this? broken collarbone for sure, and likely the shoulder has been crushed... both of them in shock... someone get me the IV kit, get blankets ready... Pedro, could you build up the fire in the stove, please?...*

I was awed by his quiet competence. And Hannah seemed to be able to anticipate his requests, with Cat a quiet, interpreting shadow at her side. I at least knew where things were and was glad to be able to fetch and carry; that seemed about all I was good for.

"Tessa, use your gift," Hannah sent me a fierce whisper as I stood watching Doc insert the IV into Pedro's left arm. She nodded toward the second examining table where the second victim was stretched out, breathing but unconscious.

"You're hanging back because you think your gift is gone," Hannah said. "That is no excuse!"

Right then I admitted to myself, deep down as deep as the lake, that as awful as it was to be pretty sure the gift was gone, it would be even worse to try to heal someone, and to find myself just sitting there, useless, knowing it *was* gone for good. But I had to try.

I walked over to the second victim—he looked as young as Billy, and I thought I'd seen him at Billy's a few times, young and carefree, a little shy but with a quick smile. The name Jimmy came to me. I thought of Augie in what seemed like a lifetime ago. How to scan someone as Gram had taught me. I stretched out my hands and kept them just a few inches above Jimmy, trying to quiet everything in me and focus. But I was a blank inside. Nothing.

"Tessa, what the hell are you doing?" came Doc's voice from behind me.

I jumped a little and automatically said, "Nothing." And it was the truest thing I had ever said. I really was doing nothing.

~

I had fallen asleep in the rocker that someone had donated to the hospital bed end of the clinic; I had taken night duty, watching over Pedro and Jimmy, and I'd fallen asleep. I dreamed of childhood and sitting on the radiant heated floor at our community center, Hannah on one side of me and Jesse on the other, and hearing Gram tell the Étain story. One line echoed in my mind as I woke: *And she shed from her wingtips a spray of droplets that could cure sickness in anyone she went with.* I had forgotten that Étain had been a healer during her years as a fly.

Sadie seemed to materialize at my elbow in the dim light— perhaps it was the clinic door that had woken me up—but instead of reprimanding me for sleeping on the job, she just smiled and whispered, "I was pretty sure you'd like someone to join you."

She had carried over one of the chairs from the other end of the room, and plumped down on it, close enough that her knee touched mine. She patted my arm. "Tessa, dear, you must be so tired."

I heaved a huge sigh. "I just feel so useless!"

She kept patting. "Tell me what it is."

And I told her what I'd woken up with weighing down my heart—*Once I had a gift that could have helped people, but I turned my back on it, and now it is gone...*

Sadie reached over and gave me a hug, and I didn't hold the sobs back any longer, but muffled them on her shoulder.

Then she said exactly what Gram would have said—"Some things are mysteries, dear. The thing to do is just keep on, keep doing your best. We keep trying."

~

Not long after Manuelito and Jimmy's accident—and thanks to Doc, and the efficient and comprehensive care of Hannah, they healed—Billy and I had an interesting conversation while we helped winterize project units for elders in the community who didn't have the reach for hanging rugs or weren't strong enough to staple visqueen plastic over drafty container end-doors.

I started it by saying that I'd realized that he'd help move the trees off Manuelito and Jimmy. When he tried to deny it, I told him that I came from a long line of people with odd abilities that tended to freak other people out, so I really did have some experience in that realm, even if I myself was pretty boringly normal. I understood.

He paused with a sheet of plastic in one hand and a stapler in another, looked thoughtful.

"Tessa, it's a burden. That's what it is. It's gotten me in trouble a bunch of times and I try to forget it."

"Billy, talk to Hannah and Cat. They both know exactly what you're talking about because they're in the same boat."

He looked surprised. I didn't say anything more because I knew it was better for Billy to hear directly from Cat and Hannah—which he did. That night as we were getting into our beds, Cat asked if any of us understood telekinesis. No. We agreed it was another of those mysteries.

When Billy and I started work on another unit, he grinned and said, "So, I don't feel like a freak anymore, Tessa. Thanks to you! Or at least, I'm not a lonely freak, because it turns out that I'm surrounded by them!"

Billy began calling our corner of the project *Freakville*.

As time passed, we became a family, Hannah and Cat and Sadie and Billy and me. It was the bond growing between Sadie and Billy that surprised and delighted me the most. Bit by bit, bossing him into doing jobs to help the neighbors, feeding him, teaching him Spanish, comforting him as she had comforted me, Sadie had become Billy's Gram. Watching them together—tiny, white-haired, energetic Sadie bouncing along, only about a third the size of steady and gigantic Billy—always made me smile. She was his Gram, his auntie, his *madre*, all in one. And Cat and Hannah and I were his sisters. He seemed to relate to each of us in a slightly different way. With Hannah he was the little brother who did whatever she told him, trying to please her. Cat brought out the sweet side of him, as she did with everyone. And he seemed to save his slightly sarcastic philosophizing, the deep questions he asked of the world, but also of himself, for me. I think this was because I was asking the same questions with the same protective sarcasm, so Billy and I were questing together, in a way. Usually sarcastically, but sometimes seriously.

~

And Hannah kept having dreams about Jesse. Hannah had been at Easthaven for three years and she was still having dreams of Jesse. They confounded her because she couldn't tell if they were dreams or Seeings.

"It doesn't make sense that I would keep dreaming about him," she said one morning as we sat at the breakfast table with Cat.

I wanted to joke that *I* was the one who should be dreaming about Jesse, but I couldn't joke... because so many of my dreams had been nightmares. It had been seven years since he'd been killed, and still I felt like a part of my body and soul was missing. I missed him every day with a deep ache.

"Are there any details clear enough that could help you differentiate between dreams and Seeing?" Cat quietly asked as she poured us more coffee. "Like when you Saw Tessa here?"

Hannah frowned and slowly shook her head. "For a while he was on a ship, at sea, along a coast. But I've never seen the coast south of here, so I wouldn't know. But now I'm beginning to dream of him, or See him, here in the city, which is strange, too..."

We hadn't tried to track down Emmitt and Lars since Hannah had been told they were no longer in the safe house south of the city. Now I was wondering again about that. I wondered if we should try tracking them down through Mack and Davis, but Cat told me that for now we should wait; it wasn't safe to put out inquiries.

"What do you see him doing?" Cat asked Hannah.

"That's what's so strange—he's with us. We're all running from Orion."

Cat's eyebrows shot up.

"That sounds like one of *my* dreams," I said. "One of my nightmares."

I couldn't get Hannah's dreams out of my mind. That night I couldn't sleep, and so I got up, pulled on a jacket and quietly walked out into the spring night. My feet automatically took me uphill to my sitting spot. A drift of mist moved through the forest and began spilling downward, through the shipping container homes of the project. My mind drifted for a while and began snagging on thoughts, like the mist snagged and tattered in the trees along the slope south of us.

Hannah's Sight was such a strange thing. I knew that Jesse could never have survived the train. But Hannah kept Seeing him. She had Seen me when I was flying kestrels and shooting Orion jets out of the sky, and so much of that had been strange—the hare-brainedness of it (she used the same words Jesse did) was the familiar part, she said——the idea of jets and flying off the coast far to the south had all been so strange that she had been sure it was dreams and not the Sight. Until she Saw me at the Easthaven project clinic. Because she kept Seeing me here, she came to find me.

But she wasn't sure about Jesse. Of course not. It was impossible that he could have survived the train.

I had learned a Neruda poem during Spanish lessons with Sadie that haunted me now (but I could only remember it in English) because it seemed to be my heart speaking of Jesse:

If only you would call,
a long sound, a bewitching whistle,
a sequence of wounded waves,
maybe someone would come,
someone would come,
from the peaks of the islands, from the red depths of the sea,
someone would come, someone would come.

The poem broke my heart because it had taken me all these years, but I finally knew it—I loved him. And I had never told him that. If there could only be *a long sound, a bewitching whistle* that could call him back—but he was gone.

And Hannah's doubt, her vague wonderings if maybe Jesse wasn't gone after all, if he might come back, were going to kill me.

She had told me long ago that sometimes she Saw things that didn't happen because some random event happened in the between-times to change what happened later (perhaps that explained the

Jesse dreams or Seeings—perhaps it was what Jesse would have been doing if not for the train?). A person could lose her mind trying to figure out the future. I was one to argue against determinism; it was much easier for me to believe in accidents and random events and things left up to us to muddle through.

I finally gave up and went back to bed, but I didn't sleep that night.

~

As good as it felt to be becoming a family—though Hannah and I chafed each other as much as we ever did back home at the lake—we all began to feel that things were not as good around us. Life was getting harder in the projects. Shelves were barer in the food shops down by the train station, it was harder and harder to find basic necessities such as blankets and pots to cook with, and medical supplies. Many people did what they could: there were a number of level places in our project, with fairly decent soil, where we started community gardens, and Billy and a few guys took ATVs with carts and salvaged wood from abandoned houses in the area to make more veggie boxes for people who wanted to garden on their banks, as we did. They had a "good dirt" depot as well as our excellent project compost, so gardens quickly thrived. Grateful health clinic users brought us gifts of food in exchange for our free services, and some other rather odd gifts which we in turn bartered, but the most valuable gift turned out to be a clutch of young pullets which became our chicken flock, housed in a little coop Billy built with more salvaged wood, and within a year or so there were chicken flocks all over the project. Roosters crowing at 4am didn't bother anyone too much because, as Billy said, it was the sound of dinner.

But as life got harder for the people in the projects, the people got angrier. I think it was mostly the people who didn't know about the resistance quietly working behind the scenes, or who knew about it but had lost faith in it, since nothing had visibly happened in decades. It was the guys Billy's age who were the angriest. We began to hear about sabotage at the jetport, at the city docks, at the city train station. Suicide bombers, setters of booby-trap bombs, hidden snipers, almost always young males who been never known freedom and were desperate for revenge. It was chaotic, sporadic, hopeless; Billy said it was guerilla warfare, and I knew enough Spanish to know that the word *guerilla* meant *little war*, a word born hundreds of years ago when oppressed indigenous people rose up against the Spaniards in South America. Now when it happened, Orion reprisals were swift, brutal, indiscriminate.

We knew it was bad, but we didn't quite understand how bad until Orion soldiers pursuing some shooters shot three ten-year-old boys at the Easthaven train station. Witnesses said the soldiers gunned down children for no reason except that they happened to be there.

Venid a ver la sangre por las calles,
venid a ver
la sangre por las calles,
venid a ver la sangre
por las calles! (Come and see the blood in the streets... Neruda)

Two died right there, but one survived and his father brought him to our clinic, hoping we could save him. Doc was there in the clinic, thank God—we were all gathered, discussing how we might safely procure more essential supplies, with our link to Davis tenuous at best now that Orion scrutiny had increased at all the train stations——when we heard the snarl of an ATV running full power up the hill toward us.

Hannah, Cat and I heard it first, looked up, looked at each other.

"It's bad," Cat said quietly. More and more she was picking up on things happening some distance away, *breaking in on me, and I can't keep them out,* she said.

The boy's father clutched him, riding on the ATV behind the boy's uncle. They rushed him in when we opened the clinic door, put him on the table we had just cleared for him. The boy was bleeding out of a hopeless wound to his chest; his face was white, drained, his spirit was only half there, half of it already departed with his friends. Looking at him, I suddenly wanted a gun in my hands so I could kill in brutal, bloody revenge.

We tried as hard as we could, but we couldn't save him. Such grief filled the tiny clinic. Cat and Hannah wept together in one corner, I stood at a back window with cold murder in my heart, ashamed that this is how I reacted. Sadie put her arms around the grieving father and said a few words in a soft sing-song voice, gentle and comforting.

Then she said more loudly, so that we all heard her, "We can't understand it. But we know it is not right to kill the killers; if we do that, we have sunk to their level. We must go on and hope that in time we will know what to do."

~

It was the spring of my seventh year at Easthaven when the raven came. Hannah and I were out working in the vegetable boxes, now more than a dozen of them running all along the bank below Billy's and our unit, all the way down to Sadie's and Pedro's and Manuelito's.

Soft spring rain fell from low gray clouds. Hannah leaned forward next to me, industriously thinning baby lettuces, frowning with concentration, pinching the unlucky ones with her thumb and forefinger, uprooting them and tossing them a few inches away where she hoped they'd wither away and die. As usual she'd wound her thick black braids up on her head so they didn't get in her way. Industrious and purposeful Hannah.

I heard the guttural gronk of a raven somewhere up there in the gray sky. It took a minute for the sound to register in my brain since we hardly ever had ravens at Easthaven, even in the woods above us. They kept closer to the mountains.

The raven called again, and again. Billy and Cat and Sadie were outside, too, and we all looked up at the sky, craning our heads around as we tried to spot him. Hannah caught sight of him first and pointed him out to the rest of us. He was flying in from over the forest above us, coming closer and closer, calling all the while.

He tilted his wings against the gray sky. I thought of the young raven who flew away out of my hands long ago on the shores of the lake and tears filled my eyes until the circling raven became a small black blur against the gray clouds. I felt his voice all through me. Somehow I knew what he was about to do, and I stood very still, almost holding my breath.

The problem was that I'd been away from ravens for so long that I misjudged the size of them. Standing there I had this image in my mind of a raven gracefully alighting upon my shoulder. Actually it didn't work out that way. I felt the brush of wings against the air around me and then BAM!

When I could think again, I was lying flat on my back on the soft dirt with the sensation of an elephant sitting on my chest. I raised my head a little to see, and was looking right into dark raven eyes. He was leaning toward me, peering at me, and it didn't feel at all like he was bringing a soft message from the spirit realm—it felt more like he was thinking at me, *What the hell are you doing lying around? Time to get moving, girl!*

A message from my spirit helpers if there ever was one.

"Wow." I laughed a little weakly, with the small amount of air still in my lungs. Then I said softly. "Welcome. You're welcome to stay for as long as you want."

There was a squeaky rustle of feathers as he straightened up; the talon digging into my left breast moved slightly. Then with a sudden burst of wings he launched himself off my chest. Gone. Powerfully beating wings carried him over the project, headed west. He circled once, calling one last time with his hoarse voice, then he flew off toward the sea.

I raised weakly up on one elbow and found myself looking into Hannah's dark eyes.

"Well," she said. But that was all. A long, quiet moment passed.

"Do you think that might have been a sign?" I said, and we started laughing.

She reached out to help me up and she didn't need to say anything more.

~

The raven visitation was a topic of meal-time conversation for days. Billy and Sadie saw it as a sign, and the possibilities were endlessly debated. So many questions ran through my own mind. It could just have been a tired raven who happened to fly down from the mountains, seeing that interesting grid of square boxes, and that person who maybe looked like she needed knocking down. It might even have been the raven I helped heal at the lake, an elderly raven now and recognizing me, stopping for a quick though clumsy visit. It could have been pure chance. Or I suppose it could have been a sign sent from our ancestors. A sign to somehow motivate me to do something. I wished they'd made it a little clearer.

Over seven years, as the days and nights had spooled out into a tapestry of clinic, community gardening, reading, learning Spanish, becoming a family, and as we had faced increasing Orion violence and oppression, Hannah and Cat and I had periodically checked in with each other: *are we in the right place? are we doing the right things? is there something else we should be doing?* And it had seemed that yes, we were in the right place and doing what we should be doing... until the raven. And then we all got to wondering. And we knew that if there was somewhere else we were headed, we wouldn't go without Billy and Sadie, for now we were a family.

Over seven years the dinnertime conversation had always circled back to the latest news of Orion, and of the resistance. And I almost always asked the burning question *Why hasn't the resistance done more against Orion?!* It had been decades now. Surely the resistance could have come up with more by now. Why weren't we hearing anything?

Billy and Cat could fill us in on the larger picture, even the news from around the world. In our seventh year at Easthaven, Orion wiped out all of the heads of state in the Far East, reprisal for the ChinJapKor alliance daring to challenge Orion in the world courts. Needless to say, Billy added, no more Asians allowed into America; the only immigrants or even travelers allowed now were white Western Europeans. For decades Orion's rallying cry had been *America First!*, but now everyone said unofficially it was *Shoot first, ask questions later.* Especially if it involved anyone from the Near East or Far East.

The night Billy told us this—about Orion poisoning, shooting, making accidents happen to leaders of other countries who might have stopped them—at the dinner table, I couldn't stop myself from slamming down my fork and shouting, "Then why can't we stop these criminal fuckers!?"

There was a moment of silence. Billy set his fork down carefully and turned in his chair so he was looking directly at me. "Tessa, we're trying, but it's in ways you can't see. That's the problem. The good guys—everybody south of the city, everybody in the little villages that we see in the news getting burned because they're labeled seditious— they can't see what we're doing and so they don't think we're doing anything."

"So, Billy, what *are* you doing?"

Billy hardly ever talked about his job with the resistance. He kept looking intently at me, and then said, "I've been able to break into a few of the middle levels of Orion intelligence."

"What do you mean, 'break in?'" Hannah asked from across the table.

"It's in the computer world. That's why it's not visible. You know, not every single one of their portals is absolutely secure," he said, leaning his chair back until he was resting against the blue and green wool rug that Cat had hung to the left of the window next to the dining table. It wasn't yet summer so the rugs were still up. "Think of it kind of like getting a toehold. Or maybe like just getting your fingers on the ledge of an upstairs window and being able to slip in so you can burglarize the house."

"Oh dear!" from Sadie.

"But..." I said, "how do you *do* it?"

"You mean like how with my laptop?"

I nodded. That would be good for starters.

"Well, being up on the hillside, I can intercept a lot of different signals," he said. He looked more carefully at my face. "They're invisible, Tessa. Radio waves. You know, like light is waves?"

I nodded. I did remember that from school long ago. The speed of light and all that.

"And it's one big network of networks out there," Billy went on. "With all sorts of entry points, whether it's government or businesses or just regular people like me. Whether we're wireless or using carbonoptic cable—they have cable in the cities, not out here, we're the have-nots—we're all connecting to the network. And some of the connections aren't encrypted well enough to keep me out."

"How can it be both cable and radio waves?" I asked.

Billy dropped his chair forward, leaned his head in his hands. "Oh for God's sake, Tessa! Could someone please bring me another beer?"

Cat burst out laughing and went to the refrigerator.

Cat, of course, picked up all kinds of things in her time at the Information Booth right smack in the center of the Fayerport train station. She had to work on filtering, she said, or she'd lose her mind surrounded by so many people. *Just imagine that a hundred people, or more, around you are all talking at once.* When pressed, she would tell of overhearing people thinking about sex—*sex is one of the biggest topics, believe it or not* (and Billy grinned at this)—or all of the worries: worrying about being late, or getting lost, or forgetting something, or (a hard one for Cat) not bringing enough food home to feed their kids. She was getting better and better at filtering out this buzz beneath the surface and paying attention instead to spikes of thought, usually caused by emotion. I was familiar with this from childhood, feeling the steady state of the people around me and feeling sudden emotions' spike of intensity.

Cat spoke of the increasing Orion surveillance—the tiny drones flying everywhere in the city, as well as at all of the train stations, even ours, and the high-flying drones as well, but these we never noticed—all a response to the increasing guerilla warfare. We all were well aware of the jopters flying low over our heads at all hours of the days and nights. Strange the things one can get used to.

Cat knew the recent crackdown on third class workers entering Fayerport was coming, even before Orion soldiers started pulling people aside and scrutinizing identity cards, and arresting some people just because they felt like it; she'd picked up on suspicion in the minds of some of the Orion soldiers on duty at the station. They suspected that the resistance was using the rail lines to bring in grounders, which was true. She'd even been able to warn Mack and Davis in time and they both had disappeared; she didn't know where they'd gone but guessed to the cities in the north, where there was a bit more breathing room away from Orion's northwest headquarters in Fayerport.

But in the past two years Cat noticed more and more people connected with the resistance had the same feeling that we had—a feeling that something big was coming, something was about to happen. Cat seldom came across anyone who knew anything at the high levels, since the resistance was being so careful to keep information secured down to only what people needed to know in order to do their jobs. But still, she said, there was this sense that things were building. The resistance was getting ready for something.

We all looked at each other around the table.

"I'd love to see that," Billy remarked. "But only if it's successful."

8. April–May, 2111

A week after the latest dinner-table information update, Cat heard the name *Tessa* at the station. It had been thought, not spoken. She couldn't figure out where the thought had come from, but she said it felt sad somehow, which made her wonder if I was the one being thought of, and if it was someone close to me. In the chance that it was a regular—either a grounder or, less likely, someone in the resistance who had infiltrated Orion, which did occasionally happen——she wanted me to come in with her a few times just to see if I glimpsed anyone I knew.

As terrified as I was of the trains, I had to do it. What a slim hope! Yet, if there was any chance at all that it had been Emmitt, or Lars, I had to go. I know that Hannah still wondered if Jesse had somehow survived and was out there somewhere, but I couldn't even begin to let myself think in that direction.

"I'm coming too," Hannah said.

"Me too," Billy said. "Solidarity!"

Cat looked thoughtful for a moment as she rested in what we all called the comfy chair, with her feet on a stool, just having come in from a long day in Fayerport. Sadie was already nestled into the next-comfiest chair beside her. Billy had just walked in, ready for dinner. I was stirring some fresh herbs from our boxes into the stew on the stovetop, and Hannah was setting the table.

"We need to be careful," Cat said slowly. "I think we'd better go separately. I mean, it's okay for the three of us women to go together, but you'll need to appear independent from us, Billy."

He sighed. "The old lightning rod effect. I know."

"And I'll stay here and keep the homefires burning," Sadie said. "The clinic hasn't been quite as busy so it could be a good time for me to be orienting that new recruit."

We went the next day.

Cat had a blonde wig that she kept by the door to pull on every time she went into the city, to decrease the likelihood of anyone from her past recognizing her. It wasn't likely that she'd ever come across someone from her former circles, though. The only people who rode the workers' train, and who went through the Fayerport station, were what Billy called *the have-nots*, like us. The upstanding residents of

Fayerport didn't need to ride the trains: they used aircars and the jetport, across the north bay. In effect we existed in two entirely separate spheres.

Cat's worker's card said she was Kathleen Simmons, age thirty, five foot seven inches tall, one hundred thirty-five pounds of weight. And Hannah had been given a card by the grounders working at the safe house, when she first came to Fayerport. Helena Whitefield, her name was, and she looked old and somber with her hair pulled tight into a large bun.

"I wouldn't laugh, Ellen Gray," she said when I broke up the first time I saw her card. "Your picture isn't exactly a winner either."

We all had our identcards, we were *in the system*. It should be okay, I tried to reassure myself as Cat and Hannah and I walked through the small Easthaven square to the train station. Billy was going to take the next train in, an hour behind us. I hadn't realized quite how jumpy I was, though, until something about a foot long, whirring on its own power right over the stairway to the station, careened just past my face.

Cat soothed me after I jumped and swore, telling me that it was one of the Orion drones that were everywhere now.

"Just try to ignore them," she said.

"Easy to say as long as they keep their distance!"

But after that we didn't say anything more about Orion, or surveillance, or anything except our lives as Kathleen, Helena and Ellen, girls (that very day it occurred to me that we weren't exactly girls anymore—both Hannah and Cat were thirty-one and I was pushing thirty pretty hard) from the projects, menial laborers in the city. Cat held my hand on the platform as the high-pitched vibrations of the approaching train filled the air and I tried not to hyperventilate. The three of us sat together on a bench seat and watched out the window. All of the trees were dressed in their early April green, from the lines of low willows and alders along the streams and gullies, to the taller aspen and gnarly cottonwoods, and the shiny little birch leaves shimmered when rays of sun pierced through the spring gray clouds. Then there were fewer and fewer trees, and more and more buildings. The city skyline grew closer and closer.

"Did you know that our great great grandparents lived here?" Hannah asked Cat, who was sitting in between us.

She nodded. Before Hannah joined us, I'd told Cat about Ellen Silloway being a pilot, back in the days of Minerva, back before she and Dylan the poet knew about the extent of the industry of weapons development and sales to the terrorist groups Minerva was defending America against. Before they began to see the insidious world-wide militarization that had been planned out to benefit one corporation more than the people it was supposedly protecting.

As I looked out the window to the taller buildings and the flashing signs of shops and businesses, I wondered how people could live here and not know what Orion really was doing. But perhaps they had been lulled into not questioning. Perhaps their own safety and comfort had become so important that they were willing to not look at some things. Billy had described the steady flow of images and sounds that carbonoptic cable provided for its wealthy customers in the city: it filled their homes, and they could watch news networks (*all filtered by Orion!*) but most people chose entertainment... And the big thing was AR, augmented reality, that people lived in during their days by simply wearing glasses capable of data overlay. Orion knew that people were lulled by the thought of security, and by the pleasures that money could buy. Few today questioned like Ellen and Dylan Silloway did.

"Mine lived here too," Cat said softly. "They may have all known each other."

Ours left; Cat's stayed, among those who didn't question; or maybe they had questioned, maybe some of them also had been in the resistance long ago and Cat didn't know it. And here we were together, this day, headed for the city. Cat reached out to squeeze Hannah's and my hands.

Our train climbed up its elevated track when we reached downtown. As we took the big curve on the final stretch to the station, I glimpsed the glowing green that I had noticed seven years ago on my way out of the city.

"Cat, what is that?" I pointed in the distance, at the edge of the north bay, just before it disappeared behind some towers.

Hannah looked out and saw it, too. I felt a quick twist of pain in my gut as I watched her; no, it was fear, and then I realized it wasn't my fear, I was feeling hers. She closed her eyes.

"That's Prison One," Cat said quietly. "Not a good place. The green is the electrified Fence."

"I've Seen us there," Hannah said, with her eyes still closed.

Oh crap. I remembered now her words to me when I was not yet eighteen and told her I was leaving for the city—*killing and imprisonment and crying our hearts out.* I took a deep breath and tried to hope for the best. Hope that things weren't going to go as she had Seen.

The Fayerport train station seemed much as I remembered it, though I immediately noticed the drones. Like the one that nearly hit me on the Easthaven station steps, they were small, erratic, everywhere. As we walked through the first set of doors into the huge space, I found myself fantasizing about holding a sturdy wooden bat in my hands and smacking them out of the air, one after another. The satisfying smash of delicate electronics, the sudden going-black on a screen that somewhere an Orion soldier was monitoring.

Next to me Cat gave a small laugh and I realized she'd been following my thoughts. But with Cat, I never minded. She tried to give us all privacy, and when she sometimes slipped we didn't mind because it wasn't like she was prying; she just couldn't help it.

"Here's where I work," she said as she led us up to a octagonal kiosk in the center of the cavernous hall. It had waist-high walls lifting a wide desk that ran around all its sides, and several posts held high a large sign that read, on both sides, *Information.*

"It's an anachronism," Hannah spoke for the first time since she'd talked about Seeing us in prison.

"What's an anachronism?" I asked.

"Something out of time... from the past."

"Oh. So what kind of information are we giving people today?" I tried to joke.

Cat smiled, but her eyes said, *Careful, Tessa—anything you say here will be heard!*

"Much of this is automated," she nodded to flat touch screens built into the desk. "But no matter how much is computerized, there are always questions computers can't answer."

We entered the kiosk and sat down on the three chairs that were inside.

"I'm orienting both of you today," Cat went on. "I'm guessing that you both will need several orientation sessions before you're ready to work here."

"I'll say," I commented, and tried to settle onto my hard metal chair, wishing I'd brought something warm and soft to sit on.

Cat reached into a small cupboard under one of the counters and pulled out a couple of thin cushions she handed to us. *Thanks*, I thought. *You're really on it today.*

She just smiled. I sat there thinking that this could be pretty boring. I wanted to ask her which people hurrying past us were thinking about sex, but thought better of it.

Hannah sat quietly knitting next to me. Just like Hannah to think of bringing her knitting. She sat there with her head bent, her hair in that big granny-like bun, the kind of woman you'd expect to be thinking of her four or five children and husband waiting at home, if you didn't know better. Next to her Cat was so fair, her skin so white, with her large blue eyes and her wig of short blonde hair. She looked barely old enough to give Information. And I imagined I looked somewhere in the middle, sitting there with my spikey short black hair, my tattered jean jacket and don't-fuck-with-me look that went with the walk. I doubted anyone would be tempted to ask me for Information.

People flowed through the huge space around us, through the tall revolving doors from the street side, or through the opposite tall revolving doors from the train platform side. Smaller eddies moved back and forth from the narrower ends of the building where there were several shops, and I guessed one of those was where Davis had once worked. I wondered where he was now; I hoped he was safe. *A port in the storm*, he had said. Well, he hadn't been that for me, but it had been a nice offer. I'm sorry he couldn't have at least known I was grateful for it. There had been one port in the storm for me but it was gone. Neruda came to mind again: *If you existed, suddenly, on a mournful coast...*

I tried to pay attention to individuals in the crowd. Men and women wore somber clothes and were intent on where they were going, every once in a while one of them carefully shepherded a child; older teenagers in black jackets and tattered jeans sauntered and strutted. Black-uniformed Orion soldiers stood just inside the tall revolving doors, their eyes on the crowd, ear pieces in place and AR glasses on their faces. Short stunners hung from the soldiers' belts, and automatic weapons—long gleaming steel barrels extending from bulky ammunition packs— strapped over their shoulders. Cat had told me about the stunners: they had a range of at least fifty feet and knocked you, screaming, to the ground, and if you got hit point-blank, you might not wake up for a half-hour, and in those first few seconds of waking you'd be in so much pain you'd wish you hadn't woken up. Still that was preferable to the real weaponry the soldiers carried.

I tried to remember what it was like back home when the only time we ever saw a gun was when a parent carefully readied it for a hunting trip to bring home meat for the village.

I wanted to go home.

Billy suddenly walked past, giving us all a quick smile and a wink, then continuing on in the direction of the tech shop at the east end of the station.

Several people stopped and used the computer screens on our desk, not even glancing at us, and moved on. Then an older couple stopped at the desk opposite Cat. They looked part native; she wore a kuspuk like Gram wore on special occasions. Since it now was nearly impossible to enter Fayerport from outside without an Orion identity card, they must be living somewhere in the projects like us, far from their real home.

"What sort of information do you give for those nearing home?" the woman said, smiling as she looked at Hannah and me, too. They were resistance.

"Whatever we can!" Cat said with a little laugh. I could tell that she knew them.

The man smiled also and was about to say something, when Cat gave a little gasp, put a hand to her throat, then looked at the couple. "Quick, come in here," she gestured them to the little gate that let them into our kiosk. "Hurry!"

This was so strange, we all stared at her. But Hannah got up and also motioned for them to hurry in.

"I'm sorry," Cat said, "but something is happening... I don't know what, but I feel so much danger..."

Hannah gestured the older woman down onto her chair, then gestured to the man to crouch down next to her. "It's bad," she said. "Everyone get down and cover your heads."

"Oh, I saw something out front I was worried about..." the woman began...

And then the building lifted—it felt like the entire building lifted

189

upwards and then rocked back, toward the train platform. A deafening explosion pierced my eardrums, punctuated by glass shattering and crashing, along with huge wall panels, to the concrete floor. Our little kiosk, untethered, blew across the floor toward the train platform doors, but it held together. I felt my chair rise into the air, then someone—it must have been Cat as she had been sitting on my right—thumped against me, rolling me, and I went down and the rough wood kiosk floor slapped my cheek.

We stopped moving. Sudden silence. I wondered if that was because I had gone deaf? Then I heard people crying, a few moans, people calling for help.

I pulled myself upright and realized that I was all right—I looked at my companions in the kiosk and saw Hannah on her hands and knees, shaking her head, and Cat sitting on the floor next to me, brushing dust and glass off her shoulders. The old couple were stirring and patting each other. Beyond us, though, was devastation. Part of the street-side wall had fallen in; most of the windows on that side of the station had blown out and glass had fallen down on people. More people were lying on the concrete floor bleeding than were getting to their feet and moving around. The explosion had come from outside the building, and as devastating as it had been, I don't think there would have been anything left, had it been inside the building.

Loud voices—Orion soldiers picking themselves up off the floor near the platform doors where they'd been blown not far from us, and more hurrying in through those doors—all of them running across the station to the other side, the side the blast had come from.

Billy! I thought. And just then I saw him some distance away, looking fine, trying to navigate around bodies and debris on the floor. He must have been in the shop, thank God.

"Are we all right?" I heard Cat's voice behind me. Hannah said something; she was getting to her feet, then helping the older couple to theirs. The man had a bleeding cut on his forehead, but it didn't look too bad, and Hannah gave him a scarf from her knitting bag to press onto it.

"Oh, I knew it!" the older woman exclaimed, brushing dust and tiny glittering fragments of glass off her kuspuk. "We saw three, four young men outside the entrance when we came in... more Orion soldiers were coming over to question them... a couple of the kids were wearing bulky coats..."

"Suicide bombers," Cat said quietly. "They took out the soldiers, but how many innocent people did they kill?"

We all stood up and looked around. "Let's go help," I said, and Cat and Hannah both nodded and moved out of the kiosk with me.

"Wait," Cat turned back. She reached into the cupboard still in the kiosk, below one counter, and pulled out a first aid kit that I took from her hands, and then a pile of material. "Old curtains that came with the kiosk," she said. "Just what we can use for bandaging."

Billy rushed up to us as we stepped out into the destruction. "Thank God you're all right! Jesus!"

Sirens started up outside—at first I thought it was my ears still ringing—sirens coming nearer and nearer, not for anyone lying on the floor around us, I knew, but for any surviving Orion soldiers out on the street.

"Work in pairs," Hannah said, giving me a nudge toward Billy, "and try to stop the bleeders first."

I took an armful of faded cotton curtain fabric, and grabbed scissors and a roll of tape from the first aid kit before Hannah took it. Billy was already kneeling down next to a small child, motionless, not bleeding. I knelt down, too, and held my fingers to her wrist, and then against her neck. No pulse. Her spirit had left minutes ago, speeding off, far from us. I choked back a sob, touched her eyelids, pulling them down over her staring eyes, whispered *Go with Raven, go with the angels and your spirit helpers.* I patted Billy's back and stood up.

"Those stupid fuckers!" he said. "Stupid! Stupid! How could they do this?"

I thought I understood how someone could take their own life out of desperation and despair, but no, I could not understand how a person could deliberately take so many lives. This was terrorism, and it was just what Orion wanted—home-grown terrorism within its own borders so it could say, *See? We told you they were trying to kill you! We are your only chance for safety!*

The child's mother was dead, too, impaled through the chest by a piece of steel that must have blown from the wall. Her spirit had followed her daughter's. There was nothing we could do here. My stomach twisted and tears sprang up in my eyes and blurred the awful scene around us.

They're together and she won't know the grief of losing her daughter, I

191

thought, and made myself move on. We found a cluster of people who were more or less conscious and all bleeding from glass wounds, and we set to work tearing curtain fabric into bandages, wrapping, taping, holding pressure and instructing those who could to help hold pressure on the bleeding. It was good to be able to do something.

A whirring sound from the blasted street entrance doors—it was an aircar—it hovered right in through the gaping opening where the doors had been, and hovered about seven feet off the floor inside the building, its sides down as its occupants scanned the room. Orion brass, as Cat called them, the guys with all of the extra stars and bars on their black uniforms. They were literally scanning the room with a large black wand attached to a screen, but several of them were turning their heads this way and that, carefully looking over the people below them. The Orion officer on our side of the car looked at me, then began to look away, then looked back at me. I looked away, shivering.

"Tessa!" a hissed whisper from the other direction—it was Cat trying to get my attention. "Come here, hurry! We've got to get away!"

Billy heard her, too. We both turned and headed for Hannah and Cat. Behind us I heard a shout, but I didn't look back. The four of us began running, weaving through the piles of debris, through people still lying there, bleeding, needing help. I heard the aircar humming behind us. We were running from Orion. How could we think we could get away? But we had to try.

I stumbled over something; Billy grabbed my arm to steady me and pull me forward. Then terrible pain pulsed through me, and the last thing I remember was pitching head first toward a pile of bodies.

~

I woke up to pain in all quadrants, but the worst of it was shooting out the top of my head. *Another concussion*, I thought, but then knew that I must have been stunned. *Orion has me!* I sat up and looked around. Not just me, but also Hannah and Cat. As sorry as I was that they, too, had been captured, I will confess to feeling such a relief that we were together.

Hannah was still on her back, eyes closed, her bun undone and braids tumbled down, bits of glass in them glittering. Cat was slowly pushing herself up from the floor to sit next to me; her face was as white as the bright white walls of the room, but she gave me a smile.

White wrapped all around us, walls, ceiling, disorienting white. Lights recessed above us were too bright, especially with my head feeling the way it did. I noticed the glitter of tiny glass fragments on my shirt and jacket, even on my jeans and leather boots. It was probably in my hair, too.

I was pretty sure where we were. Yes, a glimpse out the slit of window in the wall across from me confirmed it. I saw glowing green outside. We were inside the Fence, not a good place to be, as Cat had said. As Hannah had Seen. I made a promise deep in my heart that we would all get out of here alive and soon, if I had anything to do with it.

"Yes," Cat whispered from close beside me. "Not a good place."

Hannah opened her eyes and struggled to sit up, looked at us, then laughed and said, "God almighty, Tessa, you still have glass in your hair."

"It's my new look," I tried to sound casual. Thinking—*how's that for don't fuck with me hair?* "And you do, too, as a matter of fact."

A whispered *hiss* and the invisible door behind Hannah slid open. An Orion guard stood in the doorway, all black, with shining silver stars on his shoulder, stun gun in one hand.

"You." He pointed the stun gun at me. "Come with me."

Hannah, Cat and I all looked at each other. Then I scrambled to my feet, stunned headache pounding anew. Why me? There was nothing to be done but obey the guard.

Hannah's eyes said, *Be careful!*

I felt the touch of Cat's mind, a quick comforting caress.

I followed the guard down a long, white hallway under more of the bright overhead lights. Finally he stopped and pointed with his gun to the right, and a door slid open, to a small office-type room, several chairs along one wall, desk opposite the door, a window behind the desk that looked over the Fence to the north, over dark inlet water, then miles of farmland and factories, to the distant haze of other Orion cities on the cleared-off plain, to the tall mountain range to the north, shining bright white under the spring afternoon sun.

I sat down on the chair the guard pointed to with his gun, and waited, turning my head to look out that window so I didn't have to look at the large chair against the wall opposite me. The padded headpiece and restraints built into that chair weren't easy to look at.

Finally the door opened. The person who walked in was not at all what I expected. Instead of male, grim, authoritarian, the black Orion uniform—in walked a small woman in a bright blue stretchy pantsuit that bulged in a few places, with shiny gold hair, perfectly coiffed around her round face, her lipsticked mouth wide in a smile that showed a lot of white teeth. I came close to automatically returning her smile, I was so surprised—almost, but there was something odd in all of that bright, shininess. Like there wasn't really a person there at all. I wished Cat was in the room to get a read on her.

The woman stopped just in front of my chair, intently focused on my face. I wanted to look away, to escape the brilliant intensity of her, but it was also like knowing there was a big spider in the room with you and not daring to take your eyes off it because as awful as it was looking at it, it was more awful not exactly knowing where it was in the room.

She blinked her blue eyes several times and somehow increased the wattage of her smile.

"You stunned two soldiers at the terminal," she said. Her voice matched her face—quick, pressured, as if she was listening to herself. "Now how on earth did you do that?!"

Surprise coursed through me. "I did *what*?"

"They went to pick you up to put you in the aircar and you sent them flying about twenty feet, though you appeared unconscious."

"Their stun guns must have malfunctioned."

She shook her head. "And it was just you, it wasn't any of your... comrades."

This was so bizarre I had to sit there thinking for a minute.

The woman moved past me to take the chair behind the desk. I noticed the smile left her face as soon as she looked away from me. Lines etched the skin at the edges of her eyes, and the skin below her small chin pouched a little; I'd bet she'd been dying her hair that brilliant gold for some time.

"You may call me Miranda," she smiled at me from behind her desk. "Now, who are you?"

I pulled over my head my identcard on its titanium loop and set it on the desk between us. "Ellen Gray. I live in Easthaven."

Her blue eyes flicked from my face to the card, back to my face. Then she waved it away. I pulled it back on over my head and let it drop inside my shirt.

"So, Ellen Gray," she said my name in a tone that said she didn't believe it was my name, "where are you from?"

"Glacierport, before Easthaven. I lived there a year and worked in the cannery. I came from a tiny village east of Glacierport."

"I see." Again her voice told me she didn't believe a word of it. She leaned back in her chair and watched me.

I looked past her out the window.

After a pause, she said, "Well, Ellen Gray, you are being held here for aiding and abetting the terrorists who bombed the train station, killing dozens of innocent women and children."

Surprise again jolted me. "If I had been aiding and abetting," I couldn't help saying, "why would I have stuck around and given first aid to the people I'd blown up?!" A little late, I realized she was just playing with me. I shut my lips tight together. But out of the corner of my eye, I could see that chair that she would put me into, where she could get whatever information she wanted out of me. How to stop that? I couldn't think of anything I could do.

When she motioned to the chair, I just sat stupidly in my seat. *Passive resistance...*

But Miranda just motioned to the guard inside the door, and he walked over and took my arm and pulled me out of my chair as if I were a sack to be slung onto a cart, except he slung me into the chair and clicked the restraints in place before I could blink twice. Meanwhile she had risen from her chair and walked around the desk toward me, the smile back on.

"This isn't terribly unpleasant." She touched a place on the wall and a door slid open to reveal a rolling cart, which she drew with her as she approached the chair. "Though the drugs we use do often make people quite nauseous. You're sure you don't want to just talk without the drugs?"

I looked away from her, turned my head so I could see out the window again. The mountains to the north sparkled white; so tall they never lost their winter snow. I longed to be there. The woman—Miranda, such a hard sound inside a deceptively soft word, it seemed to fit her very well, about as well as the stretchy pantsuit—stood just to the left of the chair I was strapped into. I shut my eyes and silently said *Raven, spirit helpers, Gram, if you can help me, help me now. Please help me know what to do.*

I felt her slide up my left sleeve and feel for the vein inside my elbow.

In my last conscious thought, I imagined drawing a cloak around myself and found that it became a bubble, a large bubble that enclosed me, and then I slipped, gleaming gold, under the water of the lake and sank gently to the bottom. Safe.

~

"What do you do in the resistance?" A penetrating voice, stabbing downward but sliding past. "Who is your contact?"

"I'm not resistance," I heard my own voice, slow, oddly thick.

"The lake!" Miranda's voice was loud and sharp. "Again, where is the lake?!"

I was slowly rising upward. Back to consciousness. I heard myself say quietly, "The lake is everywhere."

A quick burst of pain across my face. She must have slapped me. But I kept my eyes closed. "No one held here is ever able to hold back what we want," her voice said. It was a warning: she wasn't done with me.

I heard footsteps on the hard floor, receding.

After a moment a quiet man's voice said, "Get up."

I opened my eyes and saw the soldier who had brought me to the session. The woman called Miranda was no longer in the room. The restraints were off. I began to stand up and a wave of nausea broke over me. The soldier moved as if to pull me up, but I put my head down between my knees, held up one finger, and he waited. He'd probably learned from many other sessions that if you rushed the prisoner, you'd get thrown up on. What was an extra thirty seconds? I took several slow, deep breaths and felt better, then eased off the chair and stood on my feet. I followed him out the door and slowly down the hall.

Back in our room, I recounted the episode to Hannah and Cat, in a whisper, with our three heads close together because of course our room was monitored.

"But she'll try again," Hannah breathed next to me, looking like she was about to cry. I nodded, bumping Cat's head. True that. So what to do?

Pray to Raven, I heard Gram's voice. That was all I could do at the moment.

"Do you know where Billy is?" I asked, suddenly fearing for him.

"He got picked up, too, but he's on the other side of this wall and he's okay," Cat breathed.

"Oh, thank God." And Raven. Though I was sorry that Billy, too, had been captured.

~

An hour later the three of us were led down the hall to a room with showers and lockers. Female guards watched us as we stripped off our clothes and pulled on the gray jumpsuits and light boots they handed out. And then the daily routine began: we were kept for twenty-two hours a day in our room, which was about ten feet by eight feet, furnished only with three sleeping pads and a slop bucket. In the mornings we'd pile our sleeping pads up against the wall on the other side of Billy's room so that we had a sitting space and a pacing place. Hannah remarked that it actually was more space than we had in our bedroom end at the project. I found that if I stood right up to window slit that ran from floor to ceiling at the end of our room, I could see the mountain range to the east. I spent a lot of my time there.

We were out of our room for two one-hour sessions a day: one hour we were outside in a fenced-in pen, and for the other hour we filed into an auditorium to sit on cold metal chairs, women on one side, men on the other, to listen to what was called *Re-Education*. It was like our weekly project citizens' group on steroids, to borrow a Billy expression. Guards with stunners lined the walls but the crowd (I guessed there were about fifty of us women and perhaps twice that number of men) always felt subdued, even stunned you could say, by the loud music and bright images that played through the air in the middle of the huge room, in between us. I couldn't help watching with interest—so many places I'd never seen, glittering cities rising above the sea, and one rising in every color imaginable above a desert, people working together to build things like gardens on rooftops in the sky or praying in a church easily one hundred times the size of the auditorium, whose windows were entirely glass. There was never a sign of poverty or illness, never a person who wasn't white-skinned. And yet on a dais at the center of the room, when the pictures faded, sat a dozen natives or Hispanics—like most of us prisoners—wearing the Orion uniform. They were the ones who talked every day about how there was a new life out there for us to live, and we would soon have a chance to prove that we had

197

rehabilitated and were ready for that new life.

"They're using us against us," Cat whispered in my ear on that first day in the auditorium. "They want us to believe we have a choice."

"Doesn't seem like anyone in this crowd will opt for it," Hannah whispered from my other side.

Cat and Hannah and I all agreed that it was vital that we hide from Orion even the suspicion that any of us had any kind of paranormal ability. Cat said it was the kind of place that would keep you and experiment on you, and maybe even do things like clone you, if they had any idea that you had abilities that were out of the ordinary. Billy especially would have to work as hard as he could to stay under the radar. Cat allowed him only one thing: very slowly, over two days, as he sat with his back against the wall between us, he used his mind to thin the metal plates covering an air duct about a foot above the floor and halfway down the wall, so that we could sit on the floor with our backs against the wall and whisper back and forth.

On our second morning in that tiny room, Cat said quietly from the pile of our sleeping pads, "Oh, poor Sadie. She's going to assume the worst."

"Well," Hannah said, "she wouldn't be too far from wrong, would she?"

I couldn't help laughing. Then all three of us were laughing. When we were done, Cat heard Billy whisper from his side, "What the fuck was *that*? Send me some!"

Three times a day small trays holding bread and water were pushed through a slot in the door; at night we got an additional dish of beans.

"Maybe I'll finally be able to lose a little weight," Hannah commented, with an unexpected flash of humor.

I took hope from that. She had Seen us here, but one night she whispered to Cat and me that she also had Seen us escaping, so there *was* hope. Though when I pressed her about the details of the escape, she just shook her head, and in the thin greenish light that came through our window slit I could see that she looked troubled.

I tried not to pace the cell; sometimes I forgot, and caught a quick look from Hannah which told me to cease and desist, more loudly than anything she could have whispered. I spent most of my waking time looking forward to the one hour of every day when we were released from our room and marched down the halls and outside into a paved yard enclosed on three sides by a tall wire fence. As we were in the auditorium, we were segregated by gender for our outdoor time. If it was raining, there was an overhang of roof that we sheltered under, a long line of us shivering in our gray jumpsuits. Even on those days I was happy to be out and breathing the damp air, hearing the hush of rain falling, smelling it on pavement; standing in the rain was infinitely preferable to our tiny room. And even though we were facing the city, I could smell the sea.

We would whisper back and forth and down the line—*what are you here for? where are you from? Are you nearing home? do you know...?*— giving names of loved ones, hoping for connections, but never giving our own names because as Miranda had said, *no one held here is ever able to keep back what we want.*

It turned out that about a half of us were resistance, another handful were the unlucky in-the-wrong-place-at-the-wrong-time ones, and two never said a word and felt so distant and dark that I was sure they were terrorists, which Cat confirmed.

A captured grounder told me that she had been at P1 for nearly a year, longer than anyone else there, and she was worried because a number of people had vanished over her year there, but she'd never seen them go... no one freed, declared rehabilitated, walking away out a gate, waving at those left behind, watching, hoping for themselves. *They just disappear*, she said.

A week later, I looked for her while we were all outside for our hour, and couldn't find her. She had been small, slender, dark-haired; she'd gone by the name Roxanne; no one knew her well. We never saw her again.

Billy said that a grounder told him that the week before we arrived, three grounders tried escaping out the main gate—the only entrance or exit through the Fence—and all were shot. They'd said before they tried it that they considered a one percent chance of succeeding worth it; getting shot to death was beginning to look like the better option.

~

Days passed. I began to hope that maybe Miranda had forgotten about me. But no.

It was a different guard this time—but always they were white, and, I assumed, Christian—leading me down the hall until a door opened on my right and he pointed with his stunner for me to go into the room and sit down and wait for Miranda. And this time she sailed into the room in a pale green pantsuit, just as stretchy-tight as the other one, with the same small black shoes with heels that clicked on the floor, that oddly seemed a little like hooves.

No pleasant talk today, though; she barely bothered with the smile and the small talk, and ordered the guard to put me in the chair. She drew the rolling cart over to her side and rummaged amongst the vials and packages—I looked away, not wanting to think about what was coming next. Slow, deep breaths and pray to Raven and all my spirit helpers... I felt the needle's cold jab of pain in my left elbow, the drug working so quickly, a heavy curtain coming down over my brain. I had just enough time to see the bubble closing around me, protecting me, slipping me under the lake.

~

Bright light. A sensation of pain just on the other side... so close, but not quite touching me. I heard Gram saying, *Tessa, this is* not *the time to pay attention. This is the time to disappear...*

Miranda's voice said, "This isn't working. Get a gurney and take her to the scanner."

I drew a slow breath and saw the bubble around me. I was underwater, but there was so much light; in the bubble, I was resting on a shelf of the lake bottom, about the depth I'd been in when I went through the ice as a child, but no fear this time, the same golden light shining down through the water and a feeling of peace and protection. I was safe here. The water was darker down below me, but I felt no fear of that, either. Tiny wiggling things swam toward me as if to greet me, looking in through the bubble, salmon fry. I smiled at them. *Stay safe, little salmon. Maybe you should consider staying in this lake and not heading out to the sea... you'll be safe in this lake.*

~

I woke up on my back on a hard metal table, on the other side of a sleek white dome that was humming, but quieting, as if it had just been switched off. My feet were almost in it. I was pretty sure I'd been inside there, and I was so grateful that I hadn't been aware, since being in small spaces is—well, not exactly something I enjoy.

Thank you, Raven, I thought. *Thank you, Gram, for being with me.*

And then I remembered that Jesse had been with me. I had been back in the tent glowing with sunrise light, hearing Jesse softly tell me the story of Bluejay the healer. Tears filled my eyes and then spilled over, down my cheeks.

Thank you, Jesse, I added.

"Get up." A male voice from just off my left shoulder.

I stirred, and felt a wave of nausea. A stunner poked my left ribs. Maybe it wouldn't be so bad, throwing up on this guy, I thought as I struggled to swing my legs over the hard edge of the table and sat up.

The room whirled around me. Closing my eyes helped a little.

"Move it," the guard's voice came again.

So I slowly slid down until my feet touched the floor, but my knees buckled and I went down all the way, just barely catching myself with my right hand to keep from smacking my head on the floor. Large, strong hands grabbed at my waist and pulled me upwards. I heard a second man's voice, then felt myself being pressed into the cool, smooth plastic of a wheelchair. I kept my eyes closed against the bright light and the whirlies, and let them cart me down the halls like a piece of baggage.

Hannah had Seen us in machines, I was thinking. Hopefully just me and not Hannah and Cat. She'd said something about Orion studying our brains. I wondered what they saw in my brain. Hopefully the bubble had protected me... but there was no way of knowing.

~

A few days after this, feeling more or less like my normal self again, I was sitting in between Cat and Hannah at our regular evening Re-Education. The usual cadre of non-white Orion guards walked among us, trying to look like friendly advertisements for the good life we could have if we only raised our hands and said that yes, we'd like to join Orion. The usual holo-picture show was going on in the middle of the auditorium, with its heavily rhythmic music pulsing through us. We'd spotted Billy in the men's crowd across from us, which was reassuring. He was sitting as he usually did, next to several big native guys who reminded me an awful lot of Jesse's uncles about twenty years ago, though I don't remember Jesse's uncles having the number of tattoos these guys had. Anyway, it was reassuring to see Billy, to think, *At least we're still here together...*

Then the images changed. Blue skies over green mountains, we swooped low over thick green forests with a bird's eye view, over alpine meadows filled with nodding blue wildflowers. There was a rushing mountain stream ahead and we zoomed in closer and closer, and then we were there, in the middle of rushing water, jagged mountain peaks rising beyond, and a man was standing there in the rushing water, in a rubber suit with a fishing pole over his shoulder.

The pulsing music stopped. "Hi!" the man said. "I'm Leeland Freeman, your president, the CEO of Orion and the Forty-Six United States of America."

A stir ran through the crowd around me, a ripple of laughter— on the men's side too—this just seemed so incongruous, so faked. Near me a dark-skinned Orion guard frowned.

"I want to talk with you about how much Orion is doing for our environment," the man continued.

Oh this *is going to be good!* I thought.

"No one has worked harder over the past decades than Orion has to clean the air you breathe, to clean the mountain streams like this one..."

Anger spiked through me. What a colossal lie!

"Orion is leading the way in the protection of the forests, which protects against erosion and helps protect the wild creatures of the forests, too."

"They don't give a damn about the forests and the wild creatures!" I couldn't help saying to Hannah and Cat.

"Shhhh," Hannah said from my right.

"Orion is working hard to keep the oceans clean, to protect the fish and the sealife," the man went on.

"Bullshit!" I said.

"Shhhh," Cat said from my left.

The man looked right into the camera, right into our eyes. "We are working with you to be good stewards of the environment."

"This is bullshit!" someone yelled. "What a fucking liar!"

It was me. I was on my feet, yelling. I have no idea how it happened. Hannah and Cat were grabbing at my arms, but I was still standing there, yelling, "It's all bullshit!"

Hannah and Cat were trying to pull me down into my chair, but I shook them off. I heard shouts and some laughter from Billy's corner, and I thought, *hey, maybe the spell is broken and...*

That's when a guard stunned me. Everything went completely black and pain ran through every nerve in my body. But as I went unconscious, I thought, *This definitely was worth it.*

~

I woke up in solitary confinement. The room was about six feet by six feet, all white with the usual too-bright ceiling lights which were always on, and there was no window slit now. There was a slop bucket, but no sleeping pad. My whole body ached from the stunning.

I closed my eyes again and kept lying there on the hard floor, my head pillowed on one arm. Okay... here I was... it was doubtful that I was getting out of this room any time soon. I definitely would not miss Re-Education; I would rather die than go back to that. But I would miss that hour outside every day. And I didn't think I could live without Hannah and Cat.

But here I was, so I needed to figure out how to be here and stay myself. Stay Tessa. *They have me, but they don't have me...*

I would go back to the lake. Raven was there, Gram was there, the stories were there. It was all inside of me. Even in this god-awful room, it was with me.

The stories of raven as trickster didn't help as much as the stories of Étain in her isolation and banishment, after she had been transformed into a fly. Meditating on the old Celtic story, I was Étain. I was deep in love with the god Midir who walked among men, but the evil witch Fuamnach, who happened to be married to Midir, had cast that spell on me that changed me into a fly. Étain, as a fly, brought healing—*she shed from her wingtips a spray of droplets that would cure sickness in anyone she went with.*

The part of the story I kept forgetting. She brought healing.

I, as Étain, tried to stay with Midir, who knew and loved me even as a fly, but then the witch caused such a wind that I was blown far, far from the green land... For seven years I could not rest. I was tossed and tumbled over clouds, and when I could finally look about, all I saw was the stormy gray sea. I had no home, no family, no beloved Midir. I had no place where I could rest. It was all I could do to stay in the air above that cold sea. Alone.

Midir's foster son, Aengus, found me. That's when I slept in the sun-bower and felt the *lustre of happiness* return.

But the witch found me there, *she summoned up the same wind as before so that the fly was carried out of her sun-bower and lashed about the sky in misery and weakness.*

But again I found sanctuary, this time all on my own. I settled onto the house of the King of Ulster and dropped into the golden cup that his wife was drinking from, and nine months later she gave a new birth to me, Étaîn. I was again a woman. *And they say it was a thousand and twelve years from the first begetting of Étaîn until her last begetting...*

She was a healer. She ended up with Midir, her one true love.

This is where I was during those days or weeks of isolation.

9. May 13–14, 2111

In my sleep, I dreamed of distant explosions. I felt the floor tremble beneath me. Explosions or earthquakes. I slept on.

Then I heard Hannah's voice, whispering.

"We've got our diversion, Tess! Can you wake up and walk? We need to get moving!"

I opened my eyes. It really was Hannah, crouched next to me in my cell.

"How'd you get in here?" I managed to ask. "I thought I was completely sealed in."

She smiled. "Cat," she whispered. "She's got all of the codes." She was close so we could keep whispering in case—no, it was certain—the room was monitored. "It's been two weeks! Are you all right? Can you walk?"

I sat up. I gave her a *How can we possibly get out without being caught?* look.

"We've got a plan," she whispered.

I couldn't understand how it was possible, but I had to trust. But I kept wondering what had I missed in those two weeks? What was going on? Were those really explosions that I thought I'd dreamed of?

As Hannah led me down the empty corridor, she told me the utility door code, just in case (*just in case of what?* I wondered, but kept quiet since she was so intent). I tried as hard as I could to focus, so I'd remember it. Unlike Hannah, I'd always had a hard time with numbers, which felt like a language I'd never been able to learn. That was the real reason at Whitewater Bay that I always got the jet with the busted altimeter—I didn't need to use numbers to know how high I was off the ground, as long as I could see the ground, of course.

Cat met us in the stairwell at the end of the long corridor. *Where is everybody?* I wondered. *How can we be walking around the halls like this?*

Cat touched my cheek, her eyes smiling at me. "Tessa, dear, it's our hour break so we were let outside, but Hannah and I got back in... well, things are a little crazy here right now." Her whisper was overwhelmed by the high whine of a jopter landing closeby.

"Those explosions..." I began.

She nodded. "The resistance. Finally some big action!"

"That's the second jopter in fifteen minutes!" Hannah said in my ear. "Huge emergency response to Orion headquarters, just a few blocks away. Most of the soldiers are over there, too, so that's good for us."

I followed Cat and Hannah quickly down two flights of stairs, which by my reckoning put us on the basement level. My knees felt a little shaky, but I was ready for anything.

"Billy?" I asked Hannah, who was off my right elbow. How were we going to connect with Billy?

"We're going to wait for the men to go out on their hour break and nab him then," was all she said. I was sure glad she and Cat seemed so confident with their plan; my own brain would not work.

Through the heavy metal door and another brightly lit corridor ran straight ahead. It was quickly intersected on the left by another equally bright white corridor, with a lot of doors opening on both sides of it. We hurried past.

I kept thinking, *Okay, we got out of our rooms, but how are we going to get out of the building? And how the hell are we going to get past the Fence?*

"We're going to hijack a jopter," Cat said quietly. "You're going to fly us out of here, Tessa."

Holy shit.

Then, as we hurried as quickly but quietly as we could down the corridor, we heard a door shut behind us. We all whipped around—no one. It must have been a door on the intersecting corridor, which meant that someone was likely to come around the corner back there and see us in just a few seconds...

There were two doors on our right—closets or some other little rooms—no door handles or anything easy like that. But Cat knew the door codes. Her fingers flew over the touch pad of the first door and it slid open. The three of us tumbled in. The door sealed shut behind us. It was pitch dark.

"Jesus, Joseph and Mary!" I'd learned that expression from Jesse when we were kids and hadn't used it since then. I had to consciously take slow deep breaths or I was going to pass out.

A moment later we heard footsteps, faint through the door, pass us and continue down the corridor.

"Oh my God," I breathed. "That was close."

Cat pushed a button on the wall and the door slid open. She

slowly looked out, left and then right, then motioned us out. The three of us started down the corridor again, then heard another door slam, and loud voices this time. We scurried back to the closet we'd just left and the door sealed shut behind us, and again it was pitch dark.

"I hope we aren't stuck in here for hours," I couldn't help whispering. What if we missed our chance to get Billy?

Footsteps and voices went by outside the door. Just as they were fading away, we heard more approaching. We could only hope that Orion didn't know we were on the loose, but even if they didn't, once the women's outside hour was up, the alarm would go out for Hannah and Cat. And wasn't my isolation room monitored?

"We've had incredible luck so far," I whispered once the voices were past, "but I can't imagine that's going to hold..."

Hannah laughed softly on my left. "I don't think it was luck, Tessa."

"And you think some Superior Being is going to help us figure out what to do now?"

"No, I think it's up to us to figure it out."

"Shhh," from Cat. "I think I just heard more voices coming."

"Cat, see if there's a light switch." I had a sudden idea. "I want to have a better look around this closet."

I felt her move away so she could find the panel next to the door. The door didn't open; a light didn't come on. Instead there was a faint hum, and the dipping sensation in my stomach told me we were in motion.

"I think I hit the wrong button," Cat said.

"This is an elevator!"

"Don't panic, Tess," Hannah sounded calm and composed. "What are the chances of the doors opening on our floor—one in three?" There were two floors of prisoners and our floor had been the lowest one of the two.

"I thought you didn't believe in chance!"

"Shut up! We will either get out on our floor, or the next one above us, and maybe we can just wait in here until everyone comes in from our hour break."

"But since this is an elevator, aren't we at risk for someone calling it while we're in it?" Cat knew elevators better than we did.

Silence.

We were still rising. "I have a feeling we're going to the top floor," I said. "What's up there, Cat?"

"Orion offices," was all she said. More silence. *Out of the frying pan and into the fire*, Gram used to say.

The elevator ride was so smooth it was hard to know when we'd stopped. We waited in the dark for the doors to slide open.

"Tessa, you hold the doors open, when they open," Cat said. "As soon as I can see, I'll try to hit the right button on the panel."

"Be ready to do it as quickly as you can and maybe no one will notice us up here," I said.

We waited for the doors to open. They didn't open.

"What the hell?" I said. "Now what do we do?"

In the pitch dark I heard the sound of Cat hitting buttons on the control panel.

"Nothing's working," she said.

Silence. Then a man's voice said my name. It sounded like it was coming from above us, and it sounded like someone trying to be quiet.

"Tessa, can you hear me?"

There was no mistaking it. I'll admit that my first thought was that it was a ghost. All of the little hairs on my arms and neck felt like they were standing straight up.

"Tessa, it's me, Jesse. I'm above you."

All three of us moved, in the pitch dark, at the same time, bumping into each other.

"Don't make a sound!" I hissed to the others. "They sent someone to lure us out!"

"Shhhhh," Cat's voice said. "It's not Orion. It's someone who's telling the truth, who wants to help us."

"I've Seen this!" Hannah whispered, then raised her voice and directed it to the ceiling, "If that's you, Jesse, prove it."

There was a pause. Then the voice said, "Tessa, you liked the Bluejay story I told you on our first night on the trail."

"No!" I said, not caring if I was too loud, ignoring the hushing from Cat on one side of me and Hannah on the other. "That was a memory I had in the machine, and they could have it!"

Another pause, then, "Tessa, you felt guilty when Bobby and I overturned in the lake. You told me it was supposed to be you, not me, and you felt guilty about it. You gave me your pin."

"Oh for heaven's sake," Hannah's voice said, "that is Jesse, Tessa, whether you want to believe it or not."

There was a scrabbling sound over our heads, then the beam of a batt-light shone down on us.

"But how did you get here?" Hannah asked.

Jesse's voice said, "I was in the wall—I got over here from the Command Center, through the utility corridor and inside the walls—and I heard your voices in the elevator on the other side of the wall and I came through the crawl space door and cut the power."

It couldn't be Jesse! I'd seen him hit by a train. Seen his body tossed high in the air and hit a second time by the same fucking train. Not survivable. Not by a human.

"Do you all have a plan for escaping?" Jesse—if it was Jesse—asked.

"Yes," Hannah replied for us. "Though we're kind of stalled in this elevator."

"I think you'd better get out of there before someone forces the doors open to see what's wrong with the elevator. I'll help you climb up to me," Jesse's voice said. "I've opened the ceiling up just enough so you can get through, but I think I can close it up after you're through and hopefully no one will notice. That will give us some time."

"Believe him, Tessa," Cat whispered from close on my left. "He's telling the truth. He came here disguised as Orion, he's just shot three Orion guards and somehow made it over here without getting caught, and all of this because he's trying to get you out of here."

"It can't be Jesse," I said. "Jesse was killed by a train."

"What train?" Jesse's voice said from above us. He shone his batt-light down on me. "What train, Tessa?"

"You see!?" my voice cracked. "That is *not* Jesse!"

Hannah slapped me across the face. Tears blinded me, then anger. I wanted to hit her back.

"Pull yourself together, Tessa!" she hissed. "Trust him now. We can talk later!"

Jesse reached down through the opening. "We've got to move as quickly as possible. Tessa, you first."

I took two steps forward and reached up for his hand, put my right foot up on the railing as he told me to do, and pushed off as he pulled me up through the ceiling. He'd set the batt-light down on the roof of the elevator so he could use both hands, and it was shining on a concrete wall three feet in front of me. I saw, dimly, three more concrete walls boxing us in, but metal rungs led upward from one wall into darkness above.

There was just enough light to see Jesse standing in front of me. I stared. When I had last been with him, Jesse, at eighteen, was more of a boy than a man. Now here was a man just turned thirty, so tall, with broad shoulders, but lean. As I stared, he quickly tied back his thick, black hair warrior-style, a familiar gesture. Jesse's hair, Jesse's eyes, Jesse's voice.

Something pale in the dark was lying at his feet, and I leaned forward to see that it was a blond wig. He was wearing the black Orion uniform, and he'd been wearing that wig. He was staring back at me. Suddenly I saw what I looked like to him—dirty, in a baggy prison issue jumpsuit, don't-fuck-with-me spiky hair and attitude to match.

He reached out an arm; I moved back, automatically. He dropped his arm.

"Whatever it was, Tessa... I can see it was bad. I'm sorry, but this *is* me. I thought you were dead, too." He took a breath. "Until six weeks ago when Emmitt told me you'd been sighted in the train station. So, I've had the advantage, knowing you were alive. Though knowing you were here..." His voice trailed off and I saw him shake his head in another characteristic Jesse way, what he did when he was trying to clear his mind and think better.

I still couldn't find any words.

"Climb that ladder," he told me. "There's a trap door above it, push it open with your head and shoulders and climb through it. The small room up there is safe, for the moment."

He turned and bent down to help Cat and Hannah.

I started climbing up into the darkness. The air was chill and stagnant. I had just enough balance and strength to use one hand to push open the trap door when I bumped into it, letting it rest open on my shoulders as I clambered through it. I stayed there, holding it open for the others. Jesse came up last, with the batt-light in his teeth. In the dark he looked more like an Indian warrior than I've ever seen anyone look.

He paused next to me when he saw me looking at him, took the light out of his mouth and said, "It *is* me, Tessa. Since I heard you were alive and here, I haven't lived an hour without thinking of you." His mouth twisted more than smiled. "All my life I haven't lived an hour without thinking of you."

I opened my mouth to say something, but still I could find no words. If by some miracle this really was Jesse, it would be the happiest moment of my life, even if Orion guards were behind the next door and about to shoot me dead. But something in me just couldn't quite believe. Couldn't understand how it could be possible.

He nodded. "Hopefully we'll have time to talk later." Then he looked at Hannah and Cat, holding the light up so we could all see each other. "So what's your escape plan?" he asked.

"Tessa's going to fly us out in a jopter," Hannah said.

Jesse raised his eyebrows, then he looked at me.

"It's their plan," I said. "I've been in solitary confinement for a while so I'm kind of out of it."

Jesse blinked, then looked at Hannah. "How are you getting to the jopters?"

"After we grab Billy, we wait for dark and make a run for it."

Jesse looked surprised again. "Who's Billy?" So we all quickly explained who Billy was and why we couldn't leave without him.

Jesse shook his head. "I doubt making a run for it between the barracks and the Command Center would work, even with the guard numbers reduced as they are right now."

There was a small pause.

"I am a pilot though," I felt like I should add. "If I had a jopter, I could fly one."

Jesse smiled a little. "Why am I not surprised?" He looked at me a moment longer. "And what other hare-brained, idiotic brave things have you been doing in the past eleven years?"

It was Jesse. No one else talked that way; any last doubts in my mind vaporized. I didn't understand about the train, but this was Jesse.

Alguien vendria, alguien vendria... (Neruda came back to me)... Someone would come, someone would come... Someone had come.

Tears filled my eyes and ran down my face, all I could see was Jesse's face in front of me, the smile in his brown eyes. I took one step closer—that's all it took—and put my arms around him, reached up to lightly kiss his mouth. His arms went around me and he kissed me back, warm and deep. Home.

Then Hannah cleared her throat, and I stepped backward. Everyone was looking at me. "I'm sorry I doubted it was you, Jesse," I told him.

He reached a hand to quickly touch my cheek, and smiled. Then said, "Okay. I have a better plan for getting to the Command Center. If you all can figure out how to get Billy without giving us away."

He had studied diagrams of P1 for two weeks, planning how he'd come in and get us out when the resistance bombs went off at Orion headquarters. There was a utility corridor that ran between the barracks and the Command Center—he'd just used it. To get to it, we had to climb down four floors, inside a wall. It was going to be narrow and steep, with rungs like the ones we just came up, but for four floors. It would be pitch dark and—here he shone his batt-light right on my face—we would have to be absolutely silent so as not to give ourselves away. Then we'd have to crawl through the utility corridor that went underground between the barracks and the Command Center.

"First we have to get Billy," Hannah whispered.

~

I sat down on the cool concrete floor and let the others figure that one out. Cat and Hannah made me proud, though, in that they had most of it figured out by themselves—the small utility door at the end of the building, under the overhang where prisoners often hung out, would work if Billy could fit through it, and Cat would try to get close enough on the other side of the wall to be able to call to Billy mind-to-mind (Jesse raised his eyebrows at this, but took it all in stride). Jesse supplied the safe route through the building utility spaces.

And it worked. The four of us slowly climbed down the metal rungs built into the concrete outside wall, to the ground floor, crawled through a vent to a closet at the end of the ground floor corridor. I was voted the one to open the outer utility door for Billy, who meanwhile was edging to the end of the line of gray-clad prisoners leaning against the building wall. It was dusk now and the light at that end of the building was dim. He bent down to tie a bootlace.

I slid open the small door, praying he could fit through it.

"Hey Billy," I whispered. "We're escaping. Want to come?"

He was grinning as he squeezed in. Somehow no one saw—

maybe that was Cat. In fact, I'm sure that was Cat. She said she'd been working on *gentle distractions*, as she called them, though she promised she never used us as her test subjects.

"Good to see you again, Tessa!" Billy whispered as he squeezed past me. "I just want you to know that you're a hero to the guys in my section."

I didn't know what to say to that, except that if it was the big, tattooed native guys he was talking about, well, that struck me as pretty funny. When Billy was safely in, there wasn't space in the closet for a handshake between Billy and Jesse—the two of them couldn't fit in the closet together—but they smiled at each other in the light of Jesse's batt-light, past Cat's and Hannah's heads, and said hello.

"We're climbing down one more floor to where we pick up the utility corridor," Jesse whispered, and disappeared down the wall crawl space.

"How could that be your Jesse, Tessa?" Billy whispered as we waited our turn. "I thought he died."

I grinned. "Turns out I was wrong!"

I was the last one down, pulling the trap door shut behind me. The space at the bottom of the wall rungs was so small that by the time I got down there, Jesse had already started leading the way through the utility corridor underground between the two buildings. Cat whispered to me from the low doorway that we'd be on our hands and knees for quite some way, and it would be dark, but she'd be right in front of me. I hesitated for just a second. I hated tiny spaces.

"It's okay, Tess," Cat whispered, and clasped my hand. "You can reach forward and touch my boots. I'll be right there in front of you."

Thank you, I thought.

So we started crawling. I tried to pretend there weren't metal pipes inches above my head, that the walls weren't just a few inches to either side of me, that the concrete floor wasn't so hard and sending sharp pains through my kneecaps. The concrete smelled damp, with a hint of mold.

My brain kept spinning out disaster scenarios. We could be shot as soon as we came out in the Command Center; that's where Jesse already had been involved in a fire fight. That's where they stored all their weapons, come to think of it. But we had to go there because that's where the main gate was, and the jopters. But if we couldn't hijack a jopter, how the hell were we going to get out the main gate? I hoped Jesse had a plan of his own. He was doing so well, but what if we got there and realized none of our plans were going to work?

I made myself take deep, calming breaths. I said a silent prayer: *Raven, you've always heard me, please hear me now...*

We were all crawling on our hands and knees under the pipes. I wondered how Billy was managing to fit. We kept going. Slowly. My knees were killing me. I would have bruises on them for weeks. Still, it beat all of the alternatives.

Finally Cat's feet weren't in front of me, cooler air touched my face. I managed a stiff crouch out of the low corridor and into a larger space where I could stand up next to the others, though it was very narrow.

"Command Center utility space," Jesse whispered in the darkness.

A tiny light glowed next to me—he was checking the time on his wristpad.

"This is where we have to kill a little time until full dark," he said. "Might as well sit down, get comfortable if you can." He clicked on his batt-light and kept it partly covered with the fingers of one hand, to give just enough light for us to see each other.

Hannah, Cat, Billy, Jesse, we were all there in that tiny space, everyone with their backs against a wall. I reached out behind me to a space against a cool wall, and sat down on the concrete floor—at least it was dry here—with the wall at my back and my feet on the other side of Billy's as he sat against the opposite wall. Hannah was next to Billy, Cat was close on my left, Jesse was close on my right.

What was the plan? I was dying to know, even if Hannah jumped on me for talking.

"How did you cut the elevator power so quickly?" I had about fifty questions for Jesse, but that's the one that came out.

"For heaven's sake, Tessa—" Hannah started, but Jesse said, "I've got a knife strapped above each boot. Easy." Then he added, "I've got a gun, too."

"Good!" a whispered burst from Billy.

After a little pause, Jesse whispered, "Raven, tell me about the train."

Cat tapped soft fingers on my left knee. "Maybe I can help you both figure out what happened."

Shards of thought blew around my mind—*we're in the wrong place*...a metallic singing luring us to our deaths...a train, bigger than Earl's barn, a hundred times louder than my screaming...Jesse's body flung high into the air by it, then the cruelty of it hitting him again and throwing him higher until he disappeared into the darkness on the other side—*No, start at the beginning,* I heard from Cat, and took a breath.

"It was still dark, before dawn," I whispered. "We'd come down the trail out of the mountains but we were on the wrong trail; we'd missed the one your father told us to take. We came to the train line, though we didn't know that's what it was. There was a bridge in front of us, a bank of melted snow and moss. You wanted to climb up to see what was at the top of the bank..."

Jesse's hand touched my right hand in the dark, gently wrapped around it. "I think I might remember that," he whispered.

Cat leaned against my left shoulder.

"There was a high pitched, metallic singing sound, almost too high to hear, getting louder and louder." I was breathing as fast as if I'd been running.

"You climbed up the bank, wanting to see what it was, telling me to stay back, and the sound was driving me almost crazy... and then it was on us, so fast we couldn't do a thing. It hit you and threw you up in the air—"

The image that would haunt me for the rest of my life.

I couldn't speak.

"It was the force field that hit him!" Cat's voice whispered in the dark. "Not the train. That's why he didn't die."

"What's a force field?"

"It's like an energy envelope, sheer power created by something so big moving so fast," from Billy.

"But she said it hit me a second time," Jesse whispered.

"Right. So if you'd been standing just a step farther back, the force field would have thrown you backwards, but you must have been standing just close enough for it to throw you upwards and pulled you in a bit, where you hit the force field again, high up in the air above the train. But if you'd been any closer on the bank initially, you would have been sucked in, and, well, you wouldn't be here talking with us." Cat paused.

Billy nodded. "That's exactly right."

We were silent for a moment.

"But you must have been hurt terribly, even so!" I whispered to Jesse.

"Oh yeah. Broke both legs and got a concussion I still suffer from. Headaches."

"So you never could remember what happened?"

"No. Don't even remember the first couple days after the sailors picked me up."

"Sailors picked you up?!"

"Yeah. Resistance navy. Two of them were on an airbike coming through there in a hurry, not supposed to be there exactly, saw me and thought they'd give me a quick check. You know why they picked me up, Raven?"

I shook my head in the dark, then said, "No. Why?"

Jesse let go of my right hand, and clicked on his batt-light, mostly covered with his fingers to shine just enough light on something he held out for me to see. It was great great grampa Silloway's Viking pin. I reached out and took it from him, and turned it over in the light he was shining to see where I'd scratched on its back (with Gram's best kitchen knife) *J from T.*

"Turns out," Jesse whispered, "great great grampa Silloway had something to do with starting up the resistance navy. These guys picked me up because of the pin you gave me when we were kids. I was wearing it inside my shirt."

I started crying. When your heart overflows, there's nothing else you can do. Jesse turned and put his arms around me, pulled me in against his warm chest and held me for a long time, until the shaking sobs stopped and I could breathe without making noise.

Then I told Jesse how I'd been picked up by resistance aviators passing through with such haste that they couldn't risk picking up his body—so they said. So the air force had picked up me, and the navy had picked up Jesse.

I still had a thousand questions for him, such as how he got himself into P1, right when we needed him most, but it was twenty-three hundred hours and time to move.

"I don't suppose any of you has been in the Command Center before?" Jesse asked, before we all got up.

None of us had. He said that if all went well, we wouldn't see the inside of the building anyway, just stay in the walls like we were.

"They have regular shipments, by truck, out at midnight on weekdays," he whispered. "My plan was to smuggle you onto a truck." He paused. I noticed the past tense, and was pretty sure the others had noticed, too.

"Now there's four of you and I won't lie and say it's going to be easy, but we're going to try to make it work."

"But there are the jopters," I said.

"Yes." Jesse got to his feet. "That's plan B."

To get to the side of the building where the loading bay was, we had to climb up three floors—metal rungs in the concrete wall just the other side of Jesse, like the barracks building, but only three floors this time—then traverse the roof of the Command Center, then descend through the wall on the main gate side. The access panel in that wall opened to the bay where trucks were loaded and unloaded.

"There are surveillance cameras on the roof," Jesse said, "so you have to follow exactly where I tell you."

"How do you know these things?" I couldn't help asking as we all stood up. Hannah reached across Cat to pull on my sleeve, but Jesse whispered back,

"We've had resistance grounders undercover here from time to time."

I heard the rustle of Jesse standing up. "But if you're navy, why are *you* here?"

"For heaven's sake, Tessa!" Hannah hissed.

Jesse smiled. "I switched forces a year and a half ago, left the sea and came back here."

"Why?"

"You called me."

"What?"

"You don't remember? It was so clear—I heard your voice. I knew you were alive. I got Emmitt to start hunting for you on the feeds from all of our resistance drones in the city."

I was speechless. For the moment.

"Let's move." Jesse whispered as he headed for the rungs in the wall, and we followed.

We climbed up three floors, this time with Billy going first and Jesse bringing up the rear. We followed Jesse across the dark roof, zigzagging, using the blocky ventilator units and other taller but narrower projectile shapes for cover. The cool, damp sea air smelled wonderful. I took deep breaths, picturing the bay so close to us on this dark and drizzly night, hearing the sounds from the nearby city docks—getting bumped by Hannah for taking too long. *Get with the program, Tessa!*

Then following Jesse, who was nearly invisible in Orion black, black hair pulled back from his face, slipping through a low door into another tiny utility room where we picked up the ladder down the wall to the ground floor loading bay... It was like a dream now. Or like being in one of Gram's stories—*and they transformed into shadows and slipped out through the window bars and into the cool night and flew away...*

There were jopters out there in the dark, on the tarmac between the Command Center and the Fence, waiting for us. I was pretty sure that was how we were going to get away. If I could get a jopter going and turn on the cloaking quickly enough, we might have a chance.

Jesse opened the door to the loading bay. Light seeped through under two doors about twenty feet away on the wall to our left, and I could dimly make out stacks of boxes in front of us. Huge shipping containers rose to the shadowy ceiling to our right. Jesse turned his head and looked at us.

"I don't suppose any of you has a gun?"

We all shook our heads. And I knew that even if I had one, I wouldn't be able to use it. I had relinquished the role of the warrior for ever.

"That's okay," Jesse whispered. "We're going to make this work." His eyes met mine. I heard him saying in the green-gold light in our tent along the trail, just before we were separated for eleven years, *I've got your back, Raven.*

Okay. I was ready.

"Actually, I don't have a gun, but I do have something," Billy said slowly to Jesse, and while they talked quietly, I looked around the room in front of me.

The huge ground floor loading bay had those two doors opening in to the Command Center, and a tall garage door with a small window next to it that looked out on the tarmac where the jopters were parked. Hannah and Cat and I stayed hidden behind the seven foot tall shipping containers at the back of the room while Jesse and Billy both edged over to the window next to the garage door, carrying their camouflage, smaller empty containers that they could hide behind if someone suddenly came through one of the doors.

"Hannah," I whispered. "Have you Seen anything that would help us now? Like how we get out of this room without being seen, and onto either a truck or a jopter?"

She did not look cheerful. She just shook her head, not making eye contact. Damn, I hated it when Hannah looked troubled by something.

And then all hell broke loose.

Light flooded down through the cavernous loading bay, the two doors at the Command Center end opened simultaneously, several Orion soldiers walked in carrying guns. They saw Jesse and Billy instantly, and took aim.

Cat, Hannah and I scurried back on our hands and knees through the low door we'd come through, back to the narrow wall space. We tangled together in the dark at the foot of the ladder. I looked back at the cavernous loading bay filled with pulsing light, pulsing sound, and Billy springing out from behind the small shipping container, roaring at the top of his lungs, I could hear him even above the sound of the Orion guns.

Hannah put her arms around me, to pull me back, and Cat shut the door behind us.

Metal crashed against concrete, slammed into walls, the floor shook under our feet. I prayed that it was Billy finally getting his chance.

Then there was a pause, and Jesse shouted my name. I pulled away from Hannah and Cat and crouch-stepped through the doorway. The room was unrecognizable—metal box shipping containers thrown everywhere, lying on their sides, upended, two against the Command Center doors—Jesse and Billy climbing over strewn objects and bodies, headed my way. Jesse handed Billy an Orion blaster and bent down to pick up another from an unrecognizable heap on the floor.

"Out the door to the jopters!" he yelled at me. "We'll cover you. Get the big one running. Here!" he tossed me his batt-light.

I wasn't sure why I needed the light as we went out the door onto the floodlit tarmac, but then Jesse and Billy, back to back, started shooting out the lights along the roof. Pops, smashes, shattering glass tinkled down everywhere. Every light shining out from the Command Center roof, every light on the Fence across the tarmac. Then they turned their guns on the soldiers who came pouring out of the lighted door of the Center, near the front gate. The gate clearly wasn't an escape option. An unlimited number of Orion soldiers headed our way from that direction.

Cat, Hannah and I dashed for the jopters. It wasn't as dark as you would think, for the Fence gave off its odd green glow, and the flashes from the blasters lit up the night like fireworks. As we neared the smaller jopter, the first one, I felt the strangest illusion of it moving past me as I came up on it, and then I realized it *was* moving––it was silently hovering just off the ground all by itself and moving backwards, in between us and the line of fire. Billy! I thought, and nearly laughed.

We reached the big jopter. I found the latch and hauled open the pilot's door with such force it smacked all the way open against the carbon fiber nose. Cat and Hannah scrambled in through the rear door, into the wide back seat big enough for three.

I sat in the pilot's seat and whispered, "Ancestors, Gram, Raven." Just those three words. *I'm not trying to kill anyone this night, I'm trying to save some people from being killed. Please help me?*

My hands instinctively reached for the controls. Hannah had taken Jesse's batt-light from me and was shining it over my right shoulder so I could see. I didn't want to bum her out by saying it, but I was realizing that since I'd flown jopters there had been so many changes to this machine that very little on the control panel looked familiar.

But I found the red light switch almost right away, and flicked that on so that red light filled the cockpit, enough to see for start-up but not enough to interfere with my night vision.

"Keep the batt-light away from me now, Hannah," I told her. "Thanks."

Ignition switch down on the left where it used to be... good thing they left these babies ready to go and didn't expect someone like me to come running out to pull off a hijack job. Power up and start the rotors...

I automatically glanced out to do a safety scan. Through my still-open door, over the increasing whine of the jet engine in the back of the jopter, I heard the slap of Jesse's and Billy's feet as they ran up to us. Then nothing but gunfire and the sound of ripping metal. The smaller jopter wavered in the air between us and the Command Center; bits of it flew off in the air toward us. It crashed heavily onto the tarmac. Fuel shone wet in the flashes from the Orion blasters. Billy stumbled and fell.

"Tess, don't look! Get us started!" Hannah was screaming in my ear.

Everything blurred. I scanned the computer screen in front of me—numbers were scrolling past on the screen and I had no idea what they meant. Shit, I'd been flying jets with hundred year old gauges, I couldn't remember anything about jopter computers...

I decided to fly by listening to the rpm's of the engine, and by looking ahead out the cockpit. The Fence glowed faint green in front of me. All I needed to do was fly high enough to clear it, and fast enough to clear the gunfire. I had my left hand closed around the throttle, powering it up gradually, and I had the stick in my right hand and it felt good, it felt like I would know what to do with it in a few seconds.

My hand was on the cloaking switch. I remembered it as a best friend. We had the rpm's for it now. I flicked it on, slammed shut my door and yelled over my shoulder to Hannah to keep the back door open so Jesse could see her.

Come on, Jesse, come on!

He was there, at the back door. He had Billy over his shoulder, was trying to stuff Billy through the door. Hannah and Cat were pulling Billy's limp body in.

"Come on! Come on!" I screamed at them.

More flashes of light and I felt the buffet of a blast glance off our nose.

Jesse was in. The rear door slammed shut. He smacked into my seat just as I pulled back on the stick, my hand jerked a little and we wavered forward and right—not into the Fence!—but just then a blast went right over our heads, something so big it would have blown us to bits right then and there. But it missed because we were still low.

Then I pulled back, hard, and we shot straight up and our stomachs all dropped away, our bodies slammed into our seats with the G force of going completely vertical at a thousand feet per ten seconds.

Jesse ended up in the co-pilot's seat next to me. "Holy fuck,

Tessa, is this how you fly jopters?!"

I resisted saying anything clever because I was trying really hard not to fuck up. The flash of a huge explosion below us lit up the night—buffeted us even higher—and dropped away so fast I could hardly believe it. *Ease up, ease up*, I was telling myself. *Get this baby under control...*

Then it was calmer, and quieter. We were flying straight and level, away from the city towers.

"Seatbelts!" I announced brightly. Cat muffled her laughter in the back. Then I heard Hannah saying something to Billy.

"How is he, Hannah?"

Cat leaned forward—clearly she had disregarded the seatbelt warning—"Not too bad a hit, Tessa. Unconscious but okay. If we can get him to a doctor soon, we think he'll be okay."

I looked over at Jesse. His face gleamed faintly in the green light given off by the computers on the control panel. He wiped a sleeve across it and took a deep breath.

"Tessa." He'd seen me looking at him. "Nice hijacking job." He grinned.

I scanned the computers for a second and found things looked a little more familiar. I saw that we were on a heading of two-zero-zero at five thousand feet and holding level. I looked back at Jesse.

"I'm so glad we're back together again. We make a good team, don't we?"

He reached out his left arm and squeezed my shoulder. "And the night's not over yet."

While I was pondering the possibility of double meanings to this, he said, "You're flying too high, aren't you?"

"No, I'm not. We're fine."

"What about Orion radar?"

"We're cloaked."

He stared at me for a second, then he said, "Tessa, there've been some changes since you last flew. Radar advances. Cloaking doesn't protect us from their ground radar now."

"Well shit! Now you tell me! How the hell are we going to get away?!"

And where was our radar screen that showed incoming? I had thought we were home free, and now panic began to climb up my throat again.

Jesse's hand was still on my shoulder. He squeezed it again. "Start descending now that you're away from the big buildings. Head for the sea."

I nodded that I understood. We'd try to go below radar. But that meant going awfully low...

I scanned out our windows, followed the midnight necklace strands of city lights down below us in all directions but one—that was the sea. My turn and descent maneuver was a bit abrupt for my passengers, but my nerves were telling me that we needed to book it out there to the dark sea as fast as possible.

Jesse lightly tapped a screen in front of him and I saw pale green dots blinking. We had a tail already. We were cloaked, they were cloaked, but we could all see each other on radar.

"Tighten your seatbelts," I said over my shoulder.

Dropping fast, through three thousand feet, two thousand feet, but we didn't want to go much lower until we were over the sea, just to be safe. There might be tall, unlighted things out there in the dark... At least we were flying away from the tall cranes on the city docks. We were headed down the coast. But where were we in relation to the old airport tower sticking up out of the water two miles off shore?

"Jesse, can you tell where we are with regards to the abandoned tower?"

He looked out his window, studied the pattern of lights sliding by below. Just beyond was the black of the sea.

"We're south of it now," he said. "Good. You're clear, and we want to head south anyway."

"Where are we going?"

"To your grampa's house south of the city. But only if we can lose our tail."

"Okay, so I'm going to fly west for a while as I drop altitude, even north a bit, just to try to throw them off."

The tiny green dots on the screen were closing on us. One thousand feet. I gently pulled right, to the west. We were over the sea now and I kept dropping. It was so dark I couldn't see where dark land left off and the water began... I sure hoped the altimeter was correct. I saw a blinking red light down below, out Jesse's window—the marker in the shipping lanes that warned of the tower. Jesse saw it too and pointed out his window. Good to know exactly where we were on the map. Five hundred feet now. I headed us farther west, farther out to sea. And hoped that no big ships were running without lights this night.

"Where's Orion now?" I asked Jesse. I didn't want to take my eyes off the black below, just in case.

"Scattering, it looks like... yes, some are heading south, some are heading north, looks like they're hunting now. I think we've lost them."

I blew out a long breath. We'd hold at five hundred feet and head west for another minute, then I'd begin the slow turn back to land.

"Grampa has a house south of the city?" Somehow this was hard to believe.

"Yeah."

"And you can find it from the air at night?"

"Oh yeah."

"Sounds like you've been up in jopters a lot?"

He nodded. "A lot in the past year or so that I've been up here in the city."

"But you don't fly?"

"I'm a sailor at heart."

"Why did you leave the sea to come up here?"

"When you called me."

"But I didn't call you. I didn't think you were alive. I'd seen you killed by the train."

"You did, though. It was like you spoke to me."

"What did I say?"

"Just my name."

I gently guided us through a slow one-eighty turn so we were now flying east, still at five hundred feet AGL, the city lights ahead of us in the distance.

"Is Orion still searching?"

Jesse studied the screen in front of him. "Yes."

"How's Billy doing back there?" I asked over my shoulder.

A seatbelt clicked and Cat leaned forward, her face just off my right shoulder. "Still unconscious, but he's doing okay, Tessa. Hannah's got him bandaged."

"With what?"

"Her undershirt."

I had to smile. Then I had a thought that took it away.

"What are we going to do with this jopter after we land?" I asked Jesse.

"I'm working on it."

He knew as well as I did that jopters were traceable. Without the code, turning off the ignition and cloaking triggered the safety mechanism—the radio beacon—that enabled Orion to trace where the jopter was sitting. Right now we were flying under their radar, but as soon as I landed, we'd be traceable. Of course I could leave the machine running... but just as we'd lost the option of having Billy awake and able to crack its codes, we'd also lost the option of quickly being able to get away from it, since we were going to have to carry him. We couldn't blast out the control panel with a gun because Jesse had had to drop his gun when he picked Billy up off the tarmac...

I could not figure out what we were going to do to get rid of an Orion jopter.

The city lights grew closer. I was coming in over the very south part of the big peninsula, some miles farther south of the Southaven projects. As we came up on the coastline, lights from a highway shone on the dark water, and then I saw a river mouth. I remembered from my Fortress base flying days that a river ran out of the mountains, across the southern part of the peninsula on its way to the southern inlet. I had to climb a little to make sure we cleared anything rising up on the shore. Hopefully we wouldn't show up on radar...

"Stay on this heading," Jesse said, looking out his window. "Can you slow down a little?"

"Yes." We were cloaked, but we were certainly audible to anyone down below. Of course low-flying jopters weren't anything new in this area.

"Fuck!" Jesse exclaimed. He was focused on the radar screen in front of him, on a swarm of tiny green dots dancing toward the larger dot at the center of the screen that was us. We'd shown up on radar again.

"A whole bunch more," he said. "We've got to put down and get everyone out."

"I'm putting all of you out and then I'm taking off and drawing them away." Hopefully we could do it so quickly that they couldn't tell I'd made a quick stop. Radar only showed two dimensions well—

they might not be able to tell that I'd landed briefly. At least that's how it used to be.

I had figured out the one thing I could do to get rid of an Orion jopter: put it in the sea.

Jesse was already turned to the back seat, giving quick directions to Cat and Hannah. Head up the river's southeast bank, how to make a carry-sled for Billy out of the netting just behind their seat, who and what to avoid... I didn't pay attention since I wasn't going to be with them, and I had enough to do. I kept my eyes on my altimeter, and on the green dots closing on my screen. They weren't more than five miles away; we'd be able to see their lights very soon.

"Now, Tessa," Jesse said. "Put us down now."

I saw what he was looking at—a dark space up ahead, no lights, but what about trees?

"It's a field not far from the house. Go ahead and gently come right down. I'll look out as best I can."

Putting down in the dark? I'd never done it and never thought I'd do it. But as we got closer to the ground, I realized I could see just a little, using the ambient light from the city. I could see enough ground to settle us, perhaps a bit more firmly than usual.

"Don't start up again until I tell you!" Jesse's face was two inches away, his eyes boring into mine; he didn't even bother going out his door, but climbed through the back past Hannah, opening her door, reaching for her, then Cat (who'd pulled out the netting from behind their seat and was carrying it, bundled, under her arm), then Billy's limp, long body. He jumped back in and slammed shut the door.

"Go!"

"Wait, why aren't you—?"

"Tessa, GO!"

I pulled back on the stick and we lifted off. I caught a blurred glimpse of Hannah's face and realized I hadn't even said goodbye. I lifted us just high enough to clear the dark shapes of trees nearby, and then opened the throttle to head us farther south, as fast as we could go, while the blinking green dots closed on us from the north.

~

"If you go down," Jesse said from the darkness on my right, "I go down with you."

He was back in the co-pilot's seat. I started us climbing and also

226

slowed our airspeed—I wanted those Orion jopters on me now, I didn't want them pausing to try to figure out if I had landed or not. Hannah and Cat and Billy were hopefully safe, hunkered down in the trees already, covering themselves against any possible searchlights.

Please God, please Raven, keep them safe...

I risked a glance over at Jesse. "I don't want to lose you ever again, either, but I was going to leave you there."

"I know you were. That's why I didn't give you the opportunity. You aren't going to leave me ever again, Raven."

I reached out my right hand and touched his arm. His warm hand closed on mine.

"Have you figured out yet what we're going to do?" he asked.

"Well, we're going to draw them in on our tail and we're going to head for the sea. That's the best I can think of."

"Yeah." Jesse sounded resigned. "I suppose we could get blown up at any time?"

That's when I thought of Quinn, and the dance we'd done that day when an Orion jopter had discovered us. No, I wasn't going to give up easily this night.

"Tessa," Jesse said, "why are you smiling?" He'd let go of my hand.

"Tighten that seat belt. Orion is going to have to work to get us."

Looking out my window, over my shoulder, I could see their jopters' lights like stars in the distance.

"Switch that radar screen to close-up, will you?" I asked.

He knew how to do it; this meant he'd been in a couple of chases himself already.

We headed for the dark sea.

"They're closing," Jesse said. "Almost within range." He tapped another screen in front of him and sat quiet for a moment.

"What?" I asked.

"We've got firepower. A whole lot of it. Don't you want to blast a few of them before they take us out?"

"No." I was completely sure. "Tonight I'm not killing anyone." I looked over at him. "And Jesse, I'm so sorry that you had to kill tonight to get us out."

"There was no other way."

"There is another way now."

"There is?"

Yes... though I just couldn't quite see it yet. But I knew we were doing the right thing by running and not shooting.

We were over the dark water. I descended a little, speeding up to keep the pursuit just out of range from us.

The words came slowly because I still wasn't quite sure. "You know how Gram always used to tell me *Be quiet and listen... Pay attention to the things that others always miss.*"

"I remember, mostly because I thought it was funny since you were the one kid of all of us who never could be still and quiet."

I deserved that. "Well, over the past eleven years I've had a fair amount of opportunities to learn to listen, to pay attention."

Jesse put his hand on my shoulder.

"And I'm thinking now it's all about us seeing a bigger picture, and seeing where to put ourselves within it."

A missile flashed past us, its trail shimmering white against black. I pulled back on the stick and sent us skyward, then rolled right.

"Hold on," I said. "This might get a little wild."

Jesse made a garbled sound from the depths of his seat.

"And then," I went back to that thought, back to the big picture, "when we've done that, when we've made our choice, we let the mystery unfold."

Another missile flashed by, this time under us. I rolled left and climbed again.

"Fuck you, Tessa," Jesse managed to whisper.

We were dancing in the night, the Orion jopters and me. We were over the black sea, under the black sky. They had the numbers but I had the grace.

I never knew how much fun it was to loop and roll a jopter. Tricks I'd learned with the kestrel worked with the jopter... to a point.

A long, drawn-out murmured "Fuck you, fuck you, fuck you..." came from Jesse's side of the cockpit. Well, everyone had their own coping mechanisms.

Then I knew just what we would do. Or try to do, anyway. I pushed the stick all the way forward and we nearly fell out of the sky. I watched the altimeter unwind and noticed that Jesse had stopped making any sounds. He was probably unconscious. Even past regretting he wasn't with the others, in the trees, headed to Grampa's house.

The Orion jopters all had their lights on. Ours were off; we were totally cloaked. *Passing through two thousand feet...* I had the control panel lights as dim as they could go. Now that I had drawn all of Orion, it seemed, out over the water, I was going to go right down to nearly sea level again to see if I could disappear. It was worth a try... *Passing through one thousand feet...*

I couldn't watch all the screens at once, though. I had to keep a careful watch on my altimeter and artificial horizon so I didn't end up hitting the water. *Passing through five hundred feet...*

"Jesse! Jesse! Wake up, I need you!" I leveled us off at one hundred feet, according to the altimeter. If I stared hard, I saw an occasional white flash of foam—low rolling waves—just below us.

He groaned.

"I need you to keep an eye on the scope and see if we've lost them."

He groaned again.

"Time to cowboy up!" Another of Earl's favorite expressions. I craned my head to see behind us. I couldn't see any lights anywhere.

"I'm not a fucking cowboy," Jesse said through clenched teeth, but he sat up and looked at the screen in front of him. "They're not on us. They're hunting again."

"Good." Maybe I could turn south one last time and slip in to land just on the coast, and Jesse and I could dash out and get as far from the jopter as we could in the few minutes that we'd have...

"Bad news," Jesse said. "Some of these blips are moving faster than others. I think we've got a bunch of Orion jets coming to join the party."

Bad news was right. I knew what Orion jets were capable of.

"I have an idea," he said.

I looked at him.

"Let's ditch this baby and see if we can jump out at the last second."

Could he have forgotten how I felt about water? Lake water was horrifying enough, but jumping into the pitch black sea on a moonless, starless night, out of a moving jopter?

"Tessa." His hand was on my shoulder again, he was leaning close. "I'll help you. I think it might work."

I looked straight ahead out of the cockpit. I had been talking of choosing to step in and let the mystery unfold... if I wasn't open to this, maybe I was only talk. On the other hand, it sounded insane. How to know?

I saw a blinking red light in the distance, off to our right. We were coming up on the tower again.

"About how far is the tower from that red buoy light, do you remember?"

He looked out his window, thinking. "Maybe a half mile east of it. Not far." He turned to stare at me. "Are you thinking what I'm thinking?" he asked.

"I don't think so," I said. "I'm crazy but not insane." Okay, maybe we did have a chance to swim to that damn tower.

I kept my eyes on the red light, not much more than fifty feet below us, sent us in a circle back to it, nearer to it, keeping in mind that the tower stuck up nearly one hundred feet, not far to the east. Hitting it would sure be a bummer.

Meanwhile a whole bunch of flashing lights—white strobes, but also red and green nav lights—passed overhead, several thousand feet above us. The jets. All were flying north to south. I knew in a minute they would all turn and fly back, south to north. Orion was hunting.

I put Jesse's idea together with my idea. Slowly I pulled the titanium loop that held my identcard off over my head, and handed it to him.

"Can you take my card off this, and stick it in a pocket for me, and leave it unclasped."

He undid the loop, slipped off the card and stuck it in a back pocket, staring at me.

"Okay, you're going to tie one end of this to the stick and the other end to something close to it on the control panel..." I felt for possible projections and found a knob that seemed to be at just about the right spot.

"Wouldn't auto pilot be easier, Tessa?"

"No, I want us on a slow climb so that they pick this jopter up..."

"And shoot it down, but we'll have jumped!"

"Right." I had to swallow hard. "If you really think we can jump out of this and survive?"

"Can you slow it down?"

I nodded. "But not too much more since it needs to have

enough power to slowly climb."

We wasted a few minutes circling west of the red light of the buoy while I got us low, and at the right speed, and we tied the stick just right for a gradual climb. The cluster of jopters stayed to our south, hunting farther out to sea, and some of the jets had dropped lower and were hunting right over our heads, but so far they hadn't figured out that we could be as low as we were over the water. But I knew our luck couldn't hold much longer.

One last pass of the buoy to get us set up as close to it and as low as possible... Then I climbed out of my seat and eased onto Jesse's lap. We were going to go out his door together. I reached back to keep my hand on the stick until the last second, to keep us right where we wanted to be, but I think Jesse got slightly distracted.

He surprised me with a quick, hard kiss. "Tessa..."

The red light of the buoy was coming up on our right. Time to move!

"Oh, fuck, I forgot to undo my seat belt!" Jesse pushed me out of the way.

My hand slipped on the stick and we tilted left... I was trying to level us off, he was trying to open his door, then ease his legs out in the wind, trying to find the skid with his feet... I let go of the stick and we began climbing.

"Shit!" Jesse yelled and lifted me up and threw me out the door, into the black.

I had no idea if he followed me or not.

He'd said to hit the water feet first, if I could. How was I to know—out there in total outer space blackness—what was up and what was down?

At least I was so high up that there was time for gravity to take over, and it became pretty clear which direction was down. White foam shimmered below me. Then I hit it. Hard.

I was glad I had my boots on, and glad they hit first, but after that initial second of gladness, I realized that their weight was going to drown me. Fortunately they were loose to begin with, and the icy cold water made it easier for me to kick them off.

I flailed to the surface. A foaming wave smacked me right in the face. I gasped, and heard Jesse yell my name. Impossible to get a bearing... I was kicking hard to keep my head above water, pushing my hair out of my eyes, craning my neck in all directions to try to hear him.

Suddenly an explosion lit up the sky and a delayed thump went through my chest. I gazed up with my mouth open—it must have been our jopter!—and I got slapped by another wave.

Coughing and gasping for air, I heard Jesse's voice much closer. Bits of flaming wreckage were still falling from the sky, fortunately a mile away from us, but enough light still flickered in the sky for me to see Jesse swimming toward me. I hadn't felt such relief since I had seen Billy levitating a jopter as a shield for us.

"Tessa." Jesse swam up to me, his black hair streaming to either side of his face, his smile flashing white in the darkness. "Did you see our jopter go up?"

Men and explosions. I didn't say it out loud because I was afraid I was going to get another wave in the face.

He reached out an arm and touched a cold hand to my cheek. "You kicked off your boots?"

I nodded.

"Okay, now remember, in salt water you'll float naturally."

I risked a wave slap. "The fuck I will! I've already gone under three times!"

He had the nerve to smile. "Roll over and lie on your back. No, with your head in the direction the waves are coming in, yes, like that. Now I'll help pull you along. You'll see how buoyant you are. Just *relax*, Tessa."

I tried. It actually worked for a little while, maybe a minute, but I was too cold to just lie there in the water.

"Climb up on my back," he suggested then, when I started splashing around. "Just stay back enough so you don't put my head underwater."

That worked a little better. I held onto his long hair.

"Where's the damn buoy?" I could just barely talk.

"Long passed." He sounded cheerful. "See the tower up ahead?"

I squinted through my salt-burned eyes, through the blur of hypothermia, over the rise and fall of waves... there was something ahead of us. I could feel it more than see it. Somehow it felt powerful. Was it because it was something that had endured for so long? Or just so strange that it was standing there all alone, so much of it under the waves? Wait, there also was a terminal building still standing, just below the wash of low tide, *so it was said*...

"Can we get inside it?" I managed to ask.

"Oh yeah. And the way the tide is right now, we can just swim right in."

"Been here before?"

"Yep. No sailor could ever resist this."

Well, that was a very good thing. Jesse could take care of me, because I was past the point of being able to take care of myself. My body was shutting down from hypothermia, feet and legs long gone, arms and hands nearly useless, brain also nearly useless. All I wanted to do was sleep forever.

~

"Tessa," Jesse was calling my name. It seemed like he had been calling it for a long time. My eyes didn't work very well, but finally I saw him above me, bending over, pulling me in against him. It was nearly pitch dark. We were on a hard, metal floor which was cold, inside a large space that echoed with the wash of waves and the high humming note of the wind. We were inside the tower.

I tried to say, *How come this night feels like a week long?* but it didn't come out very well. I don't think it came out at all.

Jesse looked worried. But when I tried to speak, I could feel his relief.

"Oh God," he said, "I was afraid you'd died of hypothermia."

I'm pretty damn close to doing that right now, I tried to say.

"Lie against me," he said, "and see if we can generate some heat."

My sodden and nearly frozen stiff gray prison-issue jumpsuit against his sodden, but at least softer, black Orion pants and jacket. He was trying to pull off the jacket and wrap it around my back. Before he was finished doing that, I fell asleep with my head on his chest.

~

When I next opened my eyes it was light. I was lying on my side with my head pillowed on Jesse's chest, my cheek against his slow-beating heart. I was warm and Jesse felt warm. Dry and warm. A silver, crinkly space blanket was under me and wrapped all around us, held in place by Jesse's heavy arm. I wondered where he'd found it; I was pretty sure it had saved our lives.

If I turned my head a little, I could see straight up the tower, six or more stories to the very top, which seemed to be a ring with its center open to the sky. There must have been a ceiling once, but now I was looking up at blue sky, far far above me.

My eyes travelled back down, lingering on the tall openings in the outer walls that made rings on the outside of the tower. As I stared, I imagined the tall glass windows that once had filled the spaces. Every other floor had been mostly ringed by windows. Once this building had been beautiful as well as functional; it still was beautiful in a stark way with early morning sunlight, buttery yellow and warm, streaming through the openings above us. I thanked God that it was the May and not wintertime.

There was one other intact floor far above, a half-floor like the one we were on, but it was on the opposite side of the tower so that it didn't obstruct my view up to the sky. The curved walls of the tower that weren't open to windows were steel and concrete with metal ladders, rungs set into the concrete walls, running up opposite sides, just like the ones inside the walls at P1.

I heard the quiet wash of waves not far below the half floor we lay on. I had a vague recollection of swimming on Jesse's back into the tower through one of the open once-window rings. Waves gently washed through the tower, in one side and out the other.

Jesse was softly snoring. I tried to move just a little, to see more of the floor we were lying on, and he stirred and opened his eyes. We smiled at each other. I felt like I had come home. In yet another strange building after eleven years of being in unimaginably strange buildings, because I was with Jesse, I felt like I had come home. I snuggled back against him and put my head over his heart again.

"Do you remember how the Étain story ends?" I asked him. "How does she finally get back together with Midir?"

Jesse gave a little laugh that bounced my head on his chest. Then he thought about it. We both come from long lines of ancestors who took stories very seriously.

"After all the fly business?" he asked, and I nodded against his chest. "Well... she becomes a woman again..."

"By landing, as a fly, in a wine cup and getting a queen to swallow her," I interjected. "And didn't you ever wonder how close that is to the Raven story, the one where Raven becomes a pine needle and falls into the drinking cup of the chief's daughter, so she can give birth to him as her son?"

Jesse turned his head so he could give me a look. "And you're asking *me* how the Étain story ends?!"

"I can't remember the ending."

He thought again. "Oh, I know. She married the high King of all Ireland—I don't think she had much choice—and then Midir came back, but she wouldn't go away with him unless the King agreed to let her go. And the king wouldn't. So Midir proposed that they play a game of chess."

"Right. Actually they played, like, a month of chess games and Midir kept letting the King win, to get him off his guard," I said. "But how did Midir finally get her in the end?"

"He said whoever won the last game could name the reward, and all he asked was for Étain's two arms around him and a kiss." Jesse smiled as he said this, and rolled onto his side, putting his arms around me, and kissed me, slow and soft and deep, the kind of kiss that made everything in me say *yes*.

When he moved back just a little, so we could breathe, I said, "And the King brought in all his warriors to make sure that it was just a kiss and no more, but Midir knew what he was doing." I remembered then how the story ended, how Midir and Étain became one, for all time.

Then he took his weapons in his left hand, and he put his right arm around Étain, and he carried her up through the skylight of the house. The chieftains rose from their seats about the king. And they saw two swans ascending over the plains of Tara...

"By God, you got it perfectly," Jesse said, and kissed me again.

~

We didn't snuggle for very long because we were both being driven mad with thirst. We were hungry, too, neither of us having eaten in quite some time, but it was thirst that got us up and got Jesse hunting through the hiding places in the tower walls on our floor. There were several emergency caches kept for people in situations like ours, he said, and he'd found one already that had stored the space blanket that had saved us. I followed him around, curious that there could be hiding places when all I could see was pretty much just concrete and steel.

"Do you remember back in school, sometime when we were teenagers," I asked him, "and our teacher—it was Mrs. Mack, not your auntie—had us do an exercise on the hierarchy of human needs?"

"Hmmm." He wasn't really listening to me, but that was okay, as long as water turned up somewhere in the tower. And I loved watching how he moved, lithe, with such an easy male grace, muscles rippling under the black material of the uniform he still wore. It was Jesse, but it was Jesse as a full grown man.

"And she said that oxygen, water, shelter and food come before sex," I said.

Jesse turned and looked at me. "She didn't actually say sex though, did she? Wasn't it more like... procreation?"

We both smiled, remembering.

He went back to pulling at another panel that blended into the concrete wall.

"And you boys were all laughing and saying, 'Nothing comes before sex!'"

"Boys can be such jerks..." He poked farther into a hidden recess. "But she was a good sport, wasn't she?" Then he laughed and pulled out an opaque white plastic bladder, big enough that he had to lift it with both arms. "Does this mean that sex can come a little sooner now?"

"Only if there's food in there, too." I stepped closer to the opening to look in.

"And only if this is good water." Jesse left the water bladder sitting on the shelf, turned it around and found the spigot, carefully turned it to open with his hand under it. Water dribbled out onto his hand; he lifted it to his mouth.

"Oh God, yes," he said. "Come here, Tessa, sit on the floor and put your mouth under it."

I did. He opened the spigot and water fell into my mouth, sweet and cool. Like heaven. Jesse stayed there, opening and closing the spigot, anticipating when I would swallow. Then I forced myself to stop and give him a turn.

I watched his face as he drank and thought that dying of thirst, and being given water, perhaps was like sex all in itself—one was desperate for it, and here it was filling him with such a sweet feeling that made him tilt his head back and close his eyes, and this look of concentration on his face, of completely concentrating on a sensation inside that filled him to sweet overflowing...

I realized I was breathing quickly and my beating heart was

singing an invitation.

His hand motioned for me to close the spigot to save water. He sat up, twisting his thick black hair back with one hand, no doubt missing that leather strap he must have lost when he hit the water.

Before he could say anything, I crouched down next to him, sitting back on my heels so our eyes were at the same level.

"Jesse, do you remember that first night on the trail when you told me the Bluejay story?"

He looked a little surprised but nodded.

"I loved that story, and I still think of it a lot, but I guess what I wanted to say now wasn't really about the story, just that... you wanted to kiss me that night, didn't you?"

His dark eyes were smiling. "Oh yeah!"

I sat back a little farther, sort of feeling the weight of something there in me that I needed to say to him, but not quite sure yet what it was. "And I wanted to kiss you, too, but something else in me was stronger. I was afraid, somehow." Speaking slowly to him, as his eyes smiled at me, I finally got it. "I was afraid of change. I'd always seen change as something not so good, bad things coming of change..."

Things like my mother leaving me, though of course I didn't remember that one, but also losing Marv, and almost losing little Augie, and leaving the village and Gram, and then losing Jesse.

"But something in me changed." I saw him smile, and heard what I'd said, and laughed a little and said, "I changed how I felt about change, I guess. But that's only after you've come back into my life."

He leaned forward just a little, closer to me. "And now you don't mind me kissing you."

I smiled. "Oh no, in fact I'll be disappointed if you don't do more."

~

Much later I gazed at his body, memorizing the lines and angles of it. How hard he was in most places, but he had some soft, hidden places too. He let me stroke him all over as we lay there on the pile of our clothes on top of the space blanket, bemused by my frame of mind, enjoying the sensations I was giving him. But really I was memorizing him and making every second last as long as I possibly could.

"We should have done this a long, long time ago," he

commented drowsily.

I, on the other hand, was awake and completely energized. "No. If we had, I would never have survived losing you when you were hit by the train. I damn near died of a broken heart then. Now, I can't imagine..."

He kissed the top of my head. "We won't lose each other now."

But how could you be guaranteed something like that? In the world we were in?

Suddenly—the sound of jopters.

"Shit!" Jesse scrambled to his feet, grabbing his clothes. "I've got to go to the upper floor. They're scanning for wreckage from last night. I meant to be up there at daybreak to keep a look out."

I dressed and hurried after him. When Jesse had been hunting for water, I'd discovered the four foot wide catwalk curving around the tower wall opposite our floor as well as opposite the other floor high above us—discovered, but hadn't ventured onto it, because there were no railings and it was creepy to think that one slip and you could fall through the air and land in the sea down below. But now I hurried after Jesse on the catwalk that led to the metal rungs that would take us up two stories to the half floor high above. I tried not to look over my right shoulder, but couldn't help it: the seawater looked as dark as slate, and no little waves moved through now; I guessed the tide had risen so the water was above that open ring of windows we'd swum through.

My shoulders were both sore from the P1 ladders the night before, so I lagged behind Jesse on the climb up. I was careful not to look down until I finally reached the next floor up. Here the open ring that once was all glass looked out to the west. The sea was far below now, sparkling dark blue under the morning sun.

Jesse reached out an arm and pulled me against him as he kept to the side of one of the wide supporting posts.

"We've got to be careful in case anyone scans the tower."

"They think we died when the jopter exploded, right? Maybe we're safe now?"

"It might be better for us if they found body parts amongst the wreckage. But we can hope."

"They might come looking for us here?" I couldn't keep a quaver out of my voice. Jesse's arm tightened around me, which felt good.

"If they do, we've got some hiding places. This floor is more intact, there are some office rooms that still have walls, and closets."

Great. Cornered in a tower, in a closet. I could just picture it... And we had no weapons to defend ourselves with. Here I'd been making a big point about no more killing, and I was longing for a gun.

"What's so funny?" Jesse asked, his eyes still locked on the jopters who were sweeping back and forth, only five hundred feet above the sea.

I told him.

"I've got my knives," he said cheerfully.

"Christ on a crutch!" Another good Earl expression. "I hope it doesn't come to that."

"Me too. But we're prepared, Raven. We can do this."

His use of the plural was reassuring. We stayed on that floor for an hour watching the two jopters sweeping the water, back and forth, scanning for debris, then departing, then three more arriving to do more of the same. After a while I sat down, leaned against the wall below the window frame, and dozed off.

Jesse woke me. "They're gone. Let's climb up to the top."

We went back to the ladder and climbed above the half floor of walled offices, long-emptied of whatever had been in there, now with collapsing ceilings, cords and things poking out of walls. At least a slip now meant falling down through a ceiling onto a floor, and not four floors down into icy gray seawater.

There was nothing now above us except the ten-foot wide ring of floor curving around the top of the tower, and open now to the sky above. The ladder we were climbing went through an opening in the floor, and then we were standing with nothing but blue sky above our heads. Empty steel frames were all that was left of walls that had been all glass. The sun was warm on my hair. We were so high I felt like I was flying.

Jesse was looking at me, smiling. "Pretty cool, huh?"

I just nodded. But how were we going to get out of here? My eyes followed the mile or so stretch of gently rolling waves between us and the western bluffs of the peninsula.

"As soon as it gets dark, I'm swimming for shore," Jesse said, reading my mind as deftly as Cat ever did. "There's nothing else to do."

Damn, was it even possible? It was one thing to know how to

swim in the sea, but what about the icy temperature of the water?

"I'll stay here waiting for you." I tried to sound hopeful and positive. "I'll be the maiden in the tower. I'll make up some stories while I wait."

I turned around, taking in the three-sixty degree view while holding onto a weathered bit of countertop just to be safe, so I didn't get dizzy and go plunging off the platform that had no edge to it, though it was a good ten feet wide. The sun glinted off the snow of the tall mountains one hundred and more miles to the north and south of Fayerport, and off to the west the restless sea stretched to what was easy to believe was forever. I turned and looked east over the city to the mountain range I loved. The highest peaks still were streaked with snow, but the lower slopes were faintly showing pale green. It would be another couple of weeks, early June, before that rich emerald green would spread up their slopes until it met the rock of the higher elevations.

There would still be snow on the low north-facing mountain slopes at home. Home. My heart yearned for home, for Gram and our little house and the lake.

I turned to Jesse. "I didn't break Gram's heart, did I? You've heard from home, right? Tell me she's okay."

He'd been gazing east, too. He turned his head and smiled down at me.

"Gram's fine. She's been living with us guys, here south of the city, for the past year and a half."

"What?!"

"With your Grampa and me and Emmitt and my brother Augie."

"Augie?!"

"Yep. He's all of twenty now, tall as me and outweighs me, even."

It was enough of a jolt to see Jesse jump from eighteen to thirty; I couldn't begin to imagine little Augie at twenty years old and bigger than Jesse. And Gram in the city?

I put my hands up on Jesse's shoulders. "Start over. Start from the beginning. Tell me everything."

We lay down side by side on the floor in the sun, looking up at the deep blue sky to the west, and Jesse told me about how he and Emmitt and Augie had all ended up in the resistance navy together, each joining up separately, but by sheer luck they all ran into each other one day in Glacierport. About a year and a half ago they'd gotten a ride with some airmen in a jopter, come back up the coast to the city to become grounders on the strength of Jesse's belief that I was alive and in the city somewhere. They all met with Earl when he came in on a supply run—that's what started it. Earl went home and told Gram all that he'd heard from Jesse about me.

"Which wasn't much," Jesse said and then heaved a sigh. "All I knew was that I'd been in some sort of an accident and you were gone. I knew that something must have happened to you, too, but tried not to think of what it might have been. But I knew that I'd heard you call me." He sighed another sad sigh.

"So Gram came out with Dad," he went on. "She wanted to come to the city while I tried to find you. She came to your Grampa's house where we were staying south of the city and she took over the running of it, since he's gone so much it was kind of in rough shape."

It was almost too much for my brain—Grampa with a house outside the city, and Gram, Jesse, Augie, and Emmitt all living with him.

"Wait, Jesse," I said, "when you say 'south of the city'—where exactly are you talking about?"

"Your Grampa's house is about three miles south of the Southport station," he said. "Why?"

I started laughing. I couldn't talk for a minute, it was just too much. Then I managed to say, "I lived seven years in one of the projects in Eastport."

Jesse stared at me, his dark brown eyes widening, then he started laughing, too. "Jesus, Tessa, you mean you and I were only five miles apart for the past year and a half?!"

After we talked about that for a while, Jesse went on to blow my mind by telling me that both Grampa and Gram were card-carrying Orion citizens.

"*What?!*"

"Well, how else do you expect them to get around?" Jesse smiled at me, like he'd smile at a little kid he was trying to explain something not very complex to. "They seem to be good Orion supporters, living by the rules, your Grampa gets to fly his plane for his trade routes." His smile deepened. "And you do know that that's not all he does, right?"

"Oh geez, what else don't I know?"

"Well, your Grampa has for twenty or more years been the main contact and organizer for the bush village resistance. You know, all those little villages tucked away in the mountains or along the coast, like ours, filled with people Orion doesn't give a shit about, mostly indigenous? Well, they've all waiting for the day when they can help stop Orion in its tracks."

I truly was speechless. So much I didn't know.

"A bunch of them came in from the villages last month," Jesse was saying, "came in on the same trail in the night through the mountains you and I were on, plus a few guys from our own village. They posed as sanitation workers on the city streets and helped us blow up Orion headquarters yesterday."

Then he looked sad. "We only got about half of what we hoped for... none of Orion's systems went down, and we lost a lot of good people."

"I heard the explosions," I said slowly. "I was there in my cell, sleeping, and heard and felt them but thought I was dreaming."

"And what were you doing in solitary confinement? I've been wanting to ask you that for hours."

"Inciting riots, according to Hannah." And I told him about my outburst during Re-Education, and he laughed and laughed.

"Oh my God, Tessa, I am so relieved that you haven't changed at all."

We were both quiet for a long moment, listening to the wind blow through the open windows below us, and the gentle wash of waves against the tower. The sun felt so warm.

"So tell me how Gram is," I said. "Is she all right?" I tried to figure out how old she would be now... if I was twenty-eight—twenty-nine in August—that meant she was about... seventy-five? Getting old.

"Yeah, she's doing great. She's learned to drive and she gets around the neighborhood. With her white hair and with sunglasses on, she looks like a fit old granny who's been out in the sun a lot."

Jesse was smiling.

"She's your Gram now, too, isn't she?" I said, snuggling against him.

He put his arm around me. "Yeah, and Augie's too. So we're there living at the house as her grandsons, taking care of the place, keeping it up. Emmitt comes and goes, mostly he lives at the safe house where we work."

"And where's Lars?"

Jesse stopped smiling. "Lars. Well, he's not around much now. He's on the inside."

"What inside? In prison? Lars!"

"No, he's infiltrated Orion... It's pretty fucking scary the position he's in. He's working with the Orion brains, the guys hardly anyone even in Orion knows about, the human brains behind their computer systems." He let go of my shoulder and sat up, looking down at me.

"Listen, Tessa," he said. He looked serious, and contrite, which I didn't understand. "I'm sure Lars has heard and he's pissed as hell at me right now for taking off on my own to P1." He paused, his chin tucked a little so he could look deep into my eyes. "It was only shit luck, and you and Billy, that got us out."

"You got us out! We were sitting ducks in that elevator. Hell, we had just barely figured out that we were in an elevator!"

He smiled, despite himself.

"We didn't have much of a plan. You saved our lives, Jesse."

We stopped talking for a minute. The north wind sang a sad, long note through the open windows below us. Jesse lay back down, nodded to himself, thinking some thought. "It was some team effort that got us out... But Lars is certain to want my ass when I'm back in Fayerport. Almost as much as Orion wants it."

If Orion suspected we tricked them and weren't in the jopter when it blew up, we were all wanted now. Jesse and me and Hannah and Cat and Billy. It was a safe bet our images were streaming out over their computer network at that moment. Well, none of us planned on showing our faces in Fayerport anyway; we just had to be extra cautious now.

"We'll get to Grampa's and meet up with the others," I said, "and then we'll figure it out. I do know I'm not going back to the air force."

He was waiting for me to say more; he was wondering.

"Too much killing," I said softly. "I was too good at it, Jesse,"

He put his arms around me and pulled me in close. "Me too," he said into my hair. "I was the golden boy of the navy for a while there. No one could touch my record for ships blown up. Then I came up here to join the ground force and... well, I got real good as a sniper."

"I was your equivalent in the air," I said into his chest. I was glad he'd kept the Orion jacket off and was just in a white undershirt. "We've got to hope we can beat Orion without doing more killing ourselves."

~

We spent the rest of that long day at the top of the tower. We slept for a few hours in the warm sunlight, spooned, with Jesse's arm around me. Healing sleep with no nightmares.

He went down the ladder and brought up some food—stale energy bars that tasted awful, but did what they were supposed to do. We both had to go down for water after eating them, though. Jesse said that we'd come back as soon as was safe, or better yet, send someone who wasn't wanted by Orion, to replenish the emergency supplies that we'd used.

The sun finally set into the sea to the northwest, after flaming the mountains to the east. Everything began fading into gentle twilight that would linger for at least two hours here at the high latitudes, only five weeks away from the summer solstice. And Jesse announced that it was time for him to try the swim to shore, for rescue. He was calm and confident, but still it was an awful thing to attempt—icy water, currents, a building somewhere under the water not far from the tower... I couldn't let him go.

But then—"Wait!" I said as he headed for the ladder down.

He paused and looked down at me, his eyes questioning.

"Do you hear that?"

He stood next to me, listening.

There it was again, the sound of a motor, getting louder. We looked at each other, then we both started looking out in every direction. No lights on the water. No lights in the air. Then a quick flash of light down on the water, then another and another, some sort of signal that made Jesse grin. He was rustling in the pocket of the Orion jacket that he had brought up to the top of the tower the last time up.

"I've got a batt-light in here somewhere, hopefully still working after being in the sea."

He pulled it out—yes, it was still working!—and began flashing it in the direction we'd seen the signal on the water. Then he turned to me, still grinning.

"Raven, that's our ride down there. It's Augie."

I was about as grateful as I had ever been for anything in my life.

We climbed down the metal rungs as fast as we could.

"Thank God it's such a calm night," Jesse added.

"And he knew we were here!" I was having a hard time keeping up with him and nearly slipped, and my sore shoulders reminded me that I needed to take my time and pay attention.

"That means they got to Grampa's house okay," Jesse was saying from farther below me.

Hannah and Cat and Billy safe. What was Grampa's house like? All I could picture was home, with Gram in her chair by the fire and Jesse dozing, stretched out on the rug. I wanted to be there. Home, the lake.

"Raven!" Jesse was calling up to me, "I want to get down there quick to signal to him again, but you take your time so you don't slip, okay?"

There was the metal half-floor still several stories below, and icy seawater another level below that—my landing options if I slipped— so I took my time.

A few moments later I was down on the floor where we'd spent the night, where Jesse now crouched at one edge, and the low, throbbing sound of an engine at idle filled the tower. I smelled fuel fumes. The tide had dropped just enough for the boat, faintly lit by someone's batt-light, to slip in through the window opening that Jesse and I had swum through. Our platform was a story or more above it still, so we were looking down on it.

Jesse's batt-light was glowing on the floor next to him; I saw his smile as he looked over his shoulder at me. "Your ride is here, Raven, and you aren't even going to get wet!"

It was a sleek boat, bobbing in the gentle waves below our platform. Two men in it, one as large or larger than Jesse and the other much smaller, dressed in dark clothes, and then the large man pulled off a cap and bushy, curly pale hair escaped—it was Augie.

"Hey Tessa," he grinned up at me.

"Oh my God, Augie!" I exclaimed.

And the other man, busy with holding the boat where it was in the water, was my Grampa.

"Well, Tessa," he said, looking up at me. "Sorry it's been so many years."

"That's okay," I told him. "You're making up for it right now!"

He grinned, and Jessie and Augie both laughed, then I followed

Jessie over to the metal rungs in the wall that led down to the water level. He went first, dropped into the boat as if he'd done this kind of thing all his life, then turned and held his arms up to me. I may have let go a little soon from the rungs, because I dropped down on him pretty hard. He staggered backwards with me in his arms and almost fell over on Augie. Everybody laughed again.

He hugged me tight and then guided me to a bench seat along one side. "Raven, you are a piece of work."

Augie came over and gave me a big hug. "God it's good to see you again!"

Grampa just grinned again and began slowly turning the boat inside the tower, pointing us for the opening.

"How'd you know we were here?" I asked as I settled on the bench seat with Augie on one side and Jesse on the other.

"Hannah," Augie said. "She Saw you guys here. How handy is that?"

"How's Billy?"

Augie lifted a hand, tilted it left, right—*so so*. But safe, I thought. And Gram and Hannah and Cat are all working on him... we'll make sure he's all right.

"You two got Orion on its ear, that's for sure," Grampa said matter-of-factly as we slowly emerged from the tower, rising and falling on the low waves. "On top of Orion headquarters getting blown up, you blew up most of the Command Center on your way out..."

"What? What did you say about the Command Center?" Jesse leaned toward him. He was sitting closest to Grampa, who was at the stern of the boat with the engine.

"That's what I heard. Thought you were there! Mostly blown up, took out the Fence. A bunch of prisoners managed to get out, I heard." Grampa had upped the throttle and the engine was coming to life.

Jesse turned his head to look at me. Batt-lights were off now and it was full dark, but I could see his eyes were wide, his eyebrows lifted in surprise.

I thought back to our takeoff in the jopter... that huge explosion below us as we zoomed skyward.

"The other jopter!" I said to Jesse. "Those idiots kept shooting. Remember how it was leaking fuel all over?"

Jesse's grin flashed white in the dark. "I just love explosions."

Augie, warm on my other side, started laughing.

Smack! smack! smack! The waves were bigger now. Grampa was cackling with lunatic laughter and Jesse was grinning at me. It was crazy, and I was loving it. Except...

"How long is this going to take?" I had to shout to Jesse to be heard over the sound of the engine.

He looked a little surprised, like he thought I was complaining. "Maybe a half hour? We're headed for the town dock that's not too far from Grampa's place."

"It's just that..." Oh, man, there was no doubt about it. I staggered to the other side of the boat, as far back in the stern as possible, and threw up the awful tasting energy bars that we'd eaten.

Jesse followed me over and sat next to me, patting my back.

I watched the city lights as we bounced over the waves toward the coastline. I focused on the thought that I was going to see Gram within the hour.

A whole new life was opening ahead of me.

III. Healer

And so may a slow
Wind work these words
Of love around you,
An invisible cloak
To mind your life.
—John O'Donohue, *To Bless the Space Between Us*

10. May 14–June 15, 2111

It was full dark, as we used to say as kids, when we turned off one rutted dirt road onto a much narrower one, and jounced to a stop, and Grampa announced, "We're here."

I was so grateful to drop down from the cab of what I heard called a *pickup truck*, where I'd been bouncing on Jesse's hard knees for several miles, feeling almost as queasy as I'd felt on the boat.

There was a house just ahead of us, with golden light spilling out of its windows onto a grassy yard, and the door flung open and people began spilling out of the house—Hannah and Cat and someone smaller, moving more slowly behind them.

"Gram!" I called and ran right past Hannah and Cat and into her arms, almost knocking her over backwards.

"Tessa, Tessa," she kept saying my name and patting my back as she barely came up to my shoulder, and laughing or maybe it was crying, and I was laughing and crying all at the same time myself.

"You were there with me in prison," I told her all in a rush, "You were there helping me, and the lake was there inside me helping protect me, and all of the stories from all of the years... they were helping me, too..."

Cat and Hannah hugged us both then, one from either side.

"Oh, I'm so relieved to see you, Tessa!" Cat exclaimed.

"We're all back together, and you sound like you're ten years old again, Tessa."

I could see that Hannah didn't mean that nastily, so I bit back the return comment I was going to make. Hey, if I could come through all I came through in the past eleven years and still sound like the Tessa of old, that was fine with me. Better than fine. I was grateful.

"Oh Gram," I whispered for her alone. "I am so grateful for all the help."

She gave me one last big squeeze, then looked up. Her hair was pure white now, still in a long braid, and lines etched her face, but her eyes were bright as they ever were.

"Time to get inside and get you something to eat, Tessa."

As I turned to follow the others in, I nearly fell over a huge, shaggy creature that pressed against my legs, coming up higher than my knees. In the dim light it looked like a wolf! I nearly shrieked, then heard Jesse laughing and calling my name.

"Tessa! That's Charlie. It's okay."

Charlie sat back on his haunches and gave me an appraising look. He had to be at least three-quarters wolf, but his gaze seemed so human that I said, "Hello, Charlie. I'm Tessa."

He got back to his feet, shook himself all over, gave a little grunt and trotted ahead of me toward the house, giving one glance back as if to make sure I was following him.

Jesse and Charlie gave me a tour of the house while Gram, Cat and Hannah set out a late dinner on the long table in the kitchen.

It was such an interesting house, built into a hill so that from the front it looked like one level, but on the other side it was two levels, where most of the windows of the house looked out on the forest. There were three small bedrooms and a bathroom on the lower floor, and that's where Cat and Hannah and Augie and Jesse and I all would be.

"If you don't mind sharing my room, Tessa?" Jesse asked me almost shyly as we climbed back up the stairs to the kitchen and main room.

"It will be just like old times," I said.

"Well, maybe not quite..." He was smiling. "And I hope you don't mind sharing my bed with Charlie, too? He showed up about a year ago and kind of adopted me."

Fortunately for Jesse, I noticed he had a big bed.

"Where's Billy?" I asked Hannah when we rejoined everyone in the kitchen. "How is he?"

"He's in the bedroom down the hall," she said. "The second one. He's much better. Grampa got him some antibiotics first thing this morning, and Gram has been using some of her herbs on him, too." Hannah gave her brisk nod, confirming that the outcome would be good.

No one had sat down at the table yet, so I slipped down the hall and quietly tapped on Billy's door, then looked in. The room was nearly dark, but a night light glowed on a bedside table. Billy looked large in the small bed, covered with a quilt of colorful fabric squares. He opened his eyes when I slipped in.

"Hey Billy." I sat on the chair beside the bed. "Are you doing okay?"

He smiled a little. "Hey Tessa. Yeah, I'm going to make it, thanks to a bunch of people, including you, I hear. How come I missed out on all the action?"

"Well, some of it was just as well missed." I sat there thinking of how wild it had been, how lucky we all were. "But it was thanks to you we even got out of the Command Center."

His smile widened. "Damn, I wish I could have been awake to see it blow up."

"Actually, that one was below us so we kind of felt it more than saw it..."

The door opened wider to spill light from the hall into the room. It was Jesse. "Tessa, time to get some food in you."

I asked Billy if there was anything I could get him, but he said he was fine for the moment; I told him I'd be back after dinner.

We sat down at the wooden trestle table in the kitchen, Gram at one end and Grampa at the other, me squeezed in between Jessie and Augie on the bench below the tall windows, and Cat and Hannah in chairs facing us across the table. Gram held up a hand and everyone quieted, and she smiled at me, then at each of us around the table.

"Thanks be to God and to our spirit helpers for bringing us all together safely!"

"Amen!" We all replied, loudly. And then there was a flurry of passing food, oh, glorious food, heaped in bowls and on platters, and I kept pace with Augie and Jesse for a good part of the meal.

When the last scrap had been eaten (by Augie), Jesse and Augie and I did the dishes. Jesse and I both took quick showers and changed, me into a flannel shirt of Jesse's, which was huge on me, and jeans of Gram's, which left several inches of my lower legs showing, but it felt wonderful to be clean. Then we all found places on chairs or the sofa—Gram patted a place next to her for me—or on the soft rug in front of the woodstove and talked for a couple of hours about the last eleven years, taking breaks from time to time to sit with Billy, until some of us fell asleep in mid-sentence. I woke up to Jesse carrying me in his arms down the stairs to his room. I'm not sure I even remember lying down in his bed.

~

I opened my eyes to morning sun streaming in through the big window in Jesse's room, which faced east. Charlie was sleeping in between me and Jesse, and both of them were softly snoring. *My new life*, I thought, my heart skipping with happiness. I slipped out of bed—still in the clothes I'd had on the evening before—and tiptoed over to the window to look out.

The rising sun had cleared the mountain range to the east some time ago, now that we were only a month from summer solstice; its rays shone through the birch forest outside the window and felt warm on my face. The light flickering through the birch leaves reminded me of light shining on water. *Thank you, God, Raven, spirit-helpers, ancestors. Thank you for bringing us all safe here, together. Please help us now to do what we need to do.*

It had been too long since I had said sunrise prayers; I resolved to do this every morning, and to find a place to be still and try to get back on the path that Gram had started me on so long ago. Jesse had said there was a path through the forest below Grampa's house, a path to a small lake. I resolved to find it... after coffee.

Gram was in the kitchen, sitting at the long wooden table beneath the tall windows no longer dark with night, but now looking out over the shimmering birches to the mountains, and above them, bright sky. She smiled at me.

"I'm not quite sure what to think of your hair, Tessa, but it certainly looks easy to take care of."

I ran my hand through my hair, my usual styling method. "It grew quite a bit while we were in prison. I think I may let it grow again, like Jesse's."

"His hair is beautiful," Gram said. "In the sun it's blue-black like a raven's wing."

We both smiled at her choice of words. She settled back in her chair, smoothing the soft green robe she'd wrapped herself in, looking warm and comfortable.

"Is there coffee, by any chance?" I asked.

She nodded to the stove and tall metal pot sitting on it. "I figured you, like everyone else here, was addicted to coffee. And mugs are in the cupboard to the right of the stove," she added, and waved me off when I asked her if she wanted a mug. She had her tea.

"How were your dreams?" Gram asked, her usual morning greeting when I was a child.

"I don't remember." I sat down next to her, inhaling the aroma rising from my mug. "I think I slept too hard."

Oh, the coffee tasted good. There had been, of course, no coffee in prison. My brain kicked in and I suddenly thought of Sadie, sitting there alone in her unit at Easthaven, with ours empty above her, wondering where we were, if we even were still alive.

"We've got to get word to Sadie today that we're out and all right," I said.

Gram nodded. "Cat and Hannah talked with Augie yesterday about her, and they're going with him this morning. Easthaven's only about five miles north of here."

"I know. Jesse told me that while we were in the tower, waiting to be rescued. We'd been only five miles away from you, for how long?"

Gram gave a little shake of her head. "Oh well, it's funny now that we're together."

"How's Billy?" was my next thought as I woke up with the coffee.

"Holding his own. In a minute come in with me and see if he's awake."

Gram leaned forward in her chair, "And how are *you*, Tessa? That's what I want to know."

I set down my mug on the table. "Gram, I'm not much of a healer any more. I squandered the gift. I do what I can..." and I told her about the clinic, and working with Hannah and Cat and Sadie.

She touched my hand. "That's such a good thing you are doing, Tessa. And if you're doing all you can, well, that's what's important."

Jesse and Charlie came into the kitchen a few minutes later, after Gram had gotten up to make some breakfast for me, though I was insisting that I could make my own breakfast. Jesse paused behind my chair and put both his hands in my hair and ruffled it.

Gram smiled at him from the stove. "She just said she was going to let it grow because she thinks yours looks so good."

"I think she should get it cut short again, as short as it is in her ident photo," Jesse said. "I think that's what used to be called 'punk.'"

I reached up for his hands and guided them down to my shoulders. He got the hint and began gently massaging.

"And I am feeding you today," Gram said, turning her back on us. "Tessa, you need at least a month of extra-good meals."

"Did they feed you at all in prison?" Jesse sounded serious now.

"Oh yeah. Bread and water, then bread and water, then bread and beans and water."

Gram turned around and stared. "Oh my stars."

"I'm fine," I said. "I think Hannah and Cat are, too. Though my teeth were beginning to ache."

"Scurvy," Jesse said.

"No more coffee today," Gram pointed her spatula at me. "I'm going to load you with vitamin C. I'll get your Grampa to look for oranges for you girls today."

After we ate, Gram suggested Jesse show me the path to the lake. No one else would be up for a while, she guessed, and no one expected either of us to do anything that day anyway.

"Take as long as you want down there," she said as we got up and carried our plates and cups to the sink, and Charlie emerged from under the table and gave himself a good shaking, readying for the next adventure of the day. "Tessa, I think you'll find it's a good sitting place for you, and I'm also coming to think that you each are the best medicine for the other."

We gave her quick hugs on the way out. No one was in the hall, so Jesse pulled me against him for a warm kiss.

"Just remember that," he whispered. "I'm your best medicine."

~

A path ran around the house, down the sloping bank and into the forest. Charlie trotted ahead of us, happy to be out, and Jesse and I held hands and walked slowly. The footing was easy on the soft duff of earth and aromatic needles shed by the dark spruce. Aspen and birch wove through the conifers, and their new spring-green leaves brightened the forest. The path crossed grassy glades dotted with the earliest wildflowers—daisies, yarrow, and my favorite, fireweed, just starting to get tall, but with its flowerbuds all tight shut; it wouldn't be in spectacular full bloom until the end of summer. It was the flower we told summer by.

I loved being deep in the woods, though it felt a bit claustrophobic after seven years of living on the hillside and looking out across the peninsula to the sea. But through the trees we had glimpses of the mountains to the east. That felt sufficient for now.

And, Jesse reminded me, we needed the trees because they gave us cover from the daily jopter fly-overs. I'd become so used to hearing cloaked, low-flying jopters when we lived in Easthaven that I was in danger of forgetting that now I needed to be sure that I didn't attract the attention of one. Trees were just what we needed now.

The path led out of the forest onto a grassy bank, and there, about twenty feet below, was the lake. The water was clear and clean thanks to an inlet on the east end, a stream running in through the forest down from the mountains, Jesse said, and there was a small outlet on the south end of the lake, only about a mile through more forest to the bay to the south of the Fayerport peninsula. This lake was much smaller than our lake in the mountains. I glimpsed a couple of small houses across the water from us, nestled in more birch and aspen, but it felt very private where I stood on the bank next to Jesse and Charlie. Protected and peaceful.

I leaned my head on Jesse's shoulder. "I'm going to spend a lot of time here, I think."

He put an arm around me. "Good."

It was a place for listening to the spirits of earth and water and sky. After filling my eyes with it all, I shut them and I thanked the water that had come down from the mountains to feed the lake, and the rich soil banks rising out of it, crowned with such tall, green trees; I thanked the warm sun when it reached through the trees to touch my head and shoulders; I thanked the life stirring all around me.

"It's not quite the same as our home lake," Jesse said from just off my shoulder, "but it's here for you." He knew.

We found some dry moss perfect for sitting, and Charlie circled several times and then lay down with the tip of his bushy tail over his nose. His eyes looked almost closed, but not quite, and I believed he kept track of us while he looked asleep.

A movement in the air caught my eye—a raven, winging over the lake, east to west, silent, but I think he saw us because he veered our way. I pointed him out to Jesse. The raven flew past and I swear he turned his head to give us a good look. As he flew away, he made that wonderful chuckling, woodknocking raven sound I have never been able to imitate.

This made me remember the raven who had knocked me down in Easthaven, just before things started happening, and I told Jesse, and he laughed out loud, and Charlie looked alarmed.

An hour or so passed, and we decided it was time to head back for the house. I'd begun thinking of Billy, and of Hannah and Cat going to see Sadie, and wanting to go, too. And Jesse said he had promised Gram he'd do some put-off repairs for her. So we walked back through the woods with Charlie, and in through the front door, noting that Grampa's ancient truck was gone, which meant everyone had left to visit Sadie and run errands for Gram. Jesse headed for the kitchen and I headed for Billy's room.

He was sleeping. His face looked flushed, his bright red hair damp with sweat. I sat down quietly on the chair next to his bed and breathed for a moment, then tried to open myself to him.

Well, that's one thing I'm learning, I thought. *You have to open yourself in order to hear anything... and I have been shut tight for so long, clamped shut around myself, protective, but also isolating...*

Already Jesse and Gram had been helping me, gently guiding me in learning how to open myself. I smiled as I sat there next to Billy, thinking of Jesse as my medicine.

"What's so funny?" Billy asked, opening his eyes. "I could use some humor."

"Well. Gram has been dispensing wisdom," I slowly answered, not exactly wanting to tell the whole truth. "Already. It sure is good to be here with her."

"She raised you, didn't she?"

"Yes, may Raven and all my ancestors bless her. I can see now that I may have been a bit of a difficult child..."

Billy gave me a quick smile. "You, Tessa?"

I gave his warm, dry hand a little squeeze. "Now you're going to go back to sleep, and I'm going to sit with you. And when you wake up, Gram will have more good medicine for you."

"That does sound good," Billy said softly. "But you're medicine, too. You always make me feel better."

"I just wish I could do more!"

"You make a difference, Tessa," Billy's voice softly trailed off into sleep, "you do."

I sat there next to him for a long time, trying to open, to hear him. I kept feeling like I was missing something... I was pretty sure it was because I had closed up around myself in prison, and now I needed to relearn how to be still and pay attention. I could hear Gram's voice telling me that the healer's role is to pay attention, to see things, to hear things that others are missing. I would try.

~

Sadie arrived for dinner that day, popping like a cork out of Grampa's overstuffed old truck, followed by Cat, then Hannah, each carrying bags filled with our clothes and a few things—one lumpy bag I hoped was filled with my books!—from our container home. Sadie wrapped her short arms tight around me.

"Tessa! I've heard all about it, you inciting riots in prison and then making off with an Orion jopter..."

I was trying to tell her it wasn't just me, and Jesse was standing there next to me laughing, and then Gram marched out of the house, right up to us as if she was thinking *Okay, I'm not so sure about this strange woman...* And Sadie let go of me and looked at Gram, and they just stared for a moment, not doing anything noticeable, but it was all going on under the surface, until they both began smiling at the same second, and then wrapped their arms around each other. It was like twin sisters separated at birth finding each other after seventy-five years.

Next to me Jesse just said, "Wow."

After hugging and talking a moment with Gram, Sadie announced that she couldn't wait another second before seeing Billy, so a bunch of us led her to Billy's room and there was another joyful reunion. She sat on his bed for an hour talking with him, and he looked great, with color back in his face, and his eyes bright. *He's going to be back on his feet in no time*, Sadie announced.

At dinner we decided, among other things, that Hannah and Cat and I would go back to helping Sadie with the clinic, getting rides with Jesse and Augie every other day or so as they commuted to the safe house where they were working for the resistance. Easthaven was only two more miles from that, through the woods, and now that it was coming into summertime the trails had dried out and the woods gave plenty of cover even in the event of low-flying jopters. Jesse and Augie each had tough-looking ATV's, built for trails and for carrying two good-sized adults, so we were in luck (we decided that the three of us women would learn how to drive them so that we could all ride on one, while the guys rode on the other... though Augie complained that he and Jesse on the same ATV was going to be a bit crowded). And Sadie would come out and visit us as often as she could, either by way of Jesse and Augie, or with Grampa in his truck that he often drove for supplies, legitimately, with his Orion citizen card. By the time that first communal dinner was over, Sadie and Gram had hatched a number of plans for things to do together.

We all had plans; we were in complete agreement that we'd come together for a reason and we were going to do whatever we were being called to do, together. The big picture—the resistance working against Orion—wasn't all that clear to most of us at the moment, but the smaller picture was: Sadie said the clinic at our Easthaven project was busier than ever and she really needed us there helping, Augie and Jesse were needed to continue their jobs at the safe house (though Jesse was evasive when I asked him exactly what his job was—*working for Emmitt* was all he said), Grampa was about to head out on another of his *trips through the villages*, where he bought native art to sell in the big city: figurines delicately carved from walrus ivory and porous whalebone; masks of buttery alderwood or gleaming cedar, many painted with the bold black, red and turquoise of the Tlingit and Haida to the south; canoe paddles carved of cedar; grass and cedar woven baskets of all sizes; moosehide moccasins with their wonderful pungent-sweet aroma, covered with a glitter of beaded patterns... but at the same time, he was the point man for the resistance, particularly in the villages like ours that had no internet connection. And Billy was getting back on his feet. Gram, as usual, was quietly keeping the household running and looking after the spiritual state of each of us.

We learned more about the big picture when Emmitt came to dinner the next day. I was in the kitchen pulling hot loaves of bread out of the oven, when I sensed someone quietly standing in the doorway, watching me. It was a man who looked older than Jesse by more than a few years, older and somehow sad. He was shorter and slighter than Augie and Jesse, his brown hair carefully cut, his eyes gray like mine, and almost as pale as mine. Emmitt. I hadn't remembered noticing his eyes when we were kids.

He smiled then, which changed him completely. "Tessa, by God," he stepped into the kitchen and hugged me when I had safely put down the bread pans. "You have grown up."

I patted his back as he still held me, feeling the sadness in him, that I knew he always carried in him. How many years was it now? I wondered. Thirteen years since Marv was murdered by Orion?

"You have too, Emmitt." He was five years older than Jesse, I remembered, so that would make him just about thirty-five. But he looked older. So much had happened in thirteen years that it made sense that we were all adults now—well into adulthood even—but at the same time, since we'd been separated, it seemed hard to believe we could all be this old.

He stepped back and his smile began to fade. "Yeah, our village feels a couple of lifetimes ago, doesn't it?"

I touched his arm. "I'm so sorry about Marv. We all are."

"Thanks, Tessa."

Silloway eyes, I thought. *I bet that Emmitt and I both have Silloway eyes. Jesse's are pure Brightwater, and Hannah's are pure Ravenwing, or maybe they're Navajo from her Dad, but I bet that Emmitt and I got ours from our odd great great grandfather Dylan...*

"Emmitt!" Hannah exclaimed from the doorway, and we both turned to see her and Cat. She gave Emmitt a big hug, and then introduced him to Cat, who was looking stunning in a turquoise tunic over jeans—the tunic the exact shade of her eyes and a perfect contrast to her flaming hair. Emmitt took her hand and held it for several seconds, looking down at her, and I watched a flush spread from her cheekbones across her face. *Oh my,* I thought. *What if...* and then shut the thought down instantly for Cat's sake. Hannah and I both looked away at the same moment, and ended up looking at each other. I lifted my eyebrows the tiniest bit, and she gave just as small a nod back.

"Your bread smells good, Tessa," Hannah remarked in the most neutral voice I'd ever heard her use. "What else is for dinner?"

~

The mood stayed light and happy right through dinner, but a lot was going on under the surface. Emmitt took the chair next to Cat's and I noticed the several times they spoke just to each other. At the same time I had the feeling that there were things left unsaid, revolving around what Emmitt and Jesse and Augie were doing for the resistance out of the safe house. It had to be something to do with computers. At least that meant they weren't out on the streets risking Jesse being identified, with all of those little drones flying around at head level everywhere, even at Easthaven. But I didn't like knowing so little.

Before he left for the night, Emmitt went into Billy's room, *to talk about Billy joining us when he's back on his feet,* he said. I noticed that he shut the door while they talked. Later, when I went to say goodnight to Billy, I could feel a new energy in him.

"Tessa," he said, "I'm getting up and walking laps around the house tomorrow. I've got a job waiting for me with Emmitt!"

"Nobody's saying much about what goes on in that safe house."

I sat down on his bed. "But if you're going there, I'm guessing you'll be working with computers?"

Billy nodded. "This is the next big resistance push against Orion. It's much bigger than bombing their downtown headquarters. We're going to take them down from the inside."

"You mean with computers?"

He nodded again. "Can't say any more now..."

"*Need to know only*," we said together.

A few minutes later, in the bathroom, while Hannah finished brushing her teeth and I sat on the closed toilet lid waiting for her to finish, which she didn't seem to mind, I asked her if she knew exactly what resistance work Jesse and Augie were doing for Emmitt. Actually I'd been hoping to ask her what she'd noticed between Cat and Emmitt, but I wasn't going to push my luck.

She took the toothbrush out of her mouth and gave me a sideways glance. "Jesse hasn't told you about what he does?"

I shook my head.

She finished brushing, spit a few times and then rinsed. "Well... I haven't heard anything officially either." She patted her face with the hand towel. "But I think they're hunting Orion with Orion's own technology." Clearly she wasn't going to say anything more.

What did that mean? All I knew was that Jesse had said that he was done shooting people, when we'd talked about what we each had done earlier in the resistance. He would know there would be hell to pay if he went back on that.

The next night, as we settled into bed with Charlie on Jesse's other side—I insisted, plus his fur was damp from the light rain that he and Jesse had just been out in—Jesse said, "Emmitt asked me about Cat."

I turned my head on the pillow to look at him. "What about Cat?"

"Well, you know, if she could read peoples' minds all the time."

"Oh. What did you tell him?"

I felt Jesse shrug. "Just that she seemed pretty normal, and like you said, she seemed pretty able to block out the people she lives with."

"Perfect." I snuggled against him. I prayed for both of them that Cat's gift wouldn't get in their way. "Did you see how captivated they were with each other when they met?"

"Captivated. That's exactly the word Emmitt used. He's writing a poem for her."

Oh my God, the Silloway genes.

"That's how we would have been, if we hadn't grown up together from infancy," Jesse went on.

"How sweet." I kissed his cheek. "Extra points for you."

"No, really, and actually that's how I felt when I saw you for the first time after so many years, there in the dark in the elevator shaft."

"Captivated?"

"Oh yeah."

~

A month passed as we were all busy and as the world moved from a swift Alaska spring into glorious high summer. Jesse and I had little time alone together, except at night of course, but that didn't seem the right time for me to challenge him on what he meant when he said his job at the safe house was *working for Emmitt*. Some days, after getting home and before dinner, Jesse and Augie would spend an hour down in the rocky hollow on the south side of the house, where they had a target range. Jesse also had a special board in the tool shed at one end of the yard that he used for throwing knives. Through the open living room windows I would hear the quiet *pop-pop-pop* of the gun with silencer, and the *thunk! thunk!* of Jesse's knives into wood and I'd think that no way was this just late afternoon recreation.

And I was pretty sure that whatever they were doing for Emmitt didn't involve sitting around in some office. I stayed worried about him. At times it almost felt like he was working to seem normal, but then I would doubt that and tell myself to stop obsessing about it.

~

One mid-June morning Hannah and Cat went in to Easthaven with Jesse and Augie, to spend the day at the clinic with Sadie and I decided to stay back and be quiet and spend some time at the lake, and help Gram with housework.

"Gram," I said as I put the last of the breakfast plates into the drying rack next to the sink, "When Jesse says he's working for Emmitt, what do you think he's doing?"

Gram was looking out the nearest kitchen window which was open to the sounds of a family of chickadees flittering through the birches next to the house. You have to give chickadees credit for sounding so cheerful all the time, and you never see just one—they always move in considerable crowds, which I'm pretty sure are families, just like the jays and crows and ravens do.

Gram appeared deep in thought. Finally she turned her dark gaze on me.

"Tessa, I don't know any more than you do. Why are you worried?"

I plopped down in the chair next to her. "It's just that we talked——in the tower, when we knew we'd survived the escape—about knowing it was right not to kill any more. But now I'm getting worried, since he won't talk about it." I leaned against her for a moment. Her hand lightly stroked my back. Outside the window a chickadee sang its *phoebe* call over and over.

"Give it a little more time, Tessa... Best to focus on what you are called to be doing, and then wait for things to come clear."

That was as typical Gram advice as you could get.

I stood up and told her I was headed down to the lake for a little while.

"Blessings are woven into this house," Gram whispered. "All around you."

What a beautiful thought. I bent to kiss her cheek. "I can feel it."

~

Charlie was my companion, as Jesse preferred leaving him at the house, and Charlie seemed to comply with good grace. Daisies bloomed everywhere now, and at the borders of the path there was cottongrass with its fluffy white tufts, and the shimmery red plumes of squirrel grass. Lapis lazuli bluebells nodded in the sun, and demure pale blue forget-me-nots with their sunny-yellow hearts bloomed in the shade. I just stopped and stared, it was all so stunningly beautiful. Charlie paused near me, next to a fireweed plant with its lowest blossoms open, each cluster of delicate four papery petals unfolded, bright fuschia under the sun, so bright I could even see the myriad darker veins running through the petals.

Fireweed. Chamerion angustifolium. Also known as rosebay willowherb, Gram taught me. As a child I had seen gravelly riverbeds carpeted with it in midsummer, so that whole river valleys gleamed faintly pink from miles away. So beautiful and seemingly delicate, yet it was almost always the first flower to appear after a disaster—as witnessed after the Mount St. Helens explosion well over a hundred years ago, or as Gram told me once, nearly two hundred years ago in London where some of our ancestors had once lived, after the terrible war bombing that left streets of dust and rubble, fireweed was the first plant to take root and then blossom and offer such color and cheer.

Fireweed was a survivor. But more than that, it was a harbinger of hope, and beauty. Perhaps a few hours of contemplating fireweed was just what I needed.

Thank you, fireweed. Thank you that you help heal the soul. Oh, I wish I, too, could be a healer!

I was beginning to see that healing was so much more than channeling power and working dramatic miracles. A plant, or a person, could bring healing by simply being there, a witness to grace and beauty and hope. I wasn't sure about the beauty part of it, but I could try for the grace and hope.

Healing is putting yourself into a blessing for someone or something else, Gram had told me when I was very little. *You become part of that blessing. Sometimes you can be the vehicle for the blessing.* I remembered that. I remembered sitting with Augie and how I'd been singing Gram's song at the lake, but brought it as a story to Augie—Raven stealing the light, or bringing the light to humans if you wanted to put a more altruistic spin on it. The songs, the stories, they were all one and the same weren't they? I thought on this for some time down at the lakeshore.

~

Sitting next to Jesse at dinner at the end of that day, an awful sensation of heaviness crept over me. It felt like for a long time I had been carrying something that was making me *weary almost unto death,* as Gram would say. Then I realized it wasn't me. The feeling was coming from Jesse. He *had* been trying to hide something from me. For how long? It felt like it had been going on for a while, but something had changed, just that day. Something had happened to cause him pain. A lot of pain.

He was trying to act normal. Trying to listen to people, trying to smile and answer when spoken to—but I could feel the pain. He even looked a little smaller somehow as he sat there, slightly hunched in, like he was trying to protect his heart.

I paused next to him while picking up empty plates, and whispered in his ear, "Come down to the lake with me."

263

He looked surprised. "Now?"

I nodded. There were still a few hours before sunset and the lake would be lovely in the warm light of late day. But that's not why I wanted to get him there.

When we were done helping clean up, we walked out into the warm early evening, not needing jackets. Charlie trotted ahead of us down the path. Golden evening light warmed us from the west, but couldn't penetrate the thick spruce forest. It felt so different from how it felt in the early mornings when I walked into the light of the morning sun. Jesse felt different too. A few weeks ago I had seen him jog ahead with Charlie, playful in the way he'd been as a child. Now he felt weighed down, old. Lines ran across his forehead, carved up and down to either side of his mouth, glimpses of what he would look like as an old man.

The path was wide enough for walking side by side, and I slipped my hand into Jesse's and gave a little squeeze. I was trying hard not to say the awful words, *We have to talk.*

"I'm sorry I've been kind of distracted," I started, feeling my way. "I've been worrying about where I'm headed and maybe that's kept me from being here for you."

Jesse stopped walking and looked down at me, but I couldn't tell what he was thinking.

"It's nothing you've done or haven't done, Raven."

Ah, he already had seen past my ploy for trying to get him to talk.

"Jesse, there are things you aren't telling me, things I need to know. We're partners in this, remember?"

He sighed and gave my hand a small squeeze back. "We *are* partners. It's just that I knew you were working on your own stuff and I didn't want to hit you with my shit."

That didn't sound good. We kept walking. It was easier to walk side by side and talk, looking ahead down the trail. But Jesse wasn't talking much. Under his faded and worn flannel shirt, his shoulders were hunched, his head was down.

I gave his hand a harder squeeze. "Sweetheart, we're in this together. I want to know what's weighing you down."

We were in the darkest part of the forest, where thick spruce trees missed their birch and aspen companions, where on bright days there wasn't enough light coming through for wildflowers to grow.

Jesse sighed again. "I've been killing people, Raven."

That's all he said at first. I had to bite my lower lip to keep from pestering him with questions; I knew I needed to listen now as if Jesse's life depended on it. Perhaps it did.

"You know I said I'd been working as a sniper for the resistance," he said slowly, his words matching our pace through the dim light. "Prior to meeting up with you at P1."

I gave his hand a squeeze for *yes, I know.*

"And I was going to stop doing it. Well, I did, but then Emmitt asked me to fly what we call the death drones. Remote, from the safe house on the mountainside. I've killed three Orion commanders with them, working with Emmitt."

Death drones. I'd seen an execution at P1 by one. During our hour outside I had been walking the perimeter of our enclosure with Hannah and Cat, heard a shout, saw a prisoner sprinting down the inside-the-Fence perimeter road toward the sea, saw something flying after him only a few feet above him, a flash, a burst of blood, his body falling forward and skidding down the road. We'd all looked away, sickened and shocked. Cat heard that he had knocked a guard out, climbed a pen fence and run. He didn't get far.

My stomach clenched. Jesse was killing people like that.

"Most of the time it's just surveillance," he was saying as we walked on, through the dark spruce. "I'm assigned officers to follow and report on their every move, from the time they get up in the morning to the time they go to bed, every place they go, every person they talk to..."

I glanced over when his voice trailed off, but he was looking down at the path and I couldn't read his expression.

"The guy I've been following for the past two months, *Delta* we've been calling him since he's number four on the list of targets, I got the command this morning to terminate him. It was confirmed— *Go*, Emmitt said, *terminate him now.* So I did."

Jesse stopped walking and just stood there on the path. He was looking off to the side, to two spruce trees that had fallen over in a tangle, taking out several others, but it was just as dark around them as everywhere else. He slowly shook his head.

"No one says *kill*, they say *terminate* instead... It's somehow sanitized, you know?" He gave me a quick look.

I nodded, feeling my stomach cramp. Oh, I knew.

"I was looking right into his eyes. I was the last thing that guy saw as he stood on the balcony outside his office, talking to somebody, looking up at the last second."

He'd let go of my hand. He ran both his hands through his hair and his right hand tangled in his braid. I reached out and gently took it, held it in my hand again.

He looked at me, his eyes so dark. "Except... all he saw was a death drone moving in, but I saw his eyes... it wasn't one man against another... it was like I had the power of a god." He shut his eyes, shook his head. "I had all the power; he didn't. I shouldn't have used it. And I'd told you I wouldn't be doing any more killing, either."

We just stood there on the path in the dark forest. I squeezed his hand again.

"I shouldn't have done it," he said again. "His eyes—that's all I can see now."

I stepped in front of Jesse and took his other hand, stood there right in front of him holding tight onto both his hands and looking up at him. His eyes were closed; he dropped his head and I leaned forward and up so our foreheads lightly touched. We stood there breathing with each other for several long minutes. Tears ran down his cheeks. I let go of his hands and reached my arms around him and hugged him against me. I was feeling all the hurt in the world right then, and praying to Raven to help us find the path out.

"I love you," I whispered to him. "Let me be your medicine." Thinking *let me be the vehicle, let me be the song...*

I heard him breathe out, almost a choked laugh. "Raven, I think this is beyond even you."

I reached up and gently cupped his face with my hands so he couldn't look away.

"There are no quick fixes for something like this—how could there be? But I've learned a lot about the healing of the soul in these past few years." I paused, thinking of fireweed blooms and a raven feather I'd found at the lake, which now lay against my chest, under my shirt. "I can offer you hope."

He put his arms around me and hugged me tight, and we just stood there, holding on to each other, for a long time. His arms, his body, felt so good. Then Jesse raised his head, and I could feel him looking up ahead. He put his hands on my shoulders and gently turned me around so that I was standing in front of him, looking with him down the trail.

I'd been looking in the other direction and hadn't realized that we'd nearly reached the lake. The trail opened just ahead. Golden light was ahead of us, warm rays of the evening sun gleaming on the gold-leafed birch and aspen and turning the lake water to gold. Charlie had reached the bank ahead of us and sat on his haunches. Gold light shimmered on his fur.

~

The next morning Jesse said he wasn't going back to the safe house. He wasn't going to go back there ever again. Augie, who was pouring himself a mug of coffee as Jesse made this statement in the kitchen, turned from the range and declared that he wouldn't either. "Solidarity," he said as he sat down next to Jesse and me.

After breakfast Jesse and I walked back to the lake, and sat on the bank, mostly quiet. Charlie sat on Jesse's other side, thoughtfully watching the lake water. It almost looked like he'd done some fishing in his past and was contemplating doing it again. Maybe the wolf blood in him was sea wolf; his ancestors might be the small number of wolves that lived along the coast, smaller than the inland wolves, eating only fish and seals, even swimming from island to island. Mid to late June meant that the big silver king salmon—those that were left—should be swimming up their home streams; I wondered if they came up the small stream that connected the lake to the south bay. Maybe Charlie had noticed them.

"Damn," Jesse said then. "I should have brought a fish net." Eerily with the same thought, which seemed to happen to us all the time. Had always happened between us.

We sat in silence for another moment, and my thoughts stayed on Jesse, and moved to Augie, and Emmitt... and Orion. I was just about to open my mouth and tell Jesse I was so glad for what he had decided, when he stirred next to me and said,

"Tell me a story, Tessa."

"What?" Stories felt so far away right then. Gram had told a few in recent evenings when we'd all gathered in the upstairs living room, but I hadn't told any like I used to.

"Tell me a story."

Tell me a story, the words I had spoken to Gram so many times as a child.

"A Raven story? Or Étain?" I stalled. They all felt so far away.

267

Bits of Sharon Matthew's princess and the bears story surfaced in my mind, and I felt my lips move in a small smile as I thought of her. What had become of her? I yearned to know that she had returned to live with her family in the tall cedar and spruce forest beyond Whitewater Bay, married, maybe with children. Perhaps she was telling The Woman Who Married The Bear story right at that moment to them.

"Girl and Raven," Jesse said.

Ah. I hadn't told one of those since childhood, and I'd stopped when every story led them to the city.

"Well, they did go to the city," I said slowly. "But they got separated. The girl... lost her way. She became a fighter. She thought she'd lost her best friend in the whole world and living didn't really matter after that, so she might as well be the best fighter she could be..."

Jesse put his arm around me. Charlie had stopped watching the water, and put his head on Jesse's knee and watched us through half-closed eyes.

"The girl became a woman, flying like Raven, but using flying in the wrong way." My voice faltered. I cleared my throat and made myself go on. "Her flying killed people. They were people who were trying to kill her, and who were killing many others, but still... she began to understand that killing them wasn't what she should do. And she wanted to tell Raven this, that she finally understood this, but just then she was captured and put in a huge cage. But Raven came and visited her there, many times actually..."

I thought of all the times I had been blessed by the images of Gram and Jesse and the lake, comforting me, feeling like warm arms wrapped around me—and the day the raven actually had come and landed on me and knocked me down, and it was like I heard his voice say, *What are you waiting for, a personal invitation?*

"And it turned out that her best friend in the whole world hadn't died. He came and helped get her out of prison, in a mad, spectacular get-away, complete with explosions."

Jesse smiled, but he kept looking out at the lake.

I paused. His arm tightened around me. *And what happened next?* I could hear my small girl's voice asking Gram.

"Then she found herself in a new place," I finally said. "No, that's not right."

In my mind I saw Raven pushing his mind against the sky. That's where I was, pushing my mind against something that felt as enormous as the sky. He pushed his mind through the sky and pulled his body after him, into the world of the humans living in the dark, to the home of the old man who had all of the light of the universe hidden away in one tiny box. Talk about thresholds.

But I wasn't sure what threshold I was pushing against.

"She wasn't quite there yet," I said to Jesse. "She was still pushing against the sky. Like Raven in the story, pushing through the sky with his mind, before his body."

Jesse turned his head and looked at me. He nodded slowly. It wasn't just me, it was Jesse too.

"But she had helpers?"

I nodded too. "Oh yes. But..." Somehow when it came right down to it, one always stood alone.

Jesse kept nodding; he knew that too.

But maybe I'd been missing something about stories. For so many years I had seen them as my comfort, or as adventures that were fun to hear. That's the answer I'd given as a child to Gram when she asked me if I knew why we told stories. Of course I didn't know then; I had to spend a lot of years finding out. Maybe I took a bit longer, though, than I should have...

But now I saw it—telling stories and hearing stories helps us to listen, to pay attention, to find meaning. But more than that, the storyteller invites the audience to participate in the story. And by participating, we experience pain and suffering, but also redemption and hope.

This is why stories are our medicine. They not only connect us with our ancestors, but also they connect us with each other, and with ourselves.

I wrapped my arms around Jesse on the bank above the lake and kissed him. He leaned against me and made a purring sound.

"I have a good story for you tonight," I said.

~

That night I told The Woman Who Married The Bear story for the first time for the family. Gram and Grampa of course knew it, but for some reason it had never been a part of our cycle of stories at the lake; Jesse, Augie, Cat and Hannah—who'd all been there gathered on the living room couches—had never heard it before.

As I told it, I thought of Sharon Matthew and all of the times we'd told the story to each other in the dark, for comfort. And the sadness in the story—she'd lost so much! The spoiled princess who'd had bear shit on her shoe had lost everything at the end—her husband whom she'd come to love, her children, and even her original family and home. She'd ended up with nothing. But now I understood that we listeners needed that sadness, because it was a sadness that we all felt, it resonated in us. And, in fact, that wasn't the story's end.

I had paused long enough for Augie to clear his throat and say, "Is that the ending, Tessa?"

I looked at Gram, sitting there on her end of the couch in a soft smocky top over her jeans, worn moccasins on her feet. Grampa was close on her other side, his plaid flannel shirt open by several buttons at the top, his left arm around her shoulders. She gave me a little nod as if to say, *Keep going.*

"The medicine in this story," I said slowly, the words coming to me so slowly, but surely, "the medicine here for us is that we think we've lost everything, but we haven't, have we?"

I thought of what I had lost—childhood, our home lake, the gift that it seemed I had been born to use to help people and to find my own identity through, the integrity of my own soul because I had killed people and would never, ever, ever be able to wash their blood from my hands... But. The story didn't end there.

I kept looking at Gram, and she saw all of that in my eyes, and nodded again.

The Woman Who Married The Bear certainly ended up a long way from being a spoiled princess. She was a woman who had lost a great deal, for sure, but...

"Look at what she had gained at the end," I said softly. "She had born beautiful children —Okay, so she'd had bears—"

Augie sniggered at this.

"But they were extremely cunning and curious and good creatures who were loyal to each other and to their people. She had returned to her village with gifts: bringing to her father the dirge song of her bear husband to be sung forevermore, and his ceremonial cloak to be used as a dancing garment, and his crest to be a part of her family line, a new identity. And she was headed somewhere from there, definitely."

"I think she was going to become a shaman," Grampa declared, and then grinned at me.

Gram smiled from his side. "That is definitely healing medicine, Tessa."

Jesse, who'd been on his back on the rug, arms behind his head, gave me a smile that reminded me of Jesse from childhood.

11. June 16–July 31, 2111

Stories and songs were my medicine, as Gram said, as was sitting and quieting myself by the lake. *Because that is a balance for you, Tessa,* Gram said when I was very little and complained about having to sit still for an hour above the lake. *It is your balance, for your natural tendency is to be too much in motion!* But working with one's hands was also important, and on the days I didn't go with Cat and Hannah to the clinic, Gram made sure I did that in the kitchen. I loved using my hands to knead dough until it was soft and springy, to shape loaves or rolls or even braids of dough and then guard them carefully as they rose; I loved chopping and mixing our own vegetables into soups and stews and watching them simmer over the blue gas flame of the stove. And as these things became easier for me to do, my mind could more and more drift and ponder the medicine of the stories and songs I had been given.

And the funny thing was, it was stories and songs I was becoming known for at the clinic. Hannah and Cat were so much more medically proficient than I was, so I was finding my own ways to contribute. I was becoming better and better at sitting quietly with someone and understanding how they were feeling and where their pain was, and I was finding that many people—especially children—loved hearing me quietly sing some of Gram's healing songs, or tell a story. We even were getting repeat visitors just to again hear Raven Travelling, or The Woman Who Married The Bear, or "the fly story." Of course I took some grief for this from Hannah, but this was more like her automatically playing her role of critical older sister. She often smiled at me when we worked together—while she splinted a fracture or pulled out a nasty splinter, and I distracted with a story.

Jesse began his own trajectory toward healing. Emmitt accepted his resignation, and Augie's too, sending a message by way of Grampa, saying he was sorry for how it had all shaken out, and he understood Jesse not wanting to return to work. But we didn't see Emmitt for some weeks more because he had taken on Jesse's work himself. We didn't talk about it, but it was hard on Cat especially, because there had been something between her and Emmitt.

I asked Jesse about Billy, too: *Billy isn't doing drone work for Emmitt? Please tell me no!* Jesse smiled, shook his head and said that no, Billy's skills fortunately lay with coding and the designing of surveillance programs. He was proving incredibly valuable to the resistance in this realm.

Gram put Augie to work maintaining the house and yard—and there was plenty to do, many jobs deferred by Augie and Jesse since they'd only had a few days here and there up until now. Jesse worked alongside Augie on some of these chores, but he also was given a different assignment by Gram.

Gram clearly was planning on making an announcement as she set a plate of cinnamon rolls down on the table the morning after I told The Woman Who Married The Bear story. I had made the dough the night before, cut it into rolls and put them in the refrigerator to rise overnight, and got up early to put them in the oven so that everyone would wake up to their wonderful fragrance. I took some pride in that. But all eyes went to Gram.

"Now," Gram said. "About today..."

Jessie and Augie were helping themselves to rolls, but they both paused and looked at Gram. Under the table Jesse's free hand found my knee.

"About today," Gram repeated, sitting down across from us.

And just then Grampa walked into the kitchen, his white hair unbraided and rumpled, but his dark eyes as bright as they'd been long ago when I'd first met him. He'd wrapped and belted a plaid flannel bathrobe tight around him; it occurred to me that I'd never seen him in a bathrobe. His skinny lower legs stuck out and he was wearing an old pair of moccasins that looked like a match to Gram's.

"I'm retiring," he announced to the room.

"Wow, we never would have guessed!" Augie deadpanned.

On my other side, Hannah made a chuckling sound. Cat, still at the sink washing mugs, turned and looked at all of us, and laughed.

This was such good news. In the past month he had been away more often than at home, flying his plane, *earning the bread and bringin' home the bacon*, as he liked to say (never talking about his resistance work). I loved it—we all loved it—when he was home with us and it felt like we were one big family, sitting in the evenings in the living room sometimes telling stories, sometimes listening to stories over the radio. We didn't have *any techy stuff* as Augie put it, no streaming holograms or vids that projected on the walls for entertainment like the people in the city had. We had an old fashioned radio that we kept tuned to the native station KNAT which provided an amazing variety of shows ranging from teaching basic Tlingit (Gram loved this one) to an old-style naturalist-in-the-wild show about birds (Cat's and my favorite) to the commentary of evening rugby games in the city (the guys had to be rationed to three nights of this a week). It was Grampa who completed the feeling of home.

"And I brought something for you, Jesse, to work on in that shed of yours. It's still under the tarp in the back of my truck. Didn't tell you about it last night, we were so busy with stories. So you'd best get out there later this morning and make some room for it."

Jesse brightened. He and Augie both ate big breakfasts and planned how they'd make room in the shed.

"You sure it's wood?"Augie's characteristic grin was back as he and Jesse left us in the kitchen and headed to the shed. "You sure he didn't bring Tessa a bear?"

I heard Jesse give a short laugh as they stepped out the door, and my heart lifted a little. Thank God for Augie. I looked at Hannah and Cat, both now sitting at the table, looking at me. And Grampa was sitting next to Gram, taking a sip out of her coffee.

Blessings are woven into this house, Gram had said.

"Thank God for family," I said softly and everyone smiled at the same second.

~

Grampa had brought Jesse a three foot tall chunk of yellow cedar. Jesse put his hands to carving, which had been a gift we'd all seen in him when he was a boy. He'd never had much time for it then, what with so many farm chores he had to help Earl with, but he loved it even as a little boy, when he'd stolen away to carve tiny totems with fantastical creatures sitting one atop another, boxes that fit comfortably in the hand and opened to keep small treasures, practical stirring spoons and salad servers shaped like bear claws.

But now he was doing masks. He said he was practicing before he touched the special cedar that Grampa had brought. He would disappear into his shed at the eastern edge of the yard, where bushy blue spruce pushed against the faded wood walls as if to hold it up and keep it from falling backwards into the small, rocky ravine below. He would be in there for hours. He'd taken the time to cut window openings in all four walls, and then built screens in wooden frames that could be put in as replacements for windows in the hot summer

months, to make the shed more comfortable for working. No one
went there unless invited: it was his medicine (though he assured me
that I was still his first medicine).

After two weeks, he began talking about the carving. He came
out of his shed as Cat and Hannah and I were taking a break from
gardening, sitting with Augie on springy clover. We were just beyond
the raised bed vegetable boxes that Jesse had built and planted for
Gram in April, now nearly bursting with lettuces and kale and bush
beans and onions and carrots and beets. It was the first of July and a
hot day, humid, with no cooling breezes. And the mosquitos were
bad. I had a bottle of citronella oil, which helped marginally, that I
pulled out of my back pocket and passed around.

Charlie followed Jesse out of his shed and lay down with a happy
sigh in the clover as Jesse squeezed between me and Augie, and Jesse
started talking about the mask he was carving.

"When I got to the eyes, it was kind of like all the shit I've been
going through came out." He paused. "The eyes," he said again, and
stopped.

I leaned against him and put my right arm around him, but the
feeling that was coming from him was that steady-state peace and
calm that I remembered from the Jesse of childhood.

"I'll admit I got scared when I was carving the eye holes," he
said. "It felt like there was something in there looking out at me. I
had to actually put the mask down for two days."

Augie chuckled from Jesse's other side. "Now, does that sound
rational?"

"Absolutely," I said, a little too quickly. "Every Tlingit knows
spirits look out the eye holes of the mask."

"It's the most important part of the mask," Hannah said from
my left. "That's where the spirits look out to the world."

Jesse nodded.

"Like Raven looking down at the lakes from above and seeing
eyes looking back at him," I added. All of those times I'd been in the
air looking down at deep lakes at the feet of mountains, shallow azure
glacier pools tucked into snowy passes, tundra ponds flashing the sun
back into my eyes, all of those times came back to me and I longed to
be back in the air. Like Raven, looking down at the spirit eyes of the
world.

Jesse reached over and put his hand over mine, on my knee.

"So...what did you do?" I asked. Thinking not of the eyes of happy spirits, but of the eyes of the Orion officer Jesse had described a few weeks ago, how he had looked up at Jesse just before Jesse had killed him. I couldn't help the shudder that ran through me. But Jesse stayed feeling calm.

"Well, I guess we made peace, the spirit and I." He was looking straight ahead, into the forest. "I said to it, *If you're someone I harmed in this life, I humbly ask your forgiveness for it, and I'll let you out if you promise to do no harming yourself*—and he seemed to agree to it."

"Gotta say man, that sounds like Catholic speak," Augie said from Jesse's other side.

I saw Cat smile. She'd been quiet, sitting beyond Augie; she'd looked thoughtful and maybe a little sad, all that morning.

Jesse chuckled. "We were *raised* by a Catholic, but that's as far as that went. At least in me!"

Augie let out a long breath. "Yeah, in me, too."

I was guessing that Earl Brightwater felt the same way. The Catholic in their family was their mother, Martha. I was pretty sure that Earl quietly followed her lead in this area to preserve the household peace. Suddenly I longed to see Earl again, and was just about to ask Jesse and Augie if they'd had any message from Emmitt lately on how things were at the lake, when we all jumped at Emmitt's voice from behind us saying, "Some work detail this is!"

Charlie thumped his tail in greeting and Emmitt dropped down on the clover in between Augie and Cat. "Gram said you were all working for her today. This is my kind of work."

"Hey man, how's it hangin'?" Augie leaned across Cat to give him a light shoulder punch.

Emmitt ignored Augie's energy with the patience of Charlie dealing with the boring hours I liked to spend at the lake. He smiled at Cat, and she smiled back, looking suddenly happy.

"Hi Tessa, Hannah." He turned, his eyes holding a quiet sweetness that was at Emmitt's core, even if he was *a driven man*, as Jesse said. A man who was not going to ever stop hunting Orion. "Hey Jesse," Emmitt added. "I've wondered how you were doing."

Jesse nodded. "I was just talking about the mask I'm working on. Nearly done. It's not going to be much, though..."

"Just call it your therapy mask," Augie suggested, and Jesse shoulder-punched him, not lightly.

"I've got a really good idea for one I want to start, with that cedar." Jesse smiled when we all looked at him, then he shook his head. "Nope, not talking about it yet."

Emmitt nodded, looking thoughtful. "Some things just need to... set for a while."

A breeze stirred through the birches below us and I sighed, imagining the cool water of the lake nearby—I had been doing some bathing along with my morning prayers. Jesse put his arm around me and pulled me against him. Hannah said she was thinking of doing a little more work thinning the lettuce. I didn't want to go back to gardening and was going to propose another trip down to the lake, when Augie suddenly exclaimed,

"Whoa man, that beezo is cool! Where'd you get it?"

Emmitt held out his left arm, showing the sleek screen device on a wristband.

"Augie, it's called a wristpad."

"Oh fuck you, Emmitt. Take it off and let me see it."

Augie swiped his index finger on the screen and punched buttons with his usual energy.

"Don't break it," Emmitt said. "You break it, I break you."

After a minute Jesse asked for it, and Augie handed it to him, and I watched over Jesse's shoulder. At P1 I'd occasionally had glimpses of the wrist screens and the ear pieces the guards wore, and it intrigued me that a wearable device could connect a person both visually and with sound to any person they wanted to connect with, as well as to all of the networked information in the world. Just like that, from one's wrist, one could be anywhere in the world, knowing everything.

When I begged to hold it, Jesse handed it to me. But as soon as I held it in my hands it began buzzing and the screen began flashing.

"Holy shit, Tessa broke it!" Augie said, and Emmitt leaned past him to take a look. Cat was laughing like I hadn't seen her laugh in a long time.

I handed it back. "Sorry, Emmitt. I didn't do anything at all to it. Honest."

"No problem, I'll reboot it." He touched a finger to one corner of the screen, which went dark, and then, as we all leaned over to watch, lit up again a few seconds later. "All set."

"Can I see it just once more? I promise I won't even touch the screen. I just want to see how it works."

Emmitt reluctantly passed it back to me, but as soon as it was in my hands, it began flashing and buzzing again. Augie shouted with laughter, and even Jesse started laughing. Charlie looked up, puzzled. Emmitt did not look happy as he held out his hand for his wristpad.

"That's it for you, Tessa!"

I was relieved to hand it off, but as funny as it all was, there was something odd going on that I felt like I needed to figure out. But I didn't have time right then, since once Emmitt had his pad *rebooted*— and where the heck did that word come from? I didn't dare ask— Jesse got to his feet and said it was time to go in for something cold to drink. Augie enthusiastically seconded that, but Emmitt and Cat told us they thought they would walk down to the lake for a little while. Hannah went back to the lettuce.

"So, Tessa, I just want to know if my brother needs to take any special precautions around you when you—" Augie started in as we walked toward the house, but Jesse grabbed him and pushed him into a prickly juniper shrub.

As I followed the two of them into the house, I found myself thinking of a couple of times in childhood when I had accidentally made things jump on our kitchen table, surprising Gram mightily, and how everyone in my class at school had been given an electronic notepad (back in the days when it was easier for us to get them, and the solar film that fed their chargers), everyone but me, because mine kept breaking down. And then, of course, there had been what supposedly happened when Orion had caught me in the ruins of the train station—Miranda said I'd stunned two soldiers and sent them flying in the air. I tried not to think of that one, actually.

As Gram would say, *Tessa, there's something here you need to pay attention to.* But I didn't really want to think on it. It was too unsettling.

Except Jesse brought it up that night.

We were alone, our heads close together on his pillow, darkness wrapped around us, his arm wrapped around me.

"Tessa," he whispered, "about Emmitt's wristpad..."

I groaned. I should have pretended I'd fallen asleep. I couldn't avoid it, but at least I was not going to tell him about those Orion soldiers flying through the air.

I rolled over onto my back, looking up into the dark. "Did it make you remember?"

"Remember what?"

"Oh, that year when everything I touched seemed to break." I had to laugh a little, thinking of it. I remembered Gram wouldn't let me near our clock or hot water heater. "When the teachers at school wouldn't let me have a notepad, me, the only kid in school without one because every time I touched one I broke it."

Jesse started laughing. "Oh my God, I'd forgotten that completely. When was that? Was that before or after the raven?"

"The raven..." I knew what he meant, but somehow I needed things to slow down. Maybe I wanted to hear what he remembered.

"You know. The day my little brother Steve ran into our house and yelled, 'Tessa resurrected a raven!'" He rolled over onto his side and I knew he was looking closely at me, though it was so dark I could barely make out his face.

I was quiet for a moment. "After."

He took a breath. "So, Tessa, you called on a power that day with the raven... to help, whatever... and it's been there with you, inside of you, ever since. Despite your deepest fear that it's left you," Jesse's voice was so soft I could barely hear it, "it's never left you."

How I both longed for it and was absolutely terrified by it, all in the same moment. I felt the suffocating darkness that had pressed down on me as a child as I had held the raven in my hands... how heavy that weight of water had felt on me as I had tried to help Augie up to the surface, even lying on his bed and not even near the lake... and if that electrical current had run through my whole body when the soldiers went to put their hands on me... I had no control over it. It was too much. And yet I yearned for it to come back. But Jesse was saying it had never left.

"You really think so?" I whispered.

"I know so." He paused, then lay back on his back and I felt more than heard his chuckle, his shoulder against my shoulder. "Just a few minutes ago, when you were trying so hard not to make a sound? When I was bringing you almost to the point of screaming in ecstasy—"

I gave him a hard nudge in the ribs. I, who had been aloof physically all of my life until Jesse came back into it, well, maybe you could say we were making up for lost time. We didn't talk much about it, but my book of Neruda's one hundred love sonnets had ended up on our bedside table.

"—you were giving off sparks."

"*What?*" I was up on my elbow staring at him.

"I saw a scatter of sparks shoot from the top of your head into the dark."

I could tell he wasn't kidding.

"Were you scared?" was all I could finally say. *I* was getting scared, thinking about it.

He reached his hand up and ran it through my hair, then to my shoulder, his hand so light on my skin, down to the curve of my breast.

"No. Somehow... no. Though I can see the possibility of you carrying so much energy that maybe you could unconsciously hurt somebody, accidentally, sometime."

I'd never in my life heard anyone so gently try to say something. We were both quiet a moment, then he went on, "And I can see that that would be a scary possibility for you to carry around."

"I'll talk to Gram about it," I said, settling back down against his shoulder. He wrapped his arm around me again. I felt him nod.

"Maybe it's possible for me to learn to have some control," I said, "or at least be able to direct it somehow, safely."

Jesse kissed my bare shoulder. "I'll confess that might keep me from getting a little anxious about sex with you again... No, no, just kidding! Tessa, if you were to accidentally kill me, it would still be worth it, loving you, having been loved by you."

I had never felt so motivated to tackle something.

~

Gram, Hannah, Cat and I had a powwow at the kitchen table the next morning. I felt like I should mention the sparks Jesse had seen, so that it didn't seem like Emmitt's wristpad was just one of those freak coincidences, though no one at the table believed in coincidences, anyway. But hearing me allude to our sex life didn't seem to horrify Gram, wrapped in what looked like Grampa's plaid bathrobe, sipping her third cup of tea.

Cat was sitting in a ray of morning sun—her hair, growing longer as was mine, glowed gold-red like fire. She was smiling at me. I had the feeling that she had already known about our lovemaking, the sparks, the conversation Jesse and I had had, pretty much everything that happened anywhere in the house... and it was fine with me. Cat was Cat and she loved all of us, and we all loved her.

And I really, really wanted to know what was between her and Emmitt, but I didn't want to seem like I was prying. But she knew that, too.

Hannah, next to Cat, sat in shadow, frowning. Something bigger than me was bothering her.

"Tessa," Gram said finally, looking up at me. "You've been healing yourself. This is something to celebrate. But I'm feeling an urgency about you putting that... energy... to use."

Something settled over us. What I had seen in Hannah, and Gram's word *urgency,* added to it. I began to feel that our peaceful, very quiet life at Grampa's house might not last much longer. Something was coming.

Cat was nodding, her eyes on my face.

Damn.

Gram had stopped talking and sat quietly, staring at her cup of tea. I looked over at Hannah. "Something's bugging you," I said softly. "What is it?"

She flicked a glance my way, and didn't say anything for a moment, then, "Something's coming our way, something that we all need to be prepared for... I don't know what it is yet."

When I kept looking at her, waiting, she added, "You're not the only one who's working on your gift. Cat and I both have been working for weeks with Gram on ours."

This sounded like a challenge, but I refused to rise to the bait. "What have you been doing?"

"Both of us have been focusing by using meditation. And paying attention to our dreams."

I swear I could hear her add, *which you haven't been doing.* And she was right, too. But feeling judged by Hannah always bugged me, so I tried not to show it.

"And...?"

"And what?" She looked irritated.

"How's it been going?"

She shrugged, then nodded at Cat, who had gotten up and was putting dishes away on the top shelf of a cupboard that Gram couldn't reach. "Cat's increased her range considerably. I bet if she really concentrated, she could know your thoughts if she were down in our room and you were here at the kitchen table." *Or vice versa,* I heard.

So much for bedroom privacy. But, as we said, Cat was Cat. It was okay. If it were Hannah... that would be different.

"How about you?" I asked Hannah. "Has dealing with the Sight gotten any... easier?"

"It will never be *easy*." Ah, we were back in the classroom, Hannah and I. Her classroom that day I went to tell her I was leaving, and she talked to me as if I were one of her first graders.

"But I'm beginning to be able to call on it through meditation, or at least to feel like I'm getting some confirmation of what I think it's telling me," she added. "And it's not taking me by surprise, or making me feel helpless, like it used to."

I nodded. "I'm glad."

She eyed me warily. Then she also nodded. "We all need to get to work now."

~

That night Emmitt sent us a quick message through Augie, who had ridden over to visit him and Billy for a few hours: *Be careful— Orion has started raiding houses in Southaven now, and may come your way. They may be stepping up the search for all of you again!*

A confirmation of our fears if ever there was one.

Gram talked about how she knew where she could find convincing wigs for us—Cat would have to switch to brown now since her last one had been blonde, and perhaps a pair of glasses would help. Gram said that I should start wearing blue contact lenses. Emmitt had told her that there were lenses (illegally obtained, of course) that not only changed the color of one's eyes, but also the pattern, to confuse retinal scanners. But Orion's technology was far more advanced than just retinal scanning. Data on our body shapes and the bone structure of our faces was in the Orion data banks as well, so changing the color of our hair or eyes wouldn't save us if we were scanned.

"But of course none of us is going into the city," Gram said. "I think it's still safe enough for you to go back and forth to the clinic, as long as you keep to the forest."

Emmitt and Augie had been given forged Orion identcards when they first joined the resistance grounders, and Jesse too, though Jesse's was no good now that he'd been exposed as a resistance fighter and scanned at P1. His card now would set off alarms as fast as his face would on an Orion scanner. But finding a disguise for Jesse would be a real challenge.

"What's so funny in all of this, Tessa?" Hannah sounded sour.

"I was just thinking of us trying to disguise Jesse," I said. "Kind of hard to disguise an Indian warrior."

Cat laughed. "That blond wig he was wearing the night he came to spring us from prison... even with an Orion uniform on—"

"He'd put some makeup on his face, too," I added. "It's a wonder he got as far as he did."

"There you go, Tessa," she said, "if you ever doubted he loved you with his whole heart. He was willing to die for you that night. That was a suicide mission if ever there was one."

~

Gram found us wigs, brown for Cat, blonde for me, and a dull mostly gray one for Hannah, and a few days later Emmitt obtained my contact lenses through one of his resistance buddies. Gram had decided that neither Cat nor Hannah needed to worry about the color of their eyes, but I did, since my eyes were *different enough to stand out*, she said. I put in the new lenses, sitting on our bed with Jesse next to me, and turned to him and got a reaction I hadn't expected. He was surprised.

"You don't like me with blue eyes?" I teased.

"No, it's not that. Go look in the mirror." He pulled me up off the bed and over to the bureau in the corner of our room that had a small mirror above it.

My eyes weren't blue at all; they now were a dark greenish hazel, sort of a dark mossy color—a lot like Billy's—but with little zigzags of gold around my pupils, tiny starbursts inside the mossy green.

Jesse was laughing. "What is with you, Tessa? It's not just mechanical, it's *chemical.*"

I still had the box in my hand; I read the label again: *Blue.*

"Maybe the box was mislabeled." I just hoped Gram would let me keep these since I couldn't feel them in my eyes and I liked the new color, even if it, too, might be different enough to stand out.

When I went upstairs for dinner that night with my new eye color and wearing my new wig—shoulder length blonde hair in a rather sassy ponytail, and I'd lightened my eyebrows just a little so that they looked more realistic with the blonde hair—I made quite the splash.

"Holy shit, Tessa," Augie laughed. "You could fool anybody!"

Jesse, who hadn't yet seen me with the wig, grinned. "I'm going to feel like I'm cheating on you with another woman."

Charlie sat up, looked at me and gave one sharp bark, which made everyone laugh harder.

I tossed my head so my blonde ponytail bounced. "I think I'm going to like being blonde."

"Just... no hair color jokes, please!" Cat frowned at me from her station at the stove, where she was stirring a pot of something that smelled very good. She was serious.

Hannah refrained from comment, but she cracked a smile.

Jesse helped Gram sit down in her chair at one end of the table. She was smiling.

"We're just getting ready, that's all," was all she said, a statement which seemed as uncharacteristic as my new haircolor.

It's not that we weren't taking Emmitt's warning—or Hannah's Seeings—seriously. It's just that laughter helped lift, just for a little, that heavy sense of something dark approaching.

~

As the July days crept by Jesse started on the carving project that he had been thinking on but not talking about. He spent whole afternoons in his shed. Several times he invited me in and I found him shirtless and sweating in the summer heat as he wielded his knives on the wood. Charlie was always there with him, lying on the bare wood floor close to the open door, where it was a bit cooler. All Jesse would tell us about his project was that it was a special mask. All that mattered to me was that he was beginning to feel happy again. He was coming back to his calm, steady resolve, to his ability to see what needed to be done, and then figure out how to do it.

In the third week of July when he invited me in to see his progress on the mask, I felt such excitement, like I was a little girl waking up in the winter to see a white blanket of snow spreading over the whole world, all the way up to my bedroom window.

"It's rough still," he cautioned, opening the shed door for Charlie and me. "But I think you can see now where it's heading."

He'd been working for a few hours already, and the shed smelled of cedar. He pulled a sheet off the large object at the center of his work table and turned on his work lamp, a small globe on a tall iron pole with a wide base. In the soft light the wood glowed as golden as the sun. My breath caught in my throat as he gently turned the two foot tall mask to face me. It was a raven—no, it was a woman transforming into a raven—all soft, golden wood that looked so smooth I immediately reached out a hand to stroke it.

The base of the mask was the smooth, soft shoulders of a woman, just above her breasts. He had carved a long, elegant neck that was going to be brushed by shoulder-length rounded feathers. I could see where he had begun to carve the wood into soft, long feathers whose curving tips touched the woman's shoulders. The head was a raven's, but the beak was gentler, less blocky than the carved raven's beaks in traditional Tlingit masks. The eyes were wide and almond shaped, narrow rims around them emphasizing their beautiful curve, the irises inset and the pupils open for the mask wearer—or Raven's spirit—to look through.

The wood glowed under the soft light and my fingers could not resist tracing the smoothness of the shoulders, the sharp edges of the feathers that were just emerging from the wood, the soft curve below the liquid eye.

"Do you like it?" he asked.

"Oh, I love it!" I finally found words. "It looks alive. No, it looks like the sun would look like if it was wood!"

"Yellow cedar," he said, also reaching out to run a finger over the shoulders. "I couldn't have used anything else for this. It's the wood that conveys the idea of softness and—" He struggled to find a word, and looked at me. "It's a paradox somehow, Raven. I wanted to show vulnerability, but at the same time, power."

Again I had no words. I just kept gazing at the mask.

"I was trying to convey what feels like the essence of you."

I looked at him. "Me?"

He smiled. "Sometimes you can carry more power than anyone I've ever met, but at the same time you have such a softness about you. Tessa Ravenwing, you're so vulnerable and invulnerable at the very same time, it just boggles the mind."

We stood there silently a moment, just leaning against each other. I could feel his slow breaths. A deep contentment was rising in him and filling me. I whispered part of my favorite Neruda love sonnet to him:

so close that your hand upon my chest is mine,
so close that your eyes close with my dreams.

285

~

But in late July, I began to have nightmares. It didn't make sense. I had been feeling like I was coming back into balance, that I was using my gifts as they were intended to be used. But after the third night of dreaming about Orion soldiers chasing me through the forest, I told Gram. I was helping her put fresh sheets on the big bed in its rough wood frame, that she and Grampa shared. It was the last day of July. After breakfast Grampa had jounced away in the old truck, into town for supplies, saying that he'd be gone most of the day since he wanted to check on his airplane, make sure his buddies were taking good care of it.

Gram paused when I told her of my nightmares, frowned, then sat down on the bottom sheet we'd just stretched over the mattress. I stood there in front of her, holding the flannel folded top sheet in my hands.

"It's just dreams, right?" I knew how stupid it was to ask that question. I'd been raised on the belief that dreams are never *just dreams*; they always have meaning that we should pay attention to, and while they usually tell us about our own internal states, sometimes they also tell us much more. *Disregard your dreams at your own peril*, Gram had been known to say. Of course Hannah said this a lot, too.

Gram gave me a look. I sat down next to her.

"Sorry," I said. "I do know better. I guess the reason I'm telling you is that on the inside I feel like I'm actually fairly well balanced right now, so I'm surprised I'd be having these bad-men-after-me dreams."

Gram nodded. "They sound a lot like the Seeings Hannah has had lately, not just of you but of all of us... and that worries me." She sat there looking thoughtfully across to the row of pegs beside the doorway, where her shirts and Grampa's shirts hung neatly, mingled together.

"Orion soldiers chasing you? Catching you?" she finally asked.

I nodded.

"Let's have a conference at the kitchen table on this," Gram said. "I'll get in touch with Sadie at the clinic and see if Augie can pick her up, so she can join us, maybe for tea. We should review our emergency plans." She patted my hand. "Just to be safe."

~

I baked tiny chocolate cakes—we were going to have a special tea—and at first it was just us women sitting down at the kitchen table to eat, in a rather light mood. Jesse stayed out in his shed, but then he looked in shyly just as we started on the cakes, and Sadie laughed and waved her arm, beckoning him in.

"Oh, this handsome man must sit next to me!"

Jesse grinned and said, "I'll get my brother!" and disappeared, Sadie calling out in disappointment. But he and Augie came back in just a few minutes, looking determined to hold their own against a kitchenful of women. Charlie slipped in with them, and under the table to lie down at my feet.

I got up with my cup and plate and moved down the table so Jesse could sit next to Sadie, which made her beam.

"Your coloring is so different," she said to Jessie and Augie, "I keep wondering how you really can be brothers."

Augie was busy piling cakes onto his plate, so Jesse replied, "Augie got our mother's genes, so he doesn't look like the typical Brightwater."

"And that is such a wonderful name!" Sadie exclaimed.

"A lot of Tlingit blood on our Dad's side," was all Jesse said. He took a bite of a cake and winked down the table at me.

"Yes, it is all there in you," Sadie said. "That is a good heritage. It is a name as wonderful as Ravenwing." She and Gram nodded at each other.

Ha! The old matchmakers, I thought. Jesse winked at me again.

But then Gram cleared her throat and said, "We need to talk of serious matters for a few minutes."

"And then we can go back to having fun." Sadie beamed and nearly busted a seam in her poppy print shirt as she reached for another cake. Jesse picked up the plate and held it out to her, and her smile deepened.

Gram briefly summarized the Seeings Hannah had had lately of Orion soldiers coming to our house, and she also mentioned the nightmares I'd been having simultaneously. Jesse gave me a quick look that said, *why didn't you tell me?* But what good would that have done? He would have just worried about me.

"Never dismiss recurring dreams," Sadie said suddenly. "They are always telling you something."

Gram nodded vigorously.

"And having them at the same time as the Seeings..." Sadie's voice trailed off. She looked at Hannah, who sat on her other side. "These are gifts to pay close attention to."

We were all silent for a moment. No one smiled now.

"First of all, we should each of us be as careful as possible," Gram said. Hannah leaned forward in her chair and looked pointedly down the table at me. I'd been wearing the contact lenses full time, but I hated the wig, and I often conveniently forgot to wear it when I left the house. Hannah had chided me for this several times recently.

"I'd like us right now to review our emergency plans," Gram went on.

Over the past week we'd agreed on several plans in response to what Hannah called *worst case scenarios*. We'd heard in more detail from Emmitt about the recent Orion raids on houses in the projects and farther south, near us, when patrols of Orion soldiers suddenly surrounded a house and then entered and demanded to see everyone's identcards, used their scanners on faces, found slim excuses for arresting people and hauling them off to "detention camps." So much for how we'd once felt safe under the radar.

No one had been able to talk with Lars for weeks now, but Emmitt was sure that Orion was renewing its hunt for the five of us escapees.

Gram reviewed our action plan in case of sudden arrival of Orion soldiers at the door: those of us who didn't have identcards and were wanted by Orion (Jesse, me, Cat, Hannah) would hide in the safe closet off the downstairs bathroom, built by Jesse and Augie with shields against infrared scanners; those with proper identcards (Gram, Grampa, Augie, and Sadie and Emmitt, if they happened to be around) would comply and seem as agreeable and innocent as possible. We didn't talk about fighting back. After the drone execution, Jesse and Augie had stopped target shooting and knife throwing; there was tacit agreement throughout the house that we would not fight Orion with weapons.

"I still think Jesse needs a disguise," Augie said a bit wickedly, I thought.

"What could possibly disguise him enough?" I asked.

"A wheelchair," Hannah said suddenly. "Disguise him as an old man hunched down a bit in a wheelchair."

Augie and I both burst out laughing. Gram and Sadie smiled.

"I think I might know how to find one of them old fashioned

wheelchairs," Sadie said. "You're thinking of the kind that people push with their hands on the wheels?"

Hannah nodded, completely serious. "And get him a wig like mine."

Jesse did not look amused. "I hate trying to get a wig on over my hair, and I flat out refuse to cut it. Ever."

"There's a dye I could comb through your hair," Gram said. "It would make you look like most of your hair was going silver. It might work."

"And look sooooo nice," Augie said, and took an elbow from Cat, who sat next to him.

Jesse shook his head and got up from the table. "I'm done here. I'll be careful. I got the plan down, and now I'm going back to the shed."

I got up, too, as did Charlie, and we both followed Jesse out of the kitchen. He was moving quickly, and under his t-shirt his shoulders were taut; I felt impatience radiating from him.

"Hey," I said quietly before he got to the front door.

He turned around and looked surprised to see me right behind him.

"Hey you," he put his arms around me. I leaned in to his warmth, loved the feel of hard muscle under the thin fabric of his shirt.

"I love you," I said against him.

"I love you, too, Raven," he said.

I lifted up my face to give him a quick kiss. I could tell he wanted to get back out to the mask, so I let him go.

I went back to the kitchen, but somehow I felt restless. When Augie got up to do a chore, I got up too, saying that I was going to go down to the lake for just a short while.

"Take Charlie with you," Gram said as I left the room. I paused, a little surprised, but then I nodded to her.

"And..." Hannah said loudly.

"Yes, I will wear my damn wig," I said, sighing like a martyr.

That meant running downstairs to our room to get it—probably I should be keeping it upstairs by the front door like Cat did with hers, and then I'd be more likely to wear it, and I resolved to do this in the future—and then taking Charlie meant running back upstairs to go out the front door, the fastest way to the shed which was on that side of the house. But that was okay because it meant I got to see Jesse again.

He laughed at me in my bouncy blonde wig and waved when I told him Gram had told me to take Charlie with me down to the lake. Charlie loved the idea of leaving the shed and heading into the cool spruce forest below the house. The fireweed now was in glorious three-quarters bloom, open magenta flowers halfway up the stalks, with the sleek buds at the tops still waiting for August. Charlie gamboled down the path ahead of me. The words to a childhood song came to my lips all on their own, perfect for the moment.

Walk with the wolf,
Walk with the bear,
Walk in balance.

Walk with the wind,
Walk with the rain,
Walk with the sun.
Walk in balance.

Walk to the east,
Walk to the west,
Walk to the north,
Walk to the south,
Walk in balance.

Walk in love,
Walk in beauty,
Walk in trust,
Walk in truth,
Walk in respect,
Walk in balance.

Charlie frisked; I sang. We quickly reached the lake and my breath caught in my throat at the beauty of it. The air was so still that the lakewater had become a mirror, reflecting the puffy clouds above and the surrounding ring of dark branchy spruce woven through with summer leafy green aspen and birch. Across the water, at the top of the tallest spruce tree, a bald eagle hunched, and it seemed like he was trying to enjoy the scene I was enjoying, but he was being bugged by two dive-bombing ravens. Typical.

Charlie trotted a short distance east along the bank, his long nose down, following a scent. I sat in my favorite spot of matted dry grasses under some birches and quietly watched the water. My eyes slowly lost focus and I felt like I was back home, sitting on the mountain shoulder above our lake, a girl again, learning how to be still and pay attention.

The eagle finally had enough of the ravens, and he spread his huge wings and launched from the spruce, lazily, effortlessly soaring over the water, following the distant bank as it curved to the southeast, and out of sight. The ravens disappeared, bored no doubt.

All was calm and peaceful. Time passed, until something restless stirred in me, the same feeling that had driven me down to the lake. Now for some reason I felt like I ought to head back to the house. I sat there for another minute trying to ignore this feeling, but then I gave up. I whistled for Charlie, who was still a ways up the bank, digging in the dirt. He lifted his beautiful shaggy head and gazed down at me. *Damn, she wants to go already...*

"Charlie, I think we need to go home," I called to him.

He clearly gave that a thought—Jesse and I both swore that Charlie understood every word we said—and then he slowly trotted back to me. I gave him a good pat.

I walked quickly and Charlie padded right in front of me. We were silent on the soft path, quickly passing the fireweed, white and pink yarrow, the tufts of squirrel grass, the huge prickly leaves of devil's club.

When I stepped out of the forest and started up the path in our backyard that led to the back door, Charlie began growling. I looked up at the house and saw something that my brain couldn't comprehend at first—an Orion soldier stood outside the back door with his gun pointed at me.

I'd dreamed it, but still it didn't make sense. I stared. The soldier was still there, silver stars glinting on his shoulder, the rest of him all in black.

Holy shit!

And then all I could think was, *dear God and Raven, please tell me that my family are all in the safe closet!*

"Charlie, quiet," I said, as the growl volume quickly rose. The fear of him getting shot by a trigger-happy soldier was much worse than any thought I had for myself. My heart was pounding so hard I could barely put my hands in the air.

"Don't shoot," I called. "The dog will obey me."

I could feel that Charlie was considering making a run at the soldier. But it would have been a long run, entirely in the open, and he never would have made it. That realization probably wouldn't have stopped him, but what did stop him was the second Orion soldier who stepped out of the back door to stand next to the first one, with a second gun out.

"Charlie, you stay with me," I said quietly but as intently as I'd ever said anything in my life. He listened. He sat on his haunches and I put my hand on his collar.

"I'll shut him in the house, and he won't bother anyone," I called to the soldiers.

The first one waved me forward. Charlie and I walked slowly side by side up the bank to the back of the house. For what felt like a full minute, or more, the Orion soldiers stared at us and we stared back at them; no one looked away, all eyes stayed locked. And the guns stayed on us. It was so quiet I could hear Charlie's footsteps on the grass next to mine. He did not growl again. When I paused, a few feet from the soldiers, he sat down next to me and quietly waited.

"Please put your guns away," I said. "We aren't going to fight you."

One soldier lowered his gun, but the other didn't. Then the first soldier used his gun to point at the door. "Put the dog in."

The second Orion soldier reached out and opened the door, and stood quite a ways back as I moved forward with Charlie. All I wanted was to get him safe in the house so they wouldn't have the excuse to shoot him.

"Shut him in a room," the first soldier said from behind me. The bathroom was on my right—no way was I going to open that door, praying that my loved ones were hidden safe in there—Hannah and Cat's room was on my left. I didn't dare try to walk any farther to Jesse's and my room, for fear they'd think I was trying something.

Charlie did not want to go in, but I gave him a little push, and he seemed to realize this was not the time to try to think for himself. I patted him. "Good boy." Then I shut the door.

The second soldier was motioning me back out the door. Why outside? I wondered.

They marched me around the house, up the steep path on the hill from the backyard. A large aircar sat in our front yard. I paused as I crested the hill and felt the poke of a stunner in the middle of my back.

"Around to the front door," one of the soldiers said. "You're going in the front door."

I concluded that they hadn't wanted to march me down the dark hall and up the stairs inside the house, for fear I'd try something. But I had absolutely no desire to escape until I knew where the rest of my family was. Suddenly it hit me that Jesse might still be in the shed, and I prayed to Raven and all my ancestors that he would stay there and not open the door. Surely, though, soldiers were searching all the outbuildings... unless it was just these two soldiers and no one had even gone in the house yet...

"Why do you soldiers want me going in the front door?" I said as loudly as I could as we walked past the living room windows, hoping that someone inside would hear me and spread the alarm in time for people to hide, if they hadn't already.

A smack on the back of the head made me stagger forward, blinded for a second, nearly falling down on the stones of the front path. But it had been a fist, not a gun, and I kept my feet. I was glad for the added padding of my wig, and that it had stayed in place.

"Shut up and go inside," a voice right behind me said.

As slowly as possible, I put out my hand for the heavy brass knob of the front door, but it seemed to open on its own, and I was staring into the eyes of another Orion soldier. And standing on his other side was... Jesse. Standing there between two Orion soldiers, barechested, his arms pulled forward... I looked down and saw that his hands were in restraints.

My heart squeezed painfully.

He saw me. He gave me a quick look that said *I love you, please don't do anything stupid.*

The soldier who had opened the door turned away as the other two behind me prodded me in. The first two soldiers pushed Jesse in front of them out of the entryway and into the living room.

"Thank you for letting me put the dog in downstairs," I said loudly again, not caring how stupid I seemed to the soldiers.

Smack! Another cuff from behind knocked me forward, but I didn't care. At least Jesse knew that Charlie was safe.

The living room was crowded. Two other Orion soldiers were standing farther in, stunners drawn, with Augie, Gram, and Sadie standing between them. No Cat and Hannah. I prayed they, at least, were in the safe space downstairs.

Augie's eyes were fixed on Jesse. Sadie looked composed and quiet, a respectable little *abuela*, which meant she looked a little too Mexican to be safe. Gram looked not happy to see me. I was sure she'd been praying that I'd stay for a long time down at the lake, safe from this.

The two Orion soldiers with Jesse nudged him farther in ahead of me, stunners trained on him the whole time.

Gram suddenly came to life. She took two steps forward, to me, reached out and grabbed my arm, pulling me toward her, which the nearest Orion soldier began to react to, but Gram was determined. She pulled me over, bumping me into Augie.

"My granddaughter! These here are my grandchildren. She's not... not quite all there in the head, and tends to wander in the woods, and I'm glad she's safe!"

"Then who's *this*?" the Orion soldier with extra stars on his jacket, who seemed to be the senior officer, pointed his stunner at Jesse.

He just stood there quietly, looking down. He was shivering even in the warm room, and I was pretty sure he'd been stunned. It was killing me, not being able to wrap my arms around him. Next to me, Augie took a breath.

Jesse looked up at Augie and gave the faintest shake of his head.

Gram said loudly, "He just works for us. He's a good boy, kind of simple too."

"Huh." The Orion officer clearly didn't believe that. "Time to see your identcards. One at a time."

Cold fear gripped my stomach. What the hell were Jesse and I going to do? And I wondered about Sadie—surely she didn't have an Orion card, but perhaps she had a worker card like I had had?

Augie's arm went around me, warm and comforting, pulling me a little closer to him.

Sadie trotted off to the kitchen with a soldier following her. We all stood waiting. It was so quiet in the room I could hear people breathing.

"Here you go," Sadie chirped as she came back into the room, pulling a card out of a voluminous handbag.

The officer took it and stared intently at it, then handed it back to her.

"All right. Next."

I felt a spark of surprise from Augie, simultaneous with my own. *Good for Sadie...*

Then Gram walked across the room to the big wooden desk, where she pulled open a drawer and removed an envelope, which she handed to the soldier.

"Our cards," she said.

He handed it to the commanding officer, who opened it and pulled out two cards.

"Ellen Joseph." He looked at Gram, who nodded.

"Augie Powers." He looked at Augie, who hesitated for a second, then nodded.

He handed Gram back the envelope, and the soldier next to her prodded her back over next to Augie and me.

"So who are you?" the commanding officer asked Jesse, who continued to look down. "You sure don't look like an Orion citizen to me."

He took a step so he was directly in front of Jesse. "Answer me, boy!"

Jesse looked up, but because he was so tall, he was looking down at the officer.

"James Stephens," he said softly.

"Your card, James Stephens?"

Jesse just gave one shake of his head.

"Like I said," Gram's voice startled me, "he just works for us, he comes and goes, he's not all there in the head, but he does good work around the...."

"Shut up, old woman!" the officer threw over his shoulder at Gram. Then he seemed to be struck by a new thought, and he turned around, away from Jesse. "And why doesn't your granddaughter have a card?" He pointed at me.

All eyes were on me now.

"Where's *your* card?" the officer asked.

I couldn't think of anything to say.

"I never got it," Gram's voice again, firm and cool. "She's simple-minded, she never leaves the property."

"Not one more word," the officer said, emphasizing each syllable. "Your card!"

A long pause. Gram and Sadie were standing there side by side trying their hardest to look like innocent old grannies. It was so quiet I could hear Gram's clock in the corner of the room going *tick, tick, tick*. The clock she had jokingly told me not to go near, after that episode with Emmitt and his wristpad. I was so nervous I could feel sweat sliding down my back.

"Then you get scanned." The officer stepped close to me and held up his right hand; I saw the wrist pad that looked a little bigger than Emmitt's. He thumbed it on and moved it up to my face. Oh fuck.

I could hear someone near me shouting in her head, *Tessa, Tessa, think! think!* It had to be Gram. Suddenly I knew what she was trying to tell me.

I leaned closer to the scanner, which seemed to surprise the officer a bit, but he didn't move, so my face was almost touching it. I tried to energize as much as possible.

The scanner began buzzing.

"What the fuck?" the officer stepped back and looked at it. Punched a button. *Reboot*, I thought, remembering Emmitt with his pad after I'd messed it up thoroughly. Where the hell *did* that word come from?

The officer held it up to me again, a bit farther away. I didn't want to be obvious, to arouse any suspicion, so I tried to project even more energy toward it, without moving. Again it began buzzing.

"Someone else use theirs!" The officer snapped, and stepped back, frowning down at his wristpad, punching buttons again. "Move it!"

The closest soldier stepped up to me and held out his wristpad. Again I tried to bring as much energy forward as I could, picturing sending it outwards. His wristpad made strange sounds, and he shook it, staring at it.

"She's different," Gram said coolly. "That's what I'm trying to tell you. She's just a little different, but slow and wouldn't hurt a fly."

"Scan him!" The Orion officer seemed relieved to turn his back on Gram, me and Augie, and pointed the soldier at Jesse. "Open your eyes!" the officer shouted at Jesse, who obeyed.

I tried to send my energy outwards, I tried...

"Holy shit," the soldier with the scanner in front of Jesse said softly.

"What!?" The officer was clearly pissed off and ready to be done with all of us. Good.

The soldier held out his wristpad to the officer, who gave a low whistle as he stared down at it. My heart stopped. Jesse gave me a quick look, something in it cautioning me. *Don't say anything, Tessa. Don't say a word...*

The officer made a strange noise; he was chuckling. He grabbed at Jesse's wrist restraints, jerked him forward a step. "We've got you, you bastard. We've got you." Then, to the soldiers around him, "Let's get the fuck out of here."

They pulled and prodded Jesse forward, and he didn't resist. He was going to calmly walk out of the house to—where? prison? torture? death? Wherever he was going, they had to take me with him.

I didn't know I'd opened my mouth until I began to suffocate on Augie's shirt. He had pulled me against him, mashing my face into his chest so I couldn't breathe.

"She's a little excitable," I felt rather than heard him say. "Don't mind us."

I struggled against Augie, but he held me firm

The front door slammed. Augie let me move back enough to breathe, but kept a firm hold on my arms.

"Let me go!" I shouted. "Let me go!"

Tears rolled down his face. "No, Tessa, I will not let you go!"

I struggled as hard as I could to get free, but it was no use against Augie.

"Tessa!" he said. "We need you! We need you here to help figure out how to get Jesse back! Going there with him now isn't going to help us rescue him."

I stopped struggling and tried to catch my breath. Tried to think. No, I couldn't think. I let myself sink down into a heap on the floor and put my hands over my face as I sobbed.

"They're gone," Sadie said from the front windows.

Gram knelt down beside me, "Tessa." She put her arms around me. "You did what you needed to do. I'm so sorry."

"But we let them take Jesse!"

"We had to. That's what he wanted, too. You know that."

Oh I did. But it pissed me off that he went so nobly. I wanted to kick him, scream at him for being so noble, for leaving us. *For going without me.*

I remained in a heap on the floor; my bones liquid, useless. Quick steps into the room, Hannah's and Cat's voices, a slow, heavy, man's voice explaining to them what had happened, and I knew it had to be Augie but I had never heard Augie sound like that.

Something deep down inside reminded me that while I had lost Jesse—again—Augie had just lost his brother. Again. And he was forcing himself to function still, to help the rest of us.

"I have to call Emmitt," Augie was saying. "I have to warn Emmitt." But he seemed rooted to the floor.

I slowly stood up. "What can I do to help?"

"Tessa," Gram said, "you know where the wristpad is in the kitchen, can you get it for Augie?"

"I'll get it," Hannah said. She was moving more quickly than me, for once.

Cat came over and put her arms around me. "We'll get him back, Tessa. We will."

I let myself relax against her, heard Hannah come back in with the wristpad, heard Augie tap numbers into it and then speak quietly to Emmitt. He used the code that we'd agreed upon if Orion ever raided us and took any of us captive.

Augie clicked off the pad and looked around at us. "He's going to evacuate the safe house. We've got to clear out, too."

Sadie had walked back from the windows to stand next to Gram and me and Cat and Hannah. We all looked at Augie. All I could think was *This is the part of the emergency plan I must have missed...* We had to clear out, too? Why?

My brain creaked into gear: I remembered the restraints on my arms and feet, the feel of the cold needle sliding under my skin, the chair, the machine... Orion soon would have whatever it wanted from Jesse; resisting wasn't an option in the face of all of Orion's drugs and scanners and other means of getting inside our heads. Certainly they would quickly know the location of Emmitt's safe house and what Jesse did there, who he had worked with there, and they probably would even learn that Lars was undercover—certainly Lars couldn't take the chance that they might not get that out of Jesse. And all Orion had to do was ask Jesse *Who were those people you were with at the house when we got you?* and they would be back for us.

"Lars," I said.

Augie nodded. "Emmitt's getting the word to him. Lars has a plan for disappearing."

"And Chuck," Gram said. "He should have his wristpad with him in the truck. Can you try reaching him, Augie?"

Augie nodded and reached in his pocket for the pad.

"And where will we go?" Hannah asked.

"I have a place where you'll be safe," Sadie spoke up. "It's perfect if we can figure out how to get there."

"If we can get Grampa back here quickly," Augie said, "we'll be able to use his truck."

"We should move on the double," Gram said, "but do we have the time to close everything up? Surely we have an hour?"

"Probably. But we should be as quick as we can, to be safe," Augie said. "Just one duffle bag each, okay?"

Then he'd connected with Grampa on the wristpad, thank God, and was quickly giving him the message to come home *now*.

Gram began to move toward the kitchen murmuring, "The wristpad, clothes, and what books should I bring? Oh, Sadie, could you help me please?"

Books. We knew that anything we left behind might be pawed through by Orion soldiers on their second, more thorough, time through the house. That was a motivator. First I ran down to let Charlie out of Cat's and Hannah's room—he licked my hands and looked up at me, whining, clearly upset. *Just like I feel...* I forced myself to go into Jesse's and my room and think about what I needed to take away with me. Neither of us had accumulated much in the way of belongings, fortunately. We'd been traveling light ever since we left the lake. But I was going to pack a bag entirely of books, and no one was going to stop me.

I scooped up Jesse's leather pouch that lay on top of the bureau, and the small ceramic dish with a celadon crackle glaze where I kept a few found treasures—pebbles picked up from the lakeshore, a jade-green stone shaped like a heart that Jesse had given me a few weeks earlier, found along the lakeshore, a collection of small feathers.

I grabbed clothes from Jesse's bureau drawers; I couldn't help burying my face in his favorite flannel shirt and smelling him—*don't think of Jesse in prison! mind on the task at hand, don't think of Jesse gone!*—

but I couldn't help it.

Charlie licked my hand as I paused, brain not able to function, sobs starting up in my throat again. He looked worried. I ran my hands over his head, rubbed behind his ears where he liked it, made my voice steady. "It's going to be all right, Charlie. We're going to get him back."

I stuffed clothes from my drawers into the duffle on top of Jesse's. Then I filled the second duffle with all of my books. I looked around the room one last time for anything I shouldn't leave behind, and walked out with Charlie at my heels.

"He should be here in thirty minutes," Augie said at the kitchen door, and there was a burst of noise of pots and pans and the skidding of chairs on the floor. I looked in to see Gram and Sadie scrambling up onto the chairs so they could ransack upper shelves.

"Oh, yes," Augie added, "let's take as much food as possible!" And he went to work reaching up and helping them cram foodstuffs into boxes.

"Don't forget Charlie's kibble," I said, and Augie waved a hand in my direction to show he'd heard.

I didn't seem needed there, so I lugged my two duffle bags through the living room with Charlie and dropped them by the front door. I took a moment to wonder if there was anything I was missing. And realized there was... but it was the one place I didn't want to go to.

"Charlie, will you come with me?" I invited him as I opened the front door.

"Tessa, where are you going?" Augie's voice called after me. I stopped and looked back to see him standing in the kitchen doorway.

"To the shed. I have to get the mask."

Walking across the yard to the shed was hard; I kept seeing Jesse stunned, Jesse dragged out of the shed by the Orion soldiers.

But inside everything looked tidy and in its place. Jesse's favorite jacket hung on its peg next to the door. A tiny breeze filtered through the screens, wafting up from the ravine below, carrying the scent of the forest. I wished I could save the shed for him, *for when we have him back*, but there was nothing I would be able to take now—except for the mask. There it stood, centered on the wooden table, propped on a metal stand that had kept it upright. He had finished it.

"Oh!" My voice was loud in the silence.

Charlie gave a small whine through his nose and sat back on his haunches. He seemed to know what had happened here. I gave him a little pat and then moved over to the table. My hand reached out all on its own to touch the mask, to the woman transforming to a raven, or the raven transforming to a woman. It was both, at the same time.

Jesse had finished carving the long, curving feathers that had the appearance of soft hair touching the woman's bare shoulders. My fingers traced the wood, over and over. I looked into and through the delicate almond-shaped eyes and a little shiver ran down my spine.

"You're coming with us," I said softly. I went over to the door and pulled Jesse's jacket off its peg, then reached out and picked up the mask and stand, found them only about as heavy as a good-sized toddler, and easy to carry because they weren't squirming in my arms like the ones I'd recently held and tried to soothe at the clinic for their vaccinations. I wrapped the mask in the jacket and carried it out of the shed, closing the door with one foot, and walked carefully over the lawn to the house, Charlie at my side.

Augie met me at the front door with a heavy canvas duffle in his hands. "I'm going out there to get Jesse's knives and carving tools," he said. "Orion's not getting those, and besides, Jesse's going to want them when we get him soon."

~

A few minutes later Grampa was back, bumping into the driveway in his old truck with an open trailer attached. We all hugged and cried a little, but he looked as serious and focused as Gram, and that helped get us moving. Augie loaded the two ATVs onto the trailer. Gram climbed up into the other front seat and Sadie crammed between her and the door. Augie, Cat and Hannah and I rode in the open back with the boxes and bundles and Charlie. Tears kept running down my cheeks, and I'd look over and see tears running down everyone else's cheeks; there was a lot of snuffling and sleeve-wiping, but there also was much patting of shoulders and backs. Augie put his arms around Charlie and buried his face in Charlie's thick fur.

We were refugees again. No one but Sadie had any idea where we were going, how we were going to live. But none of that mattered. All that mattered was getting Jesse back.

12. July 31–September 30, 2111

"Does anyone have any idea where we're going?" Augie asked as we bumped down a road that was more of a path than a road, with thick forest all around us. When we'd climbed into the truck, Sadie had said we were headed for a house that had been used for the past ten years as a safe house, but it had been empty lately. That's all any of us knew.

I didn't feel like making conversation, so I just sat dumbly behind the cab, stuck in between a food box that was cutting into my leg and someone's duffle that felt like it was filled with rocks that kept shifting and bumping me... *oh,* I realized, *those are my books.*

My brain kept playing images of Jesse being stunned, dragged, beaten, until I thought I would start screaming.

A hand patted my left knee—Cat, who was nearly buried by duffle bags off to my left so I hadn't even seen her.

"Tessa, dear," I heard her soft voice just above the rumble of the old truck, "think of your lake. Go to your lake, dear."

Thank you. And I tried, but not with much success.

From Cat's other side, leaning against the side of the truck, Hannah said slowly, "I think I've Seen where we're going." She frowned, and I guessed it was one of those Seeings that was kind of strange, or unbelievable. Great. "A house built into a cliff," she said, almost a question.

"That's weird," Augie said.

When we jounced to a stop and Grampa shut off the engine, I figured we could only be a couple of miles to the south of his house, but it was hard to know. It must have been around dinnertime, so it was still broad summer daylight everywhere but where we were, in a gloomy mostly-spruce forest. There definitely weren't any cliffs around. But then I turned my head—and ahead of the truck there were no trees, there was only bright sky.

The truck cab door opened and Sadie bounced out, announcing, "Here we are!"

Augie had already climbed out of the truck bed and opened the tailgate for Charlie. Hannah and Cat and I all climbed down, Augie offering a warm, strong hand as needed.

"I don't see a house," he whispered off my left shoulder as he and Charlie joined me in staring ahead at the bright sky.

"Maybe it's built into a cliff that's right in front of us," I said.

We both took a few steps forward. We were on the southwest bluff of the peninsula, I guessed. The ground dropped away ahead, and I could just make out some side steps leading downward. There was a door the color of earth, blending into the slope to our left.

"Son of a gun," Augie murmured.

It was like Fortress base, but hopefully with more windows. I looked out beyond the bluff we were standing on, to the late-day summer sun dazzling on low waves that were rolling toward us, to shore. It was good to see the sea again.

Augie and I turned back to the others who were beginning to pull duffle bags out of the back of the truck. He leaped up in one swift, easy movement and took over the handing down of bundles and boxes. We ferried them to a big pile at the top of the bluff, then Sadie led us down the steps, through the heavy wooden door and into the cool, mostly-empty main room of the house. The early evening sun over the sea was now low enough to flood in through the line of windows that faced west. A tiny kitchen area closed one end on the room, and near it a staircase ran down to what I surmised was the lower level.

In pairs, except for Augie who didn't need help, we carried boxes and bags down the steps and into the main room. Cat and Hannah and Gram all went downstairs with Sadie to look at the bunkroom below. Grampa and Augie stepped back outside to look around. Charlie and I lay down on the upstairs floor. I didn't have the energy to even stand up. I just shut my eyes and let myself slip off to sleep.

~

I slowly surfaced from sleep to a distant *thunk-thunk-thunk!* and the sounds of someone quietly trying to light a fire. I opened my eyes to soft sunset light and Augie crouched in front of the cast iron woodstove near me, blowing softly to coax flames onto kindling. His golden hair was sticking out this way and that from a cap he'd pulled down tight over his head, bill backwards, to keep his hair out of his eyes.

Charlie was warm at my back; the wood floor was a bit hard, but I hadn't noticed until now. I slowly sat up, still leaning against Charlie, and saw Gram and Sadie sitting on rough wooden stools at a wood table bathed in sunset light under the windows, with Cat and Hannah sitting across from them, everyone busy with something— peeling apples, chopping vegetables, kneading dough—they were all working to get dinner going, and I'd been asleep on the floor in the middle of the room. Even Grampa had been busy chopping wood, and now here he was pushing in through the door with a big armful that he set down gently next to the woodstove. He saw that I was awake and gave me a little smile, and came over.

"Hi Sweetie." He slowly stooped down, then squatted next to me, wincing when his knees flexed. "Do you feel a little better?" There was such love and kindness in his eyes that I felt tears start up in mine, in gratitude, and also in feeling that I didn't deserve it. But I did feel better for having slept for a few minutes, and I nodded at him.

He patted my shoulder. "Emmitt's on his way here. We'll have a talk, hatch some good plans. Keep the faith, little Ravenwing."

I stood up and gave him a hand as he straightened up, wincing again.

"Come on out with me a minute," Grampa said, "since the chairs are taken and looks like they have it all under control."

Gram gave me a quick smile as if to corroborate his words, so I followed him out the heavy door to the stairs built into the steep bluff.

Really, you *could* call it a cliff, I thought as I looked down to the shore maybe a hundred yards below us. Long lines of gentle waves rolled in our way, the sea quiet as the calm summer evening spread over us. But if I looked left, south, I was just able to see the edge of a mountain range before the forest blocked my view.

My flying time over Fayerport's peninsula and the surrounding area told me exactly where we were on the map. This was the beginning of the southern curve of the big peninsula. I was just able to see the opening of the southern bay that led into the mountains, the long bay that Jesse and I had skied to on the day of Augie's snowgo accident. We weren't all that far from home. *If only we could sail down this bay, we'd come to the mouth of the creek that runs through the mountains from our lake... We could be home. But not without Jesse.*

Grampa beckoned me over to a fallen log across from the stairs, wedged into a flat spot to make a great bench. We sat silently for a moment. From here we could see a little more of the mountain range across the south bay. The tops of the peaks blushed in the sunset light.

"We're not all that far from home," I said softly, remembering the resistance code words *I'm nearing home.* "If we just had Jesse, and a boat, we could sail down the bay to the valley to the south of the lake..."

Grampa put his left arm around my shoulders. "Driving out here, your Gram told me that Hannah had Seen you being taken by Orion along with Jesse." He paused. "Numerous times she'd Seen that."

I thought on that for a moment. "But... it didn't happen."

"Nope. That's what's most interesting, in it all. And Hannah said she knew we'd never see you and Jesse ever again, if that were to happen. But something changed."

I turned my head to see Grampa looking intently at me, the seams and creases in his face deepening as he frowned in concentration.

"Something happened, something changed for you to not have been taken."

"Like, the scanners getting confused when they tried to scan me?" I said slowly.

"Yup, your Gram told me about that. And also, why would they have given up so easily on you?"

"What do you think? What does Gram think?"

Grampa shook his head. "Your Gram says she was working as hard as she could... and Sadie too... that gal fits right in with all of you doesn't she?"

We both smiled.

"You should have seen her and Gram," I said, "standing there, shoulder to shoulder, trying their hardest to look like innocent little old grannies."

Grampa's smile broadened.

"So, who knows?" I said, "maybe it was synergistic energy able doing a little gentle steering?"

Grampa nodded, his nearest white braid brushing my shoulder. "What we and Hannah think is—we *will* see Jesse again. We are going to be able to get him out."

"But how?!"

He shook his head. "All I know is we'll have the best people working on it."

~

While dinner was cooking Grampa and I did outhouse duty. We had no running water at the safe house, but there was a stream just a dozen yards to the south where we could draw water and boil it or UV light it to make it drinkable. So we were stuck with an outhouse, but Cat and Hannah and I were all used to that from our life in the projects. This one was a bit rougher, though. First Grampa and I had to chase a resident porcupine out of it, and then we dumped in several cans of woodshavings that Grampa had cut. He left me to finish up by sweeping it out and then putting in a roll of toilet paper and another can of wood shavings by the rough seat.

We had all just sat down to dinner—Augie and me on old stumps he'd dragged in to supplement our limited number of chairs——when Emmitt stepped in through the door. Everyone got up to hug him, Cat reaching him first and getting a hug and a kiss that were a little more than cousinly, I thought as I watched from the sidelines. Hannah, standing just to my right, turned her head and gave me a look, and I knew she was thinking the same thing. And not at all jealous either; we both hoped to see whatever was there grow and flourish, because it just felt right.

Since we'd run out of seats, Emmitt and Augie sat on Augie's and my sleeping rolls that were still lying on the main room floor, and Cat and I carried serving dishes over to them and made sure they had heaping full plates. Everyone suddenly realized they were starving, so there wasn't much conversation for the first few minutes. And then Emmitt started telling us what he knew so far.

Everything he knew was thanks to Billy, who had broken into Orion messaging and found that Jesse was taken to P1. And this was after Billy had to take a couple of hours off to quickly evacuate all of his computer equipment to an alternative safe house, less than four miles away from us, up on the hillside, and getting it all set up again there. Billy was our man who would keep us informed on where Jesse was, and how he was doing. Billy had become a god in the computer world, staring into monitors all day, every day, tracking Orion messages, finding patterns, *listening at their doors*, as he put it, trying for the elusive magic key to let him in to the Orion brain.

Emmitt said Billy was sure that the resistance was close to breaking through Orion's spiderweb of security systems. This was the planned attack we'd heard about: the resistance was going to break through Orion's security and shut down Orion all the way across the country in just a matter of minutes. I'll admit this went right over my head so I didn't think too much of it at the moment... all I could think was *Jesse's at P1 being interrogated...*

Emmitt also reassured us that Lars had managed to disappear. He'd just arrived at the new safe house on the mountainside where Emmitt and Billy had settled. He'd used two different sets of disguises involving wigs and glasses and changes of clothes—all stashed some time ago in safe places just in case he ever had to suddenly get out. He'd safely slipped out of Orion headquarters, hurried across the city, then by train out of the city, and finally on foot through the woods to the safe house. He planned to stay low for a while, working with Emmitt and Billy.

We finally stopped firing questions at Emmitt, and Gram walked over and handed him a mug of coffee, which he gratefully took from her hands.

"You're living kind of rough here, aren't you?" he said, and looked around the main room again as he took a sip of coffee, as if confirming his statement.

"No electricity," Augie said, trying not to jostle Emmitt as he sat up a little straighter. "Though there's a few places where solar film could go, would work great."

"And we have a gas range and a small gas refrigerator," Gram said, "as well as the wood stove for cooking on."

"And the outhouse is fully operational," I added.

Emmitt smiled at me.

"We'll be just fine here, but hopefully not for long." Grampa said slowly. "The big thing we need is news from the outside world, especially knowing how Jesse's doing."

Emmitt set the mug down gently on the rough wood floor next to Augie's sleeping bag. "I'll be able to come over every few days now, I think, and I'll relay whatever we know from Billy."

I risked a quick look at Cat and saw how happy she looked.

"We might even do a little rabbit hunting, Augie," Emmitt added. "How does rabbit stew sound?"

Every one of us brightened at the thought of seeing more of Emmitt, and the thought of a filling and hot stew.

~

Something in me kept me pacing, pacing whenever I'd finished helping inside the house or with the outside chores of wood stacking or building a garden box for lettuce and herbs in a sunny space near our fallen log-bench. I never realized I was pacing the main room floor until Hannah or Cat or Gram stopped me with a light embrace but a gentle turn toward the door, and a suggestion that I head outside. I could not rest. There would be no rest until we found Jesse and brought him home.

But Gram reminded me that there was more work to be done. My own.

Cat and Hannah each would slip off into quiet corners of the downstairs room every morning to meditate, sometimes for hours. I knew they were somehow exercising their gifts. I knew I, too, had to *do the work*, as Gram put it. I needed to learn patience and focus; I needed to continue to explore the healing chants and songs and stories, the repositories of so much wisdom. But there was no way I was able to sit still, anywhere, inside or out.

I always felt better, like I was making a little progress, when I was outside walking. I discovered a path that led sidehill down the bluff to a sandy beach, and I went there as often as I could with Charlie. We would walk from our end of the beach until we got to the big pile of driftwood blocking the south end, and then we'd turn around and walk back again. Charlie would chase seagulls and little shore birds, and I walked and walked. Moving helped clear the fears out of my head.

Cat and Emmitt sometimes came down to the beach, but there was plenty of space for them to be alone together when they wanted. The three of us pulled and pushed some of the tangled driftwood against huge, beached logs to make a shelter at the very south end of the beach, and we took turns sharing it. When you were inside it on the cool sand, you were looking straight ahead out at the dark water of the mouth of the south bay, with the tall mountains rising across in the distance, deep emerald green bases and higher up their rocky slopes shining under the sun. The very tallest were white-capped, and shone gold in the sunrise and red in the sunset. But I only spent a little time in the shelter; walking and putting myself into the stories as I walked, this was my medicine.

Étain kept coming back to me. Not the later part of her story that Jesse and I had talked of in the tower—the happy ending—when she became a woman again and was wooed again by Midir, who actually turned out to be as tricky as Raven in the way he stole her away from her husband the king. It was the early part of her story I kept seeing any time I closed my eyes, now that I was separated from Jesse. Étain and Midir were separated for how many years? Almost one thousand? Cursed by the witch to be a fly (but so beautiful she became! lustrous and healing, too) and cursed twice to be blown by such fierce winds that carried her away from the elven mounds and the green of the land, over stormy seas, Étain had to fight for years for her life. It wasn't so much patience this story taught as endurance—*talk about endurance*—and it was endurance that now seemed to me the most important quality a woman could ever have. And I was going to hold onto that happy ending as tight as I'd held onto anything in my life.

~

We were half-way through August and it was my birthday (*big twenty-nine*, as Augie said) and Gram asked me to tell The Woman Who Married The Bear story again. We were all in the main room, some sitting on chairs, some on bedrolls that we brought up during the day to be "couches." Cat and Sadie had baked me a cake, Hannah had knitted me a lovely light wool scarf, Gram and Grampa had given me a small star sapphire ring of my mother's that fit my ring finger as if it had been made for it, Augie had carved a palm-sized bear for me with Jesse's tools, Emmitt had written a poem. I was so glad to be able to give something back to them.

I became the story for my family, so that they could enter it themselves. And as I spoke it, I remembered something I had forgotten from the very first time Sharon told me the story—when the woman returns to her home village, her father, the chief, calls in the village artists to carve her story into his house front. And so I described the carvers at work on the cedar, the images emerging from the red-gold wood, the lovely young woman in a robe and a cloak, the bear rising up next to her on his back legs, the young cubs transforming to human children when they reached her father's village. All of it emerging from the sweet-smelling cedar wood right across the front of the chief's house. And there was the huge bear crest carved out of the wood just beneath the point of the roof: the short ears, low heavy brow, flaring nostrils, wide mouth with such big teeth—the bear of the Coast Salish, the Haida, the Tlingit. The woman's story literally became a part of the village, shared and participated in every day by her people.

I went on to tell of how her father the old chief finally died, how her restless young sons returned to their other grandfather and his bear people in the mountains, and the new chief took over and continued the use of the gifts—the song, the ceremonial cloak, the bear crest—and the people continued in balance, with the bear people's protection.

And as I spoke the words, an image grew clearer in my mind: the new chief was the daughter, The Woman Who Married The Bear. This was her role. Of course it was. And so I told this story ending, and added that one of her two restless sons returned to her village with his wife and children, and she helped in the raising of her grandchildren—part bear and part human, and they listened and danced to her story, and continued the traditions.

And so out of those moments when we think we have lost everything, I said in almost a whisper, *we find that actually we have stepped into a whole new world.*

When I finished there was silence in the room. I looked over at Gram and saw tears on her cheeks. She held up her arms to me, and I went to her and leaned down to hug her.

"You got it, Tessa," she said through her tears. "You got it."

~

The next evening as we all sat around the main room sipping coffee or tea and digesting, Emmitt walked in and said, "All right, now it's time for me to report on how the rescue plan is going."

This was the first time he had given us details on Jesse's rescue.

We circled our chairs or tree stumps and Emmitt started talking. Lars was in charge. They would be depending on the shipment schedule, the daily arrival and departure of trucks through the P1 gates, as Jesse had planned on when he came to spring us. Four grounders would be dressed as Orion soldiers, well-armed, smuggled into a shipment of large containers, moved from the docks into P1, ready to find Jesse and smuggle him out, back through the gate in another shipment. They were counting on infiltration, grounders disguised as Orion, as Jesse had done the year before for us. *Here's some irony,* I thought—*Lars using Jesse's plan, after he berated Jesse for coming up with this plan to try to rescue us from P1.*

But it seemed to me that depending on getting in and out through the front gate was a terrible weakness of the plan. If anything went wrong with getting onto the trucks, you couldn't count on jopters sitting there ready to be hijacked, especially since that had been done successfully once. There had to be other options.

"Do you have a backup plan in case they can't get back out through the gate?" I asked when Emmitt paused. I was trying really hard not to scream, *This is Jesse's life we're talking about!*

He lifted his chin slightly. "If we have to, two of our guys will hold the Command Center while the other two will get Jesse. If we have the Command Center, we have control of the gate, and the Fence."

Ah, they would be depending entirely on firepower. On the surface, it made sense. This is the kind of plan you'd expect from the resistance—warriors against warriors. Except... except... everything in me warned me that this was not the way to go. And I wasn't surprised at Lars deciding to go with firepower, but I was disappointed in Emmitt for going along with Lars, and for not trying to think of another option.

It was an odd thought, but it made much more sense to me to go to P1 to get Jesse with Hannah and Cat and Billy than go with a bunch of heavily armed resistance fighters. It would be an awful thing to have to do—I never could ask them to do it—but remembering how we got out, I knew it was our gifts that did it, not any weaponry.

Cat put her hand on my shoulder. When I looked at her, she nodded.

"Hannah has Seen us going back there," she whispered. "You and me and Hannah and Billy."

~

But Lars wouldn't let any of us be a part of it. He argued that he needed soldiers; they needed firepower. As civilians we would only be liabilities. He did agree to let Grampa help out at the docks since Grampa had connections there that would be useful in gaining access to the shipping containers headed for P1. But Augie, Hannah, Cat and I were told to "sit tight." Of course sitting tight was the last thing I was able to do. As August became September, I grew more and more restless to the point of moving back upstairs to sleep under the main room windows near Augie and Charlie—the better for getting up in the night and walking outside when I came awake and gave up on sleep.

I missed Jesse with an ache that went right through me. Of course it was physical—I yearned for the feeling of his body against mine, his shoulder I could tuck myself under, the touch of his hand as we passed each other, the touch of his eyes on mine across a room—but it was so much more, it was the feeling the moon must have, held in orbit, the reason for her existence.

I spent hours down on the beach amongst the huge driftwood logs of our shelter-fort. I can't say I meditated much when I was down there, but the gentle wash of the waves on the sand and the sound of the wind that always blew from the sea to the shore during the day and then switched back from the shore to the sea as darkness fell—these were soothing sounds to my soul, as soothing as the hours I spent gazing out at the infinity horizon line of sea and sky.

Sometimes there were ravens, but not often. Whenever I glimpsed them they seemed to be intent on heading somewhere, usually up toward the mountains.

Cat joined me down there on the beach sometimes and this was comforting, and not because she was there to comfort me—she, too, was struggling because of Emmitt's role in the rescue plan. *He's not going to stand up to Lars,* she told me, *he's feeling torn in two because his instincts are the same as ours—we should do this without weapons, if there's any way—but he doesn't have the power to disagree with Lars.* She literally was wringing her hands when she said this. We comforted each other as best we could.

Then it was September 10, the day of the rescue.

I hadn't slept more than a couple of hours the night before; I was useless as the day crept by. Gram was keeping herself busy in the kitchen, trying not to think of Grampa down at the docks waiting for dark, when he would sneak the resistance grounders into Orion shipping containers. Gram said she didn't need my help. I tried to join Hannah and Cat in planting more lettuce seedlings in our garden boxes on the south bank—just in case we were going to be stuck at the safe house for longer—but after only a few minutes and three accidental tramplings, they gently but firmly urged me to see if Augie needed any help with the solar system he was working on. But he didn't want me anywhere around delicate electronics, so I pulled on Jesse's flannel-lined, faded jean jacket and headed down to the beach with Charlie.

It was low tide and a wide expanse of brown sand lay before us like a playground, for Charlie anyway, who was delighted with our new location by the sea. His favorite pastime was chasing shorebirds, though digging in the sand for tiny crawling things was a close second. This afternoon a whole flock of dunlins had settled on the damp sand near the retreating sea, and Charlie dashed out, sending them soaring upward like swirling snowflakes. You never saw just one dunlin, I thought as I recklessly followed Charlie out onto the sand far from shore; they were a small shorebird that knew that pulling together into a tight flock meant safety. I loved their long black bills and their fluffy white underfeathers that reminded me of full petticoats. Then there were the sandpipers and curlews—I couldn't keep any of them straight yet, they all had long legs and gorgeous checky, streaky patterns of brown and black feathers.

I was coming to love this place, too, though I felt the constant pull to home and the lake. And the constant ache for Jesse. I heard myself give one of those huge sighs I was becoming known for, and then I found my feet taking me away from the sea and toward the driftwood fort close under the bluff. Charlie could play for a while; he knew where to find me.

I clambered over the smooth wood of the outermost log, so worn by the elements that it almost felt like human skin, and nestled into the sunwarmed sand in the tiny room created by a half-dozen logs that had been piled together against the bluff by the wind and the sea. Here was sanctuary, which I desperately needed. My emotions, my thoughts, my body had been out of control all day. I needed to find calm and focus. But as soon as I stopped moving, I realized what I needed most was sleep.

Hugging Jesse's warm jacket around me like a blanket, I shut my eyes. The quiet sighing of the waves on the sand sounded so much like the hush of the wind through the mountain hemlocks above the lake. I imagined I was there, wrapped up in a warm blanket in the hemlocks, and I could even hear quiet singing of ravens hidden on their nests close by. The last thing I remembered, before falling asleep, was my voice saying in that awful room at P1, *The lake is everywhere.* And Gram's voice saying, *The lake is in you.*

I dreamed I was with Jesse. He was lying on a mattress on the floor of a room that looked much like the room I'd been in in solitary confinement. A thin sliver of afternoon sunlight warmed the frame of the window slit a few feet from the foot of the mattress, and his eyes were on the light. His wonderful thick black hair had all been cut off. He'd been so proud of his braids; seeing his shorn, shaggy head brought tears to my eyes. A soft *thumpa-thumpa-thumpa* sound kept rhythmically repeating until I realized it was my heartbeat. Or his.

Jesse, I whispered his name as softly as possible.

He twitched, turned his head, looking around the tiny room— he'd heard me.

"Tess!" he whispered. "You can't be here?!"

I am here, somehow! I had to fight down a gasp of laughter. *Maybe I'm inside of you?*

He smiled. "Oh Christ, Raven, you do beat all... I'm sure I'm hallucinating. God, I long for you!"

And I long for you! I took a deep breath and tried to send it all to him, the sighing of the wind in the hemlocks, the ravens' laughs up in the sky and their quiet songs on the nest, the clear, warm sunlight shining through the lakewater down below me. Comfort and peace. Love. So much love.

We're going to get you out of there soon, I whispered to him. *Soon.*

"Don't say any more!" His whisper sharpened. "Don't tell me anything they can get out of me... but... Tell me it's true!"

It is true, my love. We are going to get you out.

"Just promise me you won't come yourself. You can't risk yourself!"

I'll keep safe, I promise. Soon, my love. Soon.

I stayed with him, in him, with no idea how it could be, but not needing to know. Just being there for him.

Jesse, tell me a story.

"Me, tell you a story!" he almost laughed.

Tell me Bluejay again.

He took a long breath, closed his eyes, looked so peaceful. *Bluejay was a healer, a medicine man... he carried her in his canoe up the river, singing his whisper song...*

And as Bluejay goes, he sings to her, and she comes back to life slowly...

Suddenly it was so clear to me. *Jesse!*

"What, Raven?"

You were Bluejay. I was dead when you found me at P1. You brought me back to life. But I am never, ever going to leave you.

I felt his surprise, saw the tears start up in his eyes.

You gave me back my life, Jesse. We're coming for you soon...

~

I opened my eyes and was looking into Charlie's eyes. He was licking my face. Sunlight slanted across my log fort, much lower and softer now. I sat up, patting Charlie, thinking that hours must have passed and it was nearing dinnertime and everyone was wondering where I was.

We scrambled over the logs and across the sand to the path that took us up the bluff. I was puffing by the time we came out of the woods near the steps to the cliffhouse, as we were calling it. No one was around. I hurried down the first two steps and in through the front door.

"I'm back!" I called.

Gram was stirring something at the stove. She turned, looked a little surprised to see me. "Oh, that's nice, dear, but we weren't worried."

I felt like a kid again, hurrying back after an afternoon got away from me, sure my whole family was alarmed that I'd been seized by a bear, or here, maybe by a whale—and then the realization that no one had even noticed I was gone. Oh well.

"Can I help?" I asked Gram, and she put me to work washing lettuce for the salad.

No one had much of an appetite when we all crammed around the small table for dinner. Outside the low sun in the west was touching everything to gold: rays of light slanted in through the main room windows and struck Jesse's mask where I'd set it on a smaller table, red-gold cedar wood burning as if it were on fire, casting a larger oddly shaped shadow on the rough wood wall behind it. I tried to keep my eyes on the mask, but all any of us could think of was it was almost sunset, nearing nightfall and time for the rescue plan to be put into action.

Cat and Hannah made small talk about progress at the clinic where they'd spent the day before—none of us could go there very often now since we'd moved two more miles farther south. Sadie had found a supplier of milk and cheese for pregnant women and children, and someone else had found a better supplier of chicken feed, which meant that more families could have better laying hens. Gram nodded several times, but was mostly silent through the meal. She looked pale and worried. I was having such a hard time sitting there, seeing and feeling her worry and sorrow that I jumped up when Augie pushed back his chair and said he was sorry but he had to go out for a walk. When I asked him if I could join him, he silently nodded his head. Charlie and I followed him out the door.

He headed for the path to the beach and I followed without a word. The gentle wash of small waves on the shore below was soothing, as was the whisper of wind in the spruce mixed through the birches and alders alongside the path. I took big breaths and thought of how we were coming up on the most aromatic time of the year, as the pungent smell of wild cranberries mingled with spicy alder and decaying devil's club. When we came out of the woods, at the base of the bluff, my nose filled with the smells of tangy salt, drying seaweed, whiffs of sea-things decomposing on the shore. Charlie ran ahead of us, snorting the scents and hoping for more birds to chase.

Augie sat down heavily on the outer log of our fort and gave up a sigh that put the biggest of mine to shame. I sat next to him and gave him a light pat on the back, but didn't say anything, not wanting to intrude. He leaned forward and put his head in his hands, sighed again.

"I'm just so worried we're not going to get him back," he finally said. "So worried he's not going to get out alive. We don't know if he's okay even now."

I leaned against him. "He is. I know he is." I hesitated for a moment, worried that it would sound hopelessly weird, but because it was Augie, I went on, "I saw Jesse today."

His head jerked up and he stared at me. "You what?!"

"It might have been a dream, but... you know, I don't think it was. I think it really did happen." And I told him about being with Jesse for a while in his prison cell.

Augie finally looked away, out to sea. He blew out a long breath, shook his head, then looked back at me. "Tessa, you really are a piece of work."

I couldn't help smiling. "That's what Jesse says."

He put his arm around me. "Well, whatever. I believe you, however the hell that worked. And I'm glad you told me. Now we just gotta pray about tonight."

And we did. We all did. I would have stayed down on the beach for the night, but it seemed better to all be together as we waited, so Augie and Charlie and I finally walked back up the bluff path to the house, and everyone sat for an hour or so in the main room as darkness fell, silent, the minutes ticking by. It was torture not knowing a thing. We hoped that Emmitt would come to us at some point... I dared not let myself think of Jesse coming to us with Emmitt.

Finally Gram stood up from her chair and said she thought she'd go to bed, try to sleep a little. She looked exhausted. Cat and Hannah went downstairs to the lower room with her, and I grabbed my bed roll and carried it down with me, thinking it might be better if we all were together. Augie said he and Charlie would stay up top and keep watch. The rest of us couldn't bear watching anymore; I just wanted to hide my head until someone told me it was all right to come out.

Each of us kissed Gram goodnight, pretending it was like any other night. She touched our cheeks and whispered, "Say your prayers, girls."

I lay down on the bunk above her and prayed to Raven and all my ancestors, tried to hold the image of Jesse from that afternoon in my mind, but found myself back home, back at the lake. I saw it as I had seen it that day I had flown over it in the jopter, how sunlight had shone down through the greenblue water, how deep it was, the mystery of it.

Somehow I slept.

And there I was, sitting in my favorite chair in the main room of Gram's and my house by the lake, and sitting next to me in the rocking chair was Grampa, comfy in his soft flannel shirt and jeans.

"I love you so, Little Ravenwing," he said. "I wish you knew how like your mother you are." Late day sun slanted in the window as it did in the summer, shining deep gold right up the valley before it disappeared behind the tall mountains to the west. Grampa's hair shone silver, and his eyes were warm brown, like Jesse's.

"Your mother loves you and she's watching you even now," he added. "She's here with you as she always is."

I looked around, but didn't see her. Grampa leaned forward in the rocker and lightly touched high on the left of my chest, above my heart. "You carry her here." His voice was soft. "Always."

As I looked down at his hand, it began to fade; I could faintly see through it. "Grampa," I said, "how could you be disappearing? What's happening?!"

He looked down at himself. "Ah. Well, I suppose it's time." He leaned forward in the rocker, again, looking at me. "Tessa, you need to tell your Gram that I love her very much. Tell her that I wasn't drunk, down at the docks," he paused, and smiled. "Really it was just part of my disguise. Though it didn't quite work... Give her my love, dear."

A horrible realization was beginning to grow in me. "No, Grampa, please stay! Why are you talking of going?"

The look he gave me was my answer. He patted my knee, but I couldn't feel him this time.

"The end was quick and I didn't suffer. I think I may have helped the guys and we'll hope they've got Jesse now. I've lived a long and full life, dear heart, and I can let it go, but I'm glad for this—you called to me."

Tears were running down my cheeks. He was becoming transparent; I could barely see him. "Please don't go, Grampa!"

"Little Ravenwing, we all have to go some time. It's the one thing in life you can count on!" His voice, his laugh, were still strong. "But I wanted to tell you that your spirit gift is strong, and we need that, we need you. Remember all that your Gram has taught you, and use it well!"

He was disappearing in front of my eyes. "I love you, Grampa," I whispered through the tears.

"I love you Little Ravenwing." And he was gone.

I woke up crying. Across the room, I heard Hannah crying, and Cat softly whispering, trying to hush her. I sat up, saw Cat sitting on Hannah's bed with her arms around Hannah, and I crept out of bed——no need to pull on clothes as we'd all gone to bed fully clothed, even Gram—and I climbed down the ladder from my bunk as quietly as I could, hoping not to wake up Gram. She seemed asleep still, curled on her side, such a small lump inside her bed roll. I went over to Cat and Hannah's bunk and knelt down next to Cat.

"She had a Seeing," Cat whispered. "She's coming out of it, but it was... oh, Tessa, it was bad!"

"How about we go upstairs to talk?" I whispered. I wanted to protect Gram for as long as possible.

Cat and I got Hannah up the stairs. She was shaking, wrapped in a warm wool shawl of Cat's, and we both kept our arms around her. Augie had left one of the oil lanterns burning, and we navigated Hannah over to the pile of cushions in the soft light, sat her down,

Cat with her arms around her and me crouching on the floor next to her, lightly rubbing her hands.

"Maybe it was just a dream, maybe it was just a dream," Hannah whispered through her sobs.

Cat made quiet soothing sounds. "We're here, dear. We're with you and we're going to stay with you."

At that moment I knew without a doubt that I hadn't had a dream, either. I softly told Hannah and Cat about my conversation with Grampa.

Hannah let out a wail, which raised both Augie and Charlie. Augie sat down on the floor next to me, rubbing his face with his hand.

"What did you See, Hannah?" I asked as gently as I could, my voice shaking. "We have to know."

"Shooting!" she sobbed. "Shooting in the Command Center! So much blood!"

"Hannah, *you have to tell us*, is Jesse all right?"

"Yes!" she took a ragged breath. "They never reached him. He's still where he was."

"Oh thank God!" Augie exclaimed next to me.

I leaned forward to rub Hannah's back. "I'm so sorry you're the one who has to see it all."

Cat rocked Hannah gently in her arms and continued her soothing whispering. I told Augie about Grampa's words to me, and we all cried for him, although everyone laughed through tears at the part where he told me to tell Gram that the drinking was just part of the disguise.

"Oh, how *are* we going to tell Gram?" I said then.

"It's all right," her voice came softly from the top of the stairs. She slowly walked over the rough wooden floor to us, her favorite wool shawl pulled tight around her. "I woke up, knowing. Tessa, you talked with him before he left for the other side..." her voice broke.

I stood up and put my arms around her, and Augie stood up and put his arms around us both. Hannah and Cat both reached out hands to pat our legs, the only part of us they could reach, and we all held each other for a long moment.

~

None of us went back downstairs; Augie and I brought up everyone's bed rolls and we snuggled into them by the stove, with

319

Charlie licking faces and thumping his tail. We waited for Emmitt. No one slept; from time to time someone would whisper something to someone else, or one or another of us would begin crying again and others would pat backs and say soothing words.

I asked Gram if she wanted to talk about Grampa. She smiled as she wiped her cheeks, her head resting on two pillows so we all could see her face.

"Tell us about how you first met him?" *Tell the story*, something in me said. *It will be healing...*

"I've told you that before haven't I?"

I shook my head.

"Goodness, that's hard to believe. Well, it was when I was living far to the south, with granny Ida Ravenwing's family," Gram began, then paused. I watched her face in the flickering firelight and saw her as a girl, short and strong, like Hannah, with an open, hopeful face and bright dark eyes. Maybe she braided tiny glass beads into her lustrous black hair, and they would sparkle in the firelight and lamplight as she sat listening to her Granny Ida's stories.

"Chuck flew up from the small city of Haines, to the south," Gram said. "His family was of the Jilkaat Kwan, from Klukwan, just north of Haines on the Chilkat river, and he had an ancient Dehavilland Beaver on floats."

"A beaver on floats!" I exclaimed, and everyone laughed.

"That's a type of plane, Tessa," Gram said. Of course I knew that, but it was fun that she did, too. As Jesse sometimes said—it was another Earl expression—*No flies on her!*

"He landed on our lake and was giving people rides in his plane for cash... I was seventeen years old, and none of the boys there was very interesting—and the boys at home, well I'd known them all my life, just as you girls grew up with the boys your age more like brothers. And here comes this very handsome man of twenty in a floatplane." She chuckled. "He seemed so dashing!"

We all smiled. I could picture Grandpa Chuck at twenty years old, a glint of mischief in his dark eyes, and a whole lot of trouble in his smile.

"And you went flying with him, Gram." Hannah said, glancing over at me with a smile, despite the tears still shining on her cheeks.

"I did. I was seventeen and thought I could handle anything, certainly your Grandpa Chuck, and maybe even a floatplane." Gram paused and turned her head to smile at Hannah on her right, and then me on her left. "I was wrong about the plane."

I laughed. "You threw up." Yes, she'd told this story before.

"Oh my, yes. Fortunately he'd come prepared with plastic bags. But I was so humiliated. I was sure he'd never want to see me again! But he kept coming back, and he kept asking for me each time he came, so I couldn't hide from him. Finally I sat him down and told him I was happier on the ground. It's never made sense to me to put yourself in the air in a machine whose motor could fail at any moment."

"You just always need to be thinking of where you'd land. We called them unscheduled landings," I said softly, missing the air with a palpable ache.

Gram reached out and put a hand on my shoulder. "You, Tessa, are more like him than you'll ever know."

There was a little pause. The flames in the woodstove wavered as wind gusted through the forest outside. I thought, *I'll take that as a compliment.*

"We married knowing that he would always be going and coming," Gram started up again. "That was all right with me, since that's the way he was. Chuck came from a family broken apart by alcohol. His mother died young of some disease, and his father died a drunk, drowned fishing off the coast. Chuck had a few brothers who all scattered, their lives wrecked by alcohol, like their father. He was a very solitary man, Chuck was, and I think that's why he had a hard time settling anywhere, but at the same time he loved finding friends who loved him just as he was, and there were many of them."

We sat there in the firelight thinking of Chuck Joseph—son, brother, husband, father, grampa. He'd lived a long and good life, and we all would carry him on in our hearts. Hannah and I each hugged Gram, who began crying again and couldn't stop. The pain she was feeling twisted through us. And what hurt even more was seeing Gram unmoored, Gram who always was rock-solid, unwavering. We all cried with her.

Emmitt arrived without a sound, with his truck's headlights off, and we wouldn't have known except that Charlie suddenly lifted his head, ears cocked, listening. Augie got up and went to the front door, then stepped out, Charlie on his heels. A minute later he walked back in with Emmitt, who looked pale and like he hadn't slept in several days, like the rest of us.

"Listen, man," Augie was saying, "we already know most of what you're going to tell us, so hopefully that can take that load off your shoulders." God bless him.

"What?" Emmitt looked confused, and he looked at us huddled close together in front of the woodstove.

Augie sat Emmitt down on his bed roll and quietly summed up all that had gone on with us over the past few hours. Emmitt kept shaking his head, as if trying to clear something out so he could understand better. It turned out that he had nothing new to add, except that Lars had taken the mission failure very badly, especially Grampa's death, feeling responsible for it. And that surprised no one.

Gram raised her arms to him and Emmitt came over to give her a hug, then he hugged Cat, and then Hannah and me. He sat down on Cat's bedroll with his arm around her.

"We're going to get Jesse," Emmitt said quietly. "You can depend upon it."

~

Hours later, when the sun was up and we were all outside, relieved to be busy with the chores of daily survival, Emmitt drove back in his truck. A man climbed out—tall, with graying hair, and paler skin than the rest of Earl's family. His shoulders looked weighed with responsibility. Emmitt had said that Lars wanted to come talk with us, and it was pretty clear to me that this was Lars. But another man climbed out of the truck behind him, bigger, with a floppy felt hat pulled down over mostly white hair, walking a little stiff at first. It was Earl.

I leaped out of the raised bed of vegetable seedlings where I'd been working with Cat and Hannah, and ran past Lars to hug Earl.

He staggered back a step, held me out so he could see me, then grinned. "Young Ravenwing, you've grown up." He hugged me again and I burst into tears. Sadie had taught me about *todas las madres*, and now I understood that there were *todas las padres* as well. Earl had always been my father in every way except the narrowest definition.

I managed to get out of Augie's way as he barreled in to give Earl a hug. Lars was standing to one side, looking older than his older brother, and I went over to him, intending to just clasp his hand, but found myself giving him a hug too.

"Emmitt's been telling us some... interesting things about you and Hannah," Lars said when I stepped back and looked up at him. "And your friend Cat too."

I just nodded, wondering what he thought of it all. He was much more closed than Earl; it was hard to know what he thought. But that didn't matter as long as he included us in future rescue plans.

But Lars seemed to be following along with my thoughts, for he said, "We want to get started on Plan B. That's why we're here to talk with all of you."

~

The day was warm and the wind had dropped, so we all sat down on the grassy slope off to the side of the house, before the bluff turned steep. Since it had a southern exposure, the grass was dry, but Augie went in and brought out the fat cushions for Gram to sit on, and Earl said he didn't mind taking Augie up on the offer of one, too. Hannah and Cat and I brought out a thermos of hot water, with mugs and tea bags, and leftover cinnamon buns from breakfast. The sun shone warm on us, and sparkled on the sea down below. The forest was close at our backs for screening, and it was filled with quiet birds readying for their migration. Yet a sadness wove through all of us that no beautiful morning could lift.

Lars first talked slowly, in somber tones, looking at Gram, about Grampa's friends who were able to recover his body. He hadn't had his identcard on him, not wanting Orion to be able to trace him if he'd been arrested, and the soldiers who had shot him had just assumed he was *another drunk Indian down on the docks*, and left him where they'd shot him. But Grampa had resourceful friends in many places and they had managed to recover his body. Lars would make arrangements to have him cremated, and would bring us his ashes.

Lars paused, then said softly looking to Gram first, then the rest of us, "I can't tell you how sorry I am about his death, and your loss."

Gram reached out—she was sitting on one side of him, Earl on the other—and patted his knee. "You did what you thought was the best thing to do. And Chuck. He sometimes took risks that he knew were bigger than he probably should take... he always had a weakness for heroic missions."

She looked past Earl to me. I wondered why, and then I saw myself sitting in the barn with Jesse when I first told him I was going to leave home to join the resistance, and what Jesse said back to me—
—*Tessa, someone's got to be someone there to talk you out of hare-brained mission*

ideas that you surely will get.

Gram gave me a small smile. I smiled back.

After a moment's pause, Lars looked over at Hannah. "Emmitt reminded me about your gift, which I imagine seems mostly like a curse."

Hannah looked up at him, but stayed quiet.

"You haven't seen anything new about Jesse?" Lars asked.

Hannah shook her head. "Nothing new, and even then, before last night I Saw so many different endings... things are so undecided, could go so many ways..."

"You've Seen us all back at your home, at the lake," Cat said softly.

"Yes, several times. But I've also Seen some other possibilities not nearly as good."

Lars cleared his throat, then said, "We've got to try again, but don't want to try too soon again, since they'll be expecting us now."

Earl rumbled, "But we can't leave him in there!"

"No one's talking about leaving Jesse," Emmitt leaned forward toward Earl.

After another pause, I couldn't help saying to the crowd in general, "I still think that somehow the air is one of the keys to our getting in or out... But I just can't see how that would be. I know we can't try the jopter route again, now that it's been done."

No one said anything.

"You don't suppose we could drop something in?"

"Like a bomb, and kill a bunch of innocent people including Jesse, while we're at it?" Augie exclaimed. "I thought you didn't want carnage, Tessa!"

"No, no, that's not what I was thinking of. It's just... is there any technology out there that works to disable things?"

"You mean like disable the Fence?" Emmitt asked.

"Exactly. The Fence is climbable, right?"

"Well, if it's turned off!" from Augie.

"So, Tessa, you're wondering if there's some technology that would let us turn it off from the outside?" Cat asked.

"Yes."

"I did glimpse something about the Fence," Hannah said slowly, "and this sounds so weird, but I Saw people—Jesse was one—somehow going through the Fence, escaping."

A number of eyebrows went up.

"I know some people I can ask," Lars finally said. "I think that's really something worth investigating."

"And I'm going this time," Augie said.

"Me too," added Emmitt.

Hannah was looking down, but Cat and I looked at each other. *And us, too*, I thought. It wasn't the time to bring it up, but bring it up I would, and I was not going to be denied this time.

~

Earl stayed at the safe house up on the mountainside with Lars and Emmitt and Billy, and he and Emmitt came over to see us every couple of days. We didn't see Lars again for a few weeks. Emmitt told us Lars was topping Orion's Most-Wanted list; his trip to visit us and talk about Plan B was the only time he'd left the safe house since Jesse was captured, and he planned to not venture forth again unless it was absolutely necessary.

Emmitt brought Billy to dinner one night as a surprise. When he walked in the door, Hannah and Cat and I all shrieked at once and Gram clutched her chest. But we quickly calmed ourselves, and the color returned to her face, and then we had a party.

We asked Billy to tell us about what he was doing, but no one but Cat and Emmitt could really understand him.

"Listening at all their doors," he said several times.

I got that... well, I sort of got that. He had found ways of insinuating himself through his computer into Orion's network of communications, though I couldn't quite picture it.

"Think of it as a huge spiderweb, Tessa," he said to me when I shook my head, both because I just didn't get it, and also maybe in that family way of trying to shake something loose in there. "It's this incredibly complex web or net that's invisible, wireless. You move around with numbers or code..."

You do, I thought, smiling. It was well beyond me!

"And I've been figuring out their numbers and their code," he went on. "I'm getting close to being able, with some of my code, to put a cascading bug into the main component of their computer network that will take it down in seconds."

There was a stunned silence around the table.

"A cascading *bug*?" Hannah and I said in unison.

"That's an organism, dear," Gram said kindly to Billy from her end of the table. "I'm not sure about the cascading part, but it couldn't possibly affect machinery."

Emmitt choked into his napkin. Augie, next to Billy, let loose a loud laugh that made Charlie jump to his feet, bumping the table with his head.

Billy laughed. "No, no, it isn't a real bug. It's numbers—a written code—a command, that worms its way inside a system, no matter how huge and complex it is, to mess it up, shut it down. Totally."

We all had to give that some thought.

"Huh." Hannah said finally. Cat smiled.

"So having the computer system go down would shut down the Fence, and the main gate, and we could get in to get Jesse?" I slowly asked.

"Absolutely."

"But soon?"

"Hopefully."

"But no way of knowing yet how soon?"

Billy held up his hands to show he didn't know. "And here's the final touch I'm adding to it—" He waited for us to all look at him expectantly. "When all the Orion computers crash? You know, that moment when all the screens go black and everyone's hit with the awful realization that things are going completely down? All that will come back up onto their screens is an image of a raven."

He must have been puzzled by the silence around the table. He added, "I was remembering that time at Easthaven when we were all outside and that raven flew in and knocked Tessa down."

I heard a startled gasp from Gram. "A raven knocked you down, Tessa?"

"Well, it was trying to land on her shoulder," Billy continued. "Anyway, everyone took that for a good sign, and since I've been working for the resistance, I've been using it as a symbol. Our resistance symbol. It's a lot more powerful than Orion's three stars, don't you think?"

Finally Gram said, "That's a wonderful touch, Billy."

I could feel her thinking hard on it, as I was. Raven as the symbol... nothing to do with me, but Raven... there was something so right about that.

I nodded at Billy. "Raven seems perfect to me, Billy." Raven the trickster. Raven of the air. Raven of the thresholds.

Cat and Hannah were nodding too. Emmitt and Augie both grinned.

"I want to hear more about that raven knocking down Tessa," Augie said.

~

Days stretched out into weeks. The fireweed had gone to seed and its white fluff blew along the sandy bluff and down to the beach. Birch and aspen leaves burned bright gold in the sun, such a beautiful contrast against the dark green-black of the spruce forest. Waves of geese and cranes passed overhead, calling joyously, heading south.

In such autumn glory we had a remembrance of Grampa. Emmitt brought the heavy urn filled with his ashes, and he brought four of Grampa's friends with him, all grizzled, laconic pilots who looked a bit uncomfortable with a bunch of women shaking their hands and welcoming them. We all walked the path down to the beach as twilight fell, Hannah and Gram, me carrying the urn, Cat, Emmitt and Augie carrying glass candle lanterns that they set on the driftwood fort walls, creating a wonderful soft glowing light. As the nighttime breeze began to blow from the land to the sea, we sent handfuls of Grampa's ashes into the air, which caught them up in greyish white billows, like ghostly spirits headed into the night. We saved half of his ashes to take back to the lake with us. *Soon*, we all said.

As the weeks passed, Charlie and I spent a lot of time down on the beach. Earl often came down with us and we'd sit on the dry sand at the edge of the bluff and watch the sea. Every once in a while we saw the plumey spout of a whale far out from shore. We only occasionally saw ravens.

Earl told me all about how family and friends were doing in the village—how his son Steve and his wife were living in Gram's and my cabin and taking good care of it until we returned; how his son Davy had built a house next door to Earl and Martha and was helping Martha manage the farm while Earl was with us. I showed him the driftwood fort and he, too, proclaimed it the perfect nap spot. Several times Augie and Emmitt wondered where he had gone, when they were looking for help with a project like erecting the panels for the solar film, or adding a water tank to the roof of the house, but I never told on him.

~

Finally Lars came back out, pulling off his glasses and graying wig disguise as he stepped out of Emmitt's truck with Emmitt and Earl.

"We've got the device," he said as Augie and I came up to him. "It should block all electromagnetic signals within about a mile radius. So it would take out not only the Fence and surveillance cameras, but also the P1 computer system, everything that runs off their computers. Most of their vehicles, including death drones and jopters, and weaponry."

The five of us walked toward the house. "Actually it will disable most of the port machinery, at that radius," Lars went on, "but it's only a temporary blocking. It'll only work for twenty to thirty minutes maximum, and of course that's only if it's undetected on arrival. You'd have to keep a close eye on your watches!"

"So Billy's computer 'bug' isn't ready yet, I gather?" I asked, thinking that Billy's route would be the better way to go, by far... completely internal, not depending on sneaking in a device and counting on it not being detected while it worked for only twenty minutes.

Lars shook his head. "It could be weeks, but I'm pretty sure it's more like months away. He hasn't made any progress in weeks now."

We were joined by Cat and Hannah and Gram, but this time we sat indoors and I made tea since the day was cloudy and there was a colder bite in the breeze.

"So, we've got the device," Lars said. "And we have the way of getting it into P1—a drone that can do a high flyover, signal jamming by Billy's crew, dropping it precisely to a target within the compound where it's least likely to be found. And now we think we have the best way of getting the team there." He glanced around; every pair of eyes was riveted to his, and I'm pretty sure that most of us weren't breathing. "The sea."

I thought, *Oh fuck, not another boat...*

Cat, to my left, between me and Emmitt, choked back a laugh.

Emmitt said, "Jesse has a buddy from navy days named Sam Riversong. Sam's out of the navy now and back to fishing for a living. He goes in and out of the city docks so often that he's not going to be noticed. He's going to go in late one evening with a different kind of load—us. We'll wait until the device hits, and the P1 lights and

Fence go out, and then we'll dash from the docks, over the Fence and in."

I remembered the docks were maybe two hundred yards or so from the north side of the P1 compound, which was basically a rectangle, with the main gate and the Command Center at one end and the barracks at the other. The big bay that curved northeast of Fayerport bordered that side of the compound—the narrow, barracks end—where the city docks came close.

"So we go over the Fence when the power's down, run to the barracks and grab Jesse, and get out, back to the boat, all within twenty minutes," Augie was saying, a little doubtfully.

Lars shook his head. "We'll have another couple of faster boats waiting off the barracks end for a faster get-away. You'll come back over the Fence and they'll be right there."

"Who's going in?" Augie asked.

Emmitt nodded at him, "You, me, and Sam Riversong. No heavy weaponry," he glanced at me. "Just knives, just in case—Sam's as good with them as Jesse. But we're going to be wearing worker clothing this time, not going as Orion soldiers."

"Billy?" I asked.

"Billy's going to stay out along the Fence, keeping an eye on the get-away boats, making sure they're ready, in communication with the guys coming out with Jesse."

Earl groaned. "Wish I could be there with Billy to help, but with my bum leg, I guess I'd be more of a liability."

Gram, next to him, leaned close and patted his shoulder. "You're going to be here, praying with me."

A few of us choked back laughter, seeing Earl's face; knowing Earl, you knew that's not how he would prefer to be put to use.

I said calmly, "Cat and Hannah and I are going to be there with Billy."

Lars frowned.

"We won't be going in. We'll stay outside the Fence," I said. "The three of us know it's important that we go. Hannah's Seen it—we have to go."

Hannah has Seen the three of us, and Billy, too, at the Fence making the difference in Jesse's escape, Cat had told me. Hannah hadn't yet Seen what exactly we were doing to help, but that was all I needed to know.

A raven called as it flew past our cliff. Right on cue.

"That's seven people going in on Sam's boat," Lars said slowly.

"Including Sam," Emmitt said. "Plenty of room. Plus we have two powerboats for the get-away."

Lars finally nodded.

"What about the problem of Orion pursuit from the air?" I asked, thinking that there probably would be a few Orion jopters on the ground at P1, or very close by, that would be used to hunt us down.

"Yeah. That's another challenge," Lars said slowly. "We have it worked out that you can only be in the boats for a short time, enough to hopefully break contact with any pursuit from the water but before the jopters are operational again, and you're in their sights. We do have one or two drones we can use for cover, but that wouldn't be enough for very long, or for more than a couple of jopters at the most."

"So we'll be getting off only a couple of miles down the coast," Emmitt said. "We're working with maps and with grounders on good spots."

Some of us nodded; everyone looked thoughtful, and serious. A lot of things could go wrong with this plan, but there didn't seem to be any other option. No one knew when Billy was finally going to unlock the last "doors" and Lars had decided that we couldn't keep waiting. We all agreed with him.

They'd had Jesse for two months now. It was time to get him out.

13. October 6, 2111

Sam Riversong's fishing boat was much bigger than I'd expected, with steps leading down to a roomy cabin with long padded benches and a little kitchenette, and plenty of room on the aft deck, fortunately, because that's where I ended up not long after we boarded off the dock near the community center. Sam himself was small and quiet, with a quick smile, Tlingit or Haida from down the coast to the south, I guessed. Under his yellow raingear he was dressed in the ugly orange Orion prison workers' jumpsuit, also worn by Emmitt and Augie.

The boat began rising and falling as soon as Sam reved the engine and headed us out of the protected water around the dock. I had started down to the cabin with everyone else—Emmitt, Augie, Billy, Cat and Hannah—but I turned around to head back for the open air. I bounced off Billy, who was trying to squeeze through the cabin door. Like Hannah, Cat and me, he was dressed all in black, with a black ball cap pulled down over his bright red hair.

"Hey Tessa," he said, "where you headed?"

"For the railing," I managed to say, and I got there just in time to throw up. Fortunately I hadn't been able to eat much food during the day. I was also grateful that no one else was on deck with me as I heaved several more times.

The weather was not the best. The wind had been rising since morning, and now we were seeing its effect on the sea. But I gathered this was one of those missions where once the plans were in place, it would take an awful lot to change the timing of it.

I leaned my cheek on my arm that gripped the cool metal railing, and found my eyes level with gray waves rolling past us, some of them foaming white in the dimming light. To take my mind off my stomach, I imagined all of the creatures in the sea out there, just beyond me, invisible to my eyes... sea otters floating on their backs with their paws clasped, rocked up and down by the waves; humpback whales swimming just beneath the surface of a wave higher than me, silhouetted against the fading light in the western sky. I wanted to see them so much, I almost did. I understood why Jesse loved the sea so much—the wildness of it, the bigness. I just prayed he would never again ask me out on a boat with him.

"Hey," a voice said from behind me. I turned my head very carefully, still keeping it pillowed on my arm, and saw Augie. He leaned against the railing next to me and tried to unobtrusively adjust the orange jumpsuit that definitely was tight on him. He'd complained to Emmitt on the dock about how he didn't think he'd be able to run in it, and Emmitt had said that extra-larges were hard to come by, so he ought to be grateful.

"You really aren't a sailor are you?" Augie said. He had to hold his black ball cap down against the wind, but his blond curls still managed to blow around.

"Just praying that Jesse never again tries to get me out on a boat with him."

Augie grinned, then took a long breath that I could hear even over the wind. He came serious quickly as he stared out over the sea to the west. "We've got to get him back, Tessa... got to, got to..."

I patted his arm. "We will, Augie. I'm sure of it."

"Just keep telling me that tonight, okay?"

I promised him I would.

"If you're all right, I'll head back to the cabin comfort," he said and started to move away.

Just then a larger than usual wave broke as it rolled past and the wind threw icy cold spray right into my face.

"Shit!" I yelled, and Augie laughed and said he'd come back out with a towel, or better yet a blanket.

As I clung to the rail and tasted salt on my lips, wiped seawater from my face, I saw the red light of the buoy marker off in the distance. I strained my eyes to see, in deepening twilight, the metal tower rising out of the waves beyond it. Nearly five months had passed since Jesse and I had done the crazy jump out of the jopter and the swim in the sea. In a way I was glad I was on this boat, even if I was sick and wet and cold. There was something right about it. As long as we could come away with Jesse.

The timing felt right. "I'm ready," I whispered into the wind and cold spindrift.

~

Clouds scudded above our heads but there was no rain as Sam's boat slowly made the turn into the northern bay that led to the heart of the city. I had slipped into the cabin, my stomach more or less under control once we left the swells along the coast. It was night, but not dark, with lines of lights along the roadways, and light spilling from millions of skyscraper windows, with beacons flashing at the tops of the tallest towers, all of this light bouncing off the clouds and illuminating the night. This lit-up world under the low clouds must look like an enormous glowing dome to jopters flying high overhead.

P1 slid past us on its low bluff above the sea. The green glow of the Fence was unmistakable; I felt a twist of fear in my gut as I saw it, as my eyes followed the light towers spaced evenly along it. I quickly looked away from the window and sat down with everyone else on the benches, going into hiding mode now that we were nearing the city docks.

"If we get boarded at the docks," Emmitt said, pointing, "that's the door to the hold. You'll have to hide in there. It's low and nasty and stinks of fish, but that's the best we can do." He began pulling on yellow waterproofs like Sam's; he was going to be the deckhand until the lights went out and they could pull off their outer clothing and sprint for the Fence.

Billy and Augie quietly whispered to each other. Each of them held an old-fashioned talkie which wouldn't be affected by the drone's blocking signal. It sounded like they were going over alternate plans, the *what-ifs*. I liked that kind of thinking and was glad they were doing it, but also was glad I didn't have to do it as I sat next to Cat and Hannah. We didn't have our wigs on because Emmitt figured we wouldn't need them—we wouldn't be moving off the boat until the device landed and took out the power at P1, and we'd be in the dark (well, the relative dark); if we got caught, our disguises wouldn't help us anyway. I was glad not to have to put up with the scratchy blonde wig. I'd pulled my just-long-enough hair into a ponytail. Cat had pulled her flaming hair back in a tight knot and covered it with a dark bandana. She patted my knee as the boat rocked.

"You don't suppose the wind's going to be a problem?" I couldn't help whispering.

"I'm sure they wouldn't be following through with the drone if they were worried about the wind," Hannah whispered back, but she didn't sound completely convinced.

My stomach started knotting up again. I tried to take slow, deep breaths. *The lake is in you.* I pictured myself nestled in Jesse's warm jacket at the edge of the mountain hemlocks, the ravens whispering and singing softly to each other above me, the lake spreading out below me, embraced by the arms of the mountains. And I was there. Without a doubt, I was there.

I sat up and let Jesse's jacket slide to the moss at my feet. I stood, eyes closed, raising my arms above my head. *Raven and spirit helpers, hear me now... I have felt powerless for so long. Abused by people who have no right to control and abuse us, watched helplessly as Jesse was torn from us... was powerless when Grampa was gunned down and left, seen as just another drunk old Indian...*

No longer! I am ready for whatever power the spirits here entrust to me. I will use it wisely.

I am ready. We are ready!

A raven gave a hoarse cry and I knew I'd been heard.

I opened my eyes to darkness, then to the faces of my loved ones gazing up at me, more than a couple of them with open mouths, astonishment vibrating through the air around us.

I sat back down next to Cat. "Ummmm. I was at the lake." As if that explained everything; but, in fact, with this crowd, it mostly did.

I had a sudden, awful feeling that I had totally made a fool of myself, but Hannah leaned over past Cat, her eyes intent on my face. "You've inspired us, Tessa." She was dead serious, as Hannah usually is.

Emmitt moved past us to perform his deckhand duties, but he paused to give Cat a quick kiss, and patted my back. The engine sound had changed and it felt like we were slowing in the water; dark shadowy shapes loomed outside the narrow cabin windows and I guessed we had arrived at the city docks.

~

Augie was on duty at the foot of the cabin steps to warn us if any Orion soldiers came near the boat, to send us scuttling for the shelter of the stinking fish hold. He sat there, his orange coveralls unzipped, the sleeves tied at his waist ("So I can run in this fucking thing!"). Emmitt and Sam stayed up on the deck after tying us to the docks in Sam's usual spot. The rest of us—Billy, Hannah, Cat and me—sat silently meditating on what we were about to do, or, in some cases, what we weren't quite sure we were going to be called on to do. I thought of Gram, Earl, and Sadie praying for us as they waited back at the house with Charlie, who could very well have been praying too. I missed Charlie and wished we could have brought him with us.

Leaving Gram had been hard; she had looked so much older and frailer since we lost Grampa. But she leaned in to me and whispered as intently as she ever had,

"Tessa, I am so proud of you. It is absolutely right, going without weapons. I see great power all around you."

She put both hands on my sleeve, holding tight. "I don't understand it, Tessa, and you probably don't either, but that is all right. It's a mystery. We just do all that we can."

I'd quickly kissed her cheek and hurried after the others. No chance to say more; but nothing more to say anyway.

I began to get nervous as the minutes ticked by. Billy and his tech guys had planned about a half hour wait at the docks before the drone flyover and the dropping of the device, extra time in case anything came up, but not so much time that anyone would get suspicious about Sam's boat just sitting there at the dock. I kept worrying about Orion soldiers on dock patrol challenging us. I worried about the wind affecting the drone, and the device not landing on the target in P1. Billy would know... I leaned forward to whisper to him, when suddenly everything went dark. The dock lights had gone out.

Augie exclaimed, "Lights are out, Fence is down!" and he sprinted up the stairs and disappeared.

He, Emmitt, and Sam now had just twenty minutes to get Jesse, and get him out, back over the Fence. We couldn't count on a full thirty minutes of protection.

Billy brushed past me. It was our turn to slip off the boat, keeping to the shadows as best we could—with the dock lights out, there would be enough dark, even with the rest of the city lights as bright as they were—onto the pavement of the wharf with its maze of warehouses. We'd gone over the route to take, the fastest route to get to the Fence.

I followed Billy up the cabin steps and out onto the boat deck, Hannah and Cat on my heels. My eyes were fully adjusted to the night and I could see ahead and to our right, waves foaming white on the sandy beach below the gentle sloping bluff. Somewhere down there two speedboats rocked in the swells, waiting for us. *I'm going to be with Jesse in just a few minutes!*... I forced that thought back so that I could concentrate on what I needed to do first.

"Come on! Come on!" I whispered to Cat and Hannah, urging

them to run faster as we hurried off the gangplank and down to the wharf. We sprinted across to the line of warehouses. Billy, ahead of us, wasn't looking back.

I heard shouting in the distance but couldn't tell if it was behind us or ahead of us. We kept running. Down the front line of sliding metal doors, some of them open—suddenly we bumped into a knot of men, talking loudly, coming out of one of the warehouses onto the docks, speculating on what had happened to the power, but they weren't Orion fortunately, just dock workers, it looked like—*Oh! please excuse us!* I heard Cat say, stunning them into silence, and we kept running.

We rounded a corner, past the last of the warehouses, Billy just ahead of us, headed for the gentle bank to the perimeter road that ran around the Fence. I could barely make out the ten foot tall Fence; how odd that it was dark, just barely visible in the night. Sam and Emmitt and Augie had already climbed it, already were running down the dark path to the barracks. *Please, Raven, help this work!* I whispered as I kept running.

Billy stopped to catch his breath when he reached the perimeter road, and he and I waited a moment for Cat and Hannah to catch up to us. The Fence was only a few feet away, still dark. Inside P1 I heard shouting and prayed it was the confusion that we had hoped for, confusion that would help the guys slip into the barracks. Then I heard gunshots. We knew that was going to happen as well; the device would jam the heavy weaponry, but there was no way to be safe from the stunners, handguns, and rifles most of the soldiers carried.

"Come on, come on!" I urged everyone farther down the perimeter road. We arrived at our mark and stood there in the dark, looking through the Fence, but there was nothing to see yet... and then I saw people running toward us.

"They have him already!" Billy shouted, but then we saw it was a crowd, a dozen, no, more like two dozen people all in gray prison-issue jumpsuits running our way. I recognized a couple of the big, tattooed native guys from Re-Education sessions. They'd been able to get out quickly, all with the same thought—*get over the Fence while it's off!*

Billy quietly said some words into his radio, which immediately crackled with words coming back.

"The boats are in place," he said. "That's good."

But Hannah sank down onto the dirt road next to me, gasping. "No, no, no, this can't happen!"

I bent down next to her. "What? What, Hannah? *Tell us!*"

Hannah was silent for a long moment, her mouth working soundlessly. She was in the grip of Seeing something. Cat squatted down and put her arms around her.

And just then the Fence lit up, brilliant garish green in the black night, illuminating our shocked faces, humming with all its pulsing current. All of the perimeter lights on the Fence came back on, blinding us. Far down the Fence from us someone screamed, some poor soul who had been climbing.

"What the *fuck* just happened?!" I shouted.

"They had a backup generator for the Fence," Hannah said in a dull voice. "Something that doesn't run on electronics."

Billy said, "Fuck." He lifted his radio again and spoke into it, "Emmitt, do you hear me? Where are you?"

I heard Emmitt's voice say "We've got him, they shot him... what's with the Fence?!"

"Keep coming, man," Billy said. Then, to himself, "What the fuck are we going to do?"

I knelt down on the dirt road next to Hannah and Cat. Jesse had been shot. The Fence was back on. Orion was hunting us down again.

"This isn't going to work!" Hannah was moaning.

"Quiet!" I said to her.

Stop! I said to time. And somehow time stopped. It must have been my own perception of time—at least that's what I concluded later—but it felt as if everyone stopped in midstep, mid-sentence, midthought.

Gram had said she'd seen great power around me. Okay, I was going to believe in that.

Everything had stopped. Everything around me had fallen away. I felt the strangest sensation of rushing movement, first away, away, out and out, the whole planet dropping away below me... and then I rushed back in, in, in through skin and bone, past pumping heart and blood singing through veins, into... space again, the vast space inside an atom, electrons orbiting a pulsing, singing sun of nucleus.

Everything I had ever done and ever would do, ever been and

ever would be, snapped into focus. I was absolutely, totally present in the moment.

I was ready, and I knew what to do. It might not work—it would work—it's just that I might not survive it, but... well, that was that.

"Billy!" I said. Time started up again.

I jumped to my feet and looked at him. "You and I can do this. Tell them to keep coming to us!"

A siren started in the distance, and the snarling sound of the motorbikes, their lights shining down the road from the still-dark Command Center. Orion soldiers headed our way. Through the green glare of the Fence I saw three men in orange running, half-dragging, half-carrying a fourth man. Jesse.

"Cat, you yell at them and tell them to stand back," I said, "and you and Hannah stand back, too."

I took Billy's arm. "You and I can do this."

His eyes were wide. "What the fuck, Tessa?"

"When I tell you to tear the Fence, do it, okay?"

He looked at me as if I was insane.

No time to say more. I shut everything out. It was just me and the Fence. I stepped closer, and closer, feeling the flow of its current like the flow of a huge river. I raised my hands. There! It was there—the flow of energy that had run through my body before. I brought it to the Fence. It was just a matter of stepping in, in just the right place, to merge the flows.

I reached up my arms—outspread like wings—"Now, Billy!" I shouted.

And I stepped into the Fence.

The surging power of the sun ran through me from my fingers through my toes and down into the earth. I was at the very heart of the sun. Pulsating, brilliant beyond imagining, heat surpassing understanding.

And it was such an honor to be in the heat of it—at the very heart of it—for that one moment. Sparks flew; a metallic rip nearly tore our eardrums.

And then it was over. Dark again, and so quiet, and cold.

My eyes refocused on faces staring at us through a huge hole in the Fence; really it was almost a door they could walk through.

"Come on, guys," I found my voice and tried to sound casual. "What are you waiting for?"

Everyone was breathing hard; someone—Cat maybe—laughed wildly. Sam, Emmitt, Augie all moved forward, pushing Jesse through the Fence to me. Shorn hair, gaunt, but it was Jesse. He could barely walk, blood soaked through his prison jumpsuit from his throat all the way down his body, he was trying to hold a hand over the wound just below and right of his throat, his hand glistening with blood.

"Raven!" he said. "You pushed your mind and made us a door..."

"Billy did the door," I said, but he pitched forward, going unconscious. Billy reached out to grab him before he hit the ground, pulling Jesse's arms over his shoulder, dragging him out of the way.

"Go! Go!" Augie yelled at me, Hannah, and Cat.

He and Emmitt and Sam burst through the hole in the Fence after Jesse, one after another. Emmitt grabbed Jesse's legs and he and Billy ran for the beach, Jesse swinging between them. Augie waved his arms at Hannah and Cat, like a hen flapping frantically to spur her chicks forward, ahead of an attacking fox. I didn't need any pushing; I was running hard after Jesse, in the dark on the gentle bluff down to the sandy beach.

Motorcycles roared up to the Fence, shining their lights out at us. A shout from the Orion soldiers. There was a shout from the other direction, from the beach. I looked down the sand and saw two men waving at us, just beyond them a rocky spit that served as a breakwater, just beyond that two speedboats bobbing in the waves.

Damn the motorcycle lights for making us targets for the Orion soldiers! A bullet whined close by on my right. I didn't know the range their rifles had, but remembered how they'd hit Billy as we ran for the jopter, and knew the damage they could do. And Jesse was already shot. As I ran I thought—Please God, keep him alive until we can get him help...

On our side of the rocky spit, one of the men—an old guy with white braids—knelt on the sand with a rifle to his shoulder. He was shooting past us. I heard crack! crack! and it got a lot dimmer along the shore. He was taking out the motorcycle lights.

Billy and Emmitt both stumbled and nearly dropped Jesse; Augie came up behind them and swept Jesse up over his shoulder and kept running for the nearest boat. So did I, though I glanced back for a quick look at where everyone was. Cat and Hannah were both right behind me, with Sam behind them, and Billy and Emmitt both were back on their feet, all of us running as fast as we could toward the water, and the boats.

The old boat driver kept shooting past us at the Orion soldiers. The other boat driver was shooting from the breakwater rocks. We'd reached the breakwater, somehow managing not to get shot by either the good guys ahead of us, or the bad guys behind us. Augie was already wading into the water on the other side, Jesse hanging over his shoulder. But the low waves slowed him down, burdened as he was and without the use of his arms for balance. Emmitt was just to my right, headed for Augie, going to help him with Jesse.

My ears were beginning to get used to the high-pitched whine of bullets going past. It was only a matter of time... I heard a cry, and the younger boat driver just a few feet away from us dropped his rifle and fell to the rocks. Emmitt reached out for him, and the old boat driver ran up and between them they carried the injured man over the sand and followed Sam and Billy, wading into the water for the second boat.

With everyone scrambling to help everyone else, no one noticed that Augie was all alone trying to get Jesse into the first boat. I have no idea how I did it, but somehow I launched myself through the waist-high water, floundered, nearly fell, staggered to my feet and flailed through icy waves to make it to the first boat just as Augie did. He was trying to lift Jesse over the side. I found the three-rung metal ladder on our side of the boat, swarmed up it and helped pull Jesse in. Then Emmitt was there, literally throwing both Hannah and Cat into the boat, then climbing in himself, but I hardly noticed. All I could see was Jesse.

He was still bleeding, his body limp. His eyes were closed, his face was pale.

Jesse! I put my hand over his chest wound and called to him, mind to mind. *Jesse, talk to me, please! Oh Raven and all my ancestors and spirit helpers, don't let me be too late to help!*

The boat's engine rumbled. Augie said, "Hey, trust me, I do know how to drive this thing!" Emmitt crouched next to him as bullets still sang in the air. "I'm your backup man!"

Cat knelt next to Hannah, who also lay in a heap on the floor of the boat. "She landed on her head," Cat shouted over the rising roar of the engine. "She's knocked out!"

Then we all slid as Augie slammed in the throttle and sent us in a curving arc away from the shore, away from the shooting, headed out of the bay for the sea. Raising up for a quick look, I glimpsed the other speedboat ahead of us. The two local guys and Sam and Billy got off a lot more quickly than we did.

I looked back and saw lights on the water behind us, from the direction of the city docks—of course Orion would also have speedboats, I thought. And like the motorcycles they weren't affected by the drone's blackout. At least the jopters should be out of commission for a bit longer.

There was nothing I could do about any of it. All I could do was concentrate on Jesse.

Jesse, I crouched back down and called to him again. *Jesse, my love.* I brought my face down to his face, pressed my forehead against his so we were breathing each other's breath—if he was breathing. Yes, he was breathing. Just barely.

Tessa, I heard him faintly. *I always said you were lit, but you were awesome back there at the Fence...*

Listen, I told him. *We need to work a healing right now, you and me. I will not let you go!*

He was my other half. He was my life. If I lost him, I couldn't live. I would give all my soul to keep him alive.

Stay with me, I breathed against his face. I was inside his head breathing, *Stay, stay, stay... I need you. We all need you!*

I could feel him think about it. It would be so easy to slip away, as easy as sleeping. Time paused again. Everything stood in balance.

I love you, Jesse Brightwater, I told him, and used his own words from that crazy jopter ride: *I will not let you go. If you go, I'm going too.*

Finally I felt him think, *Okay then. I'm not leaving. Hopefully not.*

I breathed a prayer of thanks, and then added, *Let me be the song...*

A healing song of Gram's began to fill my mind. I softly sang it, slipping my hands under Jesse's jumpsuit, feeling for the wounds on his chest and high up on his back where the bullet passed.

Trace the path
of the whorl on the shell
of the loops in the ear
of the earth 'round the sun.
Trace the path
And find completeness and rest.
Trace the path

of the snake on the sand
of the raven on the wind
of stars spangling the sky.
Trace the path
And find completeness and rest.
Find the center and rest.
Breathe from the center and be whole.
Walk the circle and be complete.
Enter the heart of the sun.

Back at the Fence I had been in the heart of the sun. It was still with us. Heat built and built and flowed through me and into him, and back again. Through my hands on his open wounds, I felt torn edges slowly pulling together, cell by cell, layer upon layer, healing beginning, moving from the inside to the outside.

We were so warm, we were radiating. We were at the heart of the Sun. I sang the song over and over, and Jesse faintly began to sing it with me. We were with the ravens in the wind, with the stars beyond the sky. *Thank you*, I said to Raven, and my ancestors and my spirit helpers. *Thank you from the depth of my heart, from the heart of the sun. Thank you...*

~

I have no idea how much time passed; I would have guessed hours but it could only have been a few minutes. But my jumpsuit that had been soggy with seawater was now perfectly dry and warm. Jesse was warm in my lap. The boat sharply spanked up and down on the waves, the wind shrieked, Cat sat with her arms around Hannah. Augie and Emmitt stood at the wheel together, talking. Then Augie leaned down to yell, "How's he doing?"

I yelled up at him, over the engine and the wind, "Sleeping, I think! Augie, he's going to be okay!"

Augie started crying. Then he brushed the tears off his face with his sleeve, and leaned down again to shout, "It's gonna get rough in a minute. We've gotta get out a ways to shake these guys!"

I almost laughed. It wasn't rough already? But I didn't feel seasick this time. I slid down a bit on the floor of the boat and cradled Jesse in my arms, kept sending heat into him. Next to me, Cat was doing the same for Hannah.

"How is she?" I asked.

Cat just shook her head, but then Hannah opened her eyes, blinked a few times, looked up at Cat and smiled, then over at me. Her smile widened.

"The get-away boat," I explained, in case she needed an explanation, but I didn't think she did. "We're getting away."

She struggled to lean on one elbow to see me better. "Tessa, never in a million years would I have Seen, or even thought possible what you did back there at the Fence... it changed everything!"

I didn't quite know what to say, so I shrugged and said, "Well, it was a team effort. And now we hope."

A sudden thought hit me. "We *are* getting away, aren't we?"

Emmitt must have heard me. He crouched down next to us, looked at Cat first, then Hannah and me. "The other boat made it to one of the safe places along the shore." He paused. We all realized at the same second what was coming next.

"But we aren't going to make it in time are we?" I asked him.

He shook his head. "That boat back there is closing in on us. But Augie has a plan."

"And what about the jopters?" I asked. "They'll be coming any time, right? How long has it been?"

Emmitt had just looked at his watch, but he looked again. "Twenty-eight minutes."

Our boat swerved in a turn and we all slid on the wet floor. Emmitt grabbed my collar since I was holding Jesse with both arms. I wondered what Augie's plan was.

"Oh!" Cat said from beside me. "You've been here before, Tessa. Tell us about the tower and the terminal under the water."

Oh my God, Augie has taken us that far out from shore... we're going to be sitting ducks again... I forced myself to take slow, deep breaths, and then try to describe it for Cat and Hannah. Augie and Emmitt knew it well, I assumed, as well as Jesse did.

"The abandoned airport terminal is closer to shore than the tower," I said slowly, "and in low tide, it's just under the surface, which is why that red warning light buoy is out here somewhere..."

"It's low tide," Emmitt said off to my right. "Very low tide."

And I could feel another mutual realization stir through us. Jesse opened his eyes and looked past me to Emmitt. "Is he planning what I think he's planning?"

Emmitt's smile flashed white in the dark. "Yep."

343

"Oh," Cat said. Nothing more.

"Jopters coming," Emmitt said. He'd been looking into the distance, past us. "But we've got time, Augie. Don't think about them, just do what you've got to do."

Everyone was praying very, very hard that Augie knew what he was doing.

I couldn't see a thing, down there low on the floor with Jesse, but I realized I didn't need to with Cat next to me.

"How close is the Orion boat?" I asked her.

"Closing fast."

"How about the jopters?"

"They're coming pretty fast, too, but still maybe two miles back."

"Hold on, everybody!" Augie shouted, and we swerved hard.

Emmitt grabbed me again to keep Jesse and me from sliding across the boat.

I could hear Augie, just above the roar of the engine, chanting, "Come on, come on, come on!"

"The roof just under the surface!" Cat said in my left ear. "Like a reef... He's hoping..."

A huge explosion lit the night and a percussive wave simultaneously shoved our boat almost out of the water, our engine sound changing as our stern lifted into the air. Augie, Emmitt and Jesse all shouted together.

Next to me, Cat started laughing. "Men and explosions. I get it now, Tessa."

The Orion speedboat had hit the roof, as Augie had hoped it would.

But there still were the approaching jopters.

And then even from the floor of the boat, I could see the tower. Augie was heading us into the tower. The tide was so low, we easily drove right in one of the openings on the back, west side.

Augie cut the engine, but we still had forward momentum with the waves.

"Hold on!" he said for the third time in five minutes, and Emmitt grabbed me again, this time my right arm. *Bam!* we hit something and rocked backwards.

"Jesus, Augie," Emmitt said.

"Hey, you have a problem with my driving?" Augie was scrambling to the bow of the boat. "Throw me that rope!"

Emmitt was scrambling, too. I saw in the darkness a darker shape above us; we were well into the tower, below the floor that Jesse and I had slept on.

"They're tying us so we don't drift around with the waves," Cat interpreted on my left. "I think he had to come in fast, hoping the jopters wouldn't see us."

"But we're sitting ducks in here!" I almost shouted. "This is the first place they're going to come looking!"

Jesse opened his eyes and looked up at me. I could feel him thinking, *It's going to be okay, Sweetheart. Somehow.*

In the silence after all of that engine roaring, now just the quiet wash of waves moving through the old window openings of the tower... and then above that, the whine and thuh-thuh-thuh of the approaching jopters.

"Tessa," Cat said, "Hannah has Seen this. She's Seen you do what you did to protect yourself from Miranda in prison, this time for all of us, to keep us safe from the jopter scanners."

"She has?" My brain felt frozen. Like the boat, I had lost all momentum; dead stop, dead tired, feeling like giving up.

Hannah cleared her throat. "I have, Tessa. You can do it."

I can't do this! I can't do this!?

Cat put her hand on my left knee, reassuring. I blew out a long breath, struggled a little to sit straighter, Jesse trying to oblige, but he was pretty much dead weight. Emmitt had come back to us, and he pulled on my shoulders to help me sit up, with Jesse still lying across my lap. Then Emmitt sat down on the floor in front of Cat and Hannah. Augie came, too. We were all together, arms around each other on the floor of the boat. We heard the jopters coming closer.

I breathed in, seeing the lake. In my ears, instead of the jopters now, all of Gram's lessons about doing my homework—the hours of meditating, of opening, of trying to see and hear what others were missing—all of that work that hopefully puts you in a position, *ready*, in case that moment comes, when you can use it.

I saw us all in the lake, not on the lake, but in the lake, in a big bubble, breathing, taking in the joyous mystery of it, safe...

Cat was quietly telling us all to put our minds at rest, to sleep if we could, quiet, quiet...

Vaguely I was aware of—a very great distance away—bright, searching lights and loud noise, but then I let that slide away as unimportant.

We were safe in the lake, together, and what a wonder that was. What a mystery.

~

Slowly I came awake. Someone was stroking my left arm. Augie's voice was saying from my other side, "I know she'll probably be pissed, but there was nothing else to do to shake them. And it's not my fault those fuckers couldn't drive their boat."

Then the thrum of engines starting up. Emmitt's voice coming closer as he said, "Cast off. Let's creep forward until we can see." The thunk of rope dropping onto the floor across from me.

I opened my eyes to near-darkness and quiet waves inside the tower. Jesse was sound asleep in my lap. Cat had been stroking my arm; even in the dark I could see her and Hannah grinning at me. Hannah started to say something, but I turned my head and said,

"Augie!"

He bent down from where he'd been at the steering wheel. "Tessa?"

"You're right—Orion couldn't steer their boat for shit. You saved us."

He grinned. "No, Tessa, just a few minutes ago *you* saved us. Twice!" And he reversed the engine and backed us a little ways into the water in the middle of the tower, then drove us slowly forward, toward one of the openings to the east.

I knew, without seeing, that the lights of the projects— Easthaven, Westhaven, Southaven—shone across the water ahead of us. The wind was dropping, calming. The waves were quieter.

"How's it looking, Emmitt?" Augie asked ahead to Emmitt, in the bow again.

"All clear!" Quick footsteps and Emmitt dropped down on the floor in front of us. "Let's go!"

And Augie opened up the engine and sent us straight for the coast.

~

The engine was running at only a quarter throttle and the waves were carrying us now, each one lifting us and carrying us and gently lowering us until the next one took over, closer and closer to shore. Cat described a small inlet we were heading for, that looked sheltered—the forest came right down to the shore. From the floor of the boat, looking up, I could see dark trees against the not-quite-as-dark sky, and it did feel protected. *Sheltered*, I thought, what a lovely word in every sense.

Augie cut the engine and we drifted, and he threw a rope, and then we bumped against something, and I heard a familiar voice—Billy—asking about Jesse. We'd found the other boat.

But before anyone did anything else, Augie suddenly loomed over Jesse and me, threw his arms around Jesse and kissed first his left cheek, then his right cheek.

Jesse's eyes flew open and he smiled up at Augie, "I was dreaming that Tessa was kissing me, but something didn't feel quite right!"

Augie burst out laughing. "Same old Jesse, except maybe the hair." He ruffled the black, rough brush of hair over Jesse's scalp.

"Takes a licking and keeps on ticking," I couldn't resist using another favorite Earlism, and Jesse started laughing and then moaned, holding his chest. Augie, Emmitt, Hannah and Cat burst out laughing, tears rolling down cheeks, loss-of-body-control laughing. A delayed reaction to the past hour's events, for sure.

"What!? What the hell?!" from the other boat, and Billy climbed over into ours, not very gracefully.

"What's so funny? How is he, Tessa? How is he?" Billy crouched down next to us.

Jesse gave a small smile. "Not bad at all. Still ticking."

Billy looked amazed. I gently unzipped the top of Jesse's jumpsuit to show him the wound... and the hole was gone. Now there was a bright red scab where the bullet hole had been.

"How's it looking, Raven?" Jesse asked softly, when no one else could say anything.

"Not bad at all." We smiled at each other, and I tightened my arms around him. "I think you're going to make it, but we've got to get some of Gram's healing herbs into you as soon as possible. The ones that help after bleeding."

Hannah and Cat both nodded vigorously.

Jesse closed his eyes, still smiling. "Raven, let's get married as soon as possible, and move back to the lake, and have at least four kids..." His voice faded and he was asleep again.

"I guess he *is* feeling better," Billy managed to say.

"How's the boat driver who got shot?" I asked him.

"He's okay too," Billy said. "It's Rusty, Sam's brother. Bullet went through his thigh but seemed to miss everything important, including his femur. It's stopped bleeding, but Sam's holding him secure, to keep it that way."

"Oh, thank God," I breathed. I should move into the other boat to see if there was anything more I could do to help, but I couldn't leave Jesse. In fact I planned on not letting go of Jesse ever, except maybe for a bathroom trip now and then.

Billy leaned forward. "Tessa, what *did* you do to Jesse?"

"She's not going to say much, but I'll tell you later," Cat said from behind him.

"Okay, how did you get away from the Orion jopters?" Billy asked. He sat back on his heels and added, "And that explosion, was that the speedboat chasing you?"

Someone started laughing—I guess it was me, but the expression on Billy's face was so funny.

"And whatever the *fuck* did you do at the Fence, Tessa?!"

Several other people started laughing.

"We'll talk about that later, too," Cat managed to say.

"And *I* want to know..." I turned and looked at Cat and Hannah. "You lied to me in the tower, didn't you? About Hannah Seeing?"

Cat looked down and Hannah bit her lip.

"You both lied to me!"

"We did lie to you, Tessa." Cat looked up. "But did we have a choice?"

I gave that a moment's thought. No. I couldn't think of anything else we could have done.

"It was ballsy," I said.

Jesse started laughing as he lay there in my lap. "*You* are ballsy, Tessa," he said.

Then we all sat there in silence for a moment. It felt like we were a thousand miles away from the city. The wind had dropped, and water lapped quietly on the hull of our boat. Sam and his brother and father softly talked in the boat next door, and here, where it was protected, just a whisper of wind moved through the trees. And then I heard a thread of song on the air, as if a bird were singing in its sleep. I knew it couldn't be a raven—they didn't nest on the peninsula—but it sure sounded like one.

I sent a quiet thank-you out into the night.

Some minutes later Emmitt announced, "The coast looks clear still. Let's motor down along to Sam's dock. We can get his brother Rusty and Jesse to your clinic. How's that sound?"

That sounded good to all of us.

Someone could quickly run down to the cliff house in a truck for Gram and Sadie and Earl—and Charlie, of course.

Billy stayed in our boat, and Augie promised me that it wouldn't be rough as long as we stayed near the shore. We needed to do that for cover, anyway. Billy sat to my right as I held Jesse, who was sleeping deeply now, which was just what he needed.

"So where are we with the resistance plan to take down Orion from the inside?" I asked Billy. "We aren't really safe yet, are we?"

He shook his head. "Not yet. But it's going to happen real soon. Within weeks, well maybe months."

Okay. I would continue to believe that that day was coming.

Hannah and Cat were near, with Emmitt squeezed in between Cat and my left side. There wasn't as much to say now, or maybe it was that there was so much to think about that we all needed to pull into our thoughts for a while.

I still had one burning question left. Could the lake really be safe to return to? If Orion had pulled everything they wanted out of Jesse's mind when they had him, how could they not know about the location of the lake and its long connection with the resistance? Might they have already found it... too horrible a thought to think.

All I wanted in life, now that I had Jesse back, all I wanted was to get home to the lake. Marry Jesse and live there and have some kids—well, maybe not four kids; I figured two kids would probably be about all I could handle.

But the lake was calling. I knew what Gram meant about the lake being in me and all of that... but still, the lake, *the place*, was calling. It seemed to be calling to Jesse too. And I was betting that it was calling to all of my family members, and to Cat, and maybe even Billy too. In a few weeks or months, when the big resistance push against Orion was over, maybe then Sadie and Emmitt and Cat and Billy could all move to the lake.

Billy was snoring on my right side.

"Emmitt," I turned my head to look left, and was surprised to see that he, too, had nodded off to sleep. Lines grooved down his cheeks on either side of his mouth, which had slackened and made him look older than he was. But his eyes opened right away and he looked at me.

"The one thing I worry about now," I said, "is how could the lake be safe? Didn't Orion get that out of Jesse?"

He smiled. "I guess I didn't tell you that piece of good news, little Ravenwing. Billy got this in his listening to the networks. The funny thing is... Orion jumped to a conclusion when they got Jesse talking about a lake, and family."

He paused.

"What? What? I don't get it." *I'm too tired to guess, I'm not a mindreader like Cat. Just for once, could someone tell it to me straight!*

"Orion thought Jesse was talking about your Grampa's lake."

We had been family there, too; though I had been there just two months, Jesse had been there for nearly two years. And that's what saved our village and our lake deep in the mountains. Emmitt described how Orion officers had put a pin on a map to mark the lake Jesse and his relatives in the resistance came from, they sent soldiers to keep a watch on it... and it was the wrong lake!

Emmitt smiled at me, then leaned away to kiss Cat's cheek. I tightened my arms around Jesse. We passed down the coast, slipping through the night, on our way to Gram and Earl and Sadie, and Charlie. There was still much to do, of course. But we were family, on our way home.

NOTES

Chapter 1: January 2091–September 2092

13   *But the heat of fire*: "The Story of Étaîn," Sean Kane, *The Wisdom of the Mythtellers* (Ontario: Broadview Press, 1994), p. 91.

14   *Its eyes were like jewels.. the Mac Oc*: Ibid., p. 92.

30   *Now when the Raven*: "Raven Travelling," Sean Kane, *The Wisdom of the Mythtellers*, p. 56.

Chapter 2: September–October 2092

41   *There were five villages...Something that was half rock*: Ibid., p. 56-57.

42   *And as soon as the people*: Ibid., p. 58.

Chapter 3: August 2096–March 2100

82   *Before there was anything*: Bill Reid & Robert Bringhurst, *The Raven Steals the Light* (Seattle: University of Washington Press, 1996), p. 19.

Chapter 4: March 2100

99-100 *Bluejay was a healer*: "Bluejay," Coast Salish artist Joe Jack, Cowichan Salish Legend (Web: www.joejack.com).

Chapter 5: June 2100–February 2104

123   *The princess of the tribe*: Haida version of "The Woman Who Married The Bear" told by Nishga mythteller Agnes Haldane, Sean Kane, p. 78.

127   *She did not recognize... Mouse Woman, in return*: Ibid., p. 80.

128   *listen as I sing*: Ibid., p. 82.

Chapter 6: February 2104

132   *Dakanku, or The Land Beyond...and Keewa.aa*: Nora Marks and Richard Dauenhauer, editors, *Haa Tuwunaagu Yis, for Healing Our Spirit: Tlingit Oratory* (Juneau: Sealaska Heritage Foundation, 1990), p.127.

Chapter 7: March 2104–April 2111

162   *todas las madres, the many mothers*: Clarissa Pinkola Estés, *Women Who Run With the Wolves* (New York: Ballantine Books, 1992), p.181.

176   *If only you would call*: Pablo Neruda, *The Essential Neruda: Selected Poems* (bilingual edition, multiple translators), Ed. Mark Eisner (San Francisco: City Lights Books, 2004), p. 39.

178   *Venid a ver la sangre*: Ibid., p. 66.

Chapter 8: April–May 13, 2111

203-204 *she summoned up...And they say*: "The Story of Étaîn," Ibid., pp. 92-93.

Chapter 9: May 13-14, 2111

235   *Then he took his weapons*: Ibid., p. 101.

Chapter 11: June 16–July 31, 2111

285   *so close that your hand*: Pablo Neruda, Ibid, p.143.

Chapter 12: July 31–September 30, 2111

314   *Bluejay was a healer...* "Bluejay," Coast Salish artist Joe Jack.

Anne Donaghy lives and writes in New Hampshire. She has imagined and written about other times and other worlds since she was a child, but in the end she usually returns to Alaska, where she grew up and where at least half her heart remains. She sends this novel out with the hope that it might help others recall home, and family, and also the hope for a world of tolerance, kindness and peace.

Any profit associated with this book will be donated to victims of government injustice, whether far away or nearing home.

DON Donaghy Anne
Donaghy, Anne
Raven, tell a story

DATE DUE			

2019

Made in the USA
Middletown, DE
28 February 2019